COLD FROM
YOUR BREATH

COLD FROM YOUR BREATH

FRANCIS JARMAN

WILDSIDE PRESS

Published by Wildside Press LLC.
wildsidepress.com | bcmystery.com

PART ONE: GHOULIES

IT WAS A DARK AND STORMY NIGHT

"You're sexy. But I guess you know that."

It was handwritten, in a neat, flowing script, on a plain postcard. It was in English. In the bottom left-hand corner was a tiny heart. In the bottom right-hand corner was a smiley face.

Sexy? Was he really? But it was definitely meant for him, there was no doubt about that. Whoever had sent it had written his name, "Richard," on the back of the card. Then they'd slipped it into the pile of student assignments for him to find.

He compared the handwriting with the assignment that he'd just finished marking. There was no similarity at all.

He turned to the next one, which was on different-colored paper. Aha! The handwriting looked a bit similar.

He started reading: "It was a dark and stormy night."

Had the stupid girl really written that? He stared at the essay. Lisa Meyer. Who was that?

The name was familiar, though he couldn't put a face to it. There were thirty or more students in his Textual Composition class—far too many—and she wasn't one that he'd noticed yet. He knew the name from the class-list, obviously. But perhaps from somewhere else, too?

He would sometimes scan the students' faces while they were writing, ignoring the boys of course. Stopping at a pretty face, he'd give the girl a grade out of ten. Seven was a good score, Eight was exceptional. It was a game that his colleague Eddie Hodgkins had taught him (and it was an effective way of staying awake and making the time pass quicker when you were supervising exams).

Lisa might be one of the blondes in the back row of his class. Sixes mostly. Dull, bored expressions. Torpid bodies. They kept their heads down, and never answered questions. They were like grazing cows. Yes, Lisa would be one of the grazing cows in the back row.

"It was a dark and stormy night."

Where had she got *that* from? The internet? None of them read books any more. Not the Germans, anyhow. Some of the Russian girls must've done, years ago, before their families emigrated to Germany, because they would sometimes react if you mentioned Tolstoy or Dostoyevsky, or even Nietzsche.

The German girls thought Nietzsche was an online clothes store; the boys thought it was a computer virus. Perhaps it was.

Their homework for the Christmas break had been to write an account of what they did over Christmas—an assignment that was so easy it was almost a Christmas present. So on what website had Lisa found *that* particular sentence?

"It was a dark and stormy night when our Beloved Savior Jesus Christ was born"?

Or: "It was a dark and stormy night in the hills near Bethlehem, where shepherds were tending their flocks"?

Hardly.

Had it been stormy at Christmas in that part of Germany? Not particularly. Richard hadn't gone home to Britain, and the winter in Reichsstadt had been very mild. But maybe Lisa Meyer had been somewhere else? In Bavaria, or on a Friesian island, or in the Black Forest, or wherever it was that her parents lived. Germany was a big country.

Tonight it was dark and stormy, though.

He skimmed down through the text. Oh dear, it was dreadful stuff. How could a girl who wrote such drivel have found the nerve to tell him that he was sexy? That didn't make sense.

He put the assignment down and walked round to check that the windows of his flat were secured. First the two in the living-room, and then those in the spare room and the little bedroom. There was also a frosted window in the cubby-like bathroom. The kitchen was a windowless niche.

He noticed how loud the rain was, thumping against the glass.

He'd call it a day and finish the marking another time, but first he'd skim through the assignments and do a handwriting check. It must have been *someone* from that class, and only twenty-odd papers had been handed in during the lesson. The girl would be banking on her writing being recognized, and on Richard responding to her cheekiness.

She *wanted* to be caught! She fancied him. Why shouldn't she? Well, it didn't usually happen to Richard, and he knew that most women didn't exactly see him as love's young dream, but on occasion girls had been known to go for their teachers. Something about the aphrodisiac of power, the allure of authority?

It would be fun tracking her down.

What he would do when he caught her, however, he wasn't so sure. Unlike some of his colleagues, he'd never been involved with one of his own students before—Sonia didn't count, because she'd been studying German, not English. It wasn't directly illegal, as far as he knew, so long as the girl wasn't underage, but it was kind of a gray area: it wasn't approved of, and it wasn't a sensible thing to do, for lots of good reasons.

Whatever happened (or didn't), it would at least take his mind off the task he'd been given only a few weeks before, by the Fat Man, the university President himself. It had troubled and nagged at his thoughts and depressed him all through the Christmas break. It was a task that *wouldn't* be fun, and he had no idea how to carry it out.

Oh, sod the assignments! They were really dismal, worse than last time and even worse than the efforts produced by his Creative Writing class. At least *those* had included some mild (anonymous) pornography: phallic, sub-Henry Miller stuff, obviously from Milo, the only boy in the group. And there'd been a poem of sorts, juvenile Gothic, which began

YOU BETTA WATCH OUT
THERES A KILLER ABOUT
HE'LL COME FOR YOU SOON
AT THE NEXT FULL MOON

and which went on to mention throats being slit, blood spurting, bodies spasming in death throes, and horribly mutilated corpses.

That was anonymous, too, and without doubt another masterpiece from the pen of Milo.

It was in very poor taste, because a local girl (who wasn't herself a student) had been murdered some short time back, while on her way home from a late-night party. The idiot who'd written the poem (Milo—Richard would bet on that) wasn't the murderer. The murderer wouldn't be a student at all. More likely he'd be some drifter passing through town, a homeless guy, a pathetic loser, a druggie, a psycho, someone with mental issues.

The students were predictably being childish about it, as if they were in some parody horror film like *Scream*. When it came to stupid behavior Milo was a natural talent, a born leader. It was all that he seemed to be good at.

Richard suddenly fancied a beer. Damn! As he had feared, there was none left in the fridge. He could go out and fetch some from the Turkish kiosk at the bottom of the road, if it was still open. (How long did it stay open on Sundays?) He thought about it. He would need to put on a raincoat, and it would be a long trudge coming back up the hill carrying the beer. It wasn't a night to be out in—unless you had a reason. You'd have to be really keen to go out in this weather. Was beer a good enough reason? Probably not.

Then his motivation took a further hit—he remembered that some of the essay assignments had been handed in late, thrown into his mailbox individually the following day. He'd even seen some students doing it, and spoken to them. ("Well well, Claudia, last chance saloon again, eh? Try to hand this stuff in on time please!")

For all that he knew, the postcard could have ended up between two assignments purely by chance, rather than being handed in during the lesson. And so there was no guarantee that it was from a girl who was in his Textual Composition class. It could be from almost anyone.

As so often with Richard, laziness won out. He stayed in, and put the kettle on for a cup of tea. No beer then! He'd make himself comfortable on his second-hand sofa—a purchase that he'd never regretted—and watch the regular Sunday night episode of the crime series *Tatort* ("the scene of the crime"). They weren't at all bad.

Or maybe he should watch a different programme, something that didn't remind him of that other business? Unfortunately he was stuck with it: he couldn't have said no to the President, not even if his job at the university had been safe (which it wasn't). He didn't have tenure. He was on a fixed-term contract; he was under-qualified for his position; and he had a boss who wasn't fond of him.

But just thinking about what the Fat Man had told him to do kept him awake at night.

The President had instructed him to look for a dangerous sexual predator. And he had suggested that he begin the search in his own backyard: the English Department.

THE SNAKE AND THE RAT

Not far away, in the same part of town, though in a more obviously expensive residential area and in a much larger apartment than Richard's, two people were fighting for control. Nothing was said, but the air in the rooms quivered.

One of them would eventually go out, despite the rain, wind, and darkness, ostensibly for cigarettes.

The other would then sit brooding, for hours if need be, hunched over papers, books and an expensive laptop computer.

The Snake had earned her nickname almost immediately she started in her new job at the University of Reichsstadt. Was it because of the way that she let her tongue slide out over her lips? In a different woman that might have seemed seductive. She was good-looking by any standards, and she photographed well. The university's glossy magazine had made the most out of the attractive new appointment as Head of English. But the period of time (after first getting to know her) in which most men found her sexually attractive—or other women viewed her as a potential rival—was generally short. After that, they would go to great lengths to avoid her, or (if they were obliged to interact with her) they would end up fantasizing killing her with a blunt instrument.

As you would want to kill a venomous snake that had slithered threateningly into your life.

Her husband had no nickname as yet, but we shall call him "the Rat" because that is what he looked like. He was a big man, but he had a thin, bony head with a prominent nose. His lips were thin and, when he pulled them back, revealed sharp, protruding teeth. His hair was black, unkempt and greasy. His movements were unpredictable: sometimes smooth, sometimes agitated ("twitchy," his students would say).

Dr. Lothar Baumgart had come to Reichsstadt because of his wife. She had secured a better job than he could now hope for, and she earned far more money. She was even taller than he was, she was better looking, her voice was stronger and more resonant than his, and she had a powerful, albeit sinister, presence.

He would have liked to be able to make such an impact on people, if only by frightening them, but instead most people merely disliked him. Enmity would be easier to live with than contempt. Somewhere along the road his wife had discovered that secret, and drew nourishment from the loathing that people felt for her.

Are there marriages made in hell? If so, this was one of them.

The rooms were sparsely furnished, and what furniture there was was ostentatiously modernist-expensive, with a few functional IKEA-type items as well.

In many homes the friendliest room is the kitchen, but here there was no indication that anyone cooked regularly (the cupboards were bare) or enjoyed cooking (where were the herbs and spices, where were the fancy Mediterranean oils and vinegars, and the cookery books?). Instead, there were normally fast food takeaway cartons heaped in a corner, and in the sink a pile of unwashed plates, some with moldering fragments of pizza or ready-meal lasagne stuck to them.

The previous week, the Snake had invited her small "team" of student assistants to the apartment for a working supper. She had served them takeaway pizza margheritas, and disgusting red wine from two jumbo-sized bottles. "A proper student feast," she had called it. "Just like when I was a student."

(Had she ever been a student? Micha, the only boy in the group, found that hard to imagine. It was easier to think of her being created by some malevolent Dr. Frankenstein, and unleashed on the world as an act of revenge.)

It was agreed that the three girls—but not Micha, who had an essay to finish—would come back the following day. They needed to collate the figures that had been presented at the meeting, and then draft an initial report on the progress of their little research project.

She'd feed them again, she promised.

The collating and drafting took quite a while that morning, but when they broke for lunch she had a surprise for them: a meal consisting of the pizza leftovers from the evening before, trimmed into neat squares and decorated with squirts of tomato ketchup; plus what was left of the wine.

At least she'd arranged the pizza squares on plates.

"I couldn't let you guys starve, could I now?"

The students said nothing, ate quickly, and then slipped away without offering to clear up. When her husband returned, he found that she expected *him* to do that. It was beneath her dignity, she said, and hadn't she provided all the food?

Though he was welcome to what was left of the pizza squares, she added, if he was still hungry.

He was not pleased. As far as the Rat was concerned, it was *her* project and they were *her* guests, and he didn't see why *he* should have to clear up after them. Also, she had made a point of keeping him away from the students the evening before. He could go to the cinema, she had suggested. There was a Polish art-film showing at the Studio. Hand-held camera-work, black-and-white, all jagged shapes and looming shadows. Impressive. Demanding. (Said the reviews.) Just the kind of pretentious crap that he liked.

"And you do know why I don't want you hanging around here?" she had said, interrupting his protests. "Cozying up to my students? You remember what happened in Dortmund, don't you? Or have you forgotten?"

He remembered, of course. What had happened hadn't been much, and it had been less than he had *wanted* to happen, but it had been enough to get him into big trouble. Yes, he remembered Dortmund.

So he had done what she suggested. (And the film had been very much to his taste: interminably long, weird, and full of sudden, violent twists and psychological cruelty.)

Furthermore, he had even chosen to go in to the university the next day, although he had no classes scheduled and she hadn't actually asked him to go. That was a positive gesture on his part.

No thanks were forthcoming. Instead, over the weekend she had been spiteful and provocative. They had quarreled over almost everything, and again it was the Rat who had left, supposedly only to fetch cigarettes, though he had stayed out for hours.

In his absence, she took over his corner of the apartment—he had a much better writing-desk than she had. She spread out her papers, but discovered that she couldn't concentrate. She found his pedantically tidy collection of art-books thoroughly irritating. Every time that she looked up from her work she would see the alphabetically arranged names on the spines of the books in front of her nose: "Chagall, Chirico, Clouet, Constable, Correggio...," with a few brochures and slim paperbacks tucked in between them.

What a pathetic excuse for a man! He hadn't even gone to the trouble of arranging his books intelligently, by epoch, or genre, as she would have done. No wonder that he couldn't get a permanent university position, let alone a Chair! When had he last published anything of interest? He was academically dead in the water.

She had tied herself to a loser. He should have been a librarian. The university librarians were equally clueless, good only for shunting books around on shelves and making lists.

Had she managed to tame him? She wasn't completely sure. She needed to be careful. She had learned in Dortmund what he was capable of, once off the leash. And now the *Frau Professor* had a seriously promising academic career to be protected.

KAJO

In a different part of the city, in a proper middle-class house with a well-tended but conventional garden, Richard's former Acting Head of Department, Dr. Karl-Johannes Christenkorn, entered his book-lined study and shut the door behind him.

Quietly. (As he did most things.)

Kajo didn't want his wife rushing up the stairs like an avenging angel to find out what was going on. He booted his desktop computer, opened Word, and wrote and printed the letter of resignation. One draft was enough. He had been carrying the thoughts around with him for weeks.

He read through what he had written; sighed; read it again—and then destroyed the letter in the shredder. He had needed to write it, yes, but it would never be sent.

Kajo was tenured. He was a Senior Lecturer—in the States, he'd be known as an Associate Professor, which sounded much more impressive— and he was second in rank in the English Department, which only had one member of staff entitled to call herself Professor. People like Kajo were never sacked, but they never resigned either, unless because of ill-health.

As a publicly-funded civil servant, he could look forward to a handsome pension when he retired.

Kajo was healthy for his age—he slept eight hours a night, every night, generally from 10.30 till 6.30; he didn't smoke; and he drank wine in moderation—mostly semi-sweet Riesling, or a Merlot if he was feeling daring. He nearly always walked to the university, leaving the car at home for his wife to use; and he went for long walks, during which he brooded over his life

Kajo's health problem was his wife, Tilde. She wouldn't leave him alone, nag nag nag, until he had finally made it to Professor, German-style. (Perhaps she wanted to be addressed as *"Frau Professor,"* by proxy, at the baker's or the chemist's, and didn't realize that no-one did that any more.)

Unlike in some other countries, in Germany the title of Professor wasn't given easily. Most academics never reached those glamorous heights. But Tilde was the sister of an eminent Professor of Physics, and the daughter of an even more eminent Professor of Biology. So why wasn't her limp-dick of a husband a Professor, too? Kajo was fifty-five, however, and his career was stalled.

He would need help from someone with genuine power or influence, either in the university or the Ministry, but there was no-one who was interested in him. And why should there be? He'd never been involved in politics, either for the party now in power or for the party that might be in power next time around. And he had no access to those magical "Vitamin B" pills ("B" stood for *Beziehungen*, or "contacts") that had helped other academics, no more deserving than he was, to a speedy promotion.

He would never make it now. Everyone knew that, except his wife. They also knew that, because of Tilde, he didn't dare to stop trying. And so they laughed at him behind his back.

Kajo chewed at a pencil. His fingernails were already bitten down to the quick. In recent months he had drafted (and then destroyed) his letter of resignation several times.

He stared out into the dark garden, where his wife's shrubs were fighting against the wind. The fruit-trees at the bottom of the garden were being shaken violently, and he could see a couple of broken branches twitching about on the lawn. That was real power! When you could smash and break and tear things at will, and no-one could stop you.

Kajo had only tasted power once. For six months he'd been the Acting Head of the English Department, after dear old Professor Timpe had retired—which was unusual, because the normal procedure would have been to bring in someone from outside as a stop-gap.

Yet one bright and sunny spring morning the President had summoned him, offered him (with unprecedented politeness) a chair, coffee and a chocolate biscuit, in that order, and said, *"Herr Doktor* Christenkorn, your department needs you. I want *you* to do it!"

For a moment, his heart had taken wing and he could have floated joyfully out of the President's window and across the Great Quadrangle to dance with the daffodils—before it dawned on him that it was not the permanent position of Head of English that the President had meant.

The *Präsi* had then been completely honest with him. As he explained, it simply wasn't worth the bureaucratic hassle to advertize what would be an interim appointment that ran for only six months. You'd do all the boring interviews, choose someone, and then have to turf the guy out when the position was filled permanently. And *that* would happen without too much delay: the application process for the permanent job would be over comparatively quickly because the position was such an attractive one, with the title of Professor (highest grade) and a salary to match.

It would therefore be easier all round, and cheaper, to make the senior academic in the department acting head for six months.

Agreed?

And it would look good on Kajo's CV, wouldn't it?

No, it would look like just what it was—some table scraps thrown to the old dog out of kindness, while a pretty new puppy was being chosen.

He didn't say anything, but the President probably read his thoughts. He spoke more harshly. Kajo was welcome to apply for the permanent position, he said, but he should please remember that in-house promotions of this nature were highly untypical, and actively discouraged by the Ministry.

As if to rub it in, the President had also asked him about his publications list.

How many peer-reviewed publications did he now have?

Oh. That's a pity.

Or book publications, apart from his PhD of course?

Really? Well, never mind.

Was he working on *anything* substantial at present?

He wasn't, and so Kajo had had to make do with those six months at the helm as Acting Head of Department.

It wasn't really "power," either, as he soon discovered. His colleagues had smirked and prevaricated. They had exchanged ironic glances, and raised points of order. They knew that the "Acting Professor" would soon be slipping back into the ranks with the rest of them. They didn't let him impose anything on them that they didn't already want.

Now the new Professor was there, and from the moment she arrived she had wasted no opportunity to humiliate him. Admittedly, she was unpleasant towards everyone, but a disproportionate amount of her venom seemed to be reserved exclusively for Kajo. Did she see him as a challenger? That would almost be flattering!

He stared out into the garden again. Yes, that was what power meant, he told himself, to be able to hurt people whenever you wanted to, to be able to bend them to your will, like the whipped and broken branches out there in the darkness.

Quite suddenly, Kajo made a decision. He switched off the computer and the shredder, and got up from his desk.

LISA

What else was happening that night? Who else was out in the storm?

Lisa Meyer (she of the essay assignment) was on her way back to the student hostel on the Südstädter Allee. She had been to badminton training at the university sports center, which was located directly on the riverbank (it also catered for the university's high-profile rowing club). It had not been a successful evening, and now Lisa was struggling to get her bike round Gallows Hill against the wind.

She was reflecting, gloomily, on what the university had to offer by way of men.

Not a lot, actually. As she saw it, the whole place was basically just a glorified teacher training college. A few trendy subjects like computer science and business studies had been tacked on, and there were hordes of awful engineers. The education students were mostly girls, and the handful of men in her institute were either pathetic pimple-cases who started stammering when you looked at them, or impossibly vain.

Like that horrible Sebastian from the Students' Union she'd ended up in bed with after the party in Freshers' Week—what a conceited prat *he'd* turned out to be! And he'd messed up her sheets, because she wouldn't let him finish off inside her.

Or Micha, even, who to be honest was the only reason why she'd joined the badminton club. Unfortunately, Micha was really good at badminton, unlike her, so when the pairings came to be chosen on club nights she never found herself on court with him, not even on the other side of the net.

Wasn't sport supposed to be about bringing people together?

That's why she'd gone to the sports center on a Sunday evening, when it wouldn't be so crowded, and when only some of the more serious sports freaks like Micha would be there, trying to put in some extra training. But he hadn't shown up.

She couldn't be *too* direct—that would be cheap. Also, her self-confidence had been dented by what had happened in the hostel back in December. It had been really frightening.

All that she needed, she told herself, was to find a way of "bumping into" Micha, somehow.

If the options within her faculty were limited, the prospects beyond it were even worse.

The computer science students were all total nerds.

The business studies students were both dull *and* opinionated—which was not a good combination.

And the engineers were unspeakable. Did they never, ever, change their checked lumberjack shirts?

Ah, she was a Princess, waiting for her Prince! Perhaps a (slightly) older man, one of the profs even?

Some of the younger lecturers in the English Department were quite tasty, she thought, but Lisa was only a First Year and she didn't trust herself just yet. She didn't want to screw up her degree by making *that* sort of mistake. Later on, she might need some of those guys as examiners.

When examination time came, she didn't want to have to rely on female profs. From what she'd seen so far most of them were awful old bags. In any case, in English there were only two of them: Dorothea total-boredom-on-a-stick Schlichting, and the new woman that they called the Snake, for some reason. Lisa saw her as more like a dragon than a snake.

Her best friend Steffi wasn't so choosy. In fact, she was a right slag. With Steffi, although she wasn't a fantastic looker, there was always something weird going on with men. You never knew quite what she was up to, but Lisa would be told about it afterwards—at length.

At the Freshers' Week party, for example, she had almost pulled the American prof, Harlan. Amazingly, that evening was the only time that Lisa had got laid, and Steffi hadn't.

According to Steffi, Harlan had had too much to drink, and she had driven him back to his place out in the Weststadt near to the *Autobahn*—she had a car, the cow!—and he had apparently groped her most of the way. The car had been swerving all over the place.

"It's not easy, you know, driving with some randy bloke's hand working away between your legs!"

Lisa, who had neither a car nor a boyfriend, found it difficult to sympathize with her.

Steffi hadn't slept with him (*she* said), "because it was the first time," but the next day he had been kind of distant and couldn't recollect anything about it. Oh, surprise, surprise. Maybe he had just remembered how small her tits were?

Steffi said he was a jerk, and thought the *Lektor*, Richard Orwell, had more to offer.

Lisa didn't think much of Mr. Orwell. That wasn't his fault—he was simply too *British*. His Textual Composition class was deadly, but it was good for snoozing in if you could find a seat at the back. She never answered questions, and as for the homework assignments, well, you could always copy some fancy shit off the internet.

Harlan Kurz, on the other hand... now *he* looked like a man who knew how to make a girl happy! You simply had to play it right. He was a live wire, always cracking his finger-joints, winking and grinning and telling strange jokes that no-one understood. He had a nice body and a tight little backside, and he stared at the girls in Translation I. Well, at *some* of them.

Lisa reminded herself that she had much better tits than Steffi did.

The trouble with Harlan Kurz was, how did you get the man on his own, and in the right kind of atmosphere? She'd need to build up her confidence before trying anything. And he too would have to be in a relaxed mood (but still sober). She couldn't see anything exciting ever happening in his office, which he shared with that other British guy, Jonathan Snoad, the one who thought he was God's gift to women. Actually, Snoad wasn't there much in the office, but nor was Harlan, except when it was his office hour.

She imagined it would probably be easier with proper Professors, the senior ones, who didn't have to share their offices with anyone. Apparently there was this old guy in the History Department where you could see the dried sperm stains on his sofa, or so it was rumored. You went to *his* office hour, they said, and he'd make it ever so nice and easy for you.

"Come in, Lisa, and take a seat. Yes, my dear, here on the sofa. You want me as your examiner for your minor subject exam? Excellent! I don't see any problem with that. I'm sure we can come to some agreement. We'll need to meet once or twice, though, to talk about your topic. And to get to know each other better."

Hard to believe, but there were girls who fell for that! Lisa certainly wouldn't. She wasn't born yesterday.

Lost in her thoughts, Lisa failed to notice that she was being watched. That she was being *observed*.

The watcher saw her thrust her weight against the pedals in the face of the wind, saw the sports bag bulked out with her kit and a used towel or two, and with the handle of a racket protruding, saw her strong, fleshy body, the firm buttocks and thighs, the long blond hair still sweaty from exercise and now plastered down by the rain.

The first box on a mental checklist was ticked.

Lisa slipped down off the bicycle and with an effort lifted it across a strip of thick grass and weeds onto a gravel side-path. This was the start of a narrow lovers' lane that led round the side of the hill and through a gloomy little plantation of pine-trees. It came out eventually on the other side, near to the students' hostel where she lived.

This was the best route back from the sports center. Naturally, you could stay on the road, but then you'd have to go round Gallows Hill the other way, and cycle past all the university buildings one after the other before you finally got to the hostel. The lover's lane was much quicker, though it was a bit spooky at night, because below it was waste ground, and the entrances to the famous caves, and everyone know about *them*.

Completely unaware that she was being watched, Lisa clambered awkwardly back onto the bike and, now better sheltered from the wind, wobbled off into the dark mouth of the side-path, pushing down on the pedals as much as she dared.

There was a moment of recognition. Well, well, well, look who it isn't! How nice! This young lady was *unfinished business.*

And a second box was ticked.

MONDAY MORNING

Monday morning was *not* a good time at the university. In fact, it was only slightly better than Friday afternoon was.

Nearly all of the Reichsstadt Professors kept to a leisurely *Di-Mi-Do* attendance schedule (meaning *"Dienstag-Mittwoch-Donnerstag,"* i.e., Tuesday-Wednesday-Thursday), which allowed for a generously extended weekend. The onerous task of organizing the departmental timetable was normally dumped in the lap of some junior member of the teaching staff, and there was no way he or she was going to be able to force the mighty Professor X to teach a seminar on a Monday morning or a Friday afternoon (unless, for some perverse personal reason, Professor X actually wanted to).

A few top-level Professors only came once a week, if at all, and let their teaching assistants and the much abused secretaries do the work for them. The rights and privileges of Professors, however lazy or absent they might be, were jealously upheld, in the name of "academic freedom," and they were still ring-fenced by German law.

Few of these rights and privileges were extended to the non-professorial academic staff, who were also teachers and researchers. That didn't stop the non-professorials trying it on too. This was despite regular reminders from the university administration that their presence in the college on *every* working day (public holidays and vacations excepted, but including, unbelievably, the long three months of the summer break) was a legal requirement.

However, anyone who took a reality check would soon discover that this was not a sensible way for academic teachers and researchers to organize their work, whatever their status in the hierarchy happened to be. And although a few Professors enjoyed bullying their subordinates, nearly all of them (except for a handful of science profs who were worried about lab rotas) grudgingly acknowledged that this particular law was an ass. Since no time-clocks had been installed, or were ever likely to be, the regulations couldn't be enforced, but lip service was paid to the law by the sending out of occasional stern reminders from the President (who thereby covered his back with the Ministry).

As for the students, if there were hardly any classes on Monday mornings or Friday afternoons, why should they bother to come in at all? Those, like Lisa and Steffi, who were neither enthusiastic early risers nor workaholics, found *Di-Mi-Do* a perfectly acceptable arrangement.

During the Christmas break, the buildings of the University of Reichsstadt had been daubed with aggressive slogans in which the name "Michael" figured prominently. Dr. Hans Michael was the misguided Professor who had tried to tighten up the last round of Sociology exams, so as to achieve more of a bell curve effect on the graph of results. (In other words, there should be fewer Grade 1's, and a small number of candidates would actually have to fail.)

Failing was almost unheard of in Sociology, however dismal many of the performances in examinations were, and any grade below a 2+ was seen as the kiss of death, although a grade 3 was officially defined as "satisfactory," and you could still pass with a 4.

The reaction to this attempt at academic rigor had been robust, and could be seen scrawled on the outside of one of the lecture halls—"NO TO MICHAELISM! WE SHALL WIN!"—and on a flurry of large, garish posters inside:

"WE REJECT MICHAEL-FASCISM"

"EXAMINATIONS: OPPRESSIVE WEAPON OF SOCIAL CONTROL IN A REACTIONARY PRE-REVOLUTIONARY SOCIETY"

"ADVANCE! ONWARDS! QUESTIONING, WE MARCH TOWARDS THE FUTURE (REICHSSTADT SPARTACISTS)"

and so on.

The Students' Union had reacted more mildly, merely announcing in their magazine that Michael was a sad but unfortunately typical example of "the white-supremacist hetero-patriarchal capitalist order."

In the men's toilets, Professor Michael had begun to figure in the graffiti—"MICHAEL SUCKS DICKS," "MICHAEL IS A POOF," "MICHAEL TAKES IT UP THE ASS" (statements that may or may not have been true, though they were not pertinent to the ongoing controversy)—mixed in with the more conventional "STATISTICS IS TOTAL SHIT," "WHY IS MY LIFE SO POINTLESS?," "HAIRY BLOKE, 25, HORNY, HERE EVERY SATURDAY 11:00," and (accompanying an obsessively detailed anatomical drawing) the plaintive message "I WANT TO DO IT WITH SABINE."

But which Sabine had the artist meant? There were so many Sabines, including a few secretaries and a couple of elderly lady profs. At least the anonymous artist wanted to do it "with" rather than "to" Sabine, suggesting a modest degree of sexual enlightenment.

The university buildings, consisting of a row of concrete bunkers with windows, were nondescript. "Ugly" would be more honest, but let the gentler word stand, as a description both of the buildings and of the whole institution. Other words, like "undistinguished," "middlebrow," or "sleepy," also spring to mind. None of this, of course, was part of the self-image of the members of the Reichsstadt *Professorium*.

Rightly or wrongly, a university is judged by the quality of its senior Professors. In Germany, Professors in the narrow sense are handsomely paid and are expected to be academically impressive and intellectually dazzling. (Or so it is hoped.)

The Reichsstadt Professors undoubtedly spent a great deal of time and energy in pretending to be brilliant. But, like the glow from a small torch, the light they projected illuminated only the immediate academic vicinity, and failed to penetrate the deeper reaches of international scholarship. This created marginally more heat—the heat of constant spiteful bickering—than light, and the light served only to cast dull shadows a very short distance.

Lisa and Steffi might still have been abed, but Richard had found his way into college late that morning. It wasn't a long walk from his apartment, down the Südstädter Ring, onto the Südstädter Allee, past the big Real supermarket where he did most of his shopping, and on to the university. His original plan had been to collect any mail from his mailbox, then take an early lunch at the university canteen, the *Mensa*, and finally go to his departmental meeting, which had been scheduled, once again, for the ridiculous time of 1 p.m.

Monday lunchtime for a staff meeting! How ridiculous! The English Department was being laughed at by the other institutes. If the Snake was trying to make herself unpopular, then she was definitely succeeding.

And the *Mensa* was generally poor on Mondays, unless it was the week (once a month) when they had spaghetti bolognese as an option. They did the sauce very nicely, Richard thought. But he had already checked that out online, and it wasn't one of those spaghetti Mondays. So he'd give the *Mensa* a miss, and get himself a sandwich somewhere, maybe from Real.

His mailbox was almost overflowing, with circulars, publishers' catalogs, and long-overdue assignments from his different classes. And there was another postcard, again in English, and in handwriting that he'd seen before.

You are...

Reliable
Interesting
Charming
Horny
Amazing
Rogish *[sic]*

Delightful

And I love you!

S.

Aha! She had broken cover! She was "S."

Who could it be?

Presumably not Lisa Meyer—there was an "s" in her name, but it wasn't an initial. His old girlfriend Sonia from the German Department? No. That hadn't lasted long, and she'd dumped him for an actor at the *Landestheater*. She hadn't been that keen on him anyway, or, if she had been, she hadn't shown it. And hadn't she gone off to South Africa with her actor friend?

Besides, Sonia's English had been superb (one of the reasons he'd fallen for her in the first place), and she wouldn't have misspelt "roguish."

"S." That gave him something to work with. It could only stand for her first name. Even in the dour north of Germany you wouldn't tell someone he was "horny" and "amazing" and then sign yourself off as "S" (for "Schmidt" or "Schröder)."

If she had wanted to do it more formally, she could have used both her initials, though that would have been too much of a giveaway. Or she could have written *"Fräulein S."* That sounded quite sexy, like a domina you'd go to for a bondage session, who'd have it printed on her business card: "FRÄU-LEIN S. / ALL SERVICES (FRENCH, GERMAN, RUSSIAN, GREEK) / PERSONAL TRAINING / WATER SPORTS / STRICTEST DISCIPLINE."

He'd go to the English Department office and get a printout of all the students' names from the secretary. He'd tell *Frau* Ludewig that he needed it for planning next semester's courses, or for the exams. (Any nonsense would do, she wouldn't ask questions.) He'd try to catch her before the stupid departmental meeting.

How many girls could there be who had first names beginning with S? He could already think of several possible candidates: some quite appealing, others less so.

WORKING HARD FOR THE UNIVERSITY

Naturally it's the "profs" and the students, the lectures and seminars, that are the main distinguishing features of a university—at least as far as the outside world is concerned.

This, despite all the best efforts of some institutions to play down the importance of teaching and turn themselves into glorious ivory towers, in whose upper chambers the chosen professorial few would breathe only the pure air of research. Ideally, undergraduate teaching would be dispensed with altogether, but if that wasn't possible the chores could be left to doctoral students and the like, scrabbling about far below the rarefied heights, and barely visible.

There were even some wild rumors about the pending introduction of a new kind of animal onto the academic scene, the "Teaching Professor," a broken-winded work-horse good for nothing else but to teach back-to-back classes. His or her exertions on the teaching treadmill would enable the *real* Professors to concentrate on fulfilling their nobler destinies.

The university would soon become a gleaming academic city on a hill, stuffed with Fulbright alumni and alumnae, international award winners and Nobel Prize contenders. Research monies would come flooding in, from dazzled corporations and national foundations, soon matched by generous funds from a shamefaced government now regretting its previous short-sightedness and stinginess.

And if anyone should dare to ask about the old "Humboldt Model" of the interconnectedness of teaching and research? It was still good for an academic paper or two, or to be trotted out in interviews with the press, but as a scholar one had more urgent concerns.

Yet the teaching staff on their own would not have been able to keep the university show on the road. For that, a hardworking, long-suffering and (in their own opinion) underpaid administration was needed. They were the auxiliary troops in the university's battle to achieve distinction, to one day climb the rankings or be awarded some seal of approval such as "élite university" (whatever that meant).

The students had most contact with the least influential of these service workers: the cooks and serving ladies in the *Mensa*; the secretaries who snapped at them that Professor Whatnot was busy; the team of janitors led by the bad-tempered *Herr* Geisler, the Head Porter; the junior librarians, stressed-out or phlegmatic, but never particularly happy-looking; the technicians; the admin people who did all the paperwork; and (occasionally) the cleaning ladies, though these were most active at times when the students were still in bed or already on their way home.

The administration (including the technical services) was divided into obvious fiefdoms like the Library, the Computer Center, the International Office, and Departments of Student Affairs, Finance, and so on. Each of these was headed by somebody assumed to be highly competent in their field. In addition, there were certain senior positions that were effectively filled at the President's pleasure; most of the functions associated with these wouldn't have been familiar to students of an earlier generation.

Thus, there was a so-called Quality Manager, *Herr* Rammler, who tirelessly collated and assessed the evaluation forms that were filled in by students every semester at the end of their courses.

There was a Performance Manager, *Herr* Grote, who encouraged the teaching staff to attend refresher courses in different aspects of the theory and practice of teaching, and organized prizes for those of them who kept the students particularly happy;

There was a Chief Information Officer, *Herr* Dr. Breitkreuz, who ruled over an online system for disseminating information about the lessons, and enabled the students to register for classes, to have their attendance checked and to receive their credit points, all from computer to computer, and all with minimal human interference.

There was a Press Officer, who spread the good news about the university to the outside world.

And there was a University Fundraiser, whose task it was to woo local businesses and wealthy private citizens for donations and funding for projects.

The names of the people occupying the last two positions are of no great interest. The media repeatedly misrepresented the university's activities, and funds seldom flowed in as they were supposed to, so these particular jobs had more than a little in common with ejector seats, and their occupants were seldom around for long enough for people to become familiar with their names.

The jobs of Rammler and Dr. Breitkreuz were both safe, because of the impenetrably complex software and statistical calculations on which they spent most of their time; while Grote, who spent his time "motivating" (i.e., annoying) the teaching staff, was *ipso facto* earning his keep.

The functions and prerogatives of these small departments overlapped considerably, just as Rammler's and Grote's did with the work of the Personnel Department and Dr. Breitkreuz's with that of the Computer Center.

Rammler and Grote disliked each other (nobody knew why).

Dr. Breitkreuz, who was shy, and terrified of most people (but especially of Rammler and Grote), seldom left his office or answered his telephone. Most of his work—such as briefing the teaching staff and the students on the constant modifications to his online system—had to be done online, or by part-time student assistants, to whom he gave instructions by email.

Breitkreuz shunned human contact as best he could. He was so timid that (according to his colleagues) he'd come off worse in a confrontation with Sukie, the university cat, or even with one of the *Mensa*'s renowned chocolate puddings (lumpy horrors that were portioned out from huge tubs every second Friday, and described in the *Mensa* menu as "*Schoko-Dessert*").

Finally, there were the two "Commissioners," the mild-mannered *Herr* Schinkel, responsible for safeguarding the interests of disabled members of the university, and *Frau* Dr. Dröge-Daschmeyer, Commissioner for Gender Equality, a lady you absolutely did not want to tangle with.

SUMMONED BY THE PRESIDENT

The discovery of the second postcard had put Richard in a thoroughly good mood. Somewhere out there was a woman who found him "roguish."

Now *that* was a new one! Did he have a roguish quality? He never danced about in front of his classes like Kurz; and Snoad seemingly had an effortless gift for making girl students moon over him. But Richard did his best as a teacher; he told the occasional joke; he flirted gently to hold their attention when the lesson permitted it; and apparently there *was* someone who appreciated his low-key charm.

He felt good, even though he wasn't looking forward to the staff meeting. And even though, on his way in to the college, he had been oppressed once again by gloomy thoughts about his other quest: the task he had been set by the President.

He had been summoned by the Fat Man in the middle of December, just before the university began the slow winding-down for Christmas. Why should His Magnificence the President of the University of Reichsstadt, Professor Dr. Dr. Isidor von Glöwing (the name was pronounced GLER-ving), respected Catholic theologian, fierce essayist, participant in political chat shows on German television, expert on the intellectual underpinnings of the Counter-Reformation, and an object of terror to most of the university staff, have asked to see Richard? ("Ask" was a misnomer—it suggested that Richard had a choice.)

New Professors would always be invited to the *Präsidium* for coffee and a brief "meeting of minds." (After which, most of them would quake whenever such an invitation was repeated.) For important visitors to the university, *Frau* Henkel and *Frau* Binsenweis would even fetch out the fancy porcelain coffee service, decorated charmingly with pink, blue and yellow forget-me-nots.

The President showed less interest in meeting the persons, let alone the *minds* (such as these were), of lower-ranking teaching staff, and had no inclination to waste either his time or his coffee on them. The members of the so-called *Mittelbau*, the "middle section" made up of the university's non-professorial academics, were sandwiched between the Professors on the one hand and everyone else (students, technical and administrative staff, cooks and cleaners) on the other. They were there to labor at the coalface, teaching whatever they were told to. If any need should arise to contact them it could be done within the chain of command, with instructions filtering down through the appropriate Dean or Head of Department.

However, the message to Richard had come directly, in writing, in the garish-colored ink favored by His Magnificence, and not through the Snake. Did she even know that Richard had been invited?

He had accordingly presented himself at the *Präsidium*, ten minutes before the time proposed.

By the time he arrived, his knees were knocking slightly.

To reach the inner sanctum it was necessary to announce yourself to the President's secretary, Kyra Henkel. If she was the Cerberus of the *Präsidium*, she was a most attractive one: trim, always smartly turned out, with a friendly smile even when she was at her most businesslike. Eddie rated her a Seven—which he would up to a Seven-plus, he said, if he ever had the chance to "do her," in what he called a "spread-eagle," on the President's desk.

"The neat way she trims her hair... I bet she trims her bush too," he once confided in Richard.

Richard didn't bother to speculate: good-looking as she undoubtedly was, *Frau* Henkel was old enough (just) to be his mother, and she was light-years past the normal cut-off point of his interest in women. (God, if you started thinking about it in *those* categories, the Snake would also be a candidate (she had a good enough body), but even Eddie Hodgkins in his wildest flights of erotic fancy never went *there*.)

Frau Henkel was expecting him, but not for another ten minutes, and she asked him to sit down for a moment until the President was ready for him. Her eyes were gleaming. She'd been reading a magazine, which she slipped quickly into the drawer of her desk, though not before Richard had caught a glimpse of what looked like beefcake. Was *Frau* Henkel a *Playgirl* reader? Well, well!

Would he like a coffee, or a cup of tea? He declined the offer—he was simply too nervous—and parked himself on the other side of the office. There was a small table there, with two chairs. Spread out on the table was a selection of glossy brochures about the university, for visitors to read while they waiting. Richard picked up the glossiest one and pretended to read it.

The doors of the two adjoining rooms were both open: through one of them he could see *Frau* Henkel's deputy, Martha Binsenweis, hammering away on a computer keyboard; through the other, which led to the President's spacious office and was only slightly ajar, he could hear someone being put firmly in their place.

A few moments later there was the scraping sound of chairs being moved and Walther Wichsler, the Dean of Education, came out of the President's office looking distinctly hot and bothered.

"*Danke, Frau* Henkel," he muttered without looking at her, as he made for the outer door.

"*Herr Professor*," she acknowledged, but he was already gone.

She turned to Richard. "You can go through, *Herr* Orwell. The President will see you now. You can leave the door open."

"Doesn't he need a moment to, er, ...?"

She smiled sweetly.

"No, of course not. He has a very busy schedule today." She added (and her smile became conspiratorial), "I'm sure he's calmed down. He won't bite you!"

Richard wasn't so certain of that.

The Fat Man was standing waiting for him, and stepped forward and clasped Richard's hand in a strong, vigorous German handshake. The presidential hand was surprisingly cold and dry, not what you would have anticipated from a man who was so corpulent. Somehow you would have expected him to be sweaty and gross; he wasn't, though.

He indicated that Richard should take a seat, not in front of his enormous desk, where to judge from the position of the chairs Professor Wichsler had just been sitting, but at a large conference table.

Had Richard been offered any refreshments?

"Yes, thank you. I'm fine."

The President smiled at him.

"Good. Then I can come straight to the point, *Herr* Orwell. I'm going to give you a little job to do! As we know, you normally receive your instructions from *Frau* Professor Reiss-Baumgart. In this case, however, you will be working directly for me, and reporting back to me, and to me only. She is not to know anything about it. Do I make myself clear?"

"Of course. Any way that I can be of help..."

"You and I are going to be friends, Richard." ("Richard"? "Friends"? Richard's eyes almost popped out of their sockets.) "And it will be in your own interests to have me as a friend. *Frau* Professor Reiss-Baumgart doesn't like you too much. You do know that?"

"Yes, well—"

"She doesn't like *anyone* very much. More to the point: she is new in the job this semester, and as you may know a newly-appointed Professor will often try to bring in some of her friends or research cronies as her *Mittelbau*. No-one can blame her for that. We all do it, don't we?" It didn't seem to worry him that that "we" excluded the likes of Richard. "Unfortunately, to bring in new people you have to get rid of some old ones first. You started here a few years before *Frau* Professor Reiss-Baumgart, and you are now more than halfway through your contract. But that contract can be renewed.

You will have been informed of that?"

"Well, yes—"

"Again unfortunately, *she* will be aware of this, too. And your lowly status as a humble *Lektor* (I mean no offense!), plus your lack of a PhD, does make you vulnerable. Unless, of course, you have someone to protect you. Basically, I'm offering you a deal, *Herr* Orwell. When the time comes for your contract to be renewed—or not to be renewed—she will be surprised to find that you have an ally in the *Präsidium*. All that you have to do in return is to carry out a little investigation for me. Do you accept?"

Without knowing what the President would be asking him to do, Richard nodded.

"Yes, of course!"

Did he have any choice?

To his surprise, the President grasped his hand once again.

"Then we are in agreement! Excellent!" His jowls wobbled enthusiastically. "So, Richard, let me fill you in on the details, as they say. Are you familiar with the sad tale of the murder of Lea Hartwig?"

Richard was. A young woman named Lea Hartwig, a trainee hairdresser, had been attacked and murdered one dark evening on her way home from her place of work. According to the press, her body had been stripped and mutilated, before being arranged by the killer in a peculiar way.

This was the girl referred to so tastelessly by the anonymous poet in Richard's Creative Writing class.

"Yes. She wasn't a student, though, was she?"

The President ignored his question.

"As a longstanding member of the Rotary Club I meet people like the State Prosecutor or the Chief of Police, and through them I learn of details that don't always appear in the media." He leaned forward and lowered his voice. Richard remembered that the door to the office was open, but the President made no move to get up and close it. "What I tell you now must not be passed on to anyone else. Under any circumstances. Do you understand that?"

"Yes, of course."

"The unfortunate child, this Lea Hartwig, was mutilated, yes." The President's voice had now dropped to a bare whisper. "There was speculation in the gutter press about, um, *genital mutilation*. Of a perverse and unspeakable kind." Then louder: "But not so! It was only her fingers that were cut off, and that was done *postmortem*. And her slip was not only removed from her body—the killer seems to have taken it away with him. So what do we have here? A murderous pervert, who is also a fetishist." He suddenly smacked the table with the flat of his hand, making Richard jump. "*That* is the monster that the police have been hunting for, so far without much success, and I don't want them looking for him *here*, in my university. Especially now that the number of student applications has begun to recover again."

Richard didn't altogether understand.

"But the murder happened months ago, and it hasn't been solved. And she wasn't a student. So why should the police now come looking for the murderer here?"

"Why indeed? What do *we* have to do with such disgusting matters, here in the comfort and safety of our little fortress? Nothing, I sincerely hope. But then again—"

He paused, as *Frau* Henkel brought him in a cup of fresh coffee, She caught Richard's eye as if to repeat the offer of refreshments; he smiled, and shook his head.

After she had left, the President told him a strange story.

Since the beginning of that semester, there had been a minor epidemic of break-ins and incidents in the student hostels.

Items of female underwear had been stolen from individual students while they were asleep. Two girls claimed that they had even been *wearing* the knickers that the thief had stolen.

Several students half-remembered being stroked, or touched intimately, or had felt someone removing their underwear, before they woke up properly and raised the alarm.

Two girls at least had glimpsed the man briefly as he fled.

In addition, a student returning in the early hours from a late-night party said that she *might* have seen someone in the corridor, but her description of the man—who *might* have been of heavy build, masked, and dressed in dark colors—hadn't been of much use, even though it matched the descriptions given by the other girls.

The porter on the night desk in each case hadn't seen anyone like that coming or leaving.

The three main hostels were run by an independent organization, not by the university, and their wardens had felt no urgent need to inform the college. Nor had they spoken to the police. Childish high jinks in the hostels, strange men roaming the corridors at night, illicit comings and goings, underwear being stolen: there was nothing new about any of that.

And no-one had been hurt, had they?

But then a student *had* been slightly hurt and, while the warden of her hostel was still dithering over what if anything to do about it, the girl's father, who lived locally, had stormed into the university to complain. He was a Professor of Medicine at the local teaching hospital, and a Senior Consultant, and a fellow Rotarian, so naturally he was taken straight to the President.

The President had fortunately been able to persuade him (and all others concerned) not to go to the police, but to "leave the matter with him."

What had actually occurred? Returning from a party, and fairly drunk, the wretched girl had stripped off her clothes and collapsed into or onto her bed. She had been woken (she claimed) by a sharp pain. There was a heavy pillow lying across her face. She had struggled and yelled out, but didn't see anyone. However, she found the door to her room open, her slip had gone, and her fingers were bleeding.

"There could be a harmless explanation for all this. After all, she had been drinking heavily. She may herself have left the door to her room open; she might have cut herself accidentally; she may have mislaid her slip. Was anyone else involved? Dozing in a masturbatory, alcohol-induced twilight zone, the girl may simply have imagined an incubus mounting her in her bed."

"That's feasible," Richard ventured, with some courage, as he wasn't quite sure what an incubus was.

"Quite. Alternatively, she might well have brought a boy back to her room. Let us speculate that, after much energetic coupling, and re-arranging of the bedclothes, she sinks into post-coital slumber, her head stuck under a pillow, while her cavalier disappears off into the night, taking her slip as a trophy and not shutting the door properly behind him."

"Also possible. But she wouldn't have forgotten having the boy in her room, would she?"

"Probably not. But she wakes in a panic, believes she has been attacked, and won't admit that her sordid little encounter is the likely explanation— she certainly won't want to mention it to the warden, or to her father. My problem is this: if she *does* go to the police with her story, they will start looking for a potential serial killer with a morbid interest in fingers. And they will begin by looking *here*."

"Not necessarily. No, sorry, yes," Richard was extremely nervous, "they would come looking here, of course, yes, but maybe not for a murderer. Maybe just for a copycat criminal, a sick pervert."

"A copycat? Interesting. But that's not likely. Only three people outside the investigation know that Lea Hartwig's *fingers* were cut off, and that it was only her slip that was stolen, and who are they? I'm one of them. You are now the second. The third is the man who did it."

Richard wasn't convinced.

"There might have been a leak. What about the police? And the forensics people?"

"Yes, but then the leak would have been to the media, wouldn't it? And not to the Perverts' Club of Reichsstadt." The President paused, and then smiled. "Good! I see that I've woken your interest in the case! Brilliant!. What I now need you to do for me is to find the person or persons responsible for this, and find him before the police hear about our latest hostel incident. If they do, they'll put two and two together to make five, and then start tramping around in the university in heavy boots. It won't just be our students who'll panic; it'll frighten the parents of *prospective* students, and we can't have that."

Richard swallowed hard.

"You're asking me to hunt the murderer?"

"The murderer? Of course not! Don't be silly! My dear Orwell, *that* unpleasant creature is probably in Spain or Australia by now. If someone has been playing silly games in girls' hostels, it won't be the same person as the murderer of Lea Hartwig. Any similarities between the two are probably an annoying coincidence. If that. The man might not even exist—our latest victim probably cut her hand in a drunken accident. Bear in mind that, if there *was* an attacker in her room, he had her at his mercy, and he could have killed and mutilated her at his leisure. But he didn't do that, did he? No, I don't see any murderer at work here, and you're not going to be in any danger, Mr. Orwell. But whatever has been going on, this nonsense needs to be stopped, before it causes the university serious embarrassment."

Richard felt much relieved, though now he couldn't see any easy way of wriggling out of the assignment.

He had one final question: "Why me? Why not hire a private detective for this?"

The President beamed expansively.

"Two good reasons, my dear boy, and not just to save money. All the girls in the hostels who have reported unusual goings-on happen to be students of English. Trainee teachers, not philology students. That can't be a total coincidence, surely? Either we have a case of mass hysteria within a closed group of late adolescent girls (not a completely unknown phenomenon!), or a prankster, someone connected to your department, a male student or an immature member of staff, a young lecturer or a technician, is targeting them. Theoretically, it could even be you—"

"Oh no!"

"—ha ha, just my little joke. I'm sure that you would never make inappropriate advances to your students." He paused ominously. "Or would you?" And then he laughed "But we need an insider to investigate this. *Frau Henkel* will give you a list of the names of four of the girls involved—the ones who are not demanding to remain anonymous—with the 'where' and the 'when' of each incident. Treat the information with the utmost discretion, please." He glanced at his watch. "And now you must excuse me."

"Of course." Both men got up. "Um, actually, you said *two* reasons."

The President giggled—a most unnerving sound.

"Elementary, my dear Orwell. You wrote your MA thesis on Conan

Doyle, did you not? By your choice of topic you have brought this, so to speak, upon yourself!"

On his way out, Kyra Henkel gave him a folded sheet of paper, and advised him to regard the information printed on it as highly confidential.

"There is the issue of data protection, Mr. Orwell. Also—," and she smiled at him with disarming sweetness, "when you go to meet these girls, please treat them gently. You probably know them all, but this is a sensitive matter. And we don't want any of them to panic. They're very young."

That was now weeks ago. Far from rushing into action, Richard had done nothing at all since receiving the confidential list of names. No, that wasn't true. He had worried endlessly about the task he'd been given, hoping that it might somehow go away of its own accord. But so far he had no more than glanced at the four names on the paper: Jeannine Garbe; Miriam Burkhardt; Felicitas Förster; and (the girl whose fingers had been cut)—Lisa Meyer.

THE STAFF MEETING

At one o'clock sharp, without the traditional fifteen-minute delay referred to as the "academic quarter of an hour," the staff meeting of the English Department began. It was the second meeting that the Snake had called since taking office at the beginning of that winter semester. It was *her* meeting, as it was *her* department.

She was a Professor of the highest rank, what was formerly known as an *Ordinarius*, the ultimate level to which a German academic could aspire. In a culture which still worshiped academic titles, she was one of the gods. In her own little department, where apart from herself only the spineless Christenkorn had a doctorate, she *was* God. She was *Frau* Professor Dr. phil. habil. Leonore Reiss-Baumgart, the "habil." revealing that she had achieved the distinguished post-doctoral qualification known as the *Habilitation*.

At one minute past one that afternoon, looking round the table at her team of lecturers and assistants, with two chairs still empty, she felt satisfied and confident, the tensions of the night before completely forgotten. Inwardly, she flexed her muscles. Those irritations were already forgotten. There was no-one here who could challenge her. They were all weak, in their different ways. She could break each and every one of them at will. She wouldn't necessarily do it, but they should all know that she could, and at any time that she chose. Yes!

This happy daydream was disturbed by Christenkorn, who had the temerity to open the discussion by addressing her without referring to her as

"*Frau Professor.*"

"*Herr* Kurz and *Herr* Snoad were told about the meeting, *Frau* Reiss, and I'm sure that they'll both be here soon."

Richard saw at once how annoyed she was. He wasn't the one who'd thought up the name "the Snake." That came from the students, who already detested her. But he thought it fitted her well. Two of her team were late for the meeting! She was the only person around the table who didn't know that Kurz *always* came late to meetings, on principle. It was a democratic statement; it was an act of self-expression. It was the way Harlan Kurz did things.

Or that Jonathan Snoad almost never appeared (but always had an impressive excuse).

Richard saw Enno Müller and Dorothea Schlichting exchange amused glances, across the empty seat that they were keeping for Kurz. They, and Kajo, had been the old guard of Germans in the department that Richard had joined. The two of them had barely tolerated Christenkorn as Acting Head of Department, and now their grins were saying, "Just who does Kajo reckon he is? Does he still think he's running things? The Snake will chew his balls off!"

"I imagine we can start without him, *Herr* Christenkorn. Wouldn't you agree?"

"*Herr* Christenkorn," without the doctorate. *Touché.*

But at this point Harlan R. Kurz burst energetically into the room. He expressed himself by ignoring the chair waiting for him and parking himself at the far end of the table, from where he apologized (in no particular direction and to no specific person) in his own peculiar version of English.

"Lot on today. But no stress: I had this one bookmarked, real-time."

Was that an apology?

He spoke in a distinctive, mock Californian whine, like no authentic American accent anyone around the table had ever heard. Was he a genuine American? Americans who met him were often appalled by him, and were sure he *wasn't*. His German colleagues often found him very difficult to understand (as did the students), whichever language he was using.

The R stood for Raymond, he had once let slip. Kurz insisted on the middle initial—like a good old US of A boy—but he normally suppressed speculation about what it stood for, maybe to make himself seem more interesting, or because "Harlan Ray" sounded too much like trailer trash.

Eddie had "researched" the whole matter by wheedling *Frau* Ludewig into asking *Frau* Binsenweis in the *Präsidium* to check the full name on his contract. He was a German—of course! Hartmut Raimund Kurz, so the "Raymond" wasn't too far off the mark. But he pronounced his name as Americans would (Kurts) rather than the German way (Koorts). Why did he have to pretend to be an American? That was the big unanswered question.

Professor Timpe, who had hired him, had (for some weird reason of his own) introduced him to the team as "Mister Kurz from the United States." No-one had questioned that. Professor Timpe was a saint. No-one ever doubted what he said.

"We had almost given you up for lost, Harlan *Schätzchen*."

Dorothea couldn't resist sticking her oar in, Richard thought, listening to the burst of banal small-talk that then followed. Behind it, there were power plays and maneuverings. Richard observed the department's group dynamics, but was neither willing nor able to join in or take sides.

Dorothea, for example, loved using diminutive suffixes like *-chen* or *-lein*, a good way to irritate her colleagues. Enno, her favorite, was "*Baby-chen*" or "*Babylein*." Since he was tiny, it actually fitted.

Harlan was her "little treasure."

Behind his back, everyone called Christenkorn "Kajo" (Karl-Johannes), which he hated, though only Dorothea used it to his face.

The Snake was fuming as the meeting buzzed along happily without her. With a dramatic movement, she cracked open a large book lying in front of her and hit it down on the table. Everyone stared at her.

"This is our main topic today. *Research.* Yes, *that* dirty word! What I have here is this year's Research Prospectus. An expensively produced volume, but a depressing document, if I may say so, as far as our own department is concerned."

"It has to be seen in context, though"—this was Enno, the educational empiricist, puffing himself up like a frog—"It was an exercise in self-evaluation. We were honest enough to focus solely on the essential research being done in this department..."

"Essential research" presumably meant Enno's endless studies of teacher-pupil interaction, and of the body language of the classroom: How many times did the teacher scratch himself, and *where*? What was the yawn rate per person per lesson?

The Snake licked her lips.

"I take it that you are referring to your own little project, *Herr* Müller? It is certainly expensive enough, if that is a satisfactory measure of quality." (All that money to pay student ancillaries to evaluate the hundreds of questionnaires! It made Enno popular with the students, though.)

Enno's chest subsided slightly.

"Naturally I was also thinking of Karl-Johannes's studies on motivation. I believe he has several publications listed as pending."

"Yeah, he's cool," Kurz added, unhelpfully.

Kajo cultivated the image of a kindly, deeply responsible man, but Richard had never penetrated this facade. Was he right to like him? Was there more to him than met the eye? With Jonathan Snoad, who was Harlan's soulmate (and Richard's *bête-noire*), there was definitely less. Behind his pretentious talk, Snoad was a vain nonentity, an empty husk, though people like that were easy to underestimate and their selfishness could be very dangerous.

Kajo was held to be the dullest teacher in the university. It was therefore ironical that he had made so many contributions to the literature on how to *motivate*. These included such papers as "Beyond the Overhead Projector: Training Learner Vocabulary with Computers" and "Nursery Rhymes—How to Make Grammar Lessons Go with a Swing."

He spoke up, perhaps to turn the Snake's baleful attention away from the subject of his publications.

"It was a difficult time for any of us to complete our projects." The Snake made a snorting sound, clearing her nose of mucus. Ignoring her, Kajo continued: "We had to cover the teaching and administrative functions of the, er, vacant professorial position."

"I appreciate the efforts you made as Acting Head of Department, *Herr* Christenkorn, though it is rather a pity that during that time your famous expertise in motivation couldn't be extended to your own colleagues"—tongue licking over lips again—"still, that is one matter that you don't need to worry about any more."

She began to read out the summary of the English Department's endeavors, as listed in the Research Prospectus. It didn't take her long, though she added numerous grunts, snorts or meaningful pauses at the appropriate places.

Like most of the rest of them, Richard hadn't had a chance to look at it. Enno had collected their information, and *Frau* Ludewig had prepared the department's submission. Only Enno and Kajo had seen the whole manuscript.

At around this time the Snake had arrived in the department, and, according to *Frau* Ludewig, she had moved like lightning to have her stuff added to the Prospectus. This was long after the file had been prepared for submission to the *Präsidium*, and almost before the formalities of her appointment as Professor had been concluded.

Later, one copy only of the printed and bound Prospectus had been sent to the departmental office, and the Snake had literally snatched it out of *Frau* Ludewig's hands: "I'll take that!"

The entry on **Professor Dr. phil. habil. Leonore Reiss-Baumgart** probably constituted more than half the entire entry for the department. Her research portfolio sounded to Richard like a catalog of the least intriguing aspects of English language didactics, and was strong on such topics as attracted little interest from anyone else in the scholarly community; her publications were many but *not* various (the whole collection could be boiled down to two or three themes, endlessly recycled); but the titles of her essays pressed all the right fashionable buttons, without giving away what the texts were *about*.

How had she obtained the Chair of English? Richard hadn't been in the committee that selected her, though he had heard that the other candidates "were even worse" (hard to believe, that!).

Maybe the Commissioner for Gender Equality, Kerstin Dröge-Daschmeyer, had supported her, as part of the initiative to increase the percentage of women in key positions?

Maybe they had decided to favor a candidate who was "stronger" on the language didactics side? Professor Timpe's doctorate had been on Oscar Wilde (and for years he hadn't taught much else, though he had reacted to snide comments by broadening his range of lectures to take in such themes as "Wilde the Educationalist" or "Wilde in America"). Kajo's doctorate had also been literary.

Next came the German academic staff. (The Snake was cagey about referring to members of the *Mittelbau* as her "colleagues," that word being used by many Professors only to refer to their peers.) First, Kajo, because of his seniority and his tenured status, and then the other two, alphabetically:

Dr. phil. Karl-Johannes Christenkorn: motivation (and, lo and behold, a couple of publications were indeed listed as pending).

Dipl.-Päd. Enno Müller: empirical research into teacher-pupil interaction from the interpersonal psychology perspective (ongoing doctoral project; a report on initial results pending).

Dipl.-Päd. Dorothea Schlichting: themes and problems in adult education (ongoing).

But *was* anything going on? Richard seriously doubted it.

The "*Dipl.-Päd.*" was a postgraduate qualification in education, often referred to by those working in more "serious" academic areas (such as philologists) as the "Mickey Mouse degree."

There followed the non-German *Mittelbau*, in no particular order:

Jonathan Edwin Snoad, MA (Oxon.): issues in contemporary intellectual culture (partly in collaboration with H.R. Kurz, ongoing; publications pending).

The Snake snorted loudly, and for once Richard sympathized with her. She didn't know it yet, but this was the familiar Snoad smokescreen. If pressed for details, he would refer the questioner to his "*cher ami et collaborateur*" Harlan Kurz for further information, while emphasizing that "Rome was not built in a day." In general, he was an expert in creating the impression of being busy, whereas in fact he would seldom do anything, beyond his fixed teaching duties, unless he was paid for it.

He was aided and abetted in this by Kurz, who despite Snoad's frequent absence at meetings would throw his friend's name into whatever was being discussed: "*Jaan*" (Richard always thought of toilets) "should be brought in on this," "This is one of *Jaan's* major concerns," "We need *Jaan's* take on this issue" (or his "angle," or his "input"), and so on. Nothing was ever specified, but it created a nebulous impression of activity and involvement.

Richard Orwell, BA (Hons.), MA: Conan Doyle Studies; a book-length publication pending.

This was the revised version of his MA thesis on Conan Doyle that wasn't *quite* ready to be submitted yet to Cambridge University Press. In fact, CUP were still blissfully unaware that such a manuscript might or might not one day be heading in their direction.

Harlan R. Kurz, AB: issues in contemporary intellectual culture (partly in collaboration with J. Snoad, ongoing; publications pending); translation studies (ongoing, publications pending).

Unlike his friend Snoad, Harlan Kurz would tell all who cared to listen that he was working on this or that "major project" or "definitive study," and waffle on incomprehensibly about it. The projects and studies tended to have in-your-face titles like *The Feminist Imperative* or *The Gay Challenge*. He had been announcing the impending completion of these epochal undertakings for years, but nothing had ever appeared in print.

Finally, the part-timer Eddie and the Taiwanese visiting scholar Dr. Dong:

Edmund Hodgkins, MA (Cantab.): research-inactive.

She slammed the Prospectus shut.

"And we don't need to concern ourselves, do we, with our dear friend *Herr* Dr. Dong? I assume that his long hours of research in the University of Reichsstadt Library will one day bear fruit! Or does someone wish to follow this up? No, I thought not."

No-one actually knew what Dr. Dong got up to in the library. Maybe he just looked for a quiet corner, in "Nineteenth-Century Church History" or "Moral Philosophy," and (inspired by what was all around him) rested his head on his arms, closed his eyes and slept.

"It isn't that we don't appreciate the honor of having a distinguished Asian scholar working among us—"

"*Herr* Christenkorn!" she interrupted him. "That is not the point. The point is that *this*," and she prodded demonstratively at the Prospectus in front of her, as if indicating something that had just been sicked up by a cat, "this document is awful. It is truly *dreadful*. And the noble efforts of our temporary guest Dr. Dong, however much we appreciate them, won't change that, one way or the other. So—what are we going to do about it?"

"Taking what we have already achieved as a starting point, there are different ways we can approach it" (Kajo was doing his best to sound magisterial) "and I am confident that in the fullness of time we shall discover that every single member of the team will have made a lasting and dynamic contribution."

From her reaction, it was obvious what the Snake thought of Kajo's input. After glaring at him witheringly, she scowled at everyone else around the table. Only Harlan Kurz, who was preoccupied with texting, and bopping enthusiastically up and down on his chair like an idiot, failed to notice.

"No doubt, no doubt," she said. "Well, since no-one has a lesson until rather later this afternoon, we are free to consider these *dynamic contributions* at our leisure."

Richard now regretted having given the *Mensa* a miss. His stomach was rumbling badly. The sandwich from Real hadn't helped. Could he slip out quietly, as if for a toilet break, and dash down to the foyer to get himself a bar of chocolate or a chocolate-chip cookie from the vending machines (if they were working)?

It would probably take too long, and it would attract her attention. He didn't want to put himself in the firing line any more than could be avoided. In her eyes, he would likely be one of the hopeless cases who were not pulling their weight on the team.

LUNCH AT THE *MENSA*

While Richard was trying to avoid having to explain the reasons for his "research-inactivity," Lisa and Steffi had met up for lunch at the *Mensa*. It was just before 2 p.m., which is when they normally stopped serving hot food. Although it was a Monday, and thus outside the *Di-Mi-Do* framework, the *Mensa* was surprisingly full. Many of them were slug-a-beds who had only just hauled themselves out from under their duvets and were lazily substituting a greasy lunch for a late breakfast.

In her reply to Lisa's text message, Steffi had insisted on meeting at the *Mensa*, and not in the hostel, where both of them were residents.

Could that mean that Steffi had spent the night somewhere else?

God, what a tart that girl was, Lisa told herself (not wholly without envy). She was putting herself about like a right old slag. She wasn't a fantastic looker, so how did she do it?

Steffi Albertz was small and dark-haired, with a flat chest and a body that looked better naked than clothed. Steffi was lithe and quick rather than athletic. She didn't keep herself as clean as Lisa did, she tended to wear the same unambitious clothes combinations a bit too often, and she wasn't over-concerned about make-up. But when she smiled, men jumped. Her grin was her principal weapon. She wasn't a Princess—more the cheeky lady's maid.

Lisa was horrified when her friend told her how many men she'd been to bed with. Steffi recited their names in roughly chronological order, substituting unflattering epithets like "Curly Dick," "Wet Boy" or "Mister Premature" for those whose names she couldn't remember. Lisa soon lost count. Her own conquests could be counted very comfortably on the fingers of both hands—with the second hand only recently having become necessary, because of Sebastian. (Now what epithet would Steffi have given *him*?)

For several years Lisa had agonized over whether, deep down, she might be a lesbian. She'd had some pretty intense crushes on women teachers or older girls at her school, and she hadn't discovered boys until comparatively late. Up to that moment, boys had not really been part of her emotional history. She had viewed them as being on a hygienic level with dogs, but less cuddly and far less trustworthy. And, like dogs, with their tongues hanging out all the time. As every girl knew, boys only wanted ONE THING (and she hadn't been prepared, yet, to give that to them).

In her life till then there had therefore been "pashes" and flirts, but no penetrations. Her "first" had been a married man, one of the neighbors, who'd flattered and jollied her along for months before pouncing on her during a street party in the early hours of January 1st, when everyone was too drunk and preoccupied with the fireworks to notice what was going on.

Afterwards, she had been disgusted, angry, and bitterly ashamed of herself.

Lisa knew that she was better-looking than Steffi, but Steffi had whatever it was, that certain something, that men liked.

The two girls met as arranged, and joined the queue for the vegetarian Option Two, which today was a sort of hash of fried noodles and chopped up vegetable gunk, over-seasoned with curry powder. It was a lot better than Option One, which was a greasy slab of luncheon meat in batter (cynically referred to as "East German Schnitzel"), accompanied by mashed potatoes and last week's carrots.

The third option was a trip to the Super Salad Bar. Salads were widely acknowledged to be healthy (yawn), but this didn't happen to be a declared "slimming week" for either girl. They weren't rabbits, and if your lunch came from the Super Salad Bar you were guaranteed to be hungry again before the end of your next class.

Clutching their trays, Lisa and Steffi wandered round the dining hall until they found an isolated table that wasn't wonky, and which was a reasonable distance away from anyone too awful. For instance, away from the prying eyes and pricked ears of other girls from English, or from a couple of long tables around which gangs of noisy Engineering students had clustered.

Lisa always had a feeling that the Engineers were gawping at her tits. She didn't hold that against them. They didn't get to see women very often, so it was understandable. Playing around all day with pistons and sockets must make them unbearably horny, and many of them probably hadn't seen a tit in real life (as opposed to online) since the last time they were breast-fed.

Steffi for her part enjoyed being stared at, but she did have certain minimum standards, which Engineering students were unlikely to meet. (I mean, if you had any real class, you weren't going to study Engineering, were you?)

She was stubborn and unforthcoming about what she'd been up to. It couldn't have been a lesson—not on a Monday morning!—unless it was one of those compulsory introductory lectures, but then Lisa would have been expected to go to that too. So it must have been a man.

Steffi refused to be drawn, and kept changing the subject.

Why had Lisa wanted to meet? They'd be seeing each other later that afternoon anyway, wouldn't they, in Harlan Kurz's translation class? *If* Steffi decided to go, she added. She hadn't forgiven Mr. Kurz for his behavior after the Freshers' Week party. She had generously given him a lift home, he'd had some drunken fun with her in the car, and then he didn't want to know? What a bastard!

(Aha, Lisa thought, maybe they'd done it after all.)

"And I'm only going if we can sit right at the back! I don't *have* to go. I can get the texts from someone after the class."

Steffi didn't say "from you." Both of them knew that Lisa's translations and annotations, if she ever made any, that is, would be pretty worthless. No, Steffi would chat up Pimply Konstantin, the star of the translation classes (and biggest nerd in the department) and get a copy of the notes that he took during the lesson. Konstantin would do *anything* to be seen being spoken to by girls in public. (He'd probably even rush home afterwards to jerk himself off. Or maybe he wouldn't, which would explain why he had so many pimples.)

Yes, they could sit at the back, Lisa said, though they'd have to arrive there early to bag some good seats. The back row in language classes was always popular, for obvious reasons.

Personally, she'd have preferred to sit right at the front, where Harlan might notice her, and from where she could enjoy watching him flouncing about. Every time that he made what he thought was a witty remark he'd spin round and twitch his tasty little backside, like a game-show host on TV. Usually he could rotate at will on the polished floor, but once he'd tried it standing at the side of the room where the floor was rough, and his foot had stuck as he twisted. Ouch! That must have hurt! She didn't share these thoughts with Steffi, though.

Of course, if you sat at the front, there was a teeny-weeny risk of being asked to translate a passage of text, but the danger was minimal. Harlan Kurz was one of those lecturers who liked to push on quickly, and get through as much of the text as possible, which meant he took answers mostly from the stars like Konstantin or Goggle-Eyed Beatrix, both of whom stuck their hands up all the time, thank God.

"So, come on, what *did* you want to talk about? Tell! I've got an office hour to go to."

Lisa took a while to explain what it was. After all, it wasn't something she was particularly proud of.

She wanted to move out of the hostel.

"*What?* Are you crazy?!"

"Sssh, keep your voice down, people are looking."

There were long waiting lists for all the hostels, especially the three on the same street as the main campus, and the *Ernst-Egon-Gutknecht-Haus* ("Eeg" or "Gutie" for short), named after the first postwar Lord Mayor of Reichsstadt, was the best of those. Both girls knew that, but Steffi reminded her of it nevertheless.

Lisa shrugged.

"So what? If there are waiting lists, that just means it'll be easier for me to find someone to take my room."

They both also knew that that wasn't the point. You were expected to take the room for the full year. That was the way it was done. There was a whole load of boring paperwork involved, which had to be coordinated between the student, the university administration, the bank (or the student's parents' bank), and the institution that ran the hostels. Forms had to be filled in, statements had to be signed and countersigned, deposits had to be arranged. The short-tempered ladies who did the paperwork absolutely hated people moving in or out other than on the designated dates. It wasn't Airbnb, they would say. The students should count themselves lucky. Now in *our* day...

"But why do you want to move out anyway?" When Lisa didn't answer, she whispered, "Oh, because of *that*."

"Yes," Lisa whispered back, "because of *that*. What else could it be?"

"Aren't you making too much out of it? After all, nothing happened, you didn't see anyone—you could have imagined it all. Come on, you'd had more than a few that night, hadn't you?"

Lisa was trembling slightly.

"I said that I didn't see him, and I didn't really. It was only a glimpse. But I saw his *eyes*."

"Oh."

"I get this feeling that he's still watching me, and I turn round dead fast, and he's not there, of course. But I don't feel safe there any more. And, you know, other girls have seen things too—"

"Ah, you mean that business about the stolen knickers?" Steffi grinned. "That's just our boys and their silly games. I mean, *look* at them," and she swiveled on her chair to indicate the nearest table of male students, who conveniently happened to be Engineers, "oozing with maturity, aren't they? They probably all collect stamps!" She sighed. "It's enough to drive you into the arms of older men."

Lisa remained adamant.

"Anyway, my dad wants me out of the hostel too. He went to the President about it. So I don't think they'll make any fuss about me moving out. He said he wanted me to live at home again."

That, of course, was out of the question. Lisa's dad might be a top doctor with pots of money and a huge house—Lisa still had an amazing room of her own under the roof, like an eyrie, Steffi had been there several times—but taking your dirty laundry home at the weekends was one thing, and having your social life monitored 24/7 was another.

Reichsstadt might be Lisa's home-town, but there had never for a moment been any question of her living at home once she became a student. There was nothing in the universe uncooler than that (except studying Engineering). Besides, having to pay for Steffi's hostel room was hardly going to bankrupt Dr. Meyer, was it?

"So you said no. OK. Look, I'm telling you, no panic, you'll be fine in the hostel. Lightning doesn't strike twice, and all that?"

"No, I can't stay there. You're right, I didn't really see anything. But there was a *presence*. There was something horrible there in the room."

Steffi was beginning to lose her patience. She glanced down at her watch. "Well, I need to go." She started clearing her stuff onto the tray; then said: "If you don't want my advice, why are you telling me all this? Why don't you just... you know, go ahead and do it?"

And then came the surprise.

Lisa's dad had a colleague who owned and rented out a very nice apartment. If Lisa wasn't prepared to come home, he had said, he wanted her to move in there at least, where she would be safer. He could easily arrange it. His colleague had just had the apartment redecorated, and it was currently empty. It was a really smart place.

However, the apartment was for two people at least. Lisa was hoping that Steffi would move in with her.

"It's huge, and it's not too expensive." She added, hopefully: "We can have some great parties. There's even a garden."

Steffi laughed. "You know me, girl, I can have parties *anywhere*. So, where is this amazing new pad of yours, then?"

Lisa blushed. Steffi wasn't going to like the next bit.

"It's up on the Nordstädter Allee. You know, near the end, but before you get to the river."

"Jesus, Lisa, no way! Fuck, that's where *they* come from"—again she swept her arm round to gesture at the nearby table of Engineers, who were clumsily loading their trays and pushing back their chairs—"that's even further out than where Harlan Kurz lives. Who on earth's going to trek out to your famous parties? Even people with a car won't be able to find it. It's beyond the Metro. It's Outer Darkness. It's like falling off the edge of the world. It's... you know what it is?"—and she used a charming but obscure German expression—"It's where the fox and the hare say 'Good night' to each other!"

Meaning that it was the back of beyond, a place too remote for anyone but Engineers and the terminally senile to want to live.

She also asked Lisa how she would manage, without a car, being stuck out there? Lisa had rather hoped that Steffi would say yes simply because of her car—it would make everything so much easier, she had thought. Damn!

The car business was a highly sensitive point with Lisa. She had failed her driving test, and her father (who as far as she could tell was drowning in money) had told her that, whatever happened, he wasn't going to buy her a car. Let her finish college, get a job, pass her test, and then he'd think about it. In the meantime, there was no hurry, the roads weren't safe, and there were buses and the Metro, weren't there?

Ironically, the modest Reichsstadt Metro system, which didn't go anywhere of great interest to most students, and wouldn't have helped much in this case either, would have taken Lisa's father almost from his front door to the main entrance of the teaching hospital where he worked. But he still chose to drive an impressive Mercedes.

Lisa was not surprised by her friend's negative reaction, but she was hurt by her vehemence. She had known that Steffi wouldn't be enthusiastic, but had hoped that she might at least pretend to be pleased.

"I'm sorry," Lisa said, sullenly, though she felt sorry only for herself.

"No, *I'm* sorry. It's a generous offer, really, and I am grateful. Honest. Hey, maybe we can we talk about this again? You're upset. But you'll get over it! Gutie's a great place. You've got all the action there, and it's only five minutes to the uni. Just lock your room next time, girl! Get yourself a pepper spray! Get a dog! Do a karate course! Get a live-in boyfriend! Well, you know what I mean, a *sleep*-in boyfriend. Whatever it was, it's done. It's over. It was a long, long time ago—like your last half-decent shag, no doubt!—and it's not going to happen again, is it? OK?"

Lisa should have laughed, but instead she went quiet. Against all the background clatter of the *Mensa*, Steffi could barely hear what she said.

"No. You weren't there. I still dream about it. And I know that he's going to come back."

"Stop it! Enough is enough!" Steffi got up. "I'll see you over at Transy I, then, since you fancy dear Mr. Kurz so much. I have to say, you're welcome to him! But I'll tell you this: we're not sitting in the front row. Agreed?"

And the two girls took their trays back, Steffi sauntering on ahead and wiggling her backside (as Lisa noticed) in a most vulgar manner for the benefit of anyone who was paying attention, be he an Engineer or not.

TOWN AND GOWN

Steffi's perception that there were parts of the city that were trendy, and parts that were uncool, was personal rather than accurate. A more objective assessment would have been that Reichsstadt was a stolid, prosperous, dull place—almost without exception. There had been regular attempts to launch "style magazines" for the local yuppies, with titles like *Trend*, *Pacesetter* or *City-Impact*. These advert-heavy publications had invariably folded almost immediately, because the genuinely "hip" was nowhere to be found in Reichsstadt.

No-one who ever achieved wealth or fame stayed very long. It was a large city, but still a backwater. What was said or done there seldom impinged on the wider world beyond. As a corporate friend of mine once put it, "Take my advice: if your company ever speculates about transferring you there, speak up quickly, because there are far better postings to be had." ("Basically, it's a shit-hole," he had added, in a whisper, behind his raised hand.)

In this regard, town and gown matched each other well. Reichsstadt, the uninspiring capital of Germany's least exciting state, was too small to be truly cosmopolitan, but large enough to have no excuse for being so boring. The *Reichsstädter* were materialistic, unimaginative, and unfriendly, without the flair of the Hanseatic cities of the north or the bonhomie of the Catholic south of Germany. (Or so said those students who came from the Hanseatic north or the Catholic south).

If Reichsstadt had been a few kilometers further east, it would have found itself in that old Communist dinosaur, the German Democratic Republic, and might have been renamed as something dreadful like Rosa-Luxemburg-City. Whatever the undereducated may have believed, however, there was nothing sinister about the "Reich-" part of the name Reichsstadt, which referred not to the notorious Third Empire (Hitler's), but to the city's

Holy Roman Imperial importance in the Late Middle Ages. Signs of this earlier magnificence were everywhere, in the form of uninteresting medieval walls and protected or reconstructed churches, and they featured heavily in the municipal tourist advertising.

The students ignored these dull monuments—theirs was a different concept of culture—and they complained constantly that the city didn't have enough bars or clubs. The presence of two cathedrals, one Protestant, one Catholic, reflecting the denominational balance of the population, a couple of small trade fairs per year, and a local cuisine that rang the changes on fatty pork dishes and different varieties of cabbage couldn't make up for the lack of a *scene*.

The university was weighted towards its two largest components—a huge faculty of engineering, stuck out on the northern edge of town, and an assortment of departments on the main campus—with a third complex halfway between them. The institutes on the main campus were grouped into several squabbling faculties and were devoted to the training of different types of teacher.

Among them were the Departments of English, French, Slavic and German Didactics, the first three of which had been set up after the war as a sop to the allied occupation forces. The majority of their academic staff expended their energy on matters didactical and pedagogic, rather than on their subjects *per se*.

The Slavic institute was tiny, there being little demand any more for teachers of Russian.

The French Department was slightly larger, a fact maybe connected with the regular injections of grant and scholarship money from Paris. Its Professor was never seen (she was usually in Paris, arranging those generous grants and scholarships), and the department was dominated by the statuesque *Lektorin*, *Madame* Plouvier, whose classes in *Civilisation française* had such resounding titles as "*La Grande Nation*," "*Le Grand Siècle*" or "*Les Grands Vins de France*," which made Richard's courses in Background Studies sound depressingly workaday. *La Grande Madame* had an intimidating reputation, and even the President reportedly stood slightly in awe of her.

The English and German institutes, in contrast, were swamped with students. English was regarded as a soft option (everyone knew *some* English, didn't they?), while German was seen as the default subject for the academically challenged (since you escaped the horrors of having to learn reams of new grammar and vocabulary).

Trapped between the twin molochs, of Engineering on the one hand and the teacher training institutes on the other, were the pure sciences, cut off from their Engineering compadres and enfeebled by a lack of third-party funding from industry, and the fine arts: among the latter were "serious" (that is to say, non-teacher-training) departments of English, German and other philologies, and an entity mysteriously known as "The Institute of Esthetic Praxes."

The pure sciences and the fine arts co-habited uneasily in a third complex of buildings, further up the Südstädter Allee near the crossroads beyond which it became the Nordstädter Allee. Even though their own buildings were much nicer, those working or studying at this (in their opinion) remote location resented the teacher trainers' occupation of the main campus and their convenient proximity to the *Mensa,* the university library, and the administration. They sneered at their didactically-oriented colleagues' academic shallowness, while complaining that they themselves (who did *proper* research) inevitably drew the short straws when it came to media exposure.

That last complaint was definitely not true of the esthetic practitioners, the most exotic beasts in the Reichsstadt menagerie. They were adept in drawing attention to themselves, with exhibitionistic displays of various sorts: avant-garde drama productions, happenings, events, and installations. These tended to involve exposed breasts, and actors clambering about on climbing frames, shouting at each other earnestly.

Unforgettable for those who had seen it was their reworking of Shakespeare's *Tempest,* with a lesbian Miranda denouncing Ferdinand as a male chauvinist pig, and artificially induced vomiting. (For the benefit of anyone who failed to grasp its significance, the symbolism of the vomiting was explained at some length in the photocopied program handed out to the audience.)

The structure of the university was less the consequence of wise, long-term planning as the result of several attempts, over the years, to give the institution an eye-catching "profile." It had certain advantages, at least for the students. At the Freshers' Week discos, the placid heifers of teacher training (or so Eddie put it) could pair off with the clumsy bullocks of mechanical engineering, and everyone got more or less what or whom they wanted. Planners couldn't have organized that better!

One serious problem that arose from the arrangement of the faculties was a recurring duplication of seminars. The teacher trainers constantly strayed into subject areas that were normally the preserve of specialists, and offered their own unique and enthusiastic take on Native Americans, The European Film, Chinese History, Western Colonialism, or the Vietnam War. It wasn't only the rival "didactic" and "philological" language departments who trod on each other's toes in this manner—the worst offenders were probably the colleagues from General Educational Studies, from whom no topic was safe.

No attempt was made by the teaching staff to coordinate their efforts, and there was no central authority charged with the fine tuning of the whole programme of courses offered by the university. What mattered was that each of the so-called "modules," or groups of classes, that made up a degree was filled with lessons that fitted the specifications for that module, and since those specifications were usually fairly vague that requirement was easily met.

In this way, a seminar on, say, Pop Culture might be offered by departments in four different faculties ("didactic English," "philological German," Esthetic Praxes, and Sociology), with none of the profs responsible bothering to look over the fence at what their neighbors were doing. Yet the students hardly cared, since the approaches were often entertainingly different. Let a hundred flowers bloom, let a hundred schools of thought contend!

Generally speaking, the seminars in teacher training came in three varieties.

The largest group of classes involved "student-oriented teaching," i.e., the dumbing down and simultaneous jazzing up of the material to satisfy the broader lumpen mass of students. This was where Lisa and Steffi felt most at home.

A much smaller group consisted of those classes that stretched the students to breaking-point but broadly met the expectations of the brighter ones, namely, that by the end of the semester they would be slightly wiser and better informed than they had been before.

The remaining classes made even fewer concessions to the slower-witted—here, the material was dumbed *up* by being refracted through dense, noxious mists of Critical Theory. The students could gape or doze as they preferred. There were no true epiphanies, no Eureka-moments of "so *that's* what it's all about!" But, as long as there were credit points that could eventually be obtained (usually with an essay cut-and-pasted from the internet), most were happy to let the gobbledygook wash over them. And the titles of the classes sounded so impressive.

One or two students listened carefully, however, learning the tricks and the terminology so that one day they too could plant their feet on the lower rungs of the academic ladder.

AFTER THE MEETING

Richard came out of the meeting exhausted, bad-tempered and hungry.

He couldn't claim that the Snake had been unfair—she had bullied everyone in turn, sneering at what they had done and demanding to know how their present activities merited being described as "scholarly research."

"When I tell *Frau* Ludewig to make me a list of local elementary schools that offer beginner classes in English, she also has to do research. But I wouldn't dream of putting the results in next year's Prospectus! Still, they wouldn't look out of place beside your research efforts, *Frau* Schlichting."

Dorothea had gone a color somewhere between pink and purple, but had said nothing.

The Snake would now have a dangerous enemy: Doro was a thoroughly nasty person, a malicious gossip and intriguer. Richard would never turn his back on her (metaphorically speaking). Arrogant but underqualified, she was highly sensitive to criticism. She liked dishing it out; she didn't like being on the receiving end.

Enno grasped her hand to reassure her. He had got off lightly, since his mammoth project was well-funded and would lead, eventually, to a doctorate. It could be sneered at, but not dismissed off-hand. He already had his supervisor and his examiners lined up, marshaled for him by the mild-mannered Professor Timpe before his retirement. He didn't need the Snake, and if he was sensible he would try to exclude her from any major role in his doctoral examination.

Sneer at his tedious project she could and did, however.

And when it was Kajo's turn, Richard felt deeply sorry for him. What did she have against *him*? She concluded her tirade with the ironical advice that Kajo should focus his researches into motivation on his own department, which was pristine territory as far as scholarly initiative was concerned. Or, if he preferred, he could go back to dabbling in his former interests, literature and culture. (She managed to pronounce "literature" and "culture" as though she was referring to things you tried not to tread in.)

"And now for our native speakers, our three gallant Musketeers, all of whom have chosen to take refuge in wishy-washy 'cultural' activities rather than researching something of practical use to the world. Man up, gentlemen! This is not good enough!"

When it came to slagging them off individually, though, it wasn't quite as easy as it had been with the Germans.

Richard's MA thesis, like Enno's PhD project, was a hard fact, and Cambridge University Press was not to be dismissed lightly. (Richard had dropped a hint about CUP to *Frau* Ludewig, who had told Enno, who had told Kajo, who had told the Snake. By a process of Chinese whispers, the august publishing house with whom Richard had day-dreamed of being able to place his thesis had become the front-runner in a battle of British publishing giants to secure the brilliant new study of Conan Doyle by a promising young expat critic.)

As for Snoad and Kurz, how do you fight a blancmange? Especially when half the blancmange isn't even there.

She had harsh words for Snoad (fully deserved, as far as Richard was concerned, and he hoped that "*Jaan*" would get to hear them). Then she laid into the wobbly mass of incoherence that was Harlan Kurz's idea of scholarship. He took most of it in silence, occasionally underlining or conceding a point with some weird expression like "I had that tagged, hundredpercento" or "You're sitting pretty high in the bleachers there, no doubtee" that no-one was inclined to follow him up on.

Richard found himself watching the Snake's hands, as she drummed on the table or poked at the Prospectus. Her fingernails were long and sharp, and painted bright red, but her wrists were scrawny, and the skin of her hands was mottled and unhealthy-looking, although she wasn't so very much older than Richard was.

Nastiness was thoroughly exhausting. It took its toll on you. Wasn't there a poem by old Bert Brecht about that?

But she was enjoying herself. She'd bottled it up, and now she was letting it all out on Kurz—for whom Richard had no sympathy at all. He was a selfish, pretentious little creep, and Richard had been the target of his sarcasm far too often.

This was no longer about anyone's research achievements or failings: she wasn't interested in any of these topics, and she despised everything "cultural." Nor could she understand Kurz's peculiar English. Yet her own English was shaky, and she wouldn't risk challenging him over his "research" in the area of translation, so with that at least he was safe, and he knew it.

The storm was therefore destined to pass over quickly, without seriously harming anyone. Kurz accepted his punishment stoically, his eyes half-closed, smiling complacently with Buddha-like inner-absorption, until she finally gave up.

Richard would have liked to have stayed behind after the meeting, to talk to the Germans. Wounds needed to be licked, and in their present emotional state his colleagues might blurt out something interesting. But he was also eager to find out whether *Frau* Ludewig had prepared the list of student names for him.

There was no sign of life in the English Department office. Ludie had locked up and gone home! Well, it had been a very long meeting, and no-one had brought her any work to do for hours. Why should she hang around?

Richard needed food. He would pop in to Real to pick up some supper.

On his way out of the university he stopped at the mailboxes, and found a large envelope containing... the list of names that he'd asked for. *Frau* Ludewig had done it after all. She was a treasure! He could look forward to an engrossing evening studying the document and making his own short-list of Silkes, Susannas and Sandras.

Then he noticed that there were other items in his mailbox that hadn't been there earlier. There was a flyer from a removals firm ("Best Prices in Town"), and a large, full-color booklet from a US university press advertizing its new releases in Anthropology. Both harmless enough.

Why did the librarians always think that information on new publications in almost any possible field would interest *him*? Was it because the books were in English? They would throw into his mailbox announcements of new releases in the most unlikely subject areas, like Physics or Soil Science or Ancient Numismatics. He'd received expensive brochures on "The Arabian Horse" and "New Developments in South Asian Linguistics," and promptly recycled them into the nearest wastepaper bin.

Feeling slightly malicious, he chucked the brochure into the mailbox of "Kurz, H." (the addition of the "H." was because there were several people named Kurz, Kurtz or suchlike on the faculty).

Here you are, Harlan baby, chew on this! A little something to further your ongoing researches into contemporary intellectual culture.

There was also a postcard from "S."

Yes!

It was a large-format card, and in English. He lifted it out of the mailbox—and found another one under it. And then a third card, this one of normal size.

She was mad, completely crazy!

All this, and the list: it was almost too good to be true. There were bound to be clues in the texts that she'd written. She'd squeezed a lot of words onto the cards, in tiny handwriting, and since the lighting in the foyer was dim, he decided to read them back in his apartment. But he could hardly wait!

He dashed into Real and (to save himself having to cook that evening) picked up some ready-made sandwiches, some beer, chocolate biscuits, and a carton of yoghurt. Twenty minutes later he was back home, studying the three messages from "S." under a reading lamp.

Dear Richard,

Do I need to say that I love you?

All right, here it is: every part of me loves every part of you: my eyes love your face, my ears love your voice, my heart loves your soul, my yearning loves your laugh. My lips want to kiss your lips, my hands want to touch your skin, my body wants to be loved by you(rs). But not only my body wants you, I do love you too. I love the way you look at me. I love your hair and your eyes, I love every little mistake of you. I love the way you walk and talk, smile and laugh, I love your weakness and your strenght [sic], your humour and your sunny nature. I would give anything to have you in my arms right now. I can't believe it has come to this: I cry myself to sleep every night.

I love you... and I wish I wouldn't...

Sometimes when you smile at me I wish I could die right at that moment. To drown in your eyes... what a wonderfull [sic] death! I want to fall asleep with you as my last thought. And then I would die and never open my eyes again. If I could do so, I would never have to live without you. I would never have to miss your smile.

So please smile at me once again.

S.

"Humour," not "humor": so, British English. But that didn't help him. Most of the students had learned British rather than American English at school.

Her English was very good, he noted, barring a few spelling mistakes. "Everything *on* you" was wrong, of course, but prepositions were always hardest to get right.

To his surprise, the message on the second card was in the form of a poem:

Dear Richard,
> It's not that I can't live without you, It's just that I don't even want
> to try
> Every night I dream about you, But in daytime I'm just too shy
> If I wasn't such a coward, Right now I'd be holding you
> There's nothing that I wouldn't do, Richard, if I only knew:
> The words to say, the road to take, To find the way to your heart!
> What can I do to get to you, And find the way to your heart?

* * * *

> I don't know how I got this crazy, But I'd do anything to say what's
> right
> 'Cause your voice is so amazing, Richard, you're the best thing in
> my life!
> Let me prove my love is real, And make you feel the way I feel
> Give me just one chance, To give my love to you
> 'Cause no one on this earth, Loves you like I do
> I beg and plead, fall to my knees, I promise I will give the world
> If only you would tell me, Richard:
> The words to say, the road to take, To find a way to your heart
> What can I do and get to you, And find a way to your heart?

Tell me!

S.

Had she adapted some crappy popsong? Surely she hadn't written the slush herself? Reading the gushing words, Richard was convinced that it couldn't possibly be a *boy* sending the messages.

Yes, that thought had indeed briefly crossed his mind. Maybe some clever-dick First Year and his mates wanting to have a laugh at his expense? Setting him up like Malvolio? But what sort of boy would have the patience to pen such soppy rubbish without throwing up? Yuck!

A gay student, perhaps? The English Department wasn't Esthetic Praxes, though, where if you were standing behind one of their students in the queue in the *Mensa* you often didn't know whether it was a boy or a girl.

Richard's gaydar was terrible, but so far he'd only spotted one obviously gay male student in English. The svelte Rico, his shirt unbuttoned to the waist (in winter!) and a chunky gilt masculinity symbol on a chain flopping against his hairless chest, had more or less propositioned him after an English Grammar class one Friday afternoon.

Rico had found the lesson so *stimulating*. He had felt an immediate kinship with Richard. And there were so few *men* in the English Department, weren't there, that "we boys" ought to stick together. So did Richard fancy a quick coffee?

Richard did not (he didn't fancy a quick *anything* with Rico). His answer must have been so brusque that the boy stopped coming to the class altogether, though his English could certainly have done with it. So much for the stimulating effects of English Grammar!

Afterwards, Richard considered whether there were any circumstances under which he might accept an offer like Rico's. He couldn't see himself tumbling on a bed with him, locked in a sensual embrace, or kissing him, but the boy probably had very soft skin, and would buggering him, for example, be so different from buggering a girl (admittedly, something he hadn't tried yet)? Briefly he tried to imagine that scenario.

No, it didn't work for him at all. The first sight of hairy thighs or glimpse of flopping testicles would be a major turn-off.

The third and final postcard was the most interesting one. It was headed "To the One Who is My Destiny":

> In the beginning was time. And we were there too. And from the very beginning I knew of your existence. I never knew weather [sic] you also knew about mine. But I waited. I knew it would come, that I would move closer, closer to the centrel [sic] of our existence, closer to the meeting point where our paths would cross. And I knew I would love you and I thought you would love me too. But love does not seem to be my destiny. You love another! I saw you with her! I shall find her and kill her!
>
> Or was I wrong? What does she mean to you? Do you love her? Or are you just a butterfly, playing with all our hearts? No, that is impossible! You are mine. Mine only. You are MY destiny, MY love. Tell me that all is not lost!
>
> S.

God, he was being spied on!

But who had she seen him with? It must be a misunderstanding. Students were always stopping him on his way to classes, asking him about this, that or the other. Sometimes he'd tell them to come to his office hour, but more often he'd try to deal with them quickly on the spot, even if it meant arriving for his lesson a minute or two late.

Nobody seemed to mind that, and he wasn't as bad as Kajo, who was *always* late for his classes. Kajo was both too kindly to brush students off, and interminably long-winded.

So maybe she'd seen him with some Final Year student? Some poor girl worried about her exams, gazing at him desperately, hanging on his every word. Some girl she didn't recognize. A situation easily misinterpreted.

Or did she know about Monika?

MONIKA

It is a truth universally acknowledged, that a young man of good education, not ugly, and with a generous salary and only himself to spend it on, will attract the attention of young women. Before Monika, there had been other girls in Richard's life, both in England and afterwards in Germany, but (other than Sonia) Monika was the closest thing to a girlfriend that he had had in Reichsstadt so far.

He had made a slow start. He'd come to the city months before the beginning of the summer semester, not knowing anyone and (after he'd moved into his apartment) not overly taken with any of his neighbors.

His colleagues had shown little interest in him, though Dr. Christenkorn had politely invited him round for tea (tea, not coffee—Kajo was an anglophile).

He liked Kajo, who reminded him occasionally of some of his more otherwordly Professors back in England. But there was at least a generation between them in age, and Kajo was plainly a timid, non-gregarious type. Mrs. Christenkorn seemed a bit of a battle-axe (Eddie Hodgkins actually called her a "ratbag") and she was undoubtedly the one wearing the trousers in that household. The Christenkorns had an attractive house, with a big garden, and a friendly cat, but no children.

Kajo was never going to be his first friend in Reichsstadt. He'd be a senior colleague; briefly, his mentor; a friendly acquaintance; his boss for a short while; but never his friend.

That honor fell to Eddie. Richard had known plenty of people like Eddie Hodgkins in his university days. Amiable bullshitters, mates, or drinking chums, they were always on hand to distract you when you should have been finishing an essay or mugging up for an exam. Always good for a laugh, their philosophy of life was: "Sod this, you only live once!"

They'd hang around the university for years, but they seldom finished their degrees. Eddie admitted that his tutors at Cambridge had dragged him by the scruff of his neck to his modest BA "for his father's sake" (Eddie never talked about his father, except to mention that he'd been at the same college).

He had afterwards "proceeded" to his MA, as they so quaintly put it in Cambridge, with something of a bad conscience. But Eddie was quite well-read. In fact, he read voraciously, if not always selectively, and he was always good for an irrelevant quotation from some obscure Bulgarian novelist or Catalan poet.

Otherwise, Eddie's conversation revolved around sex. He expressed his thoughts in a time-warp vocabulary from his days at a minor public school: sexual intercourse was *shagging* or *shafting* (a word also used metaphorically, as in "Kajo got a right shafting from the Snake, didn't he?"); girls who made the mistake of going back to your flat with you were asking to be *rogered*; and the ultimate objective of any social activity involving women was a *leg-over*. If he'd had a bedpost, he would have notched it.

Viewing the new students at the induction event in Freshers' Week every October, Eddie would smack his lips and say: "God said: 'Let there be totty. And there *was* totty.'" Yet the consensus opinion was that Eddie's non-stop blathering about sex was a cover for his not actually managing to get very much of it. And while most of the girls quietly ignored Eddie when they could, occasionally he came up against a more militant representative of the fair sex he so admired, and suffered a massive put-down.

For example, bullshitting in Murphy's Bar one evening Eddie found himself involved in a raucous exchange with Gundi, a postgrad who was the self-appointed Convenor of the Reichsstadt LGBT Initiative. Gundi was a bulky person, usually leather-clad, and sported metal-studded leather armbands as well as a variety of tattoo and piercings. She crushed Eddie in the ensuing debate (as she could have crushed him physically if she'd decided to).

Not satisfied with humiliating him publicly, she complained about him afterwards to Sebastian, the Students' Union "spokesperson for gender issues."

"The English Department are employing a shameless male chauvinist pig. So, what are you going to do about it?"

Sebastian, who knew, and didn't dislike, Eddie, and who (despite his spokesperson function) was a bit of an MCP himself, was not inclined to do anything at all.

And Gundi's timing was poor. She had just sabotaged a Students' Union

Week of Anti-Michaelist Protest by preferring to attend an LGBT Awareness Workshop instead, taking half the Reichsstadt activists, both gay and straight, with her. (Some were true believers; others were too frightened of her to say no.) Now she was demanding that the Students' Union go directly to the *Präsi* over the matter, or even raise it at the next meeting of the Senate. Dream on!

In reply, Sebastian made a perfectly sensible (but nevertheless malicious) suggestion that he knew would stop Gundi dead in her tracks, and enrage her too. She should take her complaint to the person best-positioned to deal with it: Dr. Kerstin Dröge-Daschmeyer, the ambitious, power-dressing Commissioner for Gender Equality.

As he was well aware, Gundi and "DD" detested each other. They may have shared a lot of common ground ideologically; they had similar erotic preferences, too; but the differences between them in style, in taste, in manners, in appearance, in personal fragrance, and in their respective levels of social and educational sophistication, were unbridgeable.

Sebastian knew that Gundi would never ask the Commissioner for anything. The first (and last) time that Gundi had gone to her office hour, "DD" had opened the windows for a good ten minutes afterwards to air the room—and told everybody about it.

The complaint would therefore go no further.

Sebastian let Eddie know what had happened, and gave him a friendly warning to steer clear of the "woman-mountain" in future. Eddie swore solemnly to be more careful, but naturally didn't stop bullshitting, and he told Richard the whole story of his run-in with Gundi—with embellishments, of course.

Eddie had a vivid imagination, and was only too happy to hang out with Richard (especially when Richard was paying). However, when it had come to helping him find a girlfriend—which had been Richard's main concern in those first few months in Reichsstadt, along with preparing his classes at the university—Eddie had been of no use at all.

The breakthrough, when it came, came entirely by chance. One day, Richard picked up a local newspaper that had been abandoned at his bus-stop, took it home to read, and discovered the heady world of personal contact ads. They were so much more *direct* than anything he'd encountered before! Many of the people advertising, for a partner, a friend, a spouse, or just a dirty weekend, were almost pitiful in their neediness or vulgarity. They were literally *asking* for it.

Richard wrote to half-a-dozen of the less freaky ads, e.g., **"Girl, 29, blonde, 1.65, slim, attractive, unmarried, young professional, non-smoker, seeks trustworthy friend, m, 29-45, at least 1.80, unmarried, no beard, no pervs,"** as a consequence of which he had a couple of awkward meetings with fat, lonely girls, and then a date with Monika.

He ended up in bed with her.

Not *in* bed, actually, but *on* the bed. They never slept together, and she only visited his apartment once. Their relationship was low-key. She made no emotional demands on him, they didn't talk much, and he couldn't imagine her as anything other than a regular source of physical relief.

Fortunately, she had no contacts at the university, or any good reason to go there. It would have been deeply embarrassing if his students had known that he was involved with such a plain, boringly dressed, unhip woman. Even Eddie wasn't told about his "rogering" activities with Monika.

She was a mid-level secretary at a utilities company, and she dressed and talked like a mid-level secretary at a utilities company. On their first date, they had met at a café. Richard was nervous about being seen with her, and he was delighted when she said that she'd like them to go back to her place, nearby, if he didn't mind, because the café was so crowded.

Wow! He didn't mind at all. Signals came no clearer than that.

Her flat was tiny, clean, and very dull. She made them some coffee, sat beside Richard on the sofa, quizzed him on who he was and what he did, seemed satisfied with what he told her (though uncurious), and then leant across and kissed him. While he was kissing her back, she started fingering his thigh. He put his hand down the back of her pants, then the front, and soon they were pulling each other's clothes off.

On future visits, since it was now clear (more or less) what they both wanted, they would kiss, caress and undress more sedately, though without wasting too much time.

What Richard was after was an uncomplicated sexual relationship.

Monika, on the other hand, while she also wanted to be *serviced* (Richard's word, not hers) every ten days or so, liked to be approached with an exaggerated show of respect and politeness. She wanted to be treated like a lady. She had no time for "primitive types," she said. Richard suspected that she'd made it from some crude working-class family into a safe lower-middle-class job, and was gradually re-inventing herself.

He wasn't natural marriage material for her—she'd probably noticed that he didn't change his socks or underwear every day, as she did. He also read books, and even liked talking about them: an unnecessary quality in a husband. But he'd keep her satisfied until she managed to hook one of the managers at her company.

It was very much a pragmatic arrangement.

As for the sex, Monika preferred to be enjoyed from behind. That suited Richard fine. Despite her age, she had the body of a fit teenage girl, slim and well-proportioned. She was immaculately clean, and sweet-smelling, with her pubic hair trimmed back to a small triangle on her mons. Even her sweat smelt good. Her skin was soft, but the flesh of her body was pleasantly firm.

Once, while they were fucking, a ridiculous thought suddenly crossed his mind, that her gorgeous backside was like a pair of pale Gouda cheeses, and her cunt, tucked between them, like a pot of delicious, spicy chutney, ready for dipping into! He burst out laughing at this peculiar image, and they had to stop. She was very angry with him.

Whether he was sliding in and out of her like a piston, or they were gripping each other like Velcro, their bodies were a marvelous physical fit, such as Richard had never experienced before.

He enjoyed the sex, and he was only ever put off when she occasionally turned round and *looked* at him, with a prim, schoolmistressy expression on her face, and her winged secretary-type glasses perched on her beaky nose. Her face was decidedly not her best feature. In addition, her voice, which seemed almost to have been made for nagging, soon grated on him, except for her occasional grunts of "Oh, yes" or "That's good, that's really good."

Their screwing always followed the same pattern. Richard would have liked to be more adventurous, and he felt increasingly challenged by the little rosebud of her anus—there had to be a first time!—but once when he had licked his finger and tentatively inserted the tip of it a few millimeters into her, she had swiveled round and snapped, "No!" Monika was not going to allow him to split her peach.

Her lovely bottom was simply made for spanking, but this was an activity she didn't approve of either. Nor did she like his tongue to be anywhere except in the vicinity of her mouth. She once told him how disgusted she was by people who played around with "tricks" like bondage, or leather gear, who filmed each other, who did it in groups or swapped partners, in short, people who indulged in "filthy" forms of sex.

People like that were *perverts*. She was pleased that Richard was such a nice boy, and not a pervert.

They had no social life together. She showed no interest in meeting his friends (as if he had many), and he certainly didn't want to meet hers. The idea of going to a concert, or to see a film, happily never arose. They might have bumped into someone who knew him.

As for hobbies, she collected wine-labels (German ones only), which she steamed off the bottles, though he was never granted a viewing of her full collection. He'd bring a bottle of Rheinhessen or Rheinpfalz to their trysts. Not too expensive, but with a fancy label chosen to please her. She preferred semi-sweet wines, as he soon discovered.

Richard, who came of solid but fairly unsophisticated stock (he was the first person in his family to have made it to university), had inherited what was a common British prejudice, namely, that white wine was the favored tipple of women and poofs. However, as the wine lubricated their meetings, and encouraged both his ardor and hers, he made no mention to her of his preference for dry reds.

Surprisingly, she didn't go in for any kind of sport, not even riding a bicycle. She drove to and from work in her little dark-blue Fiat, which she had bought entirely with her own money (she told him proudly).

By the time that Richard received his first communications from "S.," his relationship with Monika had become monotonous, and wasn't going anywhere. Maybe it would be a good moment to slip away, to extricate himself? He hadn't heard from her for weeks anyway. He couldn't be sure that "S." had found out about Monika—how could she have seen them together, except that first time in the café?—but he didn't want to risk anything. Monika could make a scene; she could also make a fool of him in the university.

Besides, he was intrigued by "S." This was a girl who was clearly obsessed with him. If he was unlucky, she might yet turn out to be a dumpy Five or Six from the back row in Textual Composition. Or she might be someone else altogether, an absolute scorcher. And she was *begging* for it. So why let Monika get in the way of all that? His affair with Monika was effectively over.

He still had reservations about becoming involved with a student, but he wanted to find out more. And maybe to investigate what was on offer.

PLOTS

Lisa and Steffi had gone for a coffee after the Translation class. That sounds rather hedonistic, doesn't it? You imagine croissants and lattes, and laid-back, sophisticated conversation. None of these were normally to be had in the student cafeteria, and the cafeteria was in any case already shut. The coffee therefore had to come from a machine outside the library.

You made your selection, e.g., coffee with or without milk, cappuccino, coffee with cream, coffee with extra milk, tea with or without milk, tea with lemon, herbal tea, hot chocolate, hot chocolate with extra milk, tomato soup, cream of mushroom, chicken soup, or broth. All the options were based on the same foul, gray-brownish stock, which was drawn chudderingly up out of the bowels of the machine, injected with chemical flavoring powders, according to which buttons you had pressed, pumped into a frothy mix, and squirted into a small plastic beaker Not surprisingly, all the options tasted fairly similar, and none of them tasted very good.

The least disgusting options were considered to be cappuccino and coffee with extra milk.

The girls made their choices, and then sat down on a bench to drink their cappuccinos and to review the lesson they had just come from. As usual, they didn't talk about the content of the lesson, but only about the lecturer.

Harlan Kurz had been on top form. Steffi still thought he was a creep. Even from where they were sitting in the back row you couldn't help noticing that, she said. He exuded nastiness.

Goggle-eyed Beatrix had been absent, which meant that the lesson had begun as a dialog between Kurz and Pimply Konstantin. There was nothing wrong with that, but they could hardly keep it up for ninety minutes. People would start making jokes about the "Harlan and Konsty Show." Kurz would have to bring in one or two other students at least.

Fortunately (for the likes of Lisa and Steffi) there were a couple of foolhardy volunteers, philology students of English with an inflated view of their own abilities (the classes in the Translation module were taught on a "code-sharing" basis for both English Departments, the teacher trainers and the philologists). None of these poor fools, however good they might have been at deconstructing Dickens, were much good at translation; certainly none of them had the ability of a Konstantin or a Beatrix.

Lambs to the slaughter. Why did they do it?

The first less than perfect answers were treated with cool disdain, and merely corrected. After a while, though, Harlan R. began to run out of patience. His eyes gleamed, his tongue worked like a whiplash. Then, after he had pounded and pulverized the poor creatures who had volunteered such feeble suggestions, the dreaded moment came and he started pointing at students directly, and at random, and requesting *their* inputs.

Panic set in.

Konstantin nobly continued to raise his hand each time, but in vain: Kurz had smelled blood, and now he wanted to taste it.

Thank goodness Lisa hadn't insisted on their sitting in the front row! They would have been directly in the firing-line. Kurz was less likely to go for the back row, because he preferred to be able to *see* the embarrassment and distress he was causing.

Shirin the Iranian girl was already in tears.

"If you can't answer such a simple question, sweetie pie, what are you doing in this class, might I ask? This is not one of those colleges where you buy your degree in the car park! *Capisci?*"

The malicious idea that he meant colleges in Iran and other Middle Eastern countries hung tantalizingly in the air. Kurz was a master at intimating an offensive remark without actually coming out with it.

One of the boys attempted to distract the ogre by calling out a well-meaning attempt at an answer.

Kurz turned on the young man venomously.

"Aha, someone here trying to attract my attention? So you think I'm a waiter, do you? 'Hey, *garçon*, two beers and a pepperoni pizza, *toute suite!*'

I think not, buddy! And I'll tell you this: waiting tables is what some of you guys will be doing when you leave here, because no-one in their right mind is gonna give you a fucking job! Oh, I give up! I don't know why I bother." Then, as an afterthought. "And it was a crap answer, by the way. That's the problem with you guys: you're so bad you don't even *know* that you're bad."

And more of the same. He undoubtedly had a point. Eventually he relented, and let Konstantin supply the answer that was needed.

Shirin the Iranian girl was still sobbing, but was ignored. Why didn't she just get up and walk out? I would have done, Lisa told herself. Definitely! I would even have told him to go fuck himself! But (if she was honest) she knew that she wouldn't have dared. Though Steffi might have.

Harlan had a powerful character. You couldn't mess with him; you could only submit to his will. Lisa found that idea strangely appealing. A strong man, who knew what he wanted!

He wasn't very nice to people, though.

Now Harlan was doing funny voices, mimicking his colleagues. He did that towards the end of lessons, when he was bored.

He had pompous old Dr. Christenkorn, with his stilted English, off to a T: "I am grateful for that suggestion, Mr. Stenzel" (Kajo could never bring himself to call students by their first names) "and I am of the opinion that it can hardly be improved upon. Unless it *can* be improved upon. Which is a possibility we should now take into consideration."

Or Enno Müller: "Great answer! Hands up all those who agree! Let's see what percentage level the consensus gets to!"

He mimicked his friend Jonathan Snoad, exaggerating his drawl ("Sorry, *Jaan*, buddy!"), and Richard Orwell, who had a clear British accent when he spoke German and didn't roll his R's properly. It was clear that he didn't particularly like Orwell.

But for some reason he never did the Snake.

Oh, you'd never be bored with Harlan R. Kurz, Lisa thought.

Steffi was unrelenting, though.

"No, I honestly do think he's a creep. I've seen him close up, remember? That night in the car? Still, if you fancy him—"

That was a matter that Lisa wasn't quite sure about yet. Could you *not* like someone, and find them sexy nevertheless? Lisa's handful of former boyfriends—if that was the proper word for them—had been very much "what you see is what you get" types. (Her "first," that bastard of a neighbor, didn't count.) But this situation was one that she hadn't been in before. This was *complex*.

It was easy enough for Steffi to talk! She flitted from one bloke to the next and never looked back. *Of course* she didn't like Harlan, because he'd turned her down. He'd taken a quick look, and had a little feel, and decided:

No, not this one. You could almost say that that was to his credit.

Lisa found herself admitting, "I wouldn't say no." God, had she really said that?

Steffi laughed.

"See? There's hope for you yet! Now we have a project: to my *left*" (with an outward flip of her wrist) "we have Lisa, a girl with a quest, and to my *right*" (with a flip of her other wrist) "we have Mr. Harlan R. Kurz, the object of her unrelenting passion. How to bring these two lovebirds together" (she drew her hands slowly towards each other, ending by making an obscene gesture with her fingers) "is the question that now concerns us."

"Don't be so disgusting!" But Lisa had to laugh.

"I'm doing you a big favor, girl. And, I have to ask, if you're *not* willing to go there occasionally, why do you bother taking that little pill so conscientiously? Why screw up your body if you're not actually screwing, eh?" Lisa said nothing. "Still, fair's fair, I need a project too. While you're busy seducing H.R., I personally will focus my attention on his colleague Mr. Orwell. I've had my eye on him for a while now, oh yes. Don't be so surprised! I have my own ways of doing things. I have a little plan, and now it's time to close in for the kill."

AN UNHAPPY CHILDHOOD

She was cruel, but she was also kind.

When I cried because it was dark, she would laugh and take me into her bed and hold me close. I was a big boy, but she let me suck her like a baby. She was groaning and stroking me. It was nice and warm under the bedclothes.

In the morning, she let me play with her body. Her hair was hot and sticky. It was spread on the pillow like ropes of gold.

When I tried to suck her again, she would push my nose between her titties and squash them together.

"Bad boy!"

One night after I had sucked her she went down under the bedclothes and got hold of my thing and sucked it. That was a good feeling! It went hard. But then she shouted at me, nasty words, and threw me out of the bed.

I WAS A DIRTY BEAST.

Why was I a dirty beast? I didn't understand. I only did what she wanted. Many, many times over.

She made me lick her thing under the bedclothes. It was hot and wet, and had a strong smell, like fish. Then she would push me away from her and put her own hand between her legs. She twisted and turned so much, and shouted out so much, that I was frightened and got out of the bed even though it was cold. But she would call me back.

"Here," she would say, holding out her hand, the fingers all wet and gleaming. "All yours."

And I would lick her fingers clean.

Sometimes if she was angry she would beat me afterwards, with a leather belt on my bum. Once she hit me with the wrong end of the belt, and the metal bit made me bleed.

I couldn't sit still in school, it hurt so much. *Frau* Gröne noticed, and she took me to the school secretary. They made me pull my trousers down.

Do you want to suck me? I asked.

After that I had to go to the doctor, who made me take my clothes off and touched me all over. I didn't ask *him* if he wanted to suck me, because he was a man.

And a funny man came and visited us, not like the usual ones, who were always drunk and didn't smell good and would tell me to stay in my room and keep quiet.

This one was very serious and he wanted to talk to me, he said.

He asked very strange questions, but I didn't say anything, and nothing happened.

She never hit me with the belt again, only with a wooden spoon from the kitchen. That hurt too, but not like the belt.

Sometimes she went out for the night and wouldn't come back till the morning. She always locked the door.

I was so frightened! Especially when there were noises outside, or a thunderstorm. I would go to her room and creep into the bed. I would take her nightgown, or her bra or knickers, and cuddle with them. The knickers were best because they had her smell on them.

Once she came back early and found me asleep in her bed. I was holding a pair of her knickers to my face.

Dirty! Filthy! She screamed at me, and beat me again. But then she stripped off her clothes and got into the bed to sleep. She was drunk. She made me come to her and play "our little game" before she fell asleep.

Then I stole the knickers and hid them in my room. I soon had a collection of her underwear, hidden behind the cupboard.

She was still young—I know that now—when she died. After that, there were strangers who looked after me. It wasn't the same, though, because she was missing from my life.

I was so angry that she had betrayed me, had left me! I wanted to do something bad to her.

There was a girl in the home, in another group. She was a big girl, with long blonde hair. One night I crept into the room where she was asleep. I was good at creeping.

Her golden hair was spread out on the pillow. I wanted to smell her body under the bedclothes but I was frightened to lift them up. Anything I did would wake her. I could see one of her hands. Her fingers were very still. I wanted to suck them, or bite them. I wanted to pull down her knickers and smell them, and suck at her thing, but I didn't dare.

Her clothes were on a chair beside the bed. But no underwear!

Then the other girl who was sleeping in the room started to wake up.

"Who's there? Is that you?"

I got out quickly before she saw me.

THE WAY FORWARD

How was he going to find the mysterious hostel predator? For a long time, Richard had no idea.

The search for "S." would be easy in comparison. He would spot a give-away detail in one of her messages, or he would recognize her handwriting. Or, if she really was so obsessed with him, she'd come to tell him in person.

There had been a postgraduate girl in his very first semester who had appeared in his Tuesday office hour week after week, gazing at him in devotion, until the moment came when she told him that she wanted more than his considered advice on her thesis—she wanted *him*.

He hadn't been attracted to Karin at all, and her office hour visits had become irritating—but they were even more annoying to the other students queuing up outside to see him, waiting patiently in the corridor. It became ridiculous, though, when she told him *why* she wanted him.

She had noticed that he had a good soul, she said, but that he was a hopeless unbeliever. He never went to church, did he? She wanted to save him from damnation by bringing Jesus into his life in a big way, and if she could only do that by letting him take possession of her flesh then she was more than willing to make that sacrifice—

At which point one of the girls waiting outside had put her head round the door and shouted at her, "Leave the poor guy *alone*! I've got a fucking class in ten minutes!"

He had managed to get rid of her, and had spoken to another student, a friend of hers, about the matter. The visits to his office hour soon stopped. Karin completed her thesis, married a Canadian, and moved to Winnipeg. And Jesus had still not come into his life in a big way (at least, not yet).

Yes, "S." wouldn't be able to help herself. And soon he found out a further detail about her.

It wasn't because of the list of student names that *Frau* Ludewig had so diligently prepared for him. There were simply too many first names beginning with an "S."

There were Sara(h)s, Susanna(h)s, and Silkes.

There was a Sabine (that name was a bit old-fashioned, and was more often encountered among the staff than among the students)

Rather surprisingly, there were no fewer than three Swantjes.

He counted a couple of Sonias, a Sheila, a Svea, a Sophie, and a Sophia.

There was the Iranian girl Shirin, and a Russian Swetlana.

There were some Svenjas, a Salome, a Saskia, and (predictably) a number of Stefanies or Stephanies; also, several Sandras

There were some Simones, two Sibylles, two Solveigs, and (his favorite) a Scarlett.

Altogether, there were more than forty of them, and that was not including the ERASMUS foreign exchange students. *Frau* Ludewig couldn't provide him with a list of those; to obtain such a list, he would have to ask in the International Office.

The only one he could immediately rule out was the Iranian girl, Shirin. Both her English and her German were poor, and she was desperately shy.

As for the rest, if he looked at each of them in turn, assessing their English and checking their handwriting, he would eventually have a viable short-list, but it would take an eternity. He only recognized a handful of the names. Most of the young ladies would not be in his language classes, and would not be handing in homework regularly (and many of those who did would submit computer printouts).

It was true that a larger number of students attended his British Studies lectures, and these probably included many of his Sandras, Sonias, etc., but he wouldn't get to see *their* handwriting until they took the exam at the end of the semester. Could he wait that long?

On Tuesday, Richard had his office hour (now that the departmental meetings had been switched to Mondays), followed by his only seminar, British Studies II.

On Wednesday, he had a lazy day at home.

Thursday was his big teaching day: Textual Composition in the morning, then, after lunch in the *Mensa*, two more classes, English Grammar III and the British Studies lecture, in the afternoon.

His other two lessons, Creative Writing and English Grammar I, were on Friday.

By 7 p.m. on Thursday he had done his teaching, packed his things and was ready to go home. Waiting for him in his mailbox was another postcard, which hadn't been there at midday.

My dearest Richard,

I want you so much! I sat in your class today and while you were talking a thousand erotic thoughts went through my mind! I'm sitting on you, with my body pressed as tightly against yours as I can. I feel you deep inside me. I start moving, first slowly, then quicker and quicker. I feel your hands on my breasts. I'm moving uncontrollably. Then something different: I'm lying on my back, and you're on top of me. I kiss your lovely face, and your hot lips, as you thrust into me, again and again. Then you turn me round and take me from behind, going in even deeper, really hard. You take me without mercy. I'm groaning—and then I come. Oh my god...

I open my eyes. It was only a dream, and I haven't been listening to the lesson. Oh dear. What was all that crap about gerunds and infinitives?

S.

Hey! She had been sitting there in English Grammar III all along! (Although funnily enough the topic that day hadn't been gerunds and infinitives—but maybe that just showed how little attention she'd been paying?)

Unfortunately, English Grammar III was an untypical class.

Firstly: there were roughly sixty regular students in each lesson, most of them girls, because the department hadn't been able to tweak the timetable this semester to allow for smaller parallel groups. The student representatives had already lodged a complaint about that with the Snake—much good that would do them!—and Richard was resigned to getting a lousy grade from the students when his class was evaluated at the end of the semester.

Grammar lessons were not exactly popular anyway.

Secondly: although in theory if she was in English Grammar III she would have to be at least a second-year student (because the first years had to do English Grammar I in their first semester, and English Grammar II in the summer), it didn't work like that in practice.

There were sometimes First Years or postgrads who wandered casually into Grammar lessons, even at the wrong level, if they had an hour to kill and the cafeteria was crowded. This was on the principle that hearing someone spouting about English grammar couldn't do you any harm. Even if you didn't pay much attention, by a process of osmosis (or magic) you'd still pick up *some* benefit from it.

Even so, those sixty, plus a couple of visiting students from the university's ERASMUS partners, would hardly include thirty girls whose first names all began with an "S." This was good news! This was progress! He was going to find this girl.

His other search was a different matter altogether. For weeks, Richard's peace of mind had been disturbed by the thought of the stupid assignment that the President had given him. It had spoiled his Christmas and New Year break. It was a challenging task, and it wouldn't be *fun*. He would be looking for a man who might not even exist, but if he did, would be pathetic and unstable, a pimply masturbator, a loser, not a sexually aroused young woman—and he simply didn't know how to do it.

The group of potential suspects was clear enough, though: males with some sort of connection to the girls in the English Department. Or that was how the Fat Man saw it.

He ran through the possibilities in his mind.

There were the male lecturers Kajo, Eddie, Snoad and Kurz, and the visiting Taiwanese academic Dr. Dong.

There was Jupp Wolter, the middle-aged technician who looked after the computers and the language lab.

There were twenty or thirty male students, hardly any of whom he really knew (since he had always paid more attention to the girls). Of those he *did* vaguely know, it was unlikely to be Rico! There were a couple of guys, Micha and Sebastian, who always had girls cooing and billing over them—would they need to go sneaking around in the hostels? Probably not.

Milo was weird, though, and had a sick sense of humor. He could be counted as a suspect, perhaps.

Richard knew that he couldn't completely rule out people from the university administration who had regular contact with the department. Nor could he ignore students from other subjects who mixed with the English students socially, or who were in the same hostel with them.

So where was he going to start? It was hopeless. The best thing would be to begin at the top of his list, and try to exclude as many people as possible, so that he could go to the President and say, "It wasn't any of *them*, so it was probably a student."

That wouldn't be much of a result, but it would be better than nothing. And he would have shown willing.

As he mulled over what the Fat Man had said, one remark gave him a sudden flash of inspiration. Conan Doyle! Richard was held to be an expert on Conan Doyle (as if writing an MA on a subject made you an expert on it, haha).

How would Sherlock Holmes go about it?

Like Holmes, Richard had now become a kind of "consulting detective"—though nobody who could help him actually knew that. He'd have no access to police information, or interviews, or forensics. He mustn't even do his own interviewing too openly, for fear of frightening off the target (or attracting unwanted attention to the case).

The case? Doyle normally called them "adventures." So: "The Adventure of the Purloined Knickers"? "The Adventure of the Bitten Fingers"? Neither had much of a Sherlockian ring to it.

Südstädter Ring 27 would have to stand in for 221B Baker Street. Richard didn't smoke, or use cocaine, and he had never fired a gun or wielded a swordstick in his life. On the plus side, he was more of a multi-tasker than

Holmes, and far more interested in women. And no-one could say that his brain had always ruled over his heart—quite the opposite, in fact. In his thesis he had discussed theories of Holmes's personality, for instance, that he was bipolar, or autistic. Richard was definitely neither of those.

To be honest, he didn't have much in common with Holmes, as described by Conan Doyle, but he would have to use the famous detective's method: ratiocination, reasoning, deduction, logic, or whatever you decided to call it, and here he would be at a disadvantage. Because, unlike Sherlock Holmes, he wasn't a genius.

Something else was missing: a Dr. Watson. Richard would need someone trustworthy to confide in. Someone to bounce ideas off. Someone to gather practical information for him. Ideally, this loyal assistant would be a bright, energetic (and adoring) Girl Friday, a Karin, but slimmer, better looking, and without the Jesus-evangelical aspect. A willing helpmate, and (dare he hope?) a cuddly bed-warmer.

However hard he tried, though, the only person Richard could think of for the role of Dr. Watson was Eddie Hodgkins.

Who else was there?

Kajo was distant and secretive (he was a suspect, if anything). Richard had nothing in common with Enno Müller, and found him difficult to talk to. He didn't like or trust his other male colleagues, Kurz and Snoad. And Dr. Dong, the Taiwanese visiting scholar, was out of the question. So Eddie it would have to be.

EDDIE

As luck would have it, Eddie was also "available." The Snake clearly intended *not* to renew his part-time contract, but Eddie hadn't yet gotten around to approaching other possible employers in Reichsstadt, such as the English Philologists, or the two language schools in the Old Town. He was permanently short of cash. And he had been told to vacate his lodgings, but hadn't been able to find alternative accommodation that he could afford.

Eddie had even abased himself by mentioning his problems one lunchtime in the *Mensa*, hoping that a generous colleague might be able to help him out. Instead, he had been treated to a short burst of sarcasm from Harlan Kurz, and a contemptuous smirk from Snoad.

Richard had felt embarrassed for him, and hadn't said anything, but now he would step in and help. He would offer Eddie his spare room, rent-free, until the end of the summer semester, in return for a modest weekly contribution towards beer and groceries—and his assistance in a matter of some delicacy.

It was an offer that Eddie was in no position to refuse.

Even so, Richard wasn't wholly happy about it. What did he know about his colleague? Not much that was very encouraging.

Eddie was someone who managed to be *slightly* beyond taste or reason in almost everything that he did.

If there were firmly held opinions on how wide a tie was supposed to be, Eddie's tie would always be a fraction wider.

If flared trousers were acceptable ("Are they?" thought Richard, aware that he still had several pairs moldering at the back of his wardrobe), Eddie's would go the extra centimeter beyond what could be tolerated.

Maybe this contributed to the general perception of Eddie as strange but harmless. He was not regarded by many of the female students as a potential sexual threat, let alone as an erotic temptation. Despite his lurid accounts to his male friends of "mega-rogerings" and "seismic sex," it was curious that the recipients of his attentions were never ever women that you *knew*. They were always itinerants, people who happened to be passing through, or figures from the past.

There was the Chilean postgraduate on a temporary work placement who supposedly took one look at him "and that was all that was needed."

There was the reported "thirty-six-hour bonkathon" with a voluptuous Italian exchange student.

There were the two Ukrainian girls who had taken it in grateful turns to minister to his needs.

And then there was the Norwegian au pair ("Scandinavian men are not virile, but *you,* Eddie ......").

Only one girl in the university was widely believed to have slept with Eddie, and she was such an unlikely person that it almost gave the story credence. Elisabeth was a Spartacist, an organizer of solidarity demos and Days of Action, a virulent anti-Michaelist, a sexless professional leftie who would clasp any progressive cause (without exception) to her flat bosom, but never a man. And yet...

Eddie, much the worse for wear from a Thursday evening party, had mislaid his wallet and his keys. He had found (as expected) the light still burning in Elisabeth's little apartment (which was a renowned venue for late night coffee and political discussions), and been offered (as expected) the opportunity to "crash" on her floor. The night was young, however, and Eddie's alcohol-charged ardor irresistible, and so the inevitable had come to pass—three or four times.

So, at least, Eddie's account.

It has to be said that there were many who were intrigued by the idea of Elisabeth "doing it" with *anyone*. The deed was difficult for even the most imaginative to visualize. It called for strenuously lateral thinking—though many spitefully hoped it might be true.

The story was slightly spoiled by one of Elisabeth's progressive sisters (and, had Eddie but known it, a casual lover of hers), who confessed that at three in the morning she had slipped quietly into Elisabeth's room to retrieve a volume of Gramsci that she had lent her and been astounded to find Eddie (of all people) spread out, fully dressed, on the floor, snoring and reeking of alcohol.

Elisabeth had been, as always, sleeping demurely in her narrow bed and wearing her *Liebestöter* ("love-killer") frottée pyjamas. The volume of Gramsci (with the place she had got to in the book marked by a folded political leaflet) and Elisabeth's reading-classes were on the tiny night-table beside her bed.

Not an obviously post-coital scene, but, then again, who knows?

In short, Eddie was not someone to inspire confidence.

Over the next few days, Richard summed up the arguments *pro* and *contra* Hodgkins, before making a decision.

Pro. Well, there were plenty of arguments For.

1. Eddie was intelligent. He had a vivid imagination (if it could be channeled) and was capable of enthusiasm (once you had woken his interest).

2, He knew the English Department much better than Richard did. He'd been around longer, and he taught only First Year language classes, so he got to know all the students early on. And he kept in touch with them, too: he could be seen bopping about at all the student discos and parties, invisible to most of the girls on the dance-floor.

3. Better still, he fraternized happily with the male students, boozing and drinking coffee with them. This was by no means because he preferred their company to that of the girls, but out of necessity, because many of the girls thought he was a clown. Even those who liked him tended to treat him like a slightly annoying younger brother.

4. Eddie was naturally curious, and was a mine of gossipy information.

5. Because everyone laughed at him, and no-one took him seriously, it might be a while before people started wondering why he was asking so many chatty questions. That could be useful.

6. Eddie was silly, but he was totally lacking in genuine malice. There was no way that he himself could be the predator.

7. Finally——having him in the apartment wouldn't cramp Richard's style too much. Richard didn't bring girls back to the Südstädter Ring—his romantic assignations with Monika and the like were almost exclusively "away games"—and he couldn't imagine that Eddie would often manage to do that either, however hard he might try. There was also no need for Eddie to know about "S." Tracking her down would be a task for the master detective; Watson's assistance would not be required on *that* investigation.

Contra. Yes. It had to be admitted that there were two major problems with Eddie.

1. He was a fantasist, an embroiderer of stories. How *reliable* would his reports be?

2. He was a blabbermouth. Could he be trusted to keep a secret? (And at some point—Richard suspected that it would be sooner rather than later—his yakkety-yakking would get on Richard's nerves. Massively.)

Seven arguments in favor, and only two against, though the two arguments *contra* were big ones. But these were risks that Richard would have to take.

He went to Eddie's last class of the day (Grammar Exercises I) and waited until all the students had left. He made his offer, without going into detail about the "matter of some delicacy."

Eddie accepted immediately. Wow, fantastic, too much! So—when could he move in?

PART TWO: GHOSTIES

MOVING IN

Eddie moved in over several days.

Essentially, the moving consisted of his appearing numerous times on day one carrying a large rucksack and an open sports bag, both of which were stuffed full of clean or unwashed clothes (mixed together), assorted books, and what Eddie called his "gear"—a miscellany of items that he had lovingly accumulated over the years.

Eddie would unload the contents of the two bags and then set off to fetch the next load. Studying the growing pyramid of jumble on the floor of his spare room, Richard noted a *shisha* pipe, a fake shrunken head, some foreign car number-plates, assorted decorative beer-mugs, and a selection of traditional board games.

"Umm, I thought you were bringing a bed, too?"

There was no bed in the spare room. Richard was worried that his guest might be about to make a move to annex the living-room by way of crashing on the sofa.

"Oh, yeah, *that*."

The following day a battered van drew up in front of Südstädter Ring 27 and Eddie and two other young men got out. The three of them lugged an aged mattress and multiple crates and cartons of books into Richard's apartment. There was also a grungy-looking sound system, with enormous battered black speakers held together with sticky tape, and a Toshiba laptop of a generation no longer commercially obtainable, except on eBay.

The two young men worked purposefully, though neither of them said a single word to Eddie. However, they did greet Richard. Afterwards, they politely declined his offer of a beer, or a cup of tea or coffee, or indeed any other form of refreshment, and left.

When they had gone, Eddie said, philosophically, "I think they were glad to see the back of me!"

On day three Eddie returned to the routine with the rucksack and the sports bag, though not before asking whether Richard couldn't do him a huge favor and pick up a few odds and ends for him (he was slightly apprehensive about the welcome that the two young men might give him)?

Richard politely declined the request, and Eddie managed to retrieve the last of his belongings without being subjected to any obvious physical abuse.

A few ground rules needed to be established. Richard asked him *not* to set up the sound system, please. He already had an excellent one in place, which Eddie was welcome to use, if he was careful with it.

Eddie began enumerating the virtues of his sound equipment: the incredible bass qualities, the sheer volume, it was better than the systems installed in some discos, he and the lads had even used it for an improvised outdoor rock festival...

Yes, said Richard, interrupting him, that is exactly my point. I have my neighbors to think about.

Even without the sound system, it took Eddie less than a week to reduce the apartment to chaos.

It had been agreed that Eddie's things, of which there were very many, would stay in Eddie's room. The rule was non-negotiable. Yet this sensible arrangement was not to be. Like the encroaching sands of the desert, Eddie's books (for instance) spread themselves everywhere, with a large pile of them soon occupying one corner of the bathroom.

"Don't you ever need some light reading when you're on the pot?" Eddie replied, when he was asked what they were doing there.

Richard wouldn't have regarded *Anna Karenina* or *Moby Dick* as light reading, or the *Pillow Book of Sei Shōnagon* as ideal for inducing a bowel movement.

One day, as Eddie was polishing off a plateful of Richard's expensive Swiss muesli—for supper, as it happened—he remarked, "You know what this place needs?"

"No?"

"A cat."

"A what?"

"You heard me—a nice, friendly moggie. Seriously. It would give the apartment a *spirit*, you know what I mean? You come home after a hard day's grind, hewing away at the old academic whatnot, and there is your furry little buddy waiting to give you love and affection. I mean, no offence intended, old man, but I don't see you getting too much *action* at the moment. You know, kisses and cuddles and what-we-all-know-happens-after-that."

"No."

"You mean: no cuddles? Well, I can see that—"

"No, I mean: no cat."

Eddie looked perplexed.

"Fair enough, a doggie then. But I must warn you that they're much more work. And they do tend to poo a lot."

"Definitely no dog!"

"No cat, no dog. Is it the extra work that you object to, or do you just hate all animals?"

"Of course I don't hate all animals—"

"Fine, then." Eddie interrupted him. "I can see that we're making some progress. But we must work on this a bit. It's good to know that you don't object to pets *on principle*. You need to let love into your heart! This is a nice place that you've got here, man, really it is, but it still needs something."

What it now urgently needs, Richard thought, and solely because of Eddie, is not a dog or a cat, but a full-time cleaning lady.

Richard's nerves had long since reached breaking-point, and passed beyond—in the process discovering that the human spirit was more resilient, more capable of bearing the unbearable, than he had previously imagined. But there was a more positive explanation for the fact that Richard, despite all provocation, hadn't gone back on his word and started looking for a way to evict his demanding house-guest.

It was this: that in the hunt for the "hostel predator" Eddie had made a spectacular breakthrough.

On the second evening after the completion of the move (the first having been devoted to bonding, i.e., beer, and football on television), Richard briefed him on what the President had told him, and showed him the list of four names.

He omitted to mention the Sherlock Holmes angle.

"Aha!" said Eddie, and disappeared with the list into his room. He came back half an hour later, carrying his laptop and with a smug expression on his face. "Perhaps I have something for you; perhaps I don't. That's for you to judge, *Mein Herr*."

"Oh, so you've already solved the case?" There was often something about Eddie's manner that invited sarcasm. Richard almost added "where the police have failed," but he reined in his tongue. "Fine. What have you got? Do you know the girls?"

"Uncle Eddie knows *all* the girls," he explained. "because all the girls come to Uncle Eddie's language classes in the First Year. There's no way into the Second Year without your *Sprachkompetenz Englisch*" (this was the English Language Certificate of Competence), "and you can't get that without passing the oral test, and who is it who does all those interviews?"

Richard laughed.

"Uncle Eddie! The oral tester! So you *do* know these girls?"

"Hmm, well, not quite. I know *three* of them. I don't know this Miriam Burkhardt character, but I know *why* I don't know her. Can you guess?"

"No. But I imagine you're going to tell me."

"Indeed I shall. But my throat is getting rather dry from all this talking. Would there happen to be any more of that excellent beer left over from yesterday?"

Eddie knew that there was. He must have been to the fridge several times that day to fetch milk for his tea, and he would have seen a couple of cans of beer skulking behind the yoghurts. There was also a six-pack of *Reichsstädter Spezial* squatting on the floor of the tiny kitchen next to the plastic bucket of potatoes. Eddie had exercised untypical restraint (by his standards) in not helping himself, perhaps because it was still early days in his residence at Südstädter Ring 27.

Richard fetched him what he wanted.

"Aaah, the nectar of the gods! I'm waxing poetical, this stuff brings out the Irish in me—my atavistic side! The O'Hodgkins of County Tipperary, begorrah and bejesus! But you're not having one?"

Richard guessed that the closest Eddie had ever been to the Emerald Isle was Murphy's Bar, a favored city-center watering-hole for students (when there wasn't competition from a disco or a campus party). And, no, he wasn't having one—he had a class to prepare. Also, he needed to start thinking about the end-of-term exam for his lecture course.

"So: Miriam Burkhardt?" he reminded Eddie. He didn't know the girl either. Lisa Meyer was the only one of the four who was vaguely familiar to him, at least by name.

"Miriam, yes, indeed. It's quite simple: she's a postgraduate. She must have done her BA somewhere else, so, however pathetic her command of English may be, there is no requirement for her to go to any of my classes."

"Or to any of mine, Eddie, so how does this help? You said that you might have something for me, but there's not much so far! I'm waiting..."

"O ye of little faith!" Eddie took a deep swig of beer, and then waved the list of names under Richard's nose. "This, I take it, is all the information that Our Lord and Master provided you with? How generous of him! It's not much to be going on with, is it?"

Richard was losing patience. He really did have a class to prepare for the following day.

"The list is from *Frau* Henkel, and contains the names and hostel addresses of the four girls, and the dates and times when the incidents allegedly took place. What more do you expect?"

At first Eddie ignored his question.

"Kyra Henkel! Ah, I'm going to need another beer! The wrong side of forty, true, but still capable of stoking the flames of lust in middle-aged men. Do you think that she and the *Präsi*...?"

"Eddie!"

"Very well. You asked me what more I would expect? I'll tell you what more I'd expect. Some information about these ladies, perhaps. And photos."

"You must be joking! We're not setting up a dating agency here. These girls may have been the victims of a sexual predator."

Again, Eddie ignored him.

"If you wanted to find up-to-date photos of young people, where would you look? On social media, of course! Facebook, perhaps?" He picked up his laptop and turned it towards Richard. "*Voilà!* Exhibit number one: Jeannine Garbe. What do you think, out of ten? A solid Seven, surely? Better, even, if she didn't look so po-faced. But there are men, sad creatures though they may be, who find that an attractive quality in women."

Jeannine Garbe was good-looking, there was no doubt about that.

"Are they all on Facebook?"

"Certainly." Eddie was already typing in the next name. "The better-looking ones nearly always are. Beatrix Gerhardi *isn't*" (that was Goggle-Eyed Beatrix) "and that girl in the Third Year who looks like a warthog probably isn't either. Naturally, there are some people who aren't on Facebook because they don't approve of it for political reasons. But you're on Facebook, aren't you? We're Facebook Friends, aren't we?"

"*Of course* I'm on Facebook."

Actually, Richard hadn't checked or updated his Facebook page for ages. He only had five Friends: his sister, two former buddies from school, *Frau* Ludewig (*she* had asked *him*), and Eddie. The last time Richard had looked, Eddie had more than 700 Friends, and there were dozens of photos on his timeline, mostly of photogenic young people partying or at the beach.

"See, Miriam Burkhardt, our postgrad. Look! She studied in Bremen before she came here. In my opinion, almost an Eight. Not Hanseatic at all. No cold north about *her*—she's red-hot, this girl!"

He was right, too.

"Yes, she's OK. But I don't know what you're trying to prove, Eddie, just showing me photos of these girls and saying that you fancy them."

"And you're only interested in their intellect, Brother Richard? Well how about this little poppet then? *Fräulein* Felicitas Förster—and I think I'd add another word beginning with "F." No, not *that* word! I meant: firecracker! I've danced with her, but I couldn't keep up. She's small, but everything is perfectly proportioned. What wouldn't I give for a night of passion with Fey Förster? Let me see. My liitle finger? Six months of my life? Six months *at least*! Just look at her! Isn't she a dream? A *wet*-dream? This photo is telling you Seven, but when you see her in the flesh (do pardon my French!) that's an Eight or my middle name isn't William!"

Richard stared at the photos on Facebook. Again, he couldn't deny that Felicitas Förster was a stunner.

"She's never been in any of my classes. I wouldn't have missed *her*. The lecture, perhaps? Probably she sits at the back of the hall."

"No, you wouldn't have missed her, dear boy. One is not blind. One is not a eunuch. One's flesh would have stirred, believe me, if she'd ever found her way to English Composition or whatever it is that you offer them. Now," and again he pointed to the laptop, "last but not least, because she's such a nice girl, and I personally think she's cute: Lisa Meyer."

Richard knew the name. Briefly he'd suspected her of sending him that first, anonymous, postcard, until the second card, signed "S.," had landed in his mailbox. He knew the name, and now he recognized the face. Yes, she was one of those "grazing cows" from the back row in Textual Composition. They'd always seemed so dull, but the girl in the photo was reasonably pretty.

"Yeah, she's in my class."

"A Seven? At least."

"Do you really think so?"

"I wouldn't kick her out of bed on a cold night. But I don't think she'd ever look at me. More one for you, boss!"

"Eddie, again: how does any of this help us?"

Eddie gave him an unexpectedly serious look.

"It helps us a lot, because we're *profiling* him, right? Just ask yourself, what do these photos tell us about his taste in women? That's assuming that he hand-picked these girls, and didn't simply bump into them in the hostels by chance. That's not likely, is it? 'Oops, sorry! But, begging your pardon, ma'am, may I molest you? Nothing personal of course—you just happen to have crossed my path today.'"

"No, that obviously didn't happen. He targeted them. They're all students of English. In our department. He must have singled them out."

"OK. Good. All students of English. There is some link between this character and the English Department. Or so the *Präsi* would have you believe. What else do they have in common?"

Richard hesitated, because what he was going to say sounded so silly.

"They're all quite good-looking."

"Even Lisa? You are finally going to concede that Lisa Meyer is a nice-looking girl?"

"*Yeees*, I suppose so. If you absolutely insist."

"So, the second thing we know about your pervert is that he has good taste in women."

Richard was outraged.

"*My* pervert?"

"OK. *Our* pervert. He goes for good-looking girls—he's aiming high. But there's more to come. Point number three" (Eddie was now ticking them off one by one on his fingers) "he goes for girls who are self-confident. Maybe Lisa isn't, but the others certainly are. These are girls who have plenty of friends. Who probably have male admirers. Who may even have boyfriends hanging around, trying to scare off the competition. This all tells us something about him: either this guy has a degree of self-esteem, or self-confidence; and so he takes risks; or he's being driven by some powerful urge! You really reckon that this is just a bloke who's too shy to chat up women? Some pimply loner? I don't think so! Guys like that don't try to punch above their weight! Point number four—"

"*Number four*? Aren't you reading too much into all this?"

Eddie shrugged.

"Bear with me. I think there's even more we can squeeze out of this. So, next point: what else do the girls in these photos have in common? I'll tell you! They're all blondes."

This was too much for Richard to take.

"Oh, come on, Eddie, this is getting ridiculous! How many of our girls *aren't* blondes? This is Germany, not West Africa."

"No, not true. These chicks are all the same type: real blondes, with long hair. They're not mousy blondes or pale blondes. They're not ash-blonde, or reddish-blonde, or dirty blonde, or sandy brown. Or chemical blonde out of a bottle. These are *blonde*-blondes. Naturals. The real McCoy. This is the sort of bird that he goes for! Big, attractive girls, Nordic women, Scandinavian types, with long blonde hair."

He leant back on the sofa, looking pretty pleased with himself. Richard, however, was far from pleased. Who was supposed to be playing Sherlock Holmes in this scenario? And who was it who was supposed to be the slow-witted, unimaginative Watson?

"Well," he nevertheless conceded, "it sounds moderately convincing to me. But where do we go from here?"

"If this is what he fancies, we can warn all the girls in the hostels who look like this—"

"Oh no! That's precisely what the President *doesn't* want. It would start a panic. And for that same reason we can't go to the police."

"Then we'll have to investigate this ourselves."

"And how is that going to work? I can't swan about chatting up all my students!"

Eddie sighed dramatically.

"How unfortunate! Then the task of investigating these ladies will fall to me." He raised his hand, unnecessarily. "No ifs or buts! I'm willing to make the ultimate sacrifice. 'Into the valley of death' etcetera etcetera. But I do know three of these girls. I'll just have to take it nice and slowly. We don't want to raise any suspicions."

Eddie suggested, however, that it might be better for Richard to speak to the postgrad, Miriam. He was only a lowly part-timer, while Richard taught the odd class that postgrads occasionally attended, on a voluntary basis, if they had nothing better to do. It would therefore be easier for Richard to find an excuse for approaching her than for him.

Richard agreed. He felt completely deflated. The "briefing" had not gone quite the way he'd imagined it would. So much for Sherlock Holmes!

He didn't even need to ask where Eddie had picked up his acumen as a criminal investigator—he'd seen the dog-eared copies of sundry detective novels scattered among the other volumes in Eddie's book collection, a collection that was now spread across all the rooms in Richard's apartment.

But before he drove Eddie back into his own room, so that he could finally get his lesson preparation finished and his exam paper started, Richard did manage to salvage a little of his pride after all.

It came to him suddenly.

"There is something else," he said.

"Yes?" Eddie put down the volume of *manga* that he'd found conveniently tucked behind Richard's sofa, of all places. "Did we miss something?"

"Not exactly. But it just struck me that he goes for big girls. Doesn't that mean that he's probably quite a big man himself?"

"You're right: point number five!"

"And there's more. Point number six: if our profile, *your* profile, is correct, then he made a mistake. All four girls are blonde, and pretty. That's his type, agreed? Big, Germanic, long-haired blondes. Except for one girl—"

"Felicitas Förster!"

"—who is small. So I'm guessing that Felicitas wasn't his intended target that night. She shouldn't have been there. He'd been expecting somebody else, and something went wrong. How did he come to make that mistake? If we can find that out, we're closer to knowing how he operates. And we're closer to tracking him down."

Richard already felt much better. Though at the same time he was beginning to feel worried that the man they would be "hunting"—now profiled as a big man, self-confident or manically driven—could prove to be dangerous after all.

Eddie must have had the same thought.

"You ever do any martial arts? No? Just asking, no special reason."

OF MATTERS DIDACTIC

The exam paper that Richard needed to start preparing was for British Studies. Whereas in British Studies II, which was a seminar, the students normally earned their credit points by doing presentations and writing them up afterwards as homework, in British Studies I, which was a lecture ("Britain: A Survey"), there was a written examination that had to be passed.

This exam, in the form in which Richard had inherited it from his predecessor, was a disaster zone. Few of the students, he discovered, could express their thoughts well in written English, so it was frequently unclear what on earth they were trying to say.

To get around this problem, Richard had changed the format of the exam from straightforward essays to a cocktail mix of multiple-choice questions, simple maps or diagrams to be drawn, and various questions to be answered concisely in one or two sentences.

Yet the results were still dreadful.

Question: What are the British Isles?

Lena's answer: The Brittish Iles are ilands surounding England. (How could Lena have managed to mispell a word that was given in the question?) And she had included Gibraltar (correctly spelled) as one of the British Isles.

Question: Who was Mary Queen of Scots?

Heidi's answer: Mary Q of S was a queen of Britain who killed her sister because she was Catholic. Then there was a Civil War, but I can't remember who won.

Question: Who was Lloyd George?

Florian's answer: Some stupid dude. I don't know and I don't fucking care. (Florian was anticipating—correctly— that he was going to fail the exam. For which he'd be able to obtain a degree of revenge by giving Richard a 5 in the end-of-the-course evaluation.)

Question: In what ways did Britain benefit from the Transatlantic Slave Trade?

Lisa's answer: Millions of blacks came to Britain. Cool! So the benefits were reggae, hiphop, rap, curry, loads of football stars, Martin Luther King.

Martin Luther King?

Richard was past despair, but there was no-one he could turn to. After all, he was testing what the Germans called *Faktenwissen* ("fact-knowledge"), a procedure that these days was not educationally respectable, so it would be better not to make too much fuss about what the students were producing.

Fine, it was worthless, but when they left the university they wouldn't have much of anything else in their heads either (most of them). There wasn't a lot he could do about that. If he was honest with himself, he ought to fail two-thirds of them, but there was no way he could do that. Look at what had happened to poor old Professor Michael!

He'd get no support from his colleagues. They had discussed the format of the examination, at the time that Richard had dared to change it, in the departmental meeting.

Snoad, putting in a rare appearance, had sneered about it being an "anachronistic exercise in positivism," and Kurz had suggested replacing the whole banal lecture course with a project on Ethnic Britain. Cool Britannia?

Enno Müller and *Frau* Schlichting had yawned all the time, and exchanged exasperated glances, as if to say that these pathetic squabbles among the "native speakers" were a waste of time that didn't concern them.

Kajo, who had chaired the meeting, had remained resolutely on the fence, unwilling to offend anyone.

Richard had finally got his way, though only by taking a massive gamble. He had acknowledged the criticism from Kurz and Snoad, but then cunningly invited them to come up with a detailed proposal of their own for a restructured version of the British Studies course—and of the exams. This would involve them in lots of extra work, and it raised the distinct possibility that one of them might then be asked to teach the new product.

As he had foreseen they would, his colleagues quickly backed down.

In situations like this, Kajo invariably refused to commit himself. Richard remembered an oral Finals Exam that he'd taken part in, earlier on in his Reichsstadt career, together with Kajo and *Frau* Schlichting as the other two examiners. (Schlichting was sitting in for her buddy Enno, who had gone down with 'flu.)

The candidate was a bright but pushy young woman, Anne-Marie, who was known to be a favorite of Enno's, and her explanation of how the percentages were collated in Enno's research project was predictably impressive. But the girl's English (in Richard's part of the exam) was disastrously bad.

After the exam, Anne-Marie was sent out of the room, so that the examiners could discuss her performance and try to reach agreement on a grade.

Frau Schlichting promptly suggested a 1, which was the highest grade that they could give. For her own section, that might even have been a fair mark, but she proposed a 1 for the *whole exam*.

Richard was gobsmacked. Despite all temptation, he didn't dare suggest a 5 (Fail) for the language section. According to the regulations, if a 5 was given as the grade for any one part, the whole exam had to be declared a Fail. Instead, he suggested a mixture of grades that would lead to the end-result 3+, which seemed reasonable to him, generous even, under the circumstances.

Frau Schlichting refused to budge (Enno must have exacted a promise from her). It had to be a straight 1, there was no alternative. The young lady, she said, was intellectually outstanding, and excellence needed to be rewarded!

Richard argued that it was an English examination, and the first stage in the training of the students to be schoolteachers. How could the department give its seal of approval for someone to become a teacher *of English* whose own grasp of the language was so poor?

Frau Schlichting pointed out that, without at least a strong 2, Anne-Marie couldn't proceed to her postgraduate diploma, after which she was hoping to complete a doctorate. If her examiners couldn't find the decency to give her that grade, they would be destroying a promising young woman's academic career before it had even started. *She* couldn't take that responsibility upon herself; could Kajo, or Richard?

In any case, Anne-Marie would probably never work in a school, if that was what Richard was so worried about. She was aiming for much higher things than that.

Actually, Richard was perfectly willing to take the responsibility upon himself: the thought of Anne-Marie as a potential Professor of English seemed even more grotesque to him than the thought of Anne-Marie as a schoolteacher. Standing in front of a class, she'd be unable to spot her pupils' language mistakes and (even worse) might have her own English corrected by some younger version of Pimply Konstantin. But he couldn't say it too loudly, if only because many of the university *Anglisten* that he'd encountered in Germany were much weaker in English than they ought to be.

Then it turned nasty.

First, *Frau* Schlichting played the "language-classes-don't-really-matter-so-much" card. It was true that hardly any German *Anglisten* were interested in practical language classes—their scholarly concerns were in English Linguistics and English Literature, with British or American Background Studies coming in last behind Language Teaching Theory. Actually, since quite a few of the academics involved in teacher education had less than dazzling scholarly credentials (and a corresponding inferiority complex *vis-à-vis* the pure philologists), this whole subject was rather sensitive.

Secondly, Anne-Marie was a self-confident young woman from a highly respectable local family. They needed people like her! Her father was a member of the state parliament. What committees might he happen to be on? Failing her might cause the President embarrassment next time that he was called to a hearing at the Ministry.

Finally, like the magician whipping a rabbit out of a hat, Dorothea Schlichting produced her clinching argument.

As she had already said, Anne-Marie was known to have academic ambitions. If the young woman's progress to the academic heights were thwarted over a few banal language mistakes (a *few*?), word would soon spread that *certain people* in the English Department were small-minded—and sexist. The Commissioner for Gender Equality might be informed. Once that dreaded harpy had sunk her fangs into the issue, it would be a no-win situation for all of them. Did they want to risk that? The fact that they were without a Professor (this was during the "Kajo Interregnum") made them especially vulnerable.

Throughout this whole discussion, Kajo had said very little. He had begged them to come to a sensible agreement. Significantly, he hadn't used the word "compromise," although Richard's suggestion had actually been just such an offer—in an honest world, Anne-Marie would have received the 5 that she deserved, and an opportunity to repeat the examination one semester later. (When she could greatly improve her chances of success by asking for a different examiner for the English language section.)

Richard noticed how, gradually, Kajo's pleas for an agreement had shifted from being addressed to both of them to being addressed only to him. He had even hinted that it would be "gentlemanly" for Richard to give way to his lady colleague.

Kajo had also pointed out the time: their deliberations had already lasted longer than the exam itself had done.

Finally, Richard had caved in. Kajo was so spineless! And *Frau* Schlichting had no integrity—all that the wretched woman cared about was getting a good grade for her buddy's protégée! But they were his colleagues, and he had to get along with them. If he refused to sign the minutes of the exam, there'd be a huge scandal (in which he'd probably be the one who was hurt most), and it might delay but it wouldn't stop Anne-Marie getting her grade 1 in the end.

He was ashamed of himself—when it went down to the wire, wasn't he just as spineless as Kajo was? All he wanted now was to go home, have a stiff drink and forget it all.

However, before he could do that Anne-Marie needed to be given the good news.

She obviously knew what had been going on, for over an hour, behind that closed door, and she was bright enough to be able to reconstruct what the positions of her three examiners had most likely been.

Kajo told her her grade, and apologized clumsily that, because of the lateness of the hour, they wouldn't be able to go into the details of the examination. No matter, who cared? She was the cat that had got the cream: Richard had never seen such a look of triumph on a student's face. He felt sick.

If that was bad enough, there was worse to come. After they had shaken hands, and wished Anne-Marie all good luck for the future, and she was about to leave, she suddenly turned in the open doorway and spoke to Richard directly. Behind the spectacles, her eyes flashed challengingly.

"*Herr* Orwell, I know that you are critical of my English! Though perhaps that element in the examination is given too much weight? But even during my schooldays my teachers took it into account that I have a known problem with dyslexia. Students with such problems shouldn't be discriminated against, should they?"

Richard wanted to say: "Students with such problems shouldn't be studying for the qualification to teach children a foreign language, should they?" But the words wouldn't come out.

Kajo's face said: "See, Richard, that explains it, now everything's fine. How relieved I am!," and *Frau* Schlichting's said: "You stupid boy, wasting our time like that!"

That evening, over a couple of those stiff drinks, Richard had tried to repair the damage to his nerves and to his self-confidence. He hadn't known about the dyslexia, but Enno must have done, since Anne-Marie had been working on his project with him for months. Snoad would have let it go through without a murmur, but he was overbooked for the exams (for that very reason!); Harlan Kurz was wholly unpredictable, and was avoided like the plague at examination time; so the hot potato had landed in Richard's lap. Enno, advising the girl on whom to choose as examiner, had misjudged him.

Well, slightly. In the end he had backed down, he thought ruefully.

Dyslexia apart, Anne-Marie wasn't such a bad student. Many of them, to Richard's mind, were far, far worse. Should they even be at a college? They had no intellectual curiosity whatsoever, they never read anything, they could neither summarize a detailed argument nor construct a convincing argument of their own. But could the university be expected to repair what the schools had already messed up?

He'd supervised a group of students on a teaching practice at a local comprehensive school. It was his very first teaching practice, to be precise. He'd still had certain expectations about what should go on in English lessons, if only in contrast to the lousy French and German lessons he'd experienced during his own schooldays in Britain.

First, they'd watched the class's regular English teacher in action. This gentleman spent so much of the lesson fussily "involving," "motivating" and "interacting" with the rowdy fifteen-year-olds, and trying to get them to work (i.e., stay quiet) in groups, that (as far as Richard could tell) the sum total of English that the kids had been introduced to, after an hour, amounted to not more than a couple of straightforward items of vocabulary.

When it was the turn of Richard's students, even less was achieved. The boy who went first was a huge, good-looking young man who was in the junior cohort of the local American football team, the Reichsstadt Emperors. He had picked a ridiculously simple and undemanding lesson to teach them, and by some miracle even managed to get through it on schedule.

The girls in the class had gazed at him adoringly; in jealous reaction, the boys had speculated nastily about the size of his dick, though not so that he could hear their comments. (Richard, sitting at the back, a notepad perched on his knee, had heard every word.) In the group discussion afterwards, Richard—thinking also of the class's regular English teacher—had emphasized how little English the student had actually offered the pupils.

Those well-meaning words contributed to the disaster that was the second attempt by one of his students to teach the class.

The protagonist this time was an amiable girl with a very serious weight problem. She had picked an ambitious but deadly boring grammar topic. Right from the start, the noise level in the classroom was such that she could barely make herself heard. No-one was paying her any attention, except to snigger about her appearance. When she pushed a bit too insistently on the grammar exercise, the lesson disintegrated.

A satchel flew in a grand arc out of the window (they were on the second floor), followed by a book. The noise level was now deafening, but individual contributions could still be made out.

"*Fotze!*" (This was the 'C-word'.)

"*Ich kriege dich!*" ('I'm gonna get you!')

"*Leck mich!*" ('Kiss my ass' would be a polite translation.)

When the student teacher asked them to be quiet, *please*, there were shouts of *Fettsack* ("Fatso!"), and one boy declared loudly that this wasn't a proper teacher, was it? It was a "fucking elephant baby."

The class's English teacher made no attempt to intervene. When Richard therefore stood up and bellowed "That's enough!" he was probably breaking the rules.

The subsequent group discussion in a quiet corner of the staff-room was awkward in the extreme. The teacher accepted that his class had behaved badly, but it had been an "unfamiliar learning interface" for them and Richard's intervention had been... *unfortunate*.

Then a loud gong sounded, and he excused himself—he had another lesson to go to.

"Fatso" was understandably upset, her double-chin wobbling dangerously, though she was not quite in tears yet. Richard tried to build up her spirits by pointing out that her lesson had been much more substantial than the teacher's had been, and that some of the pupils (those who had been listening) would have picked up many useful things from her. So: *Nil desperandum!*

Richard stayed behind in the staff-room after his students had left, helped himself to a milky coffee, and got involved in a conversation with some of the teachers—in the course of which he made his second big mistake of the day, by asking who "*Frau Jano*" was.

The school entrance hall was defaced with graffiti, none of which had been cleaned off during the time that he'd been coming to the school, and one of these declared "*Frau Jano = Stinkfotze.*"

Frau Janowitz, he was told, was a geography teacher. But she had left long ago.

And nobody had tried to remove any of the graffiti?

No.

A couple of the teachers shrugged, and one said, "If you do, the shit goes straight back up a week later. So what's the point?" In any case, *Frau* Janowitz wasn't there any more.

That seemed to be the consensus view.

Richard argued against it, mentioning the slippery slope, Rudy Giuliani, and zero tolerance, but to no avail. The men's toilets were full of graffiti, too, and you expected that (it was just the same at the university), but the *entrance hall*?

A few days later, Kajo asked to talk to him. Given that they shared an office, and talked to each other all the time, this could only mean something serious. And, sure enough: the school director had complained about his "arrogant" and "unprofessional" behavior.

Richard told his acting boss what had happened. Kajo merely shrugged. It was too late to do anything about it now.

"I don't think that you found a common wave-length with the teachers. Did you really refer to the school students as 'pupils'? We don't use that term any more, the students find it so patronizing."

Did they indeed? Perhaps it would do the "students" no harm to be *patronized*, Richard thought. And to be *taught*. And to be subjected to a bit more *discipline*.

But what he said was, "I didn't know that."

Kajo had arranged for him and his group of students to switch schools with Jonathan Snoad. When he and Snoad bumped into each other a few days later, he discovered that his colleague was far from happy with the new arrangement.

"Thank you for *nothing*. In fact: fuck you, Orwell!"

Richard didn't realize why Snoad was so annoyed until the following week, when he and his team of students went to their new teaching practice school. It was a so-called Middle School, located in a smart middle-class suburb of Reichsstadt. The children were younger, there was an immaculate lawn in front of the school, the teachers were serious about what they were doing, and there were no graffiti in sight.

A cushy number! It was no surprise that Jonathan Snoad, a world-class avoider of hard work, had been displeased.

MAKING PLANS

The two girls met again in Steffi's room in the hostel.

Lisa never felt completely at ease there. She wasn't the tidiest person ever to grace this earth (as her mum always liked to remind her), but she did make a constant effort to have her room looking so that she wouldn't be embarrassed by an unexpected visitor of the mother or aunt variety. It helped that she had a second pad, the eyrie that Steffi envied so much, where she could keep a load of her stuff; also, that she got her clothes-wash done for her whenever she deigned to spend a weekend at home.

Actually, it was a real bore going home, but it made her parents so amazingly happy. Their eyes would light up, her mum would cook all her favorite food, and her dad would try to engage her in "serious conversation," and invite her to watch boring television documentaries about the Second World War with him. She didn't want to rob them of what had to be one of their few pleasures in life, did she?

Their lives must be pretty miserable, she thought. Her dad was work-crazy (if some of her profs could only see hard how he worked, they'd get a shock), and her mum fussed and worried about everything imaginable. From one of the lectures, Lisa half-remembered that someone had a theory about work expanding to fill the time available for it, and her mother would be the classic example of that, except that with her it would be worrying, not work, that was always expanding.

What would her mum think of her friend Steffi's room? The thought made Lisa chuckle.

Steffi's duvet and pillow would be anywhere—except on the bed.

There was no obvious place assigned for dirty washing, no basket or cupboard space, and so discarded tops, jeans, and socks would lie scattered haphazardly about the room. (Lisa tried not to sit too close to them.)

Coffee mugs were never washed up, but might if they were lucky eventually find themselves moved to outside the door, where the nice cleaning lady would presumably deal with them. (Or some altruistic passing stranger.) They were of different designs, shapes and sizes, but all of them were badly cracked or chipped. Steffi's favorite mug was inscribed "FUCKPUSSY" on one side, while on the other side was a cartoon drawing of cats copulating.

Not satisfied with the regulation venetian blinds and the cheap hostel curtains, Steffi had tacked up black drapes over the window. She had found the heavy material folded up and squeezed between two of the recycling bins, waiting for collection with the garbage, and garbage is what it looked like. But Steffi thought her drapes gave the room "atmosphere," and who needed natural light anyway? Or fresh air?

She had also tacked up two posters of her favorite rock bands.

The members of Thong were skinny young men with Jagger pouts. They posed aggressively on the poster, almost bursting out of their leather pants, especially in the crotch area, and thrusting their guitars upwards (could they play them if they held them like that?). *Thrust* was in fact their magnum opus; *Attitude* was their most recent success.

The other group was named Razorblade. The figures on the poster for their album *Midnight Visitor* were shadowed in black and looked more like corpses than people.

Lisa's own taste in music ran more to gentle soft-rock, and the soulful ballads of singer-songwriters. She had given up trying to convince Steffi of the delights of melody and harmony, and hoped only that Steffi wouldn't actually play any of her own "faves" while she was there.

Lisa was not alone in her lack of enthusiasm for Steffi's pet bands. Agathe, the girl in the next room, who was an active member of the Catholic Student Community, was not over-fond of Thong or Razorblade either, especially when they were played at high volume. The warden of the hostel had already been called in several times to arbitrate.

On one famous occasion, there had been some angry words between the two girls, culminating in Steffi telling her neighbor that the real cause of the problem wasn't music.

Oh no, Agathe's real problem was that her boyfriend (naturally, there was no such person, as Steffi well knew) wasn't *giving it to her* properly. As a solution, Steffi recommended a "good, hard fuck" on one of the flat tombstones in the nearby churchyard of St. Benedikt: "cold stone under your bum—and there's no escape when he goes down on you and goes in *deep*. That *really* opens you up. You should try it sometime, young lady!"

To Lisa, however, she confided that she didn't understand why the "Blessed Agathe" didn't like Thong.

"They're so sweet. I mean, what is there *not* to like? The stupid bitch can probably only masturbate to Gregorian chant, and *that's* why she doesn't like them." She conceded: "I can understand why she doesn't get Razorblade. I mean, they're an acquired taste. You have to work on it."

But Lisa didn't like Thong or Razorblade either.

Steffi graciously refrained from playing any of her music, even at low volume.

So: what should the first step be?

"First step? What do you mean?" Lisa asked.

The first step in their campaign for Lisa to get to know Mr. Harlan R. Kurz a bit better.

"No," she quickly corrected herself. "A *lot* better."

"And you and Richard Orwell too!"

Oh, *that* would be far less of a problem.

"When I want a bloke, I get him" (she explained, conveniently forgetting her previous fiasco with Harlan Kurz). "The only minor complication here is that Mr. Orwell doesn't really know me. I'm not exactly an active participant in his classes, am I?" (Or in anyone else's, Lisa thought to herself.) "The first move, the first contact, needs to be something fairly harmless, something casual. He is my teacher, after all. I can't just *go for him*, like, can I?"

Which was more Steffi's usual style, at least with students. Once she had walked up to a handsome sports student at a party and said, "You Tarzan, me Jane?," inviting him to grab her and carry her off to his jungle lair. As he had done. (But this turned out to be "Mister Premature," and it had only been a once-off—literally.)

"So...?"

"We do it softly softly, catchee monkey. *Your* way. Some getting-to-know-you stuff, then a date. As I said, the first moves need to be planned carefully. You and Harlan: no probs. Mister Jiggle-Bum will cream himself if he thinks you fancy him. All you have to do is be a touch more pro-active. Send him the right signals, and he'll jump. As for Mister O—"

Lisa couldn't see that happening so quickly.

"He's more conservative than Harlan! And the profs aren't suppose to date students anyway." (Steffi snorted loudly in disagreement.) "OK, a lot of them do, but they're the ones we know about. How do we know that Mr. Orwell's like that too?"

Steffi laughed.

"Hark at you: 'Mister Orwell'! He's a man, isn't he? That says it all. Leave him to me. I have reason to be more optimistic than you seem to be."

"I don't know why you fancy him. He's not the usual type that you go for, is he?"

That was a stupid thing to say, as Lisa realized immediately. There was no "usual type" with Steffi. She went for all sorts of men.

"He keeps it all well buttoned-up. I like that. It makes a change. I find it intriguing..."

"Maybe he's gay?"

"Rico says: no. And he's already tried."

"No!" Lisa was genuinely shocked. "But maybe he's got a girlfriend?"

"Not to my knowledge. And I have made certain enquiries. There was a girl from the German Department, Sonia Something-or-other, that he was knocking around with, but she's out of the picture now..."

Lisa was impressed.

"How do you find all this stuff out?"

Steffi gave a dismissive wave of her hand.

"Call it *research*. Call it *planning*. This is how military campaigns are won—before the first shot is even fired!"

"Wow!"

"So—here's an idea. How about this for a first contact? You know that horrible gray pullover that he wore for Textual Composition last time? And in the lecture?"

"Yes, the one with a hole at the elbow. Yuck!"

"Indeed. Hey, you're bright today!"

"Well, what about it?"

"Next time he wears it, go up to him after the lesson and offer to darn or patch it for him! All men like being mothered. He won't say no."

Lisa was indignant.

"Why me? I'm not his granny! *You're* the one who fancies him!"

Steffi gave her familiar "long-suffering older sister" sigh, and Lisa realized what was coming next: it (whatever it was) was now going to have to be spelled out to her.

"Firstly, do I look like someone who would care about a hole in a pullover?" A glance at the way Steffi was dressed, and the state of her room, would disabuse anyone of that notion immediately. "Secondly, if I go up to him after the lesson, what are the odds that I won't be able to control myself, and he'll notice, for instance, when my eyes start slipping down to his crotch? We don't want to frighten him off! This is Richard Orwell, not Harlan baby."

"OK." Lisa was convinced. "I'll do it. But you must do the darning! I haven't got a clue about stuff like that."

"And you think that *I* have? Isn't this what mums are for?" Lisa was lost for words. Steffi pressed home her advantage. "And *your* mum is a short bus ride away. Mine is at the other end of the country, in Passau, and you know how long it takes to get *there* on the train. And it's too far to drive." She paused, then added in a conciliatory tone, "Look: I can drive you home with the pullover—if my car's still working—and come and collect you again."

"What will I say to my mum?"

"Just tell her I offered to give you a lift from the uni—"

"No! What will I tell her about the pullover?"

"Tell her it's your boyfriend's."

"Not a hope! Then she'll want to know his name, and loads of details about him, and she'll tell me to bring him for Sunday lunch, and all that crap."

"Just tell her the truth. Which is, that it belongs to a favorite lecturer of yours."

"*What?!* Holy shit, that's even worse! And my dad will freak out completely. He's already been to see the *Präsi* once. I can just hear him: 'My daughter has been molested in that hostel of yours, and now one of your Professors is stalking her! Your university is no better than a brothel!'"

Steffi treated her to a pitying smile.

"You poor girl! But now you understand why I never even considered going to the uni in Passau (not that they would have had me). I can't have my parents cramping my style." She thought for a moment. "Fine. Tell her that it belongs to a fellow student of yours, who is very nice, and who often helps you with difficult homework assignments—you know, a sweet boy, a better-looking version of Pimply Konstantin—but who is unfortunately completely gay."

"Hmm."

"And if she *still* wants you to bring this paragon home for Sunday lunch, to reward him for his noble assistance to her daughter, tell her that he's switched unis at short notice. He's an alpha student. Guys like that can get a place anywhere." She paused. "And before I forget: does your mum actually do patching and darning?"

"Oh yes, it's one of her favorite intellectual activities, along with Doctor-Novels" (the German expression for romantic fiction for women) "and doing the flowers for the church."

"Sounds familiar!"

And they both laughed.

"But what then?" Lisa asked. "Mending his pullover isn't going to get us a date. And I don't want a date with him; *you* do. I don't see the connection."

Again the sigh.

"Mend his pullover, and he'll owe you. So that when you invite him out on a date he won't be able to say no." Lisa started to raise an objection, but she nipped her protest firmly in the bud. "Stop, listen—hear me out! Not *that* sort of date, obviously. No, something that *he* wants to do, but harmless. Like a bloody classical concert, or a museum. We need to research what kind of stuff he's into. And because it isn't a *real* date, and you're a nice girl, ha ha, you'll be taking along some other students who are interested in his boring museum or whatever. Once we have it set up, I'll speak to dear Harlan and get him to join the party too. I'll tell him that Ulrike Sandmann will be in the group. I'm sure he fancies her; they all do! Then a few people like Ulrike will, er, drop out at the last moment, how sad, and, oh dear, it's just the four of us: you and Harlan, Mister O, and your chaperone—me. And then let the fun begin!"

Lisa was still skeptical.

"I don't think Harlan likes Orwell very much. Not from the way he talks about him, at least. And this museum business doesn't sound terribly romantic to me."

"Then it's up to you to *make* it romantic. And don't worry about whether the boys like each other or not. Harlan Kurz is basically a simple creature, governed (like most men) by his prick. You know, men are barely one stage up from single-cell organisms. All his attention will be focused on you. And I shall take care of dear Mr. Orwell. You can leave that part of the project to me. You'll be surprised. I'm already working on it."

She leant across and starting stroking Lisa's hair.

"Hey! What's this about? You a lezzie now?"

Steffi sighed.

"I think I need to grow my hair. Long-haired girls get more *action*."

A LETTER (AND A PHOTO) FOR ADONIS

Richard's class wasn't till the afternoon, and so he could treat himself to a lie-in and a late breakfast. Eddie was still snoring and grunting under his duvet when Richard left the house.

They had both been satisfied with the "briefing session." (Richard perhaps slightly less than Eddie.) They had agreed to have another session at the weekend, and to talk about the possible suspects this time. This would be harder work because, apart from their nebulous "profile," they had nothing to go on. And if their profile *was* correct, they would be dealing with someone who was potentially dangerous, and not with a shy, lonely misfit.

In the meantime: Eddie had already said that if he was going to interview the girls, Richard would have to investigate the boys.

His English Grammar class went well. None of the four girls they'd been talking about were among the students, although Rico had shown up again, and had stared at him sulkily throughout the whole lesson. He hadn't been forgiven yet! Or was Rico still living in hope, and playing hard to get?

There were several girls with long blonde hair in the class, one of them at least spectacularly pretty. He longed to warn them, but of course he couldn't. The pretty girl's name was Ulrike Sandmann. Not Sandra or Susanna or Silke Sandmann, unfortunately. Even so, he'd keep an eye on her. (It would be harder to keep his eyes *off* her.)

Before he left the university he checked his post once again, and found that "S." had sent him a whole package, inscribed "To Richard, from S." It was a large brown envelope, so big that she'd had to fold it at one end to get it into his mailbox. There was a note; some postcards with twee photos of cats, rabbits and butterflies, accompanied by sentimental poems; and a smaller envelope containing a long, folded letter, which had been written on a typewriter or printed out from a computer.

It was early evening and there was no-one else about. Richard stood in front of the mailboxes, holding the items awkwardly and wondering what might be in the letter. But first he looked at the note.

> Dearest Richard, my Adonis!
> I've missed you so much, I've thought about you so much! For example, when I took this photo (on the other side). It's a kind of selfie. This is how I look when I think of you. What it is I'm thinking you can read in the letter, my darling.
> This time I wrote it on the computer, because my hand was shaking so much while I was writing that my handwriting came out funny. I hope you don't find that too impersonal? By the way, I've retouched the photo a tiny bit—I don't want you to recognise me. Not yet! I love you!
> And I want you!
>
> S.

Her English was excellent, he noted again, which might help him to narrow the field, and it was British, which wouldn't—very few of them would have learned American English at school.

He turned the note over and was shocked to find, on the other side, a computer printout of a photo of a naked girl. She was lying on her back on a double-bed, her legs spread wide apart, her head turned to one side. Her breasts were large and well-shaped. She was masturbating with something (a bottle?). Her eyes were shut and her mouth was wide open in ecstasy. The photo had indeed been retouched, the contours rendered fuzzy so that her face and what was going on between her thighs couldn't be seen clearly.

Richard was shocked by how much the body of the girl in the photo resembled that of an old college girlfriend of his back in England. It wasn't her, of course, just as it probably wasn't "S." either, merely some girl in a dirty photo downloaded from an internet porn site.

He had to admit that the photo turned him on. "S." knew how to turn him on! Who was she? How well did she know him?

While he was staring at the photo he failed to notice Enno coming up behind him.

"Ah, Richard, another of those tiresome love-letters from your students, eh?"

Something about the manner in which Richard had been staring at the note must have prompted him. He almost always addressed Richard in a jocular or facetious way. There was no dislike between them—they had never once spoken about the Anne-Marie business—but they had nothing much to say to each other, and each regarded the other as *unnecessary*, as being, in the greater scheme of the universe, rather a waste of space.

Nevertheless, colleagues had to talk to one another occasionally.

Caught off balance, and before he could stop himself, Richard foolishly blurted out "Yes," just as Enno, now standing quite close behind him, caught a glimpse of the photo.

He was flabbergasted.

"Is that, er, what I think it is?"

"Yes. It's a photo."

"From a student?"

"From a student. Of a student. Yes."

"Students send you *that* kind of photo?"

Richard was swimming. He had no idea how to deal with this. One step at a time?

"Yes. Now and again. Don't you get them, too?"

Enno looked at him with a quizzical smile.

"No, I don't. And I doubt whether Kajo does either."

"Why shouldn't he? It's not illegal. I can't stop them. If girls want to send me photos..."

"Of course. Of course, Richard. No-one said it was illegal." He paused. "Well, I must say, you young fellows have all the luck. Do enjoy your evening."

"You too, Enno."

When he was gone, Richard read the letter. This time there was no "Dear Richard," there was no chatty preamble. "S," whoever she was, got straight to the point.

> I'm in your office. We have something boring to discuss, I can't remember what it is, because I can't concentrate on our discussion, all I see the whole time is your beautiful face. After a while I can't stand it any more. I go over to you and kiss you lightly on the cheek. You sieze [sic] the opportunity, take me in your arms, and cover my mouth with your lips. It hits me like 100000 volts when you finally push your tongue into my mouth and show me what kissing is all about! At first I can hardly trust myself. I just kiss your lips.
>
> But then you stick both your hands under my top, and I really let go. The kisses get wilder, longer. Our hands are busy, stripping each other.
>
> After only a few moments I'm standing there in front of you in my white lace underwear. It's so thin that you can see how stiff my nipples are.
>
> You like what you see, oh yes! Slowly, you take off my bra.
>
> My tender, juicy breasts fall forward. They're yours! I feel your hands stroking and caressing me.

Your stiff tongue licks tenderly at my nipples. I groan. I don't want this to stop, ever. But at the same time I want more of it. I kiss your neck, your shoulders. My hands are pulling on your arse.

I slip my hand into your trousers, searching for the object of my lust. I pull down the zip and your prick leaps out at me, proud and stiff like a soldier. Your body is trembling, your prick pushes against my hand. At last! At last I can enjoy you, Richard.

I'm out of control, rubbing, licking, sucking. My groans gets louder and louder. How your weapon turns me on! I'm working on you with both hands, my lips and my tongue until you shoot hot come all over my tits.

I lead you over to your desk. I climb onto it, open my legs and lift them up. "Aren't you interested in this? This lovely jewel? This sweet little slit? It can all be yours!"

I lick one of my fingertips and slip it inside. I'm almost masturbating.

I whisper, "Richard, come and take me, just once! Do whatever you want to do with me!"

My legs are spread wide to invite you, but instead you go down on one knee in front of me. I feel your tongue licking my thighs and then breaking into my slit. I groan.

You're kissing the tiny tuft of hair that I've left above my cunt. Your lips are glued to my labia. I spread my legs even wider for you. Your head is completely between my thighs.

You whisper something. I can't hear what it is, but I can feel it. Your tongue licks at me, your mouth is sucking on my clit. Your tongue goes right in inside me and causes a storm!

I'm losing all control, I shout "Richard!" and I come, waves of lust breaking over me, amazingly strong and intense.

OH YES, OOOH...!

I just need a moment to catch my breath. Then I put myself on my stomach on the desk. I pull my arse-cheeks wide apart. Both holes are offered to you. Take whichever you want, they're all yours!

"Do it," I croak.

You grab me and push your thing centimetre by centimetre into my wet cunt. Good—you made the right choice! It's hard like an iron rod. You're taking me. You're moving inside me.

But too slowly.

"Please: quicker, harder!"

But you don't. You take advantage of having me at your mercy. You go even slower, enjoying your power over me. I can hardly stand it. I'm jerking from side to side, pushing my arse against you, screaming and begging.

Then with a mighty thrust you fill me up completely. Your prick is deep inside me. Now at last you go quicker, now you're really *taking* me—brutally.

I'm gabbling pure sounds, not words, as I have the biggest, longest orgasm of my life. Everything inside me is exploding as you fuck the life out of me. And we finally peak... together.

YES YES YES YES...

I turn around and cuddle you, and we stay like that for a while. Exhausted and satisfied. But I want more from you.

I lie on the carpet on my back and start to touch myself. You watching me do it makes me totally horny. My hands are wondering [sic] about, touching my tits and my cunt and your eyes are following them! My fingers go faster and faster. I'm imagining that you are touching me.

My eyes are almost closed, but I sense you coming over to me. You climb onto me and put your weapon in between my breasts. I grab the tits with my hands and make them into a slit for you. As you thrust between them I try to catch the tip of your penis with my lips. Soon he realises that he likes it there even more than between my breasts! I'm licking and sucking even wilder than the first time and you push him deeper and deeper into my mouth. Surely you can't hold out much longer?

Suddenly you stop and pull out. You stretch out on the carpet beside me. Your prick is stiff and twitching, he's inviting me to go down on him. I climb into the saddle!

I stretch my legs over you and sit down slowly, guiding him with my fingers between my lower lips and into my cunt. First I move slowly, then faster, riding you as if I am in a trance, getting wilder and wilder. My whole body is shuddering.

Your hands are playing with my nipples. I feel one of your hands going between my legs to play with my little pearl.

Then everything goes black, I'm exploding, all I can feel is your massive tool deep inside me.

YES!!!

I am beside you. I'm in your arms. I feel your warm body. I can hardly breathe. Everything is still black. You have fucked me sore, Richard Orwell. When I can finally speak, all I can say is, "Thank you!"

S.

There was a bench beside the mailboxes. Half way through reading the letter, Richard had had to sit down. He was shocked, but shaking with excitement. He realized that he was horribly, horribly aroused.

Who was this girl?

And how could he find her?

RULING OUT DR. DONG

It was a nuisance for Richard to have to turn his mind to the Sherlock Holmes investigation. Eddie left him in no peace, though. He switched off the television in the middle of the main evening news, positioned himself challengingly in front of him, relieved Richard of his mug of coffee and packet of potato crisps, and then shoved a handwritten List of Suspects for Investigation under his nose.

"My Losfi list," he called it.

Jesus wept! But Eddie needed to be humored (just as Holmes had always had to humor Dr. Watson).

He had listed the suspects, and indicated who they should be investigated by. Thus:

(1) Male members of English dept: K. Christenkorn, Dr. Dong, J. Snoad, E. Müller, H. Kurz, J. Wolter = Richard (to do).

(2) Male students in English dept = Richard (to do).

(3) Male members of admin with contact to English dept = so far unassigned.

(4) Male students from other depts = so far unassigned.

"And here is the Lowfi list!" he added, and gave Richard another scrap of paper.

"Low-fi, as in Hi-fi? Ha ha!"

"No, don't be silly. It stands for List of Witnesses for Investigation."

The second list was shorter, and consisted of the four names that Richard had been given by Kyra Henkel.

(1) Undergraduates: Felicitas Förster, Jeannine Garbe, Lisa Meyer = Eddie (to do).

(2) Postgraduate: Miriam Burkhardt = Richard (to do).

"Jesus, we can't do all this," Richard said. "It'll take us years. And I notice a lot of 'Richard-to-do' and not much 'Eddie-to-do'. So you get to investigate the pretty girls, and I get to do the men? Nicely organized, I must say!"

Eddie protested that he was only trying to save a full-time lecturer from compromising his reputation. And Miriam Burkhardt was pretty enough, wasn't she? However, as a concession, he would take on Losfi (3) and (4), if Richard absolutely insisted.

It was still too much. "Male students from other departments"? There were hundreds and hundreds of them. They were going to have to be creative right from the start. To triage the lists. To cross off names that were really unlikely. And they could start with the English Department.

"You'll notice that I've already excluded two names: Hodgkins and Orwell. Or should I have left our own names on the list? Like one of those postmodern detective stories where the narrator is the murderer, or the detective is the killer?"

"Postmodern? Stupid, you mean. However, we live in the real world. I'm happy to accept that you are *not* a psychopathic sicko, even if some of your books," and he held up one of Eddie's *manga* volumes that lay conveniently to hand, "might seem to suggest otherwise."

"And I am happy to return the compliment. Even though you have a tidiness fetish that is reminiscent of Obsessive-Compulsive Disorder, that doesn't make you a murderous schizo."

They stared at each other.

"Well, I'm glad we've sorted *that* one out!"

"So am I. Let's get to work."

The easiest name for Richard and Eddie to cross off their list of suspects was that of Jupp Wolter, the technician. He was a kind-hearted family man, much loved by the students, whose laptops he was always being asked to repair. More to the point, he had been knocked off his bicycle at the beginning of the winter semester. First, he had been away from work, with his leg in plaster; then he had selflessly come back to work, long before he needed to, but had hobbled about on crutches for weeks.

A cunning ruse, to distract attention away from him? In a novel, perhaps, but not in Reichsstadt. His leg (or his foot?) had definitely been broken. Besides, he was the least cunning person either of them knew.

It was almost as easy to cross Dr. Dong off their list.

The Visiting Scholar from Taiwan no longer attended departmental meetings. In fact, he now only came to the university late at night or on Sundays. It was because of *face*. Not his physiognomy, which was unpleasantly blotchy and which resembled a battered pumpkin, on top of which lumps of greasy hair had been glued, but face in the Oriental sense.

He had been cruelly done by, for which Jonathan Snoad was to blame.

Snoad had heard that Dr. Dong could play squash, which was hard to believe, and he had challenged him to a game. There had even been a modest wager, "to make it interesting."

Jonathan himself played several times a week (to keep fit, he said), sometimes watched by a small audience of admiring female students, and he was regarded as a pretty good player. He was probably seen more often at the Squash Center and at the local gym than he was at the university. His normal opponents included young lecturers from other departments, sports students, and *Herr* Rammler, the university's Quality Manager.

In his early days in Reichsstadt, Richard had accepted an invitation to a game at the Squash Center, after Snoad had asked him whether he knew how to play. He was not much better than a beginner, he replied, and apologized in advance: playing him wouldn't be much of a challenge for Jonathan. But on the night he discovered that that wasn't important, since the main point of the exercise was for him to be humiliated.

Later, Eddie told him that Snoad had given him more or less the same treatment.

"You public school bods are all pretty good at games, aren't you?" he had sneered. "Or does one play a different version at Eton?"

Eddie had indeed gone to a minor public school, and not to Eton. And he didn't care much about games, he said, because of the kind of douchebags at his school who *had* cared. However, he knew how to play squash reasonably well, and he had accepted the challenge out of curiosity. He had been beaten, but he hadn't disgraced himself, and as a consolation, when they went in the sauna afterwards, he had got to see Snoad's current girlfriend, a young architect, in the buff.

"Nice. Very nice. Beautiful legs. Intelligent, too. Completely wasted on him. Where does he find them? And what do they see in him?"

She had been playing another girl, and had paid no attention to the battle royal between Eddie and her boyfriend going on on a different court. But they had been watched by a group of Snoad's female admirers. Between games, Snoad had encouraged one of the students to venture onto the court and, giggling, attempt to make the racquet connect meaningfully with the ball.

"She's a regular," he explained.

Richard wondered whether Snoad's fan club ever joined their hero in the sauna afterwards. They hadn't done so that evening.

On the night of the Snoad-Dong showdown, only a couple of members of the fan club showed up, which was fortunate, because Jonathan was thrashed mercilessly. The girls could only bear to watch so much of that. Both of them left well before the end, by which time Jonathan had been reduced to stumbling about the court in a sweaty daze, as the ball zipped past him at an impossible angle or dropped tantalizingly short of his outstretched racquet.

Snoad lost the match, his money, and his dignity. And afterwards, in the sauna, came a further unpleasant surprise.

Jonathan had his revenge, though. He recounted the story of his defeat to Harlan, Rammler, and other cronies of his, embellishing it with humorous remarks about the Yellow Peril of the squash court, the Asian Juggernaut that had steamrollered him so ruthlessly. In the course of his narrative the expression "Donkey Dong" was used, and this was not in reference to stupidity or stubbornness but to another quality popularly associated with the (male) donkey.

The story spread like wildfire. When the Asian researcher realized that he was being pointed out and laughed at, and even before he found out *why*, he tried to save his face (in the figurative sense) by hardly showing his face (in the literal sense) anywhere where students might see him. He even stopped going to the University Library, except on Sundays, when only a handful of earnest doctoral students and local "researchers" ever used it. Regular students generally had better things to do on a Sunday, like "chilling out" or catching up on sleep.

The Snake could not have cared less. The man was a bore, always wanting to talk about his wretched project (whatever that consisted of) in lousy English or even worse German. There was no need for him to be seen all the time in the college. It was sufficient that his name appear in print, and online, so that people could read that her department, unlike some others that she could name, actually had an international Visiting Scholar.

Richard and Eddie agreed that Dr. Dong was not the man they were looking for. Except on the squash court, he was slow and clumsy in his movements. Flitting in and out of student hostels would not be his thing, and he avoided meeting students as much as possible anyway.

When he had arrived in Reichsstadt that autumn, the Snake had delegated Kajo to organize a little staff welcoming party for him. He had been greeted with the usual modest spread of home-made nibbles: grapes skewered onto cubes of cheese, bits of ham or fish on salty crackers, and poorly-seasoned meatballs; to drink, there had been mineral-water, orange juice and cheap supermarket *Sekt* (Germany's answer to champagne).

The whole event had been characterized by embarrassment and poor communication.

Kajo's long-winded speech of welcome had been excruciating—whenever he was called upon to speechify in English he had a tendency to slow down and over-enunciate.

Enno, in comparison, rushed through his own speech, which was in German, as though it had been agreed beforehand that Dr. Dong wouldn't understand a single word of it anyway, so why waste time?

Doro Schlichting had ignored the guest and stuffed herself with the canapés. Social politeness was not her strongest suit.

Kurz and Snoad had talked only to each other, and were obviously amused by the three speeches: Kajo's, Enno's, and Dr. Dong's laborious and incomprehensible reply in German.

The evening had been a disaster, until Dr. Dong suddenly fetched out an album of family photos and showed his new colleagues his dumpy little wife, wearing some exotic local costume and staring with stern concentration into the camera, and his two grinning, moon-faced daughters. He was clearly very proud of them.

No, the Visiting Scholar from Taiwan was not the nasty pervert they were hunting.

Which left Kajo, Enno Müller, Snoad and Kurz to think about. Eddie made a further concession: he'd add them to his list of "to do"s.

COFFEE AND CONVERSATION

Eddie decided that it was generous of Richard to let him stay at his flat like that—thank you, Richard!—and on the whole he found him quite good company. OK, he was a bit unadventurous and humorless sometimes. In fact, to Eddie's mind he could be a right prune. But his offer had been a godsend, and it was a laugh playing detectives with him and hunting for a villain.

If only Richard had more *imagination*. Eddie put it down to the books that he occasionally saw him reading: they tended to be of a serious nature, yet Richard didn't read *enough* books, even of the dull kind. Eddie, for his part, always had several books on the go simultaneously. He was a great skimmer of books. He knew that Richard didn't think much of *manga*, say, or science fiction, or Conan the Barbarian, or Dan Brown, but what Richard didn't understand was that you needed to have some fun in life, too, and that there were books that made you feel good.

Another area of disagreement was that Eddie liked talking, while Richard didn't. At least, not with Eddie, it appeared, or on any of Eddie's favorite topics.

Eddie had assumed that they would have some good gossipy sessions talking about sex. Fair enough, he didn't get to *do* it as often as he'd like to, but the subject had unlimited potential for discussion. Women were so interesting! Yet Richard would quickly clam up whenever it became too specific. He was secretive about his girlfriends (of whom there must surely have been one or two). He never mentioned names. And he never gave Eddie's lively imagination anything to work with.

Eddie was fascinated by lost kingdoms, unsolved mysteries of the past, and aliens. How could Richard be so sure that aliens didn't exist? There was so much that traditional scholarship couldn't explain. But Richard would simply switch off and stop listening whenever Eddie started to fill him in on what *might* have happened. Or, even worse, he'd shut him up with a supercilious reference to Ockham's Razor and the need to keep things simple and sensible.

Eddie rather liked the Nazis (as a topic of conversation, that is), and he was well-informed about the weirder aspects of the Third Reich. Here, Richard showed slightly more willingness to listen. He had a bad conscience, he said, admitting that he had only a patchy knowledge of modern German history, despite living in Germany. He hadn't even been to look at the local Nazi concentration camp, Flossengamme, which was just up the road from Reichsstadt. (Nor, to his shame, had Eddie ever been there.) It was apparently well worth a visit, and they agreed that they'd do that sometime, when the weather got better.

Freaks and horrors were another fun topic—not for Richard, though.

What was the cruelest form of execution he could possibly think of? Richard showed no sign of wanting to discuss it, but finally, under pressure, came up with hanging, drawing and quartering. Yes, OK, pretty nasty, that. An obvious one that you'd think of if you were British. You wouldn't want to be on the receiving end, would you? But not as nasty as being flayed alive, though, surely?

Richard barely lifted his nose out of his book on English grammar.

What about impaling? Did Richard know that after the Second World War some guys had got their hands on an unfortunate Hungarian general, who was understood to have been involved in wartime massacres, and had *impaled* him?

No, Richard didn't know that (and didn't seem very interested either).

Richard was hard to shock. Or was it just hard to gain his attention? Eddie couldn't believe that he was finding his book on grammar more interesting than information on the Twenty Most Awful Tortures of History, courtesy of one of Eddie's favorite websites.

Eddie tried again, with scaphism. This is what the ancient Persians would apparently do to you if you got on the wrong side side of them, and it was pretty heavy stuff. Eddie began to explain the gruesome procedure...

Richard said, "Enough!" and slapped his grammar book down. "That is vile, and I really don't need to know more about it. But I do have a lesson to prepare—with your permission, of course?"

Ooh, sarcasm!

Eddie beat a retreat to his room. If that was how his flatmate wanted to have it, fair enough, he would leave Richard to his own devices and bury himself deep in *Anna Karenina*, if you'll excuse the turn of phrase! (Yes, he did read the heavy stuff, too, not just *manga*. He was finding *Anna* hard going, though, but he'd definitely finish it.)

An hour or so later there was a firm knock on the door: it was Richard, bearing a mug of coffee and a plate of biscuits as a peace offering. He didn't go quite so far as to apologize, but he did ask Eddie what, if anything, he had managed to find out from the girls.

It wasn't a lot, to be honest.

Eddie had so far only managed to speak to Jeannine Garbe, and it hadn't come about in the way he'd intended.

It had been after one of his regular English Conversation classes. Eddie normally referred to these as his 3Ds (or Deadly Dull Doings): rarely, there might be a dialog between Eddie and the star of the class, a Beatrix or a Konstantin perhaps (if one of those paragons had bothered to show up); more often, the lesson would consist of a monolog by Eddie, interspersed with desperate appeals for comments, questions, or input of any kind whatsoever, *please*, from the students.

This had looked set to being a lesson of the former, slightly more satisfying, variety, and the star was obviously going to be Jeannine, who was widely regarded as an exceptional student. Eddie had been delighted to see her—attendance at the English Conversation lessons fluctuated wildly, and you could never be sure who would turn up—and he immediately hatched a plan to get them talking about "traumatic events."

That was an excellent topic for the lesson anyway. It certainly beat "What I did over Christmas" or "Pets," he didn't want yet another discussion about pop music, and there was no point in expecting them to discuss political or social topics intelligently. Jeannine would probably be only too pleased to tell the group about her terrifying visit from the pest of the hostels; and as a bonus he might even be able to squeeze a few monosyllabic revelations, about dental horrors or minor car accidents, out of some of the other students in the group.

But it was not to be. How had he described Jeannine Garbe to Richard? Po-faced? That was very apposite. Yes, she was a physically handsome specimen, to be sure, but she was totally and utterly humorless, and she had a ridiculously high opinion of herself. Most of the time she had only one expression on her face, an expression that announced to the world: "I'm the only one here who matters—so get used to it!"

That may have been an accurate summary of her whole CV. Her daddy was presumably some small-town bigwig, someone wealthy or powerful in a little provincial nest. She'd been the queen bee in the only half-decent local school. She'd been quite good at athletics, and music. She'd been the queen of the prom. If they'd had cheer-leaders, she would have been one. She'd been Princess of Hearts at the *Karneval* celebrations. Her photo had been in the local newspaper several times, with reports about her voluntary social work activities, or how she'd been a member of a delegation to their twin town in France. Her professors were going to recommend her for a Fulbright grant when she graduated. And so on, *ad nauseam*.

The other students were predictably happy to let Jeannine do all the talking. Except for one of them. Had Jeannine rubbed this girl up the wrong way? Was the girl suffering from that pre-menstrual thingie? It reminded Eddie of those dogs that take an instant dislike to each other for no obvious reason, going in seconds from amiable doggy good nature to snarling, yapping fury—

"Yes, yes," Richard said. "Get on with it."

Well, this other girl, a real live-wire, a sexy little bundle whose name was Steffi—

Richard sat bolt upright, with a sudden look of interest on his face, for no good reason that Eddie could think of.

"You all right, mate? Do you know this girl?"

"No, no. Go on."

Well, this other girl kept on interrupting Jeannine. Not exactly *interrupting* her, more like making snide comments to distract her, to break her concentration, meaning that she couldn't impress the teacher as much as she was hoping to.

And what did Jeannine do?

"Nothing, at first. You know, she was just getting on to what had happened that night, and I was encouraging her to tell the whole story. She ignored Steffi, until Steffi did her Jeannine imitation."

"Her Jeannine imitation?"

Jeannine normally talked in a cool, sovereign manner, focused on what she was saying and without looking at the other students. Except that, after a statement that was more assertive, she *would* look at them, and blow out one of her cheeks slightly. Whenever she did this, she looked like a squirrel hoarding nuts. And each time, Steffi would stare back at her and give her the squirrel routine.

She was a brilliant mimic.

After the third or fourth time, Jeannine got up and shouted (in English, he was pleased to say), "Are you OK in the head?"

"Are you calling me a psycho?" Steffi had replied, also getting to her feet and knocking her chair over with a clatter.

Jeannine was much taller than she was.

"No, you're just stupid!"

"Who you are calling stupid, *Fotzengesicht*?" "*Gesicht*" meant "face." "*Fotze*" referred to a female body part somewhat lower down.

Jeannine glared at Steffi; Steffi grinned back. Now the other students had got up, too, pushing their chairs back.

"Fight, fight!" (That was Milo, naturally.)

And then Steffi had stepped forward, reached up, and *tweaked Jeannine's nose.*

God, violence in the classroom! A girl-fight in English Conversation Group C! It never came to that. Although a couple of feeble punches were swung, they missed, because other girls had already grabbed Steffi and Jeannine and pulled them apart. But more chairs went flying, the noise level went through the roof, and just when it seemed that it couldn't get any worse, it did.

The classroom door was flung open, and a majestic figure stood in the doorway. *Madame* Plouvier! There was instant silence. The *Grande Madame* snorted "Humph!," glowered at Eddie, once she had identified him as the teacher—and therefore (theoretically) the only responsible adult in the room—and turned and departed imperiously.

Jeannine had burst into tears, Steffi shouted "Cry-baby, too!" as she flounced out, and Eddie had brought the lesson to an early close. He offered Jeannine a paper-handkerchief, and invited her to the cafeteria for a coffee. She had been telling her story so nicely until that other girl had caused the disturbance—he'd like to hear the end of her account.

"Would you really?" she had sniffled.

And so it was that Eddie had been able to collect some information about the hostel intruder from a first-hand witness.

"Well? And?"

Unfortunately, there was nothing much worth telling. Jeannine had been sleeping very deeply, as she normally did, and hadn't been woken at first by the presence of a strange man in her room. She had *felt* rather than heard something, she said. Someone had taken off her, her, you know—

Eddie had gallantly supplied the word that she couldn't bring herself to say: "Slip."

Yes, and that had woken her. She was naked, the bed-clothes were thrown back, and she caught a flash of movement as someone opened the door and exited her room.

But she hadn't seen the intruder directly, at least from the front.

Her underwear had been taken. The item had been expensive—she wore only the very best next to her skin.

And that was all she could tell him.

"You probably had your eyes still gummed together, and it was all over so quickly."

Yes, she'd hardly seen anything. Except—

"Yes?"

Well, she had gone over it again and again in her memory, and all she could say was, that there was something unusual about that movement of opening the door. It wasn't the way people normally did it. Was he slightly handicapped? Or left-handed?

Maybe it was nothing.

"That's all she could tell me," Eddie said.

He added that it wasn't much to be going on with, and Richard agreed.

He didn't want to know more about Jeanine, but he kept asking about the other girl, Steffi, which seemed a bit strange to Eddie.

"What's the big deal? She's not one of our witnesses, you know! Though I have to admit she's a little sex-kitten. Not in Jeannine's league, naturally, or Ulrike Sandmann's, but a solid Six-and-a-half perhaps? Why the sudden interest in Steffi?"

But Richard wouldn't say. Try as he could, Eddie couldn't extract anything more from Richard about Steffi Albertz. How peculiar! Was he hiding something? This too would have to be investigated!

Instead, Richard changed the subject by pointing out that he too had progress to report: the prospect of a meeting with another of the witnesses, Lisa Meyer.

"What, my little Lisa? (And how I wish she were!) How did you manage that?"

Lisa (though what was little about her? Richard wanted to know) had approached him after a lesson, and made him an offer.

"Wow, these women can't leave you alone! I thought *I* was the chick magnet around here! Ricardus, you underestimate yourself!"

But it had not been *that* kind of offer. No, she had drawn Richard's attention to the state of his pullover, and offered to repair it for him. The hole seemed to get bigger every week, she had said, and she had learned from her mother the importance of putting things right quickly, before they got any worse.

"A stitch in time saves nine, eh? And she's got you sussed, lonely boy. She's seen that you don't have a woman in your life to darn your clothes, so this is her chance to move in!"

Richard didn't think so. Why did Eddie always see *sex* lurking in every situation? There were other things that could motivate people. More likely she was hoping for a better exam grade as her reward.

Eddie shrugged.

"Who knows? Women are a mystery! So—you gave it to her!"

"Er, the pullover? Yes, why not?"

But Eddie was disappointed to hear that they hadn't talked about what had happened in the hostel that night—yet.

"But that was your big chance!"

No, Richard would wait until she returned the pullover—when it would be downright rude not to invite her for a coffee and a snack, wouldn't it? And, whatever she told him or didn't tell him, at the very least he'd have a nicely repaired pullover, wouldn't he?

STEFFI FOLLOWS THROUGH

Steffi hadn't been enormously proud of herself over the business in the Conversation class. But she had a bit of a history with Jeannine Garbe.

The highlights included her spilling O-juice over Jeannine's fancy knitwear top at a disco (this had been unintentional); a nasty little confrontation in the *Mensa*, in which Jeannine, surrounded by male admirers (from Engineering?), had directed so many sneering comments at her that she'd got up and gone to sit at another table (she knew when she was outnumbered); and an unpleasant scene in the changing room at the sports center, the less said about which the better (but for which Steffi would have to accept most of the blame).

However, the full extent of the scandal only became apparent to her when a couple of mates of hers grabbed her in the corridor and congratulated her on "putting that snooty bitch Garbe in her place."

How had they heard about it?

Who hadn't? It was the talk of the French Department!

Of course. *La Plouvier* had gone and stuck her nose in, hadn't she? As the *Grande Madame* told anyone who was happy to listen—and many who weren't particularly bothered, like the students in her French classes—this was yet another example of the *desolate* condition of the English Department. That institution had slumped into terminal decline under the unobjectionable but *ageing* Professor Timpe (she didn't actually say "senile"), it had gone to the dogs under his temporary successor (she didn't mention Kajo Christenkorn by name), and it was now, under the new Professor... well, words failed her!

She had thrust out her beaky lips, they said, like a vulture that had discovered a moldering corpse that was too far gone even for her delectation.

Those young men in the English Department, she had added, they just did what they liked, taking no account of discipline or order in the classroom! It was anarchy. A typical Anglo-Saxon state of affairs!

So who was it who'd been teaching the lesson, then? Steffi's friends were very keen to know. If such excitements occurred regularly, that might be a class worth attending!

Since many of those who studied French also studied English, word of the Conversation class meltdown was spreading like a bush-fire. And now Steffi was beginning to get worried. Eddie Hodgkins was only part-time, and he was a bit of a joke anyway, but she didn't want to get him into trouble. After all, he was one of the "good guys," as far as she could tell.

For instance: what if the Snake heard about it? It was her department, and she was now getting slagged off in public. She hadn't been there long, but she'd already made it clear that she didn't like students, and that her bite was as bad as her bark. If she now got it in the neck from old Plouvier, she'd go looking for someone to hurt.

Who would that be? It would be (A) Eddie Hodgkins and (B) the stupid student who'd started the trouble, and that certainly wouldn't be Queen Jeannine, who had "I'm a privileged bitch" tattooed all over her snooty face—it would be *her*.

There wasn't much she could do about the Snake, but she could go and say sorry to Eddie, so that when he started getting shit poured all over him from a great height he could at least say that he'd taken steps to put things right, and that the naughty girl had apologized, had *groveled* even (could she do groveling? She wasn't sure about that), that the situation had now been happily resolved, and so on and so forth, blah-blah.

If she was nice to Eddie, and explained it to him in the right way, perhaps he'd talk to Jeannine too. Because that was a step that Steffi definitely *wasn't* yet prepared to take.

Eddie proved very easy to talk to. He was so wet that he loved it when girls—*any* girls—chatted him up, preferably in public. It didn't happen very often.

Steffi was aware that this was going to cost her a helluva lot of face. It wouldn't do her social image any good at all. But she was a big girl, and it needed to be done

And so she found herself one afternoon not long afterwards buying Eddie a coffee and a bun in the cafeteria and telling him how it had come about that she'd lost her cool with Jeannine Garbe.

Surprisingly, that part of the conversation was over in a flash. Wasn't he at all worried?

No, it seemed he wasn't.

She was slightly concerned that he'd draw the wrong conclusions from *her* having invited *him* to the cafeteria. Eddie Hodgkins making an obvious pass at her in public, and her not being able to slap him down (because she did need to keep him sweet!), the way you normally would with Eddie—that would be a massive social disaster that might take her months and months to put right.

Instead, again surprisingly, nothing of this sort happened. Eddie was the perfect gentleman. What he *did* do was quiz her about his colleagues. What did she think of Harlan Kurz, for example? Did she like Mr. Snoad? Did she have many classes with Dr. Christenkorn?

Hmm. Was he so terribly insecure that he wanted her to build up his self-confidence by trashing everyone else? Or was this some kind of trap? How could it possibly be? There was nothing he could gain from what she said, and, besides, she didn't see Eddie as the cunning type. But she decided to play safe.

Mr. Kurz's translation classes were very strenuous, but of the highest quality. He was such an energetic teacher! He obviously knew what he was doing, and he asked a lot from the people who attended his courses.

Dr. Christenkorn was an excellent teacher. He was very kind, and he took a lot of time over students and their problems. He was very patient, and always willing to explain things twice or even three times if need be. Perhaps she would ask him to be one of her examiners.

And Mr. Snoad? She didn't really know him. Because of timetable clashes, she hadn't been able to take part in any of his lessons so far. But it seemed that he was an inspirational and charismatic teacher, and she'd heard only good things about him. (Which was untrue.)

Predictably, Eddie couldn't restrain himself from commenting on his colleagues and, from what he said, Steffi, reading between the lines, drew the conclusion that he didn't much like either Snoad or Kurz. So they were on a common wavelength there!

And Mr. Orwell?

She needed to be careful. She knew that he and Eddie hung out together.

Yes, well... Mr. Orwell was a really nice guy. She'd always enjoyed his British Studies lectures. He knew so much about Britain! She liked the comparisons that he made between Britain and Germany, although she thought that sometimes he wasn't completely fair. There were some things, she said, that you couldn't get from books, weren't there? Or did Eddie disagree?

No, Eddie agreed with her completely. He himself liked traveling, and meeting people, but Richard was more of a stick-in-the-mud (and he meant that in the nicest possible way). He'd never made it to Berlin, for example. And how many years was it that he'd lived in Reichsstadt, and he'd never been to Flossengamme? (Though he'd really like to go, he always said.) Eddie was trying to get him interested in local history.

When Steffi finally got away, after four coffees and the stale bun, she texted Lisa: WE MUST MEET. URGENT. SEVEN? YOUR ROOM?

That was because her own room was *ripe*. Ripe as in fine old French cheese, or unwashed socks, or last week's knickers. She made a mental note to change her underwear more often. Fair do's, it was a no-brainer, it was just that she was a bit forgetful about things like that. And she'd have to go on a massive clearing up and washing bender at the weekend, maybe on Sunday morning, when everyone slept in late and she'd have a clear run at the washing machines in the laundry room. Until then, her room would be a biohazard, and other members of the human race should keep away.

Lisa texted back: YEAH.

Steffi: BRING IT ON BABY.

Steffi arrived at Lisa's room on time, clutching half a packet of biscuits as her contribution. But instead of organizing coffee for both of them, which was the usual ritual, Lisa plunged excitedly into a narrative of achievement.

She had spoken to Richard Orwell, and persuaded him to hand over his pullover.

"Wow!" Steffi said. "Well done! I didn't think you'd have the nerve. So—our plan is moving. Have you got it here? Was it very sweaty?"

"How should I know?"

"Well," Steffi suggested, maliciously, "I thought you might be cuddling up with it at night!"

Lisa was rightfully indignant.

"Of course not! You're the one who fancies him, not me. And I've already given it to my mum. I met her in town for some shopping. She said it'll be ready at the weekend."

"Good girl! I'll drive you, if you like."

That suited Lisa fine. She would prefer not to be crossing town on her own, especially if it was late.

"I don't feel good."

"Whadya mean?"

"I get this feeling, sometimes, that I'm being watched. Or followed. I turn round quickly, and he's just slipped out of sight."

"He?"

"Yes, it's definitely a he."

Steffi laughed.

"Isn't it always? Same with me," she confessed. "It happens every time I dump a guy. They cling. They won't let it be. There was this Lutz, or Lasse, or something like that, who stalked me for weeks and weeks. You have to be harsh, really spell it out to them—"

"No, no," Lisa said, shaking her head. "I think it's *him*."

"*Him?* Oh."

"But I'm not panicking. I know I could be imagining it. Maybe it's just me. Anyhow, why did you want to meet? You wrote 'URGENT'. What did you mean? What's so urgent, then?"

"Ah," said Steffi. "If you think *you've* been busy, wait till you hear this, *Fräulein*. Auntie Steffi has not been wasting her time."

And she told Lisa about the chat she'd had in the cafeteria with Eddie, and how she'd *sort of* apologized in order to repair some of the damage from the Conversation class, and how Eddie had started rambling on about his colleagues, asking her what she thought of them, and telling her all kinds of stuff, including ("Fasten your seatbelt, young lady!") that Richard Orwell *had never been to Flossengamme*, and that *he wanted to go there*.

"You mean, the concentration camp?"

"Indeed I do. Not that I've been there myself—a girl-about-town like yours truly has more urgent social activities listed in her diary." She saw that Lisa was showing zero enthusiasm. "But you've been there, I take it? Come on, it would be ideal!"

Lisa didn't seem to think so.

"I went there twice with the school. We *had* to go. Didn't you ever do a trip like that?"

"My school class went to Dachau. But I had 'flu that week. It wasn't *that* bad, was it?"

"No, no, it was fabulous. A once-in-a-lifetime experience... I do not think! It's out in the sticks, you know, on the moor. It rained both times, all day, non-stop. They lecture you about how many Jews are buried in *that* mound, how many gypsies over *there*, what they died of (the ones who didn't get murdered), they bang on about all the torture, and killing, and disease, and how little the prisoners were given to eat, and then they let you go off and enjoy your packed sandwiches. A really fun day. Marvellous. An unforgettable experience—and not once, but twice. They make you feel so good about being German. In fact, I couldn't in a million years imagine a *less* romantic place to go on a day trip."

Steffi was not to be discouraged.

"OK, it's not an amusement park, I get your point. But for us it's absolutely ideal."

Lisa peered at her in disbelief.

"Did I just hear you say *ideal*? How'd you work *that* one out?"

"Because he can't say no, can he? This is a must-see, unless you're a Neo-Nazi, of course. He can't refuse to go. And it's completely safe—no-one will suspect anything! Who would ever suggest going on a *date* to a concentration camp, eh?" She gave Lisa a nudge. "Even better: it's the kind of trip you do with a group, so it'll be plausible if we say that other people will be going. Which they won't, of course. It'll just be us. And Harlan won't be able to say no either, without looking like an Antisemite. Unless he's already been there—I'm not sure about that. But I doubt it."

Lisa looked thoughtful.

"Do you think he's Jewish? Harlan, I mean. A lot of Americans are. Kurz isn't a Jewish name, is it? He doesn't *look* Jewish."

"You mean, he hasn't got a big nose? That's just a caricature. Lots of Germans have big noses, and lots of Jews have small ones."

"So—is he Jewish? What do you reckon? You've got up closer to him than I have."

"How should I know? Oh, now I can see where this is heading! Look, I never got to see his dick, if that's what you're getting at. *He* was groping *me* in the car, remember, not the other way round. It was stiff, that's all I can say on that particular subject." But she added: "In any case, they say most baby boys in the States get cut, whether they're Jewish or not. So get used to the idea of the delights that are waiting for you."

"Hey, you don't need to go into detail!"

"I thought you fancied him?"

"Yes, but there's a time and there's a place."

Steffi wondered whether Lisa wasn't a lost cause after all.

"Look, if you like we can stop this right now. Let me have the pullover when your mum's done it, and I'll take it from there with Mr. Orwell. Rain. Moors. Dead bodies. Who cares? He might even get emotional. I can take him in my arms," she said, with a theatrical gesture of motherly comforting, "while the poor guy sobs his heart out. You don't need to come, if you don't fancy Harlan-Sweetie that much, or if you're worried that he might be Jewish."

Lisa was indignant.

"Of course I don't care whether he's Jewish or not! I'm not a Nazi!" She paused. "It's just that I've never met anyone Jewish. They're supposed to be very sensitive, and artistically-gifted."

Steffi couldn't help laughing.

"Harlan Kurz and *sensitive*? Oh wow, now I've heard it all!"

AN AWKWARD MEETING

Richard had a bad conscience that he wasn't chasing up the other girls on *Frau* Henkel's list, but his life had suddenly and painfully been put on hold. By toothache.

Back in Britain, he had always been one for regular dentists' checkups. He had good, regular teeth—good by British standards, that is, in a country where so many kids ruined their teeth with sweets, sugary drinks and junk food—and he brushed his teeth as often as the next guy.

He hadn't bothered to find himself a dentist in Reichsstadt. He'd always tried, on his irregular trips back home, to get an appointment at short notice with old Mr. Grainger, who'd seen to his teeth since he was small, and usually he'd been lucky.

So, when the pain hit him, Richard was helpless.

Eddie was generous with his sympathy, but of no help.

"I haven't been to a dentist for years. They're all sadists! Keep away from them—they're not good for your well-being! My last dentist was a Freemason friend of my dad's. A Mr. Payne, believe it or not. *Nomen est omen.* Sorry, old chap, I can't help you there."

It was *Frau* Ludewig who had come to the rescue. What *didn't* that wonderful woman know? Not only had she recommended a good dentist in the center of town, she had even rung him up on Richard's behalf and made an appointment for him. He would see Richard *that very same day.* Unbelievable!

The surgery had been spotlessly clean, and the waiting-room wasn't crowded. There were wooden children's toys heaped on a low table in one corner, and a pile of not too controversial magazines on another low table in the center of the room. Best of all, you couldn't hear the squealing sound of the drill while you were waiting, as you could at Mr. Grainger's surgery. (While you didn't actually hear any screams of pain, you sat there *listening* for them, which was just as bad.) The dentist himself was brisk and professional. He was a *Herr* Dr. Somebody-or-other, and didn't hurt Richard any more than was necessary (and much less than he had feared).

He must find out when *Frau* Ludewig had her birthday, and get her some fancy chocolates!

On his way back from the dentist's, Richard had a surprising encounter.

He was walking along the Metzgergasse, one of the narrow lanes that led out of the Market Square and which were named after the different trades—*Metzger* meant "butcher"—except for the Judengasse ("Jew Street"). You could deduce quite a lot from the names about what Reichsstadt must have been like in the Middle Ages.

With his head tucked down, and mulling over what (little) he and Eddie now knew about the terror of the hostels, Richard nearly collided with—Monika, of all people! She was walking in the other direction, arm-in-arm with a tall young man.

This was highly embarrassing. Richard normally made efforts to avoid such awkward meetings, by crossing the road quickly, or suddenly discovering a fascinating shop window. But this had happened too quickly, and the Metzgergasse was much too narrow to allow such maneuvers. Monika obviously had a new beau, and since they had almost fallen over each other there was now no way that Richard could fail to acknowledge this fact, or get out of greeting them, without being monstrously rude.

Monika herself pursed her lips primly—the shape they formed reminded Richard immediately of the pucker of her anus—and introduced her new friend as Hans-Robert, an "executive accountant" (whatever that was). Under her disapproving stare, the two men shook hands.

Hans-Robert was gangly and surprisingly young, younger than Richard would have expected his successor to be. He was nattily dressed, like someone who made good money and wanted people to know it. He had a disconcertingly square face and head (a type more frequently encountered in Germany than almost anywhere else in the world), and a ferocious handshake. Richard could imagine him being into martial arts.

Richard was introduced as an "old acquaintance." Let Hans-Robert make of that what he liked! Actually, to judge from his friendly grin Hans-Robert seemed to have no problems with it. He seemed wholly at ease in Monika's company. When had she granted *him* access to her honeypot?

Had Monika told Hans-Robert about him? If she had, it didn't seem to worry him at all. They made awkward small-talk for a few minutes. Richard was very aware of how swollen his mouth must look from the painkilling injection. Eddie had taught him a disgusting German expression for men who'd slept with the same woman: they were "brothers-in-law of the hole." Could that explain Hans-Robert's hearty manner towards him?

Be that as it may, there would now be no going back, and (to look on the bright side) the chance encounter in the Metzgergasse might have spared them both a mildly unpleasant terminal telephone conversation. (Or would she have sent him an excruciating "Dear John" letter?)

The Monika chapter was definitely over. Yes, there were certain things that he would miss—voluptuous images flashed across his mind—but it had been bound to end soon, and there were now new and exciting developments in his life.

He had received another letter from "S."

Tuesday, 1:32 a.m.

Dear Richard,

You are my first thought when I awake in the morning. I always fancy that you are kissing me before I open my eyes. Oh how I would enjoy being woken up this way!

During the day I always miss having you around me—although up to now I had no chance to be really close to you. I hang on your lips whenever I have the chance to listen to you but—deprived of the power of speech—I am just not able to say a word in your presence.

Only once I was able to catch a short glimpse of your hands. Immediately wild amorous thoughts crossed my mind. Oh God, it really turned me on when I started to imagine how your gentle fingers would stroke me. I thought how experienced these hands must be and what a pleasure it must be to feel them on my naked body—that idea made my head swim.

Richard, my dear Richard, I want to feel your body against mine. I want to spread kisses among your cheeks, your neck, your brest [sic]. I want to kiss you all over not stopping until my lips have cosseted each millimetre of your pleasing body. I want to share an orgasm with you. I want to satisfy all your wishes. Please believe me: I would do ANYTHING you wish for! Absolutely anything. Just one little word from you and I would give myself to you.

My desire for your closeness keeps me awake every night. Just like now. And just now I am doing what I nearly always do when the very thought of you haunts my mind: I am writing a letter to you.

I must confess that I do not always write something when I am thinking of you while being in my bed. Sometimes I touch myself fancying that these are YOUR hands teasing me everywhere, not my own hands... never mind, I'll stop now. You might find it disgusting that someone is thinking about you while mas... sorry, Richard... I didn't want to embarrass you. Just bin this letter into your wastebasket and forget about it—as you probably did with all the other letters. I know they do not mean anything to you anyway. But please try to understand that I just need to write them. Otherwise I will burst from love and desire. Have I nice day [sic]!

Love, S.

P.S. I am sorry for my bad English... I am very tired... L U.

Richard spent the weekend recovering from the trauma of dental treatment and mulling over his little collection of cards and letters from "S." He had made a list of female students whose names began with an S, using the complete list of students that *Frau* Ludewig had prepared for him, but he hadn't got very far working on it yet, apart from crossing out a few names of "very unlikelies" like Shirin.

He stared at the name Stefanie Albertz. He must look into this girl, who sounded from what Eddie had told him like the sort of lively creature who might indeed write him sexy letters. Who was she?

He wasn't looking forward to Monday. The Snake had sent everyone a brusque and unfriendly email, calling for an unscheduled departmental meeting, Monday, usual time and place, to discuss some recent "untoward developments." Everyone (underlined) must be there (and there was no "please" anywhere in the text). She would accept no excuses for absence from any of her staff. She used the word *Mitarbeiter* (strictly speaking, "co-workers," but seldom used in that democratic sense) to remind them that they were her subordinates, not her colleagues.

Ah, the insistence on attendance was an obvious side-swipe at Snoad, Richard noted with mild satisfaction. It was an ill wind that blew *nobody* any good!

CRISIS IN THE DEPARTMENT

Frau Professor Dr. Reiss-Baumgart would definitely have preferred not to have had another departmental meeting so soon after the last one. She had much better ways to spend her time than with that ragbag of academic losers and joke-figures that made up her "team."

The only one she found at all tolerable (in small doses) was the secretary, Ludewig. The woman hated her, but she was highly efficient, she did what she was told, and she kept her mouth shut. One couldn't ask more of a secretary.

To make it worse, on this particular afternoon *Frau Professor* wasn't feeling at her best. However, to call off the meeting at such short notice would be taken as a sign of weakness.

Lothar had been up to his tricks again.

Why on earth had she married the man?

There was no one reason that she could blame it on.

He had been intellectually outstanding, for his age and for someone at such an early stage in his career, and there had been no-one else of comparable calibre who took an interest in her.

In those days, her level of self-confidence had been lower than it was now.

Her family expected it of her.

She wasn't a lesbian.

Lothar was further advanced in his *Habilitation* than she was in hers (that fact alone had commanded her greatest respect)

She found that the way that he presented his unorthodox views on modern art theory, urging his ideas with passion and irony, was refreshing; stimulating, even. He was a witty iconoclast.

In the beginning, their sex-life had been quite good.

Finally, he had an air of danger to him that she liked. Everyone else was boring, especially her fellow post-docs. Others noticed that edginess, too, and she gained in status as the women he had chosen, who presumably knew how to handle him.

But did she?

By the time she noticed the "tricks" it was too late. It had started in New York, where they were attending parallel conferences, so that she lost sight of what he was up to.

She could bring herself to excuse his behavior. He had an artistic temperament, unlike her, so she couldn't expect to understand him fully. He was brilliant (or so she had then believed), and a lively dog like him needed to be let off the leash occasionally.

But there had been serious trouble in New York, and again back in Germany.

He had made solemn promises to her—and he had not kept them. There had been further incidents, and by now his *Habilitation* had been abandoned. If you made enemies the way he did, that was the price you paid. And as she overtook him academically, her respect gradually turned to scorn.

Dortmund, the huge world congress on new paradigms in social theory, where to her immense satisfaction she had had a paper accepted, had been the worst, and it was amazing that no-one who mattered in the institute where she was working at the time had noticed. Some nights she would wake up bathed in sweat, after dreaming that her boss or her colleagues had found out about it.

Increasingly, he hid himself away in the apartment, slipping out only for short visits to bookshops or libraries, and for the pitifully few teaching hours that the University of Reichsstadt had granted him, on her initial recommendation.

Their living arrangements became difficult. Within the apartment, areas were silently acknowledged to be either his or her "zone," into which the other wouldn't intrude without invitation. The kitchen was shared or neutral territory. They both needed to use it, and often in the mornings both of them would need to use it at the same time. But they couldn't be in the kitchen simultaneously. She would sometimes be left screaming silently, her rage bottled up and turned inwards—and perhaps he occasionally felt the same.

It was almost as though he was doing it deliberately. Marriages have been known to fail over different ways of squeezing the toothpaste tube. Everything that he did in the kitchen seemed designed to infuriate her.

For example, the choreography of their movements was a disaster. Whenever she turned to do something, she found him turning *into* and not away from her. Frequently, he would be holding one of the kitchen-knives, not point upwards or downwards, as anyone sensible would hold it, but extended horizontally, as if to keep someone at bay. It was only a matter of time before she would be impaled on it, accidentally.

Or they would blunder into each other, one of them holding a cup of hot tea or coffee, much of which would then be splashed painfully onto legs or messily onto the kitchen floor.

Did he do it intentionally, to annoy her? He wasn't naturally clumsy. Far from it—he could move quickly and silkily when he wanted to. And he was powerfully muscled (which was one of the things that had attracted her to him in the first place).

Was it because he was left-handed, and so did everything (from her perspective) mirror-reversed, without being able to help himself?

Or did he just enjoy doing things "his way," contrary to expectations, "in your face," rubbing people up the wrong way, as he so liked to do in his critical writing?

When she had received the offer of the Chair of English in Reichsstadt, she had known that it would be difficult with him in tow. If she was to advance her career further, aiming eventually for a "call" from a major university, she needed to have an impressive, dynamic man at her side. Not too dynamic, of course, so as to distract attention from her dazzling upward trajectory, but charming and presentable.

It would be hard enough, even then. Her theories tended to be controversial—you didn't make waves by recycling the obvious, did you?—and there were others working in her field who didn't take her ideas seriously. She knew that she was often laughed at, by the small-minded and the bean-counters. And she had always had plenty of enemies, because she herself took no prisoners socially.

If she and Lothar stayed together, it couldn't be done. It was as simple as that. But how to get rid of him without it becoming too messy (which would also hold her back)?

He had gone out on Saturday evening, after a blazing row, and had stayed out all night. When he reappeared, early on Sunday afternoon, she could smell the drink on him, and he was visibly nervous. He told her straight out that if anyone should come along asking questions, she was to give him an alibi to cover the whole night.

Whom did he mean by "anyone"?

Then he had disappeared into the bathroom, locked the door behind him, and stayed there for two hours. She had heard him talking to himself, and the sound of sobbing.

She would like to be able to say that she didn't care, but that wouldn't be true—the bastard no longer had a career of his own, but he was doing his absolute best to ruin hers.

If there were a cliff to push him off, or a train to throw him under, or an easy way to poison him, she'd be sorely tempted.

With problems like these, what she *didn't* need now was any extra trouble within her department. She would have to stamp on it immediately, and crush the whole stupid pack of them into trembling submission. That was why she had called for an unscheduled departmental meeting.

It therefore gave her satisfaction, on Monday at one o'clock, to see that the full-time members of staff had all come—even that lazy good-for-nothing Jonathan Snoad. *Frau* Ludewig was also present, to take notes. Only Dr. Dong was missing, and the wretched part-timer Hodgkins, the cause of the whole crisis.

There was just one item on the agenda, she announced: a scandalous outbreak of violence in one of the lessons. This had become a damaging topic of gossip within the university and it was symptomatic of a growing lack of discipline within her department. This lack of discipline was evidenced not only by student thuggery, but also by the sloppy behavior of certain lecturers who *should* be setting an example to the students; instead of which, however, they came and went as they pleased, and even had to be bullied into attending departmental meetings.

And with that she glowered in the direction of Snoad—she had to start somewhere. It was her intention to pick them off one by one, and Snoad was an easy target. Also, she had a gut feeling that he would prove to be the most difficult to handle. She recognized a streak of spitefulness in him that was missing in the others, except for the pathetic Schlichting woman.

Snoad put on a disingenuous "Who, me? What did *I* do?"-expression, but didn't say anything.

To her surprise, it was his friend Kurz who responded, in his own inimitable version of English.

"*Jaan* shouldn't have the book thrown at him just because some guy goes mentally AWOL."

"I'm sorry?"

This hadn't started quite as well as she'd hoped—she had no idea what the demented American was talking about.

Christenkorn came to the rescue.

"I believe that what *Herr* Kurz is suggesting is that the colleague in question suffered a momentary lapse of concentration. The young man means well, and tries so hard to motivate the students! But sometimes, at the end of a long teaching day, we may loosen our grip on a lesson, and allow the classroom situation to become a little chaotic."

Kurz muttered, "You speak for yourself, buddy."

Snoad, still playing the innocent: "I can't say that it's ever happened to me."

Enno Müller expressed the opinion that it had been a once-off event, and statistically speaking—

"Yes, but I'm not speaking statistically, *Herr* Müller! I'm speaking about a lesson in *my* department in which physical violence occurred, violence which the teacher responsible (an oxymoron in this case!) did nothing to prevent! No," she raised her hand in warning, "be quiet, *Herr* Orwell, I haven't finished yet! I'm also speaking about a certain busybody from the French Department—where they have nothing better to do than stick their noses into other people's business—who made a complaint about my department to the Dean! And I'm speaking about a short but unpleasant conversation that I have recently had with the President, in which I promised to deal with this matter firmly and uncompromisingly!" She paused. "*Now* you may speak, *Herr* Orwell, if you have anything constructive to tell us."

Orwell looked up. After she had told him to be quiet, he had resorted to shifting papers and pens around on the table in front of him.

"Well, I just wanted to say that sometimes when students have got it in for each other there's not much you can do. Eddie Hodgkins is a very good teacher. He has a good rapport with the students."

"*Thank you, Herr* Orwell. You have saved me from having to name the delinquent person myself. I think that there can be no doubt or hesitation about the next course of action to be taken: the incompetent young man must be removed from our department without further delay. How did he come to be here anyway—"

Snoad audibly mouthed the words, "Good question." And Orwell glared at him. They were taking sides, she noted.

Christenkorn cleared his throat.

"*Herr* Hodgkins was appointed by *Herr* Professor Timpe, shortly before *Herr* Timpe went into retirement."

Damnation! That was highly inconvenient. She had assumed that the miserable Hodgkins was a Christenkorn appointee, from the time when he had been Acting Head of Department. That way she could smack him down, too. But Professor Timpe—that was a wholly different matter. and, unfortunately for her, the saintly Professor was still seen as being above all petty criticism.

She tried again. Perhaps she could still get Christenkorn.

"We do all make mistakes. I'm sure that my predecessor had his reasons. But why was it that no-one picked up on the incompetence of *Herr* Hodgkins afterwards? And what deluded individual was it who enabled Hodgkins to stay on by renewing his contract?"

Unfortunately, that back-fired too.

"You did!"

Frau Professor's eyes swiveled round immediately, and drilled holes in the person who had spoken.

"I *beg* your pardon?"

It was Dorothea Schlichting, grinning like a crazed gargoyle. God damn her insolence! How dare she? But before Schlichting could be obliterated by a lightning-bolt of professorial wrath, someone else spoke up.

"I'm afraid that is correct, *Frau* Professor," *Frau* Ludewig said. "You yourself approved the course catalog for the coming semester, at the end of the last calendar year. The package included the hours for our part-time lecturers, and the funding for those has already been confirmed. It was approved by the faculty council early in the New Year. The President has already been informed."

This was getting ridiculous! But the secretary was right. She had indeed initialed the listings, immediately after Enno Müller, who was in charge of course planning, had submitted them to her. There had been no discussion, except about the advanced classes that she and Christenkorn would be offering. Who needed to waste time talking about First-Year language courses?

That had obviously been a mistake.

"Then I shall have to *unapprove* the hours for *Herr* Hodgkins. Do we actually need his classes?"

Oh yes, they certainly did. It was pointed out to her that *Herr* Hodgkins taught multiple parallel lessons, all of which contributed to the English Language Certificate of Competence, without which no First Year student could progress to the Second Year. And he was also useful as an examiner for the oral tests that the students had to undergo. No-one else was keen to do all those interviews! Besides, without his hours they would be unable to meet their contractual obligations to English Philology for modules like Translation.

"We can't do without him," Orwell said, "and that's a fact."

"Very well. We keep *Herr* Hodgkins's lessons, but we replace *Herr* Hodgkins as the person teaching them!"

There was silence.

Finally, Christenkorn said, "It isn't easy to find suitable people for these part-time positions. They are paid at the lowest possible rate we can get away with. But perhaps you yourself know someone?"

She didn't, of course. Despite having chosen a career in English Studies, she had had little contact with native speakers of English, except for the academics that she met at conferences—and none of them would be prepared to do such banal teaching for such a pittance. (Or be very good at it, either.)

In theory, the lower-level part-timers still earned substantially more per hour than the national minimum wage. In practice, however, if you took into account the time spent preparing the lessons, marking student assignments, counseling students, and possibly setting and marking examination papers as well, not to mention the traveling time to and from the university, it worked out at about the same.

With tips, you could do a lot better working in a bar.

"If you mean, do I hang out with young people of the calibre of *Herr* Hodgkins, then no, I don't know anyone suitable. Do you?" Christenkorn shook his head. "*Herr* Snoad, perhaps?"

Snoad shrugged his shoulders, a gesture that she was learning meant that he didn't want to be involved. He made as if to say something, thought better of it, and then Kurz butted in, again in English.

"*Jaan* is like right out of that scene. Totally. You guys don't realize how many commitments he has!" He turned to Snoad. "Sorry, man, but you know me: I call it the way it is! But maybe I can help. I know a guy who is an alpha-plus academic communicator, and an outstanding human being."

Against her will, she found herself responding carefully in English.

"Really? Which person is this?"

"His name is Dwight G. Hackensack, III. He has a Master's in Lifestyle Anthropology from Hubert H. Humphry College, Wallace, South Dakota. And a doctorate in life!"

"But no qualification in English?" Christenkorn asked. "Not even a Bachelor's degree?"

"Can he teach English?" Enno Müller wanted to know. "Just being a native speaker is not enough."

"And can he keep our students under control?" the Schlichting woman added. "Like Hodgkins *can't*."

How pathetic! Suddenly they were all blabbering away, demonstrating their command of English. Were they trying to show her up?

Kurz was becoming quite excited. "Dwight is cool. He fronts a jazz-hiphop fusion combo. He ain't heavy, he's my brother! Nuff said?"

He turned to Snoad, his hand raised for a high five.

Snoad reciprocated.

"Nuff said!"

"Wow! Though begging your pardon, *Jaan*, this would shift the balance mightily in a US of A direction. You can live with that, dude?"

"That's heavy shit, man, but I can live with it."

She noticed that Kurz had addressed only Snoad, and ignored Orwell. She was beginning to understand the constellations and interaction patterns within the department.

The whole stupid business was now threatening to spin out of control. For a start, she had barely understood a word that Kurz had said, although she had grasped that his friend Dwight didn't have a relevant qualification.

That was all to the good—there could be no question of paying him a single cent more more than the lowest level of remuneration. Hodgkins with his degree from Cambridge earned slightly more than that.

She switched back to German.

"Then perhaps we should take a look at this friend of yours. Where is he at the moment?"

"Wallace, South Dakota."

Orwell burst out laughing.

"We'll send him a plane ticket, then!"

Angry though she was, she was almost tempted to join in. My, oh, my, what a bunch of cretins they were! And *this* called itself a university department? What a circus!

"When I called this meeting, I had envisaged that it would be over *to-day*. And that we might even come to some sensible and practical solution.

You may have time to waste, but I don't. I am therefore instructing you all to look actively for a suitable and well-qualified alternative to *Herr* Hodgkins. That gentleman will remain in place until the end of the summer semester— it seems that we have no other choice in the matter—but you will mentor him at all times, *Herr* Orwell, so that there is no repeat of the disgraceful scene in his language class. Is that understood?"

"I'll do my best."

"Then let us hope that your *best* is sufficient, *Herr* Orwell. People in this department doing their *best* has not produced the *best* of results, in my humble opinion. You will keep me informed."

"Of course."

"And you, *Frau* Ludewig, will remind me, without fail, when the time comes for me to approve *Herr* Müller's draft of the course catalog for next winter semester, that there is still a problem needing to be dealt with. By then, however, I hope—no, I am confident!—that you will all have brought me your suggestions for an appropriate candidate to replace the unfortunate *Herr* Hodgkins. And someone reasonably *local*, please. No applicants from Alice Springs or Vladivostok."

She looked around the faces at the table, to make sure that her message had sunk in, and then closed the meeting.

UNRELIABLE ALLIES

The moment Richard had turned the corner, he was grabbed from behind by Dorothea Schlichting. Enno was right behind her, though struggling to keep up.

"A word, Richard dearest? But not here."

Was he *frogmarched* to the office that Schlichting and Müller shared? Would that be the right word to describe it? Not exactly, but it was how it felt to Richard.

Once they were inside the office: "Sit down! Richard. (No, *Babychen*, let *him* have the chair. And shut the door.) You see what she's doing, don't you, Richard?"

"No?"

Richard had no idea where this was going, but Doro was clearly excited about something that had happened during the meeting, and he knew that she detested the Snake almost more than anyone else did.

"Divide and rule, Richard, divide and rule. That's what she's doing. She is trying to set us against each other. You and the Hodgkins boy against Harlan and Jonathan. The Germans against the English native-speakers. Everyone against Kajo."

Enno added, "She tries to make him look like a fool. You saw that, didn't you?"

"Why should she do that? I mean, everything, not just the bit about Kajo."

"Because everybody hates her, and no-one respects her. How did she become Professor? You do remember that, don't you?"

He didn't, actually, so she told him. They had wanted a woman at all costs, and preferably someone who was more interested in teacher training than in English. (Who was "they"?) The Snake had had the weakest formal qualifications of any of the shortlisted candidates, and the least impressive publications list, but she was the only woman who was left in the running.

The Commissioner for Gender Equality, *Frau* Dr. Dröge-Daschmeyer, had pushed it through. Yes, there was a fight, but none of the men on the selection committee had wanted to be labeled as a male chauvinist, or as the guy who pulled the plug on a brilliant young woman's career. So, one by one, they buckled.

That was how Doro Schlichting told it, at least.

Richard didn't trust her an inch. He remembered the Anne-Marie business, and how often Doro had made unpleasant fun of him in departmental meetings, or sided with Snoad and Kurz against him.

She and the Snake hated each other. As far as he could tell, they were both mediocre as academics, and neither of them were much good at English. The Snake had crazy ideas; Doro didn't have any ideas at all. One of them had achieved remarkable, but undeserved, success; the other had found herself a cushy job that didn't require her to do anything memorable or significant. They could almost be sisters!

What did his two colleagues want from him?

"All we want, my dear, is to know that, when the moment comes, you will be on our side!"

Of course he would, he said. (But would they ever be on *his*?). However, he would naturally expect them to help and support Eddie if they could. Eddie hadn't been treated fairly.

Doro said, "Well, he rather brought it on himself, didn't he?" and Enno grunted noncommittedly. Obviously no real help from them would be forthcoming, unless it was part of a broader move against the Snake. And Kurz and Snoad would now be actively engaged in getting rid of Eddie by finding a replacement for him.

That, it seemed, was the end of the discussion, and they let him go.

Richard shambled across to the mail-boxes, feeling distinctly gloomy. He'd have to tell Eddie that the Snake would now be gunning for him, though Eddie would probably already have worked that out for himself. Whatever happened, his days in the English Department were now numbered.

Richard didn't feel good about it at all. The deal that he'd made with Eddie—that he could stay in his apartment until the end of the summer semester—now seemed both harsh and brutally prophetic.

Although Eddie could be very annoying, he'd miss him. He realized that there was an element of selfishness in this: Eddie was helping him in the task he'd been set by the President, and when he left he wouldn't have a single real friend among his colleagues. Or even someone that he *liked* (with the possible exception of Kajo).

This mood of gloom didn't last long. Waiting for him in his mailbox was another card from "S."—just what he needed to raise his spirits.

Her handwriting was tiny, and she had only just managed to squeeze the text onto one side of the card. (The other side was a painting of two playful black kittens, with the caption "LITTLE DEVILS.") He had to tilt the card towards the light to be able to read it.

> My dearest Richard,
> Every time I look at the stars, I think of you. Every time I look at you, I think of the stars glimmering in your eyes. And every time you smile, I realise how it would be if you fetched all the stars down from the sky for me. At this moment I'm standing at the window and asking myself: do you see the same stars as I do? Does the moon dazzle you as it does me? I dream of those passionate hours that we didn't spend together. I dream of your hands and your lips. But they are dreams that come to nothing. There's a storm rising in me, full of sadness and pain. I collapse, crying bitterly: "Get out of my thoughts! Get out of my heart! You're hurting me so much. I must forget you—because I love you so much!
>
> S.

That made him feel a whole lot better!

The more he thought about it, the more confident he felt that this girl Steffi Albertz had to be "S." Eddie's characterization of her as a "sexy little bundle" sounded really promising. He couldn't remember her from any of his lessons, but perhaps she had barely attended any of them (except for the British Studies lecture) because her English was so good and she didn't need to.

He'd Google'd her in the hope of finding a photo, but she was nowhere to be found, except (if that was indeed her) for a mention on an old website of a school in Passau—a class list without any pictures (not even a group photo).

The card from "S." wasn't the only message that he received that day. When he retrieved the remainder of his mail from the mailbox, he found, tucked in between the announcement of an end-of-semester concert in the Music Department and a flyer from a removals company, a small, sealed envelope, neatly addressed to "MR. RICHARD ORWELL, MA." It didn't look like "S."'s handwriting.

The letter contained a pastel-colored card with a short message from Lisa Meyer!

Her mother had darned and patched his pullover (she was much better at that than Lisa was), and now she would like to return it to him. She'd bring it to Textual Composition and give it to him after the class. Would he then have a few spare minutes to talk to her? There was something she wanted to talk to him about. It wouldn't take long—he could still get to the *Mensa* afterwards. But she would understand if he didn't have time.

Aha! The mountain was coming to Muhammad! What was it that she wanted to talk about? He didn't think she had a crush on him. He'd seen no evidence of that in her manner towards him and, besides, if he was really honest with himself, he was more intrigued by the prospect of finding out who "S." was. It wouldn't be Lisa Meyer—not just because of Lisa's name, but because her English wasn't good enough.

Maybe Lisa wanted to chat him up in the hope of getting more lenient treatment from him in the English exams? That would be the most likely explanation.

Or—and it was maybe a long shot—perhaps she needed someone older and more mature to talk to about the traumatic events in the hostel?

Whatever it was that Lisa wanted, it would be a good opportunity to get her talking about what had happened to her.

On the way back to the apartment, Richard popped into Real and bought some pork chops, some fresh vegetables, and a tub of ice-cream. His conscience needed to be assuaged: he'd give Eddie a night off from his usual tinned soup or baked beans, and cook for them both. There was plenty of beer, and he had a bottle of wine too.

His mood was now excellent, though this didn't chime too well with the difficult conversation that he knew that he had to have with Eddie about the departmental meeting.

Before he had even unpacked the groceries, he put on a stern face and announced: "Eddie, there's something that we need to talk about, and I need to get it off my chest—"

But Eddie barely gave him a chance to begin.

"Me, too," he said. "I should have told you days ago, but you had all that toothache business, and you were worried about the meeting. How did it go, by the way? No, I can see it was a total bummer! So let *me* cheer *you* up a bit!"

With a wicked twinkle in his eye, he told Richard that he'd had an intimate *tête-à-tête* with a certain young lady that Richard had recently been showing a lot of unexplained interest in: a Miss Stefanie Albertz.

And Miss Albertz had confessed to him that she thought Richard was a "really nice guy"!

Richard punched the air. Had there ever been a day in his life that had swung round so completely as this one?

PART THREE: LONG-LEGGEDY BEASTIES

YOU SMILED AT ME

Dearest Richard,

YOU SMILED AT ME! We met in the corridor outside the cafeteria, and you smiled at me! I don't beleive [sic] you recognised who I was, but even so you smiled at me. Perhaps because I smiled at you? Never mind, for a brief second you looked at me and smiled. You can't imagine how much this meant to me.

And after several days I saw you again. What good fortune that your lectures are so full. Hiding in the anonymity of a full lecture hall I can sit there quitely [sic] looking at you and enjoying you. I wish I could get nearer to you, but I don't trust myself to speak to you, because I can't get a word from my lips when I'm standing there in front of you. Although I would love to make myself known to you. But all I can do is go to your classes, sit there, and dream: You, me, and a four-poster bed!

Richard, dearest Richard, I have missed you so much, suffered so much, and written so much. Am I getting on your nerves? I must be! But you must know that I *have* to write to you, or I would just burst with passion and longing. I am so happy that I can go to your classes and hear your wonderful, warm, sexy voice. But what will I do in the holidays?

S.

Her next letter was in German.

My dearest Richard,

Forgive me that this time I am not writing to you in your language, but I am so sad, panicky and confused that I can hardly think straight, let alone formulate correct sentences in English. The semester is drawing to a close, but I can't feel happy that the holidays are coming. I won't see you for many, many weeks.

Of course, I'll try. I'll come to the uni every day and roam about in the corridors, pretending to be busy with something or other, in the hope of bumping into you. I'll write every day, but I won't post the letters. There won't be many students in the uni, and what if you saw me near the mailboxes? I don't want that to happen—not yet. But with a bit of luck I might catch a glimpse of you.

Now the holidays are coming! How will I be able to survive for so long without hearing your voice? I can't stop crying. My friends think I'm depressed, because I'm sad and tired all the time—day and night I have to think of you—and because I'm not looking forward to the holidays. But

I can't reveal the truth, not to anyone. And so I write to you sometimes. I'm sorry if I'm getting on your nerves, but I have to let it out somehow, otherwise I would simply explode.

Loving you hurts me so much, Richard! I wish I could just ignore you, I wish I could make a clean break and end it, but you are simply so wonderful that I have to love you, I have no other choice.

I should stop writing—I've already taken up too much of your precious time, please forgive me. I just want you to know that there is someone who thinks of you. I love you, Richard, and the moment I have my degree certificate I'm going to march into your office holding it in my hands and tell you that to your face. Before I leave the uni forever, you have the right to know who your secret admirer is!

Thank God that I still have plenty of time before I finish here, and that I'll be able to enjoy a few more of your courses.

But that's enough now! Have a wonderful day, Richard, and spare a thought for that girl who loves you, so madly and hopelessly.

S.

COLD AND GLOOM

The long winter semester was trundling to a close. It was a season loved neither by the students, who were swotting for the upcoming exams (or *not* swotting, and feeling bad about it) nor by the lecturers, many of whom were busy preparing those same exams. Professor Michael was agonizing over whether to set a much easier examination this time around, or to grade it more "traditionally," since he didn't think he could take another semester of the mobbing and harassment that he'd just suffered.

The weather was (as usual) contributing its own early-February cold and gloom.

In the *Mensa*, the staff were bracing themselves for the end-of-semester rush, because exams meant a massive student presence on campus in a way that classes usually didn't, and stressed-out students were generally hungry students.

At the Real supermarket, they anticipated a run on bars of chocolate, potato crisps and other "comfort foods."

Many in the administration were looking forward to six weeks (after the examinations, which overlapped ten days or so into the holidays) with barely a student in sight, and peace and quiet on the campus. What bliss! Some would even take a week or two of vacation, to sunbathe in the Canaries or catch up on whatever needed to be done around the house.

For a few, however, a great, gooey, twice-yearly slodge of work was about to be tipped over their heads.

Quality Manager Rammler and his team would soon be overwhelmed by thousands of end-of-course evaluation forms that needed to be collected, scanned, processed and evaluated, before the information (in summary) was passed on to the relevant committees, and the *Präsidium*; the lecturers themselves would also be informed of what their classes thought of them and their teaching efforts, both in the form of grades and statistics, and in a scan of the "free commentaries" (if any) scribbled by the students.

Tenured Professor Graeber in Philosophy would probably glance at their puerile comments, snort "stupid little prats," and delete the email.

Jonathan Snoad would read "Why doesn't Jon wear even tighter pants?," accompanied by a sketched smiley of a grinning face with its tongue hanging out, and remind himself to show it to Harlan. (Or, on second thoughts, maybe not—it might have been from Rico.)

Young Stefan Heimlich from German Philology, worried about his contract being renewed beyond the current academic year and making slow progress on his doctorate, would read "Lousy teacher," "Waste of time going to his class," "Hasn't got a clue," and similar remarks, and burst into tears.

If Rammler ever stopped for a moment to reflect on how he was administering a system of anonymous denunciation—of the qualified by the unqualified, of the adult by (in many cases) the juvenile—that would be worthy of a police state, and which could have potentially life-changing consequences for some of its victims, he didn't share that thought with anyone. The politicians had decreed that evaluations should take place, since the students were now "customers," and someone had to organize these. That chalice had been passed to him. But he did cancel his mid-week session of squash with Jonathan Snoad for the following two weeks. .

Chief Information Officer Dr. Breitkreuz would be even busier, collating the information he would soon be receiving from the lecturers about exam results and credit points, and organizing online registration for the various classes to be taught in the summer semester.

Even Performance Manager Grote would be embattled, setting up in-service training courses for increasingly reluctant members of the teaching staff, who were all utterly convinced that they had better things to do during the Easter break.

All three gentlemen dreaded the "round-table meeting" in the *Präsidium* that they would soon be invited to, when His Magnificence, visibly enjoying their discomfort, would require them to bring him up to speed on the work of their departments during the semester. For a theologian, he had a remarkably firm grasp of their procedures and algorithms, and woe betide anyone who slipped up!

Eddie was feeling gloomy too, at least by his own standards. Generally speaking, he was like a *Stehaufmännchen* (a "little-stand-up-man"), one of those dolls with a rounded, weighted base that always spring back up when you knock them down. His glass was normally half full, and he was happy that way. ("He's like a village idiot," Snoad used to say, but Eddie could live with that.) Even so, the news that his days in the English Department were now numbered had come as a cruel blow. He knew it had been coming, of course, but that stupid Jeannine-Steffi business had tipped the Snake over the edge.

He didn't really blame Richard, and he was grateful for being allowed to share his apartment, but couldn't Richard have spoken up for him a bit more?

Well, maybe he couldn't have.

Eddie would miss all that sitting around in the *Mensa*, chatting to the students. He'd miss the rubbishy coffee, and the stale buns. Soon he'd have to start looking for a new job, perhaps in a different city. He might have to start getting up earlier in the mornings. He wouldn't have much time any more to help Richard with his quest. And just when it was getting *interesting*.

Because Eddie had a suspect—in the English Department. Richard would be amazed. He'd had a bit of a bad conscience about interviewing the pretty girls, except for the postgrad Miriam Burkhardt, and leaving Richard to do the male students in the department, plus their colleagues. Eddie had therefore recently turned his attention to the teachers.

Actually, those "interviews" with the girls hadn't led to a massive breakthrough, although every little piece of the mosaic might yet count.

Apart from helping to lose him his job, Jeannine Garbe had cost Eddie a paper-handkerchief and a coffee. With what result? She had speculated that the "intruder" might have been handicapped, or perhaps left-handed. Or maybe not.

Felicitas Förster hadn't wanted to meet him at all—the young lady was on the up, socially and academically. If she had had a "life trainer," *not* being seen with Eddie would have been one of his first and strongest recommendations. But he'd bumped into her at Murphy's, and Miss Felicitas had deigned to grant him a few moments of her oh so precious time.

("It was only about one of the courses in the summer," she'd reassured her incredulous friends afterwards, "that was all he wanted."

"Oh, you poor thing," they'd commiserated, "that guy is such a toad. Ugh!")

The "fire-cracker" had told him that she'd switched rooms in the hostel just before the unpleasant event had happened. She'd wanted a quieter room (for being able to work on her term papers, and—Eddie guessed, though she didn't say it—for "chilling" after parties) and so she'd done a swap with another student, who didn't care one way or the other. She'd even forgotten to change the name-card on the door for a couple of days.

Well, that confirmed that Felicitas almost certainly *hadn't* been the intended target. And it probably ruled out the male students living in the hostel, because they would have seen the regularly updated list of rooms and their occupants on the notice-board in the foyer. Knowing which girl was in which room was important when you were on the late-night coffee prowl.

Meaning that the attacker had probably come from the outside.

If he'd had a list of student names, it would have been an outdated one, obtained from the university administration, or from the organization that ran the hostels.

That was good to know, though how it would actually be of use to them Eddie wasn't sure.

Nothing much had happened. She'd woken up with him in the room, looming over her bed. Before she could even get her eyes open properly, let alone scream for help, he had gone. For some of the other girls it had apparently been worse.

Who was the student that Felicitas had swapped with, he asked? It was Lisa Meyer! So it looked as though he'd come for *her* twice—and on one of his visits had found Felicitas instead, clearing off immediately he realized his mistake..

Lisa was obviously important, but here Richard had forestalled him, though not by any intention of his own. The girl had approached him after one of his lessons and offered to darn his pullover for him.

Funny, that. Eddie wouldn't have imagined Lisa having a crush on Richard. And Richard was obviously more interested in Steffi Albertz (not a good match at all, to his mind). She had given him back the pullover—very expertly repaired—after his Textual Composition class, and accepted his offer of a quick coffee. But when Richard had tried to quiz her about her traumatic experience in the hostel, he had ballsed it up completely. No, she didn't want to talk about it, absolutely not, it was all too unpleasant. No, really.

But there *was* something that she wanted to talk about. She and a group of her friends, including Ulrike Sandmann, were going to organize a trip to Flossengamme. Would he like to come along? She'd heard that he'd never been there, and it was something that you absolutely *had* to see. She'd been there twice with her school, so she'd be their guide—not that a guide was necessary, because everything was explained in detail on posters and signboards. And they gave you a brochure, too.

It would be a day-trip, at a weekend or in the holidays, and they'd be back by the evening. Perhaps Saturday week, right at the end of the semester?

Richard had already said "yes."

Eddie was fuming. The cheek of it!

How had she heard that Richard had never been there? From Eddie! Though she hadn't thought to mention that to Richard, of course.

And was Eddie invited? No, Eddie wasn't!

And it got even worse. *Ulrike Sandmann* of all people would be going: the only unquestioned Eight-and-a-half in the whole English Department, a wet-dream on legs... (He knew he didn't stand a snowflake in hell's chance with her, but just *looking* at the goddess was enough to make you drool.)

Life was so bloody unfair.

What was the wretched girl up to? First the pullover, and then this. Surely she wasn't targeting Richard?

He quite liked Lisa—he even fancied her, in a mild sort of way, though she was a bit out of his league—but he'd never had her down as a sophisticated type, a predator. Ah well, there would probably be some perfectly boring explanation. Maybe she was trying to set him up, longer-term, to be her examiner? When students got friendly, that was often what it was all about.

But why go to all the fuss? Richard had the reputation of being strict and conscientious in examinations, and there was consequently no big waiting-list that you needed to be on (as there was with Snoad) if you wanted to secure him as an examiner. Weaker students tended to avoid him: that he was known to be "fair" in exams didn't make him a more attractive prospect as an examiner.

Perhaps it was all completely innocent. Flossengamme in February would be a pretty dull excursion—not the sort of place he'd have chosen, if he'd been in Lisa's shoes and with ulterior motives with regard to Richard. And if she really did have designs on him, she'd be crazy to invite Ulrike Sandmann to be in the group as well.

When the sun's shining straight in your eyes, you don't notice someone waving a torch.

Lisa's lively little friend Steffi Albertz would apparently also be there, doing the driving, and Richard seemed to have some kind of thing about her. Did he even know who she was? That wasn't good planning either. Goggle-Eyed Beatrix and the warthog-lookalike from the Third Year would surely have been more sensible choices to make up the numbers!

Eddie decided that he would talk to Richard about this. If going on a weird concentration camp "date" with Lisa was what was needed to unlock her memory on the subject of the hostel intruder, then so be it. But he didn't want his friend to be taken advantage of by a confused student. He'd tell him that. And he would fill Richard in on his new discovery about the suspicious behavior of one of their colleagues.

However, when Eddie got back to Südstädter Ring 27 he found no-one

there and, to judge from the kitchen, no sign that Richard intended to organize supper that evening either. Where could he be?

THE GUEST LECTURER

Richard had certain academic commitments that he had not mentioned
to Eddie, and was now facing what was likely to be a long, painful Thursday
evening.

He had been ordered by the Snake to attend a lecture by an eminent
visiting speaker.

Dr. Dr. Alois Piesacker was Professor of German Literature at a renowned south German university. Strictly speaking, Piesacker would be the
guest of the Philosophy Department, but the President (a former colleague
of Dr. Dr. Alois) had let it be known that he expected a good turn-out from
the *Anglisten*, and the *Germanisten* too, and he had instructed the respective
departmental heads accordingly.

Although the renowned gentleman would be addressing the philosophers on the riveting subject of "Cyclical Approaches to Cultural-Historical
Theory" (Oh no! Richard groaned inwardly. All those incomprehensible
German Idealist philosophers...), he was nevertheless a Professor of German, and not of Philosophy, or even of History. He was also known to have
a weakness for all things "typically British," including pipes and deerstalkers, knickerbockers and tartan accessories—everything, that is, except for
British philosophy, which as everyone knew wasn't up to much.

Kajo had likewise been told to attend.

The Snake herself wouldn't be going—she regarded matters literary and
cultural as a complete waste of her time. And as for the others: Enno Müller
was desperately busy "quantifying," or "collating," his wife had said on the
phone; the Schlichting woman's literary interests didn't extend a millimeter
beyond "songs and rhymes for the elementary-level English classroom";
the useless Eddie Hodgkins had made himself scarce; and Kurz and Snoad
would take so long to chase up that the visitor would have been and gone
before anyone found them.

Christenkorn, however, had once been a solid literature specialist, before he switched to motivation, and Orwell had an MA on some pointless
literary topic. Let *them* carry the flag for the English Department!

The lecture was going to be held in a teaching classroom rather than a
lecture theater. There was no way that students would turn up in numbers
for such an unexciting topic (especially on a Thursday evening, when there

would be parties and discos as competition), and a near-empty lecture theater would be a painful affront to the guest.

When Richard and Kajo arrived at the classroom, Richard's faint hopes of being able to snooze peacefully at the back were soon dashed. The safe, coveted seats to the rear of the classroom had already been bagged by those few, sad, untypical students—postgraduates, foreigners, or "mature students"—who had indeed shown up.

The front row was occupied by the President and his retinue, and by the Philosophy Professors, with little folded paper "RESERVED" notices placed on the few chairs that were still unoccupied. Richard had to smile. As if anyone would *want* to sit there!

But most of the seats in the second row, also a relatively dangerous zone of exposure, were unfortunately still free.

The President was standing talking to the speaker, a tall, tremendously imposing figure in a suit that was a shade too tight around the stomach. Thankfully, there were no knickerbockers or deerstalkers in evidence. To Richard's horror, the President acknowledged the two new arrivals as they took their seats in the second row, announcing loudly to his guest that, look! some representatives of the *Anglistik* had also come: Dr. Karl-Johannes Christenkorn, until recently the acting head of the English Department and well-known for his interest in cultural theory, and (slight pause) a young British *Lektor* from the English team.

Both of them accordingly felt obliged to lean forward, rather awkwardly, across the philosophers sitting in the front row and shake hands with Dr. Dr. Alois.

Despite its appearance, that little charade was not about politeness. What it *was* about was the President making a show of pointing them out to the speaker. They were members of the audience who could be relied upon to participate in the questions and discussion after the talk (just in case there wasn't much response, after the couple of predictable questions from the Philosophy Professors). And it was simultaneously a hint to the *Anglisten* that they were expected to "do their bit."

Damn it!

Richard would now actually have to listen, and that would be hard going. As for questions, what could he possibly ask the man? He had nothing whatsoever of value to contribute. He knew nothing at all about this tedious stuff (and didn't want to, either). He had neglected to do the most basic homework, so he wasn't even sure where Dr. Dr. Alois was coming from academically (which might have helped a tiny bit). He'd hardly be a Marxist of any kind, what with all the fuss the President was making over him. Was he more of a Traditionalist, perhaps? Or a Critical Theorist? From his pompous, old-fashioned manner, Richard would have guessed the former, but appearances could be misleading.

His own preferred position in such situations had nothing to do with ideology, and was literal rather than metaphorical—it was to keep his head down and try not to be noticed.

If that wasn't possible, there was always Plan B.

Plan B entailed falling back on the wise advice given in the writings of Stephen Potter (on "Gamesmanship," "Lifemanship," and so on). The cardinal rule here was to distract attention away from your own ignorance while still managing to sound impressive. Basically, you put up a smokescreen of bullshit. You watched for clues—if the Traditionalist sneered at Lacan, you threw him Lyotard or Althusser or some other impenetrable Continental fruitcake to chew on. If you were in doubt, you lobbed the guy a soft ball for him to smash to the boundary.

For example: "With regard to the question just raised" (whatever that was) "does the speaker see any concordances/homologies in the British and US-American responses, or are we best advised to remain focused on the European dimension?"

That could be answered in almost any way imaginable, and at happily time-consuming length.

Inviting the speaker to spot the "carnivalesque," the "transcultural," or a "paradigm shift," or inserting a buzzword like "hegemonial," "feminisms" (only in the plural, though) or "sexualities" (ditto) into an otherwise harmless question was also usually quite successful, in a Pavlovian sort of way.

The question could even be asked in English, with an apologetic explanation that this was only to ensure *absolute terminological precision* in the formulation of the question (whereas the intention of the questioner was actually the complete opposite—though no-one in the audience, as the speaker waffled on in response, would realize that).

The distinguished lecturer began (as they so often did in Germany) with a reference to Goethe. In his wisdom the Sage of Weimar had, it appeared, anticipated the very same problem that the speaker would be elucidating, and in his this-that-or-the-other commentaries (book six, the so-and-so edition being preferred) had even hinted (with his usual astuteness) at the *rightness* of approaching the subject from the very same standpoint that the speaker would be adopting.

So Professor Dr. Dr. Piesacker had Goethe on his side—that was good to know! With the Master's imprimatur, the subtext to the lecture was now: "Back off! And don't you *dare* to disagree!"

But this didn't help Richard to understand any better what then followed. There was a lot of gumph about cycles of decadence and renewal, and obscure parallelisms between different cultural circles. Quotations from all the appropriate big guns were rolled out (the very writers and philosophers that Richard always steered away from whenever he possibly could).

At one point the speaker noted that "Our British cousins, sadly, but as so often, I regret to have to say it, lagged behind the European impulse." Kajo (the traitor) muttered "indeed, too true" as several in the front row turned to note the reaction of the *Anglisten*.

Richard didn't react.

Was that a flicker of disappointment that had crossed the speaker's face?

The lecture went on. And on. And on. The students at the back were beginning to slip away.

Then Dr. Dr. Alois returned to the British connection. He mentioned a number of authors, and especially their shortcomings, then said, "As an illustrious Victorian once put it" (and he switched to heavily accented English), "'The world has grown cold from your breath'."

Safely back in German again, and fixing his gaze on Richard, he landed his killer blow: "That is a reference, I venture to add, that his modern British compatriots would almost without exception find it hard to recognize, of course, let alone to comprehend."

There it was! The typical, not completely unexpected, dig at the token Brit, the poor, semi-qualified *Lektor* who was allowed to be a hewer of wood and drawer of water in the gloomy plantations of English Grammar and Textual Composition, but who was incapable of appreciating his own literary tradition! *Gott sei Dank* that that tradition was in the safe hands of such luminaries as Professor Dr. Dr.!

The Professor had already moved on when Richard picked up the challenge. He stage-whispered, as though to no-one in particular: "*Gray* from *thy* breath, of course!"

He regretted it immediately. What had come over him? What had been riding him at that moment? But there, too late—it was done!

Like the Eye of Sauron on the heights of the Dark Tower, the professorial gaze swung around to pin down the source of the interruption.

"I beg your pardon?" Though his *Wie bitte?* was more of an admonition ("Come, come now!") than a question.

There were loud murmurings. One of the students giggled. The President, turning slightly, was visibly displeased. While Richard's correction had been unseemly enough (he was among his elders and betters, after all), his echoing of the professor's "of course" was downright insolence.

"Sorry, it's not important."

"I think you'll find that it's *very* important to get such matters right, my young friend. It's the difference between scholarship and dilettantism. We need to be clear about that. But our time is limited, and we should better move on—"

Richard concurred with a nod, and he couldn't help admiring how the

Professor had extricated himself from embarrassment. Indeed, why make such a fuss over a trivial error? The front row clucked in support of the guest, nodding to him to continue. None of them, Richard was certain, would bother to check the reference on their smartphone, or later at home on the computer.

The Professor was right in believing that hardly anyone in Britain to-day would recognize a Swinburne quotation. That included every British student of English literature that Richard had ever met, and most lecturers too. Like Kipling and Rupert Brooke, Somerset Maugham and Wyndham Lewis, Swinburne was completely off the radar as far as the curricula were concerned. But Richard liked niche authors. That was how he had ended up writing his MA thesis on Conan Doyle.

Nor did Swinburne play any role in British popular culture. If, on one of his trips to England, the Professor happened to wander off the beaten track of cultural tourism into the Public Bar of some working-class pub, and attempted to try out his literary quotations on the clientele, he might get away with a Kipling *bon mot*, or even a bit of Rupert Brooke, but with Swinburne he'd be risking a roughing-up in the Gents from feral proles ("fucking poof!"), or a Liverpool Kiss on the pavement outside.

Once the lecture was over, and the discussion had petered out—only the Philosophy Professors having asked a few lame questions, to allow their distinguished guest to hold forth a little longer—Richard tried to make a dash for the door, but he found the great man blocking his path, with the President by his side.

"You are a Swinburne scholar, I take it?"

"Er, no, no," Richard stammered, "just someone who enjoys poetry. Not just Swinburne."

"So rare, in these sad times," came the reply, "But I'm afraid I didn't catch your name, *Herr* Dr.—?"

"Orwell."

He was about to add, "and just Mister," when someone effectively did that for him.

"*Herr* Orwell," the President boomed, "is a language teacher, and I have heard that he is an excellent one, but he is not one of our Reichsstadt *Gelehrten* or *Wissenschaftler*. Alois," he added, "you will join us in the foyer for some light refreshment?"

And he moved off in that direction.

Richard became aware of Kajo hoveringly nervously beside him. He was genuinely puzzled by what the President had said, and asked Kajo what the difference was between a *Gelehrter* and a *Wissenschaftler*. Didn't both words just refer to someone who taught and researched at university?

For some perverse reason, Kajo chose to explain the difference to him in English. Was it because Professor Piesacker was still there, listening to their conversation?

"They are not the same, Richard. The *Wissenschaftler* has obtained a doctorate. He has proved that he can work in an academic context. But the *Gelehrter* has earned the higher distinction of the *Habilitation*. He is therefore more than just a mere academic—he is a scholar."

"So what is the word then for someone who *doesn't* have a doctorate?"

"Ah, Richard, you must realize that the German system would not recognize such a person as a proper academic teacher or researcher. I know, I know, you have that path before you still! But only when you have achieved the PhD have you truly begun. And the title of 'Doctor'—that is a distinction that we Germans have always taken very seriously, and worn with pride. It is not earned as easily, or given as lightly, as in some other countries. For us, it is always a badge of honor!"

That was meant to be helpful, kindly even, but Richard took it the wrong way. Why did Kajo feel the need to put him in his place? Was he trying to ingratiate himself with Dr. Dr. Alois? Was this an indirect way of apologizing for his young colleague's behavior ("He means well, and, you know, his language classes are really quite excellent. Inexcusable rudeness, though, *Herr Professor*")?

Richard was angry at being patronized again, and for the second time that evening something snapped, and he forgot himself. But this time he let rip.

"*Always* a badge of honor, Kajo? What about all those Nazis with doctorates? *Dr.* Goebbels? Mengele, the Angel of Death in Auschwitz, with *two* doctorates? Or *Dr.* Dirlewanger—the worst monster in the SS?"

The hours of listening to Eddie rambling on about the Nazis had finally paid off!

Kajo was quite nonplussed.

"Ah, but those were exceptions, Richard. Horrible men, yes, but rare exceptions."

"Then what about the Wannsee Conference, you know, where they decided how to murder all those Jews? There were fifteen people who took part, and *eight* of them had 'badges of honor'! Doctor this and Doctor that. I'm sorry, Kajo, I just don't buy it!"

People around them were now listening intently, and Piesacker was still there. He heard someone say, "He's been drinking," and there were some laughs. Oh wow, he'd really put his foot in it this time!

But as he walked out, he realized that he didn't care. If the President got to hear about it and was annoyed with him, so be it. He'd given Richard a job to do, and he needed him, so he wouldn't take the matter any further. Kajo might say something, though, in his pompous way, the next time he saw Richard. Richard wouldn't mind about that.

Maybe someone would report back to the Snake on how he'd disgraced the whole department with his rudeness. She could call him to her office, or tell him off at the next departmental meeting. But who was she to complain? She was the rudest person he (or anyone else in the English Department) had ever met, and that's how his colleagues would see it, deep down, even as they smirked or made fun of him over it.

So, who cared?

What Richard *wasn't* expecting was the reaction that he found next morning on a familiar-looking postcard in his mailbox.

> What a stupid cunt! Even I knew it is "grey," not "cold." But you showed the arrogant bastard! When you told him, I wanted to fuck you right there, in front of everyone. I was soaking wet. Well done, my hero!
>
> S.

God, *she* had been there! Now he regretted not having checked out the students who'd been sitting behind him. But surely she wasn't a Philosophy student? Had he missed someone?

Who had definitely been there?

There was that Brazilian postgrad, who apparently couldn't speak German properly, let alone English. That couldn't be her, could it?

There were a couple of doddery pensioners, who paid a semester fee and were allowed to sit in on classes and lectures (this little scheme was known as "Senior Studies").

There was Eddie's friend Mike, who lived in a commune and who'd been repeating the same Philosophy Department classes for more than ten years. No-one knew whether he was still registered as a student. He was high most of the time.

There was a Spartacist Rottweiler who was vaguely familiar to him and who had no doubt come to crush the effete guest lecturer with some ruthless Marxist logic. She had probably thought better of it when she realized that she was on her own (there had been a demo out of town that day, and the comrades were still on their way back, or had gone to one of that night's parties). She might also have noticed that her target was pretty good at spouting Hegel and Feuerbach, and could probably do Marx and Engels equally well. So she had glowered at the Professor, but she had sensibly kept her mouth shut.

And who else had he seen? He couldn't remember.

Had someone slipped in quietly after the lecture had begun, and stood at the back (because there were no seats there)?

Hell, he should have paid more attention, instead of trying to be such a hopeless clever dick!

BREAKFAST AT THE
SÜDSTÄDTER RING 27

Eddie was still feeling miffed, but over breakfast Richard was surprisingly apologetic about the Flossengamme business.

No, he hadn't thought of suggesting Eddie as an additional member of the group, because he didn't know how they would be organizing things with the transport, or how many people could be fitted into the car (or cars). It was wrong of him, though, he admitted that. Everyone knew how interested Eddie was in the Third Reich.

But he and Richard could go together in the summer semester break (at Whitsun), couldn't they? The weather was usually much nicer then than it was in February.

In any case, he wasn't looking forward to it all that much, he said. Apart from the (probably) dismal weather, he'd have to listen to endless explanations and mini-lectures on concentration camps from Lisa Meyer—who despite her charms didn't exactly strike him as being a person of *intellect*. No dazzling insights into Nazi Germany could be expected from that quarter! And, to crown it all, Lisa had intimated that Harlan Kurz would likely also be taking part in the excursion.

Eddie almost choked on his toast.

"Kurz? No shit!"

They'd be stuck in a car with him for hours, Richard said, with slight exaggeration (Flossengamme wasn't terribly far away), and his self-opinionated whining would be unbearable. On that score, Eddie agreed with him completely. If the loathsome, preening Kurz was going, Eddie wanted nothing to do with it. Even a day in the company of the lovely Ulrike Sandmann would be no compensation for that ordeal.

What idiot had decided to invite *him*?

"Lisa said that he's always banging on about the Nazis in his classes, but that he obviously knows sod all about them." Richard paused. "Look, you see what they're doing, don't you? They're trying to educate their profs! Taking their revenge by lecturing *us*! And they crossed you off the list because they know you're already super well-informed about all that Nazi gumph!"

If Richard was trying to make him feel better about not being invited, he appreciated it, and—hell—Richard might even have a point. On Nazi Germany, Eddie did know his stuff.

He had ploughed his way through several fat biographies of Hitler, massive tomes like William Shirer's *Rise and Fall of the Third Reich*, and countless books about the SS, the Gestapo, Auschwitz, and related topics. Not to mention all those constant history programs about the Nazis on German TV, endlessly repeated. OK, so he'd never been to Flossengamme, shame on him, but he could probably hold his own on the subject with any of the history profs (he believed). Having him in the group would almost be like taking coals to Newcastle—the Germans, more quaintly, said "owls to Athens"—and maybe young Miss Meyer simply didn't want to be upstaged by someone more knowledgeable about the Nazis than she was?

So he'd willingly give it a miss. No, it was not a case of the fox and the grapes. If Harlan Kurz was taking part in it, the expedition would be a disaster right from the start. Richard would see!

And Richard could expect little joy from the ladies. He seemed not to like Lisa; Ulrike Sandmann probably wouldn't give him the time of day; and as for Steffi... Richard might be intrigued by her (for reasons Eddie didn't understand), but there were alarming rumors among the students that she's had a brief fling with Kurz.

Could *that* be the explanation for inviting him?

Personally, Eddie was not inclined to believe the rumors (and had no wish to), but you never knew, did you? Everybody made mistakes.

She wasn't Richard's type, though. There'd be no chemistry there.

"But you said you had something important to tell me!" Richard's voice cut sharply through his musings. "So: go ahead!"

Which was how their breakfast chat had actually begun—with Richard complaining how Eddie had let him down by not showing up to hear some stupid guest lecturer, and Eddie deflecting the criticism by saying how busy he had been helping him with *his*, Richard's, investigation, and how he might (incidentally) have made a spectacular breakthrough.

He began by explaining to Richard that he thought that Lisa Meyer was an object of special interest to the man they were tracking. It was only a theory, though.

But he had more than that to offer. As promised, he had been taking a closer look at their male colleagues. Eddie only had a few teaching hours, so he had time to check on what they did after some of their classes, what time they went home, and so on. He'd been *tailing* them, like a proper private investigator.

He'd also enlisted the help of Dermot, a friend of his from Murphy's Bar. Dermot was a happy-go-lucky young Irishman, currently "between jobs" (his way of putting it), who had plenty of time on his hands. Nobody really knew why he was in Reichsstadt, but until he earned some money he wouldn't be leaving. He was full of charm—he was even better at cadging drinks than Eddie was—and well-endowed with the gift of the gab...

"But he's a complete and utter layabout!" Richard broke in. Dermot had visited the Südstädter Ring early on in Eddie's period of residence. He had made a lot of noise monkeying about childishly with Eddie, and they had ignored several heavy hints that it might be time for him to go, as Richard had an early start the next day. Richard had not been impressed, and he had indicated to Eddie that he'd prefer not to have any further visits by Dermot if possible. But it wasn't just that. "Who said you could tell other people about what we're doing? This whole business is supposed to be confidential!"

Eddie quickly reassured him that Dermot knew nothing. He'd explained to him that one of his colleagues was badmouthing him in the college—he wasn't sure which one yet—and that he was collecting dirt to use on the bastard when the right moment came.

It was a very tall story, but Dermot had fallen for it. He was delighted to help—"Anything for a mate!"—in return for the odd tankard or two of liquid refreshment. Also, he was dating one of their students, Rita—

Richard: "What? Not Useless Rita, surely? He's spongeing off *her*? As if the poor girl didn't have enough problems!"

Eddie: "Indeed, the very same girl. The Rita who has set a record by failing all her exams so far, including the oral test twice, and who is therefore hoping for some *Kulanz* from Uncle Eddie next time."

Kulanz was an interesting word that referred to someone being "obliging" or "accommodating"; in practice, what it meant was: finding some leeway, some wiggle room, turning a blind eye, giving a poor girl a break.

"So you have Dermot over a barrel, so to speak?"

"A barrel of Murphy's best stout? Yes, or of *Reichsstädter Spezial*, if that is your preferred tipple!"

It was agreed that Dermot could continue to assist in the investigation, provided that Eddie made sure that he remained in the dark about what the investigation was really about, and that he was kept away from the Südstädter Ring whenever Richard was at home.

"But what have you found out? If you've got some dirt on Snoad or Kurz, let's hear it! Some entertaining smut, perhaps? Even if it has nothing to do with night-time visits to hostels. Tell!"

No, Eddie had to disappoint him there.

Snoad had a new girlfriend, a lawyer this time. They could be seen sitting around a lot in cafés, sipping lattes and frappés, and "trying to look sophisticated" (Dermot had said).

"She's quite tasty, he says. A redhead." She was older than him (the usual story with Snoad) and seemed to have expensive tastes. She was a power dresser, and went in for pant suits with wide shoulders. "A successful career woman (or so she wants people to think)."

"So dear Jonathan is busy with her?"

"I bet he's spending a lot of money on her, so he's probably looking for new part-time jobs on the side."

Snoad was notorious for spending more time on little "money-earners" than on his university work.

"And Kurz?"

Eddie had a sensational piece of news about him. He had been seen visiting motorbike salesrooms and looking at... guess what?

"I have no idea."

"Harley-Davidsons!"

Richard was astounded.

"No! Really? Come on, Harlan Kurz as Easy Rider? I don't believe it!"

"More like Easy Pillock than Easy Rider. But he hasn't bought one yet."

"They'll have to rename them Harlan-Davidsons!"

This was genuinely weird, but it was weird behavior that went in quite a different direction to what the hostel intruder was doing.

Enno Müller was easy. He didn't do *anything* except teach, and work on his diss. He had lots of meetings with students, but only to talk about his research. There were thousands of students (well, quite a lot), most of them girls, working for him as ancillaries, evaluating questionnaires, collating results, creating tables of statistics.

"But there's never any hanky-panky. We've never heard a whisper of scandal about him. He works late, and then he goes home to his wife and the baby. What a life!"

"For him? Or for them?"

"But you can cross him off your list, Sherlock."

At which point Richard gave him a very funny look.

"Look, just because I did Conan Doyle for my MA doesn't make me Sherlock Holmes."

"Oh, I think you're doing a pretty good job, maestro." He paused, to make sure Richard wasn't offended. "Anyway, to get back to Enno, he's much too small to be the intruder, even in murky lighting conditions!"

So whom did that leave?

The Snake, masked and in drag, breaking into hostel rooms and assaulting innocent girl students in a lesbian frenzy? She was big, and probably quite strong. She was a nasty piece of work—there was broad agreement on that—but somehow it seemed a bit far-fetched. Such things happened in horror films, but not in real life.

"If we're going to rule *her* out," Eddie said, "we must certainly rule out *Frau* Schlichting, who's much smaller than she is. And she's nasty in a different way: snide, spiteful, but that's all."

"Agreed. She could sneer for Germany, and she'd probably win a medal, too, but more than that? I don't think so."

"Which just leaves Dr. Dong—"

"No it doesn't."

It also left Kajo.

"Kajo Christenkorn? No way!" Richard simply refused to believe it. "That guy is kind, and helpful, and conscientious. He was the only person who was nice to me when I started here (until you came along, of course). He wouldn't say 'boo' to a goose."

And yet Kajo had been behaving very strangely, as Dermot had reported to Eddie. He had (in Dermot's opinion) a "secret life," with sneaky comings and goings. He would rush off after his classes, leaving the college but not going home until very late.

How could Dermot be so sure?

Because on two occasions he'd rung the Christenkorn home, pretending to be a student or a colleague, and asked politely to speak to "Professor Christenkorn, please," only to be told by *Frau* Christenkorn that her husband was still at the university: "He's always working late, these days, he must be so busy, the poor dear."

Richard: "She said 'the poor dear'? I don't believe it!"

But according to Dermot she had.

So where was Kajo if he wasn't at home and he wasn't in the college?

First, and most suspiciously, Kajo was seen visiting the New Hostel.

("New" was just part of the name—both the New Hostel and the neighboring Old Hostel were dilapidated in comparison with the *Ernst-Egon-Gutknecht-Haus*, which wasn't exactly a model of modern luxury either. And all of them compared badly with the smart, genuinely new hostel built for the engineering students, out in the wilds, a few years ago.)

Dermot had lost him each time, so he couldn't be sure which student's room he had gone too, but he'd posted himself in the foyer of the hostel, the only entrance/exit (as had been intended by its designers in those earlier times of single-sex student accommodation and stricter supervision), and he had stayed for as long as he honestly could.

Second, Kajo was seen entering a downtown hotel and, again, staying there for longer than Dermot was able to keep up the surveillance.

"Well," Richard suggested, "he's probably writing a book with someone, and he doesn't want the university to know about it. A secret, nerdy hobby that he hides from everyone, you know, like collecting cheese labels. Or he's learning the violin, and he dosen't want people to hear him practising. Or he's in an activist group—they often meet in hotels."

"Yes, but this is not the Reichsstadt Sheraton or the Marriott that we're talking about. It's the Kronprinz Johann Hotel."

"So what? And?"

"The Kronprinz Johann is a sleazy downtown hotel which rents out rooms *by the hour*. And doesn't ask embarrassing questions." Eddie gave

Richard a moment to digest this information. "You know what that means?"

"No?"

But surely he did. No-one could be that naïve.

"It means that your friend Kajo is cheating on his wife. And probably with someone else's. Or that he's entertaining prostitutes."

"Kajo? No! I can't believe that."

"I'm going to start making a list of things that you can't or won't believe that I happen to know are true!"

Richard's first reaction had been spontaneous, and silly, Eddie thought. But what he said next wasn't silly at all.

Even if it were true, wasn't it Kajo's right to do what he wanted, provided he wasn't directly harming anyone? Wasn't it solely Kajo's business—and nothing to do with them? What was Eddie suggesting: that they should burst in and take flash photographs of Kajo coupling on the bed with, whoever?

"No. I just think we need to rule him out so that we can move on. That means finding out what he's up to."

"But even if he's shagging prostitutes, or Professor Graeber's wife—or Professor Graeber!—what's that behavior got to do with our investigation?"

Eddie agreed with him, 95 per cent. But:

"There is the question of why he's flitting in and out of the New Hostel. And that behavior *does* have something to do with the investigation."

They reached a compromise. The next time that Kajo went to the Kronprinz Johann, or (less likely) he was in the New Hostel (and Dermot knew which room he was in), Dermot would ring them, and one of them at least would rush over to the Kronprinz Johann (or the Hostel) and stay there until Kajo (and his mystery friend, if there was one) came out of the room.

"Very well, if we must. But we shouldn't be seen. We're just trying to shut down one lead in our investigation. And, seriously now, Eddie, you don't really believe that Kajo is the hostel attacker? I would credit you with more intelligence than that!"

Eddie thought that that was a rather hurtful thing to say, and said as much. There he was, busting a gut to help Richard, and he'd unearthed the only real suspect that they'd found so far. OK, not a *real* suspect, but suspicious behavior that did need to be explained.

He'd also followed up on Jeannine Garbe and Felicitas Förster, he pointed out.

And what had Richard been doing in the meantime? Not a great deal. Lisa Meyer had come to him, before Eddie could talk to her (she would have been next on his list), but she hadn't revealed very much. In fact, she had clammed up completely on the only topic that mattered. Sherlock hadn't handled that very well, had he? And was she likely to open up in Flossengamme, with Harlan Kurz (among others) listening in?

Richard had had *one* homework assignment. They'd agreed that he'd talk to the good-looking postgrad, Miriam Burkhardt. Not an arduous task, that! And had he? Er, no—he hadn't.

Richard took the criticism surprisingly well. He would try to get his homework done. He'd do his very best.

Miriam Burkhardt. They wouldn't need to remind him again.

AN UNHAPPY MARRIAGE

I hated my marriage. I hated being trapped in it, with her. Or did I hate *her*?

Had I chosen her because she reminded me of my mother?

The shouting and the violence. Do this! Don't do that! Don't be so clumsy! Eat with your *right*, you little bastard, how many times do I have to tell you? The left is Satan's hand. The hand you wipe your bum with.

But afterwards, the loving, the embrace. She would open up her arms and take me in, enfolding me. Most women wouldn't, I knew that. My mother had told me, "You haven't got a chance, you nasty freak. Don't raise your hopes. Who would want to marry *you*?"

She had married me, though. She had chosen me just as much as I had chosen her.

I had energy, and ambition—because of my childhood. She liked that. And she liked the sex: the hammering and devouring that left both of us with bruises on our thighs and blood smeared onto our clothes from the scratches on our backs. I gave her all the pain and the anger that I had bottled up for years, and which I properly owed my mother, except that my mother had always held me back, and now my mother was gone.

Eventually there came a time when she began to hold me back, too. Was this when she started to enjoy success, and to feel superior to me, and began to find me an embarrassment? Or perhaps it was when my lovemaking finally became too brutal for her?

Very well. I went in search of other outlets, and I had no trouble finding them: there were places you could go to, contacts that could be made, hungry, amenable women who *wanted* what I had to give. The world is full of sick, crazy women. But even then she couldn't stop interfering with what I was doing, the bitch, holding me back, and spoiling it for me.

There were a few wonderful moments when I got what I wanted, almost in full—and afterwards there was always big trouble. I would come back to her like a whipped dog, and she would make sure that there were no consequences for me. (Because such consequences would be bad for her too.) So far, she had kept me out of danger.

I had certain needs. I had urges.

Weren't most of the great men of history driven in a way that the little people aren't? It was a price that you paid for greatness. No, I hadn't fulfilled myself yet—as she constantly reminded me, comparing what she had achieved so far with the little that I had. But I would, I really would. It was coiled inside me, waiting for release. What she sneeringly called my *Ausrutscher*, my "slip-ups," were a natural and unavoidable part of the great plan. Why couldn't she understand that? She was actively holding me back, preventing me from achieving my destiny.

I ought to destroy her, crushing and flattening her as I had once, when we were younger, driven her into the mattress, pounding her like a steamhammer. Then nothing would be left of her! I would pulverize that arrogant, sneering face. She still had one terrible weapon: her voice. But I would obliterate it by ripping out her throat.

I had warm fantasies of blood and squelching guts, of trampling on her splattered brains, of cutting at her body. That went too far, I knew that, but, once I started, would I be able to slam on the brakes?

How many times had I been one step, just one second away from that explosion. It wouldn't happen, though. My balled fist would unclench itself. The tautness in my body would suddenly be gone. The red mist of anger that was clouding my mind would evaporate. I would always come to heel. There, there, good boy! My mother had laid the groundwork for that only too well.

It always came down to mothers, didn't it?

WEED

Richard had made promises, but getting hold of Miriam Burkhardt was easier said than done.

He wasn't sure which classes she attended—none of his, for sure—and he had no wish to do too much lurking about outside seminar rooms where she might be listening to the Snake expounding on "New Developments in English Didactics" or Kajo holding forth on motivation. She was a postgraduate, but he didn't know what her speciality was. Her postgrad thesis could be on linguistics, or literature, or educational theory, or almost anything else.

Even so, he had tried a couple of times to see if she was in postgraduate seminars that seemed to be likely classes for her to be attending, but without any success, and each time the lecturer had spotted him and asked (in their different ways) whether they could be of help.

Well, Kajo had asked, politely.

The Snake on the other hand had glowered at Richard and demanded, "To what do we owe this honor, Mr. Orwell?" Before he could reply, she added, "If you're trying to fill some of those enormous gaps in your knowledge of English Didactics, well, bravo! Good for you—it's never too late! But I do suggest that you then *take part* in the lessons, rather than just skulking about outside."

Alternatively, he could have tried to obtain Miriam Burkhardt's email address. What would he write, though? And he couldn't email her out of the blue. He needed an excuse for wanting to talk to her, something connected with her thesis, perhaps? If only he knew what her topic was! He couldn't just ask her straight out about (what was it again?) her being molested in her room late at night by a stranger, could he?

Or he could have left a note in her mailbox at the hostel. But, same problem: what would he write?

And he'd been so busy, not only with preparing his own exams—he'd also been roped in to help with exams in the French Department, because that awful Plouvier woman had gone down with some bug. What a surprise, that there was a life-form (albeit a very small one) that wasn't terrified of the *Grande Madame*! And what immaculate timing for her to throw a sickie.

A lucky chance now came to Richard's rescue. On his way to *Frau* Ludewig's office, to stock up on his supply of stationery, he found the room packed with students. Some were queueing for the return of mid-semester tests that they had done for Harlan Kurz (he was too lazy to return these himself, and usually dumped that job on the secretary), others were waiting for application forms for this or that. And some were asking where *Frau* Schlichting's class was: it wasn't in the usual seminar room, so where was it then?

Richard was in no great hurry, and he parked himself democratically at the back of the line, where he could spend a few pleasant moments appraising the girl's bums (those who were wearing tight pants or jeans). Then he heard *Frau* Ludewig say "Miriam," and he looked up.

"Miriam Burkhardt?" he asked, as, a few moments later, the girl *Frau* Ludewig had spoken to tried to step past him.

"Yes?"

But "girl" was a long way off the mark. Miriam Burkhardt was all woman, and perhaps six or eight years older than the girls surrounding her. She was definitely the "type" that the intruder liked: tall, handsome, with long, blonde hair. She was rangy and bony, pale-skinned, and with small, high breasts, a Scandinavian woman, a no-nonsense Viking. Her makeup was heavier and more sophisticated than the casual slap favored by most students.

It was now or never.

Richard introduced himself.

How nice to meet him! But, no, she had never been to any of his classes. So how could she be of assistance? A faint smile played on her lips. Richard was very aware of the other students, hovering, listening in to their conversation. *Frau* Ludewig probably was too. He would have to take a risk.

A senior colleague of his had suggested that he might be able to help her with her thesis in some small way? (If pushed, he would say it was Kajo. Kajo was often forgetful, and if he did query it Richard could always say that he'd definitely mentioned Miriam to him in passing, and that Kajo must simply have forgotten.)

"My thesis? Oh, you mean, my PhD dissertation? I finished my MA in the summer." (Damn, Eddie had only mentioned a BA. So much for *his* sleuthing skills!) "So you're into Habermas too? Fantastic! Pleased to meet you! So few people really *get* Habermas."

Whoa! Richard was *not* into Habermas. He'd heard somewhere along the line that the eminent German social philosopher had once given the postmodernists a thrashing ("Good for him!"), but otherwise he found the man nigh on impenetrable. Let the likes of Professor Graeber do battle with him. And what did Habermas have to do with *English*?

"Er, well, no, not exactly. Habermas is not one of my direct areas of expertise. I think my colleague meant more... the *formal* stuff, you know, and things like work organization and time management."

If she had then pointed out that, to her own best knowledge (and everyone else's), Richard hadn't even started a doctorate of his own—so who was *he* to be doling out advice?—if she had even dropped a hint in that direction, he would have died on the spot. It was bad enough that she sighed and said, "Of course," which the students who were listening would interpret as meaning "Dear oh me, this is the most feeble chat-up line I've ever heard!" Which it would have been—if that had been its intention.

She glanced at her watch.

"Sorry, must dash now, Richard (you don't mind me calling you Richard, do you?), I've now got two office-hours to get to, and I have to pack tonight: I'm off early tomorrow morning to check up on the old folks! But you can look by for a chat at the hostel if you like. I'm in Gutie, you know? I'd love that. Feel free. Any time after eight."

And she was gone.

Richard didn't actually hear any "tut-tuts," but they seemed to be quivering in the air around him. Suppressing an urge to whimper, he beat a fast retreat. *Frau* Ludewig might or might not gossip about it, but the students were absolutely bound to.

Who would ever have thought? The uptight Mr. Orwell chatting up a postgrad (and you wouldn't believe how *pathetic* he was). Well, well, well. What a total loser that guy was!

Nevertheless, at a quarter past eight that evening Richard found his way to the *Ernst-Egon-Gutknecht-Haus*.

It wasn't a place of particularly happy memories for him. Once or twice, really excruciating committee meetings had been held there, on busy days when the normal meeting rooms had been overbooked and alternative venues were needed. He'd never been inside a student's room, though (heaven forbid!). His only "adventure" with a student (Sonia) had been facilitated by her having a small flat of her own.

Sonia had been a lot older and more mature than most of her fellow-students—not unlike Miriam Burkhardt?—and it was she who had made the running. Yet if she'd lived in a hostel it would probably never have happened, since Richard wouldn't have dared to go there and risk being seen, and he didn't like taking girls back to the Südstädter Ring.

The evening started badly (and would get worse).

As he advanced nervously into the foyer, Richard was spotted, and first by Milo! Milo was wearing his all-black, "Gothic" outfit—the sinister look. He gave Richard what could best be described as a combined wink and leer.

"Na, boss, you on the prowl again? The night is young, eh?"

Richard didn't deign to respond.

A childish voice piped, "Hi, Mr. Orwell!" It was Shirin, the Iranian girl.

And then another girl brushed clumsily past him. She turned back, not to apologize but to grin at him. Who was she?

"Hi Richard, you are OK for our trip, right? Flossengamme?"

Could this be the famous Steffi Albertz, who would apparently be driving them? It wasn't Ulrike Sandmann, but he didn't know who else, apart from them, Lisa Meyer and Harlan Kurz, would be in the group. How big was Steffi's car? Or would they have two cars, or a minibus?

If it *was* Steffi, she was rather plain, he thought, and not the way he imagined "S" ought to look, despite the cheeky grin. He felt rather disappointed.

Where was the main notice-board? And where was this bloody girl's room?

His last visit to Gutie had been during the winter semester Freshers' Week, back in October, and it had not been a notable highlight of his year. As a favor to Kajo (whose wife's birthday it was), he had agreed to stand in for him at a "get-together" for new students at the hostel. The event was jointly hosted by the Catholic Student Community and the Federation of Evangelical-Lutheran Students, in a feeble display of ecumenical goodwill.

There were so many new English students that someone from the English Department really ought to be there, Kajo had said, and no-one else had volunteered. What he *didn't* say, of course, was that it would be totally deadly. There were student parties that night, so (as Eddie reminded him) no totty worth mentioning would be attending, despite the free drinks. There wouldn't be anyone there that you'd want to get together *with*.

The "get-together" was to be held in the Large Community Room. The whole hostel was a hymn to concrete and plastic. Whoever had designed it had been in a position to spend a lot of money to produce something down-right ugly.

The Large Community Room was a rectangle. One of the two long sides (the side without any windows) was dominated by a decorative installation of multicolored, floating blobs. Were these supposed to make you think of clouds? Or maybe they were intended to represent thoughts or ideas, as in a comic-strip, but without any text? To Richard, they looked like what would happen if a dozy giant drank sips from different buckets of colored liquid plastic and then spat them out, spraying gobbets of the stuff onto a wall. Modern art!

Eddie had been right. The Christian Union types were much in evidence, plus a few unhappy-looking younger lecturers who (like Richard) had been roped in for Freshers' Week duty. In obvious charge of the event was a horsey-looking woman clutching a large rubber ball.

Horsey lady made everyone form a big circle, and then explained that they'd be passing the ball from person to person. Whoever was given the ball must introduce themselves. It was a well-known technique used in therapy and AA groups, she said. (Drunks and loonies, Richard thought.) She kicked off by holding up the ball, like the kid with the conch in *Lord of the Flies*, and announcing: "*Ich bin die Moni.*" I'm the Moni [Monika?].

Richard shuddered—the twee and unnecessary use of the definite article, so popular among young people (and those trying to be ingratiatingly informal), always set his teeth on edge. "I'm a social worker with the Federation of Evangelical-Lutheran Students," she added. (That figured, he thought.) "And the mother of two sweet little girls."

There was a slight stir as the circle expanded to include a latecomer: the Snake, Richard's new boss! What the hell was she doing there? Had Kajo mentioned it to her too, and she'd just assumed that it was the sort of function she'd be expected to attend? She was new, so perhaps she wasn't sure of the rules yet.

Moni bounced the ball across the circle to a Christian Union type standing opposite her.

"*Ich bin die Agathe,*" the girl declared solemnly. It was hard to understand her. Did she have braces on her teeth?. "I'm a keen member of the Catholic Student Community!"

Ah! Another Bible-basher! Moni was getting things off to an ecumenical start.

Agathe dared to bounce the ball to a Fresher. (You could spot the handful of Freshers from the nervous, fidgety way they were standing. Were they already regretting not going to one of the parties instead?)

"Ich bin der Simon."

God, was he pimply, the poor guy! His whole face seemed to be eaten up by angry red blotches. And so it went on, until the ball reached the Snake, bouncing awkwardly in front of her. She lunged for it, missed, and then kicked it away angrily.

"OK. Enough of this. I'm Professor Dr. Leonore Reiss-Baumgart—and with no need for a definite article. I'm the Head of the English Department. If you need to speak to me, come to my office-hour. If you don't—don't. Whatever you prefer. And now I have better things to do, and in the company of adults. I wish you a pleasant evening."

She walked out. Had she glanced at Richard briefly when she made her contemptuous remark about adults?

To compound his misery, someone immediately threw the ball to, or rather *at*, Richard, and he heard himself saying, *"Ich bin der Richard..."*

That had been a disastrous evening, and this one had also started badly, with the embarrassing meetings with Milo, Shirin, and the over-friendly girl who might be Steffi Albertz. What was he doing? He shouldn't be here. It was asking for trouble in so many ways.

Did Richard's unsettled emotional state contribute to the calamity that was about to engulf him?

He found Miriam Burkhardt's room fairly easily, and without any further unwanted encounters. He rapped on the door. There was no answer.

He knocked again, and waited.

He was just about to walk away when the door opened and Miriam peered out. She was bleary-eyed, and looked as if she was about to go to bed. As she opened the door slightly wider, he saw that she was wearing a fluffy dressing-gown, over what looked like pyjamas, and fluffy slippers. And no make-up.

"Oh. God. It's you. I'd completely forgotten."

Which was obvious. She didn't sound very enthusiastic.

"Sorry. I'll come another time."

Something about that must have struck her as funny. She giggled,

"No. You're here, so you're here."

She reached out, grabbed his collar, and pulled him into the room, closing the door. She may have been looking disheveled, but the room was in utter chaos—and it stank of dope.

He was alone with a half-undressed girl who was one of his students.

They were four feet away from a rumpled, unmade bed. Somewhere in the room there were illegal drugs. A multitude of excellent reasons for him *not to be there* flashed through Richard's mind.

"Look. I think—"

She held up an admonitory finger.

"No! Don't think. We do too much thinking. You... just... sit." And she pushed him onto the bed. "Oh, sorry about the sheets, but you don't want to sit on my knickers, do you?" She indicated the chair, which was piled high with items of clothing. Beside the chair was a suitcase. She had probably been packing. "Or maybe you do?" she added, and giggled again.

"I'm sorry, I think there's been a misunderstanding."

"Rubbish! You Brits: always thinking, and saying 'sorry', and having misunderstandings. Just relax, man, just go with it. You wanted to see me, OK, you're here, you're seeing me. Now it's up to you, Mr. Orwell. Mr. O. *Story of O.* We all know what *that's* about, don't we?"

More giggles.

Richard tried to bring the situation under control.

"Actually, I'm here for a very good reason. Not to talk about your thesis—sorry, I mean your dissertation—and not about Habermas either. But about something much more serious."

"There's nothing more serious than Habermas."

"I'm afraid there is."

"Oh." She pouted, looking exaggeratedly disappointed. "Oh dear. And there I was believing that you wanted to chat me up! You weren't doing very well back there in the office, were you? A bit shy? I quite like that, though."

"We need to talk."

"Fine, we can talk. About anything you like. Even *serious* things. That's not very flattering, of course. You aren't gay, by any chance?"

"No!" Richard blurted out, too quickly—under the circumstances, it might have been wiser to say "yes."

"Good. Just a teeny-weeny bit shy. A bit *virginal*"—Richard wisely didn't respond to that—"and a guy who likes talking. Nothing wrong with that. You're a lecturer. That's what lecturers do. But you need to get relaxed, like me."

She stepped over to the little bedside-table and picked up a large cigarette—oh God, a joint!—and a lighter. She lit the joint, inhaled pleasurably, and offered it to Richard.

"No! Of course not!"

"Oh! Isn't my dope good enough for you? This is very nice shit. Don't say you've never smoked weed before? Well, no smoke, no talk. Your choice, mister."

Of course he had smoked before. He'd been a student, hadn't he? And at a progressive new university in a town with quite a "scene." But smoking dope as a student was one thing; doing it when you had a job to lose was another. In fact, he'd stopped going to most student parties after his first six months in Reichsstadt, because there'd usually be some pothead there lighting up, and he didn't want the students to gossip about him "doing drugs."

But maybe he needed to calm his nerves. Reluctantly, he took the joint from her and puffed at it.

"Just this once, then."

Wow! She was right, it was good shit.

"See! Not so bad after all. You don't believe in *kiffing* with students, do you? Quite right! I wholly approve. Where would we be if the profs were all turning on and shagging and getting drunk with their students? But then I'm not a student, I'm a postgrad, and that's different." She sat down on the bed beside him. "Now tell Auntie Miriam what this 'serious' thing is that you so much want to talk about."

He started to feel mellow, and calm, and—relaxed. Maybe she was right? He started to tell her about the hostel intruder, how that guy had molested several other girls, not just her, and how he was trying to piece together what it was all about. Why was he so interested? He told her about his MA on Conan Doyle. He didn't mention the President.

"Oh, Richard, there I was thinking that you'd fallen desperately in love with me! But it's not sex that you want to talk about, is it, it's violence!"

And they both laughed. That was the dope working.

"How could I have fallen in love with you? I'd never seen you before until you went to Ludie's office!" They laughed again. "You haven't been sending me love-letters, have you?"

It was surely worth a try. He didn't think she was "S," but anything was worth a try.

"Love-letters? No! Why should I? I'm a hardworking postgraduate with a diss to write. You think I've got time to write love-letters to strangers?" She paused. "Now don't tell me: some horny girl in one of your lectures has been sending you sexy notes!" She put on a funny voice: "'Dear Mr. O, I want to suck your big, knobbly dick!'" And again they laughed. It might be vulgar, but now it all just seemed funny. "Well, sorry to disappoint you. I'm not averse to sucking big, knobbly dicks, when the mood takes me, but I'm not your mystery girl!"

Richard made a great effort to get back to the topic.

"Look, did you see this man? Can you tell me what happened?"

"Oh, you're so impatient! Let's finish this little sweetie here, and then I'll *show* you what happened. Isn't that the way your friend Sherlock Holmes would go about it?"

He had to agree. Richard was now very pleasantly light-headed. He was *high*, but not so high that his brain couldn't work. Especially laterally!

They finished the joint. Miriam told him to get up, which he did, feeling decidedly woozy and unsteady. She herself got up, more athletically than he had done, and took off her dressing-gown.

"Er..."

"No, it's all in the interests of authenticity, Richard. You and I are going to *reconstruct* what happened. Please step over to the door, and perhaps it would be better to lock it? We don't want anyone to come in and get the wrong impression, do we now?"

"No, we certainly don't!" Which was true (whatever she had meant by it). He did what she had asked him to.

Next, to his surprise, she took off her pyjamas! But not the slippers. She was wearing only a tanga.

Oh! Richard goggled in disbelief. The fact that she kept her fluffy slippers on made her nakedness even more stark. Yes, a Viking, was all he could think. His head was spinning, but his throat was dry.

She got onto the bed and lay back, her legs apart.

"This is how I was sleeping that night. In this position. Now: you are the nasty man." She sniggered. "Though aren't all men nasty? You approach the bed, With Evil Intent." Richard took a cautious step forward. "No, more Intent, please! And try to look more Evil!"

Richard approached the bed—with unsure intent. Blowzy, disheveled, no makeup? But she was gorgeous.

"Like this?"

"And now you look at me. Take a good look! You look at my tits, my cunt. You're trying to decide what to do, you pervert. I'm asleep, I'm at your mercy! What would you choose to start with?"

Her breasts were small and flattened out, but she had a beautiful waist and a flat, smooth stomach. The thin strip of the tanga barely covered her sex, with tufts of pubic hair peeping out above and at the sides. Her legs were slim and graceful.

"I don't know."

"Well, let me help you then. What he did was take off my slip. So: take off my slip, Richard!"

She shouldn't have used his name. That spoiled the illusion.

"I'm not Richard, I'm—"

"Yes, yes, my mistake, you're not Richard, you're a dirty pervert who wants to smell my knickers and lick my cunt. So do it, Mr. Pervert!" When Richard didn't obey, she herself slipped the tanga down over her legs and the slippers, and threw it at him. "There, that's what you wanted, isn't it? Take it! Now, come closer!"

Richard found himself standing over her. A sudden twinge of dizziness made him lose his balance, and he toppled forward towards her, catching himself on the bed as he fell, his hands either side of her body. His head was now directly above her groin.

A hairy Viking girl. A warrior queen.

"You look very nice."

"I know I do." She grabbed his head with both hands and pulled him down onto her. "Now *eat*."

And he did. She was lovely and welcoming, hot and wet (and the wetness was not only from the actions of his lips and tongue, he was sure). One thing naturally led to another. This was no longer a scenario reconstructing a crime; this was simply an amazing fuck.

Or was it? Richard was so high that he wasn't sure how long they were at it, and he couldn't remember the details too clearly afterwards. He did remember how, at a particularly juicy moment, she had called out "Derrida!" and they had both burst out laughing.

Afterwards, they slept. Richard was obviously no longer the intruder. He was a delightfully exhausted lover, his body and mind both blown as they hadn't been for a very, very long time.

Later, she shook him awake, and offered him a mug of coffee.

"That was nice, Mr. Orwell, but I do have to get up early tomorrow. Correction, *today*. So drink up, and then I hope you can find your own way out without being seen by too many of your students."

He took the coffee.

"Thanks."

He had meant the coffee, but she misunderstood him.

"Don't thank me. I'm sorry that I couldn't help you much with your Sherlock Holmes investigation. I barely caught a glimpse of the man, and all I know is that he took my slip with him. I don't know whether he did anything else to me—as you did!"

"But aren't you frightened?"

"No. Should I be?" Richard decided not to tell her about the finger-cutting. "I'm a big girl. I don't frighten easily. Anyhow, *I* should be thanking *you*."

He liked the sound of that. Had he been *that* good?

"Oh, don't mention it."

Pride comes before a fall, and now everything came tumbling down.

"I shan't yet mention it yet—I'm not finished with my research."

"I beg your pardon?"

And she explained. To his mounting alarm, he learned that not only was she researching Habermas for her PhD; she had a second, more personal, project, which was to sleep her way around the university, department by department (lecturers only, and mostly the male ones, with a few ladies thrown in for variation). She was jotting down their foibles and predilections, and awarding grades. When she wrote it up, it would constitute an interesting alternative guide to the university, and be a modest contribution to research into Sexual Behavior. It would make for entertaining reading, too.

"I'm pretty well done with the social scientists. They were dead easy to get through. Not a moral qualm in sight! The psychologists were pretty good. They were recommending me to each other, really getting into the spirit of the thing. Mathematics is proving difficult: they don't seem to be interested in anything that isn't *abstract*. And English? I'd barely started, and then, happily, you came along."

Richard swallowed hard.

"But you had already started?"

"Yes, with your colleague Jonathan." He was horrified. "Oh, don't worry, no comparisons need to be made! In point of fact, I'd give you about the same grade: a slightly above average. He was more energetic, he had more stamina, though maybe the weed slowed you down? But he's a smug bastard—you seem to me like a nicer person, with a better sense of humor—so perhaps I'd score you just a fraction higher, if that makes you happy. By the way, who should I try next?" She paused, then looked at him quizzically. "Are you shocked?"

Richard was indignant: "Of course I am!"

"But why should you be? I'm only doing what lots of men do: screwing around, and keeping score. Or *not* screwing around, but still bullshitting about it—like your part-time colleague Eddie. I'm going to give little Eddie a miss. Likewise, that runty American, Harlan Something. Yuck! A girl has to have *some* standards. How about your German colleague Enno Müller? He's a statistics freak, isn't he? I'll have to give that one some thought. A bit too much like the mathematicians, I suspect. And I don't fancy the ladies in English very much. Maybe I should move on to History or Philosophy? There's apparently a Professor in History, a bit old, but—"

"I'd better go."

"Yes. I think so too. Don't bother to look by again—you were OK, but there's so much new material waiting out there to be tested that I can't offer seconds. The results will eventually go online, but, have no fear: anonymized. Pity I won't be able to call you 'Mr. O'. That would be our little joke."

"Online?!"

"Yes, but not open access. I have a private blog, members only. You can join it if you like. But now, if you'll excuse me..."

She showed Richard the door.

He had just destroyed himself: his job, his career, his reputation, not to mention his pride. Members only, she had said? Half the students in

Reichsstadt would be members, and how difficult would it be to identify the shy English lecturer Mr. X (not to be confused with the vain Mr. Y or the statistics-obsessed Mr. Z)?

Whether anyone saw him on the way out of the hostel didn't matter to him any more (actually, nobody did). All he wanted was to get home, urgently, and *sleep*.

EXAM TIME

Lisa and Steffi were on their way to the first (and last) of their end-of-term exams. "Their way" amounted to only a few hundred meters, from the hostel to the lecture theater in which they'd be making their first attempt to pass the written part of *Sprachkompetenz Französisch*. Nevertheless, it took in a substantial detour to the Real supermarket, where they had coffee and croissants at the little stand-up café—and talked.

They had an urgent need to talk.

As neither of them had the remotest chance of passing the exam, at least without an enormous effort—the *Grande Madame* took no prisoners—you might think that this would be a final desperate opportunity for them to talk about (and even *in*) French. But, no, they had even more urgent matters to discuss.

It was definitely on with Flossengamme. All systems were go. Steffi would be doing the driving, and she'd already persuaded a gormless engineering student (who had a hopeless crush on her) to give her car the once-over. No problems there!

It wasn't a huge distance to Flossengamme, even if it was in one of the shittiest bits of countryside that you'd ever seen. The Nazis had built several of their camps quite close to major cities (like Dachau, near Munich), but in places that were still way off the beaten track. It would be a comfortable drive for the four of them.

Why four?

Because, in the end, only the two lecturers had been invited. There was therefore no need to "de-" or "uninvite" anyone. A few of their fellow students (including Ulrike Sandmann) had been drawn casually into discussions about whether it wouldn't be a nice idea to show some of the foreign lecturers a few of the local sights during the holidays? However, any initial spark of interest was immediately extinguished for some by the mention of Flossengamme; in the case of Ulrike Sandmann, the mention of the names "Kurz" and "Orwell" had had the same effect.

But the desired overall result had been achieved: the student rumor mill was soon putting it about that Lisa Meyer and Steffi Albertz were organizing a "big excursion" to Flossengamme.

Steffi had the details all worked out. Military planning had been called for!

They'd pick up Richard Orwell first, because he lived nearby, on the Südstädter Ring; they'd meet him at the Real carpark. Steffi would ask him to sit in the front passenger seat and help her navigate.

She didn't have a sat nav, but she did have maps. He'd be much better with them than Lisa (she'd tell him), because Lisa couldn't read a map if her life depended on it. And, just between ourselves, Harlan Kurz was such a flippertigibbet, wasn't he? He'd only make her nervous while she was driving (which was *not* advisable!).

They'd pick up Harlan last of all, from his pad out in the Weststadt—which was logical, because he lived close to an *Autobahn* access point and they'd need to drive on the motorway for the first stretch of the journey. He'd have to sit in the back with Lisa. Everything would be just cozy!

And Steffi started to sing "Love is in the Air," to the surprise of a couple of plumbers, out on a circuit of repair jobs, who were standing at the next table and taking their first coffee-break of the morning.

Lisa was not so sure. She was beginning to get cold feet about the whole business.

Steffi looked very displeased.

"What's got into you, Princess? I thought Mister Jiggle-Bum was the object of your dreams? Have you suddenly gone off him? It's a bit late to be telling me that, don't you think?" She paused. "Or is there a new man in your life?"

Obviously there wasn't. Steffi would be the first to be told (and she'd probably find out beforehand anyway). No, Lisa was just wondering: "Is Harlan really what I'm looking for?," and she said so.

"Well, that depends on what it is you're looking for, doesn't it, my dear? I bet he's a great lay, provided you keep him off the drink. Oh, and just to make it absolutely clear," she added, "we *didn't*, you know, back in Freshers' Week. OK? The moment came, and it went. He's yours for the taking, if you still fancy him."

Lisa mulled it over.

"Yes, he has got an amazing bum."

"Turbo-charged, wanna bet?"

"And I reckon, when he gets going, that he's..."

Lisa didn't know how to finish the sentence. Steffi punched her playfully on the arm.

"You *see*. That my's girl. You can do dirty talk after all! There'll be no problem shifting Harlan into the right gear, I promise you that. Dear Mr.

Orwell may be slightly more of a challenge, though."

They left it there. The dreaded hour of the exam was fast approaching, and the trip to Flossengamme was still a good few days away.

The lecture theater was packed. It seemed that every second student in Reichsstadt had decided that now was the auspicious moment to go for French.

But where to sit? There weren't many seats still free, and they might not be able to sit together.

Sitting in the front row—where there *were* still some seats—was out of the question, because you'd be right under the nose of *La Plouvier*, who'd be invigilating most or all of the time. (After all, she was the one who'd set the wretched exam, and didn't she just love watching students suffer?)

The front row did have one advantage: you didn't have to watch too many people all scribbling away fluently and confidently, reminding you of how poor your own chances were. But in French that didn't apply, because there wouldn't be many confident scribblers in the room, and the number who failed would be enormous.

The *Grande Madame* was impervious to pressure to get her to grade more leniently. Her name was not Michael! Her views on the subject were well-known. The French language had to be respected. And it had to be mastered, with no ifs or buts, because the subsequent rewards were immense. Mastering French (if you were so unfortunate as not to have been born French) meant: gaining access to civilization! It was not a blah-blah subject like, well, to her mind, most other subjects. And it was not English. Surrounded as they all were by the guttural grunting that was German, why should anyone choose to learn yet another ugly, sloppy Germanic language, when French was also an option? French was a thing of beauty. And so in the French language competence examination, those who failed, failed.

Actually, a lot of her students, even as they cursed her, reluctantly agreed with her. If you wanted to do languages, you had to learn them. (Though English was something of a soft option.)

The back row was already completely full. This was because of the foolish (though widespread) perception that, if you were going to cheat, it was best to do it as far away from the examination proctors as you could get. Why was that foolish? Because any proctor worth his or her salt would move round the lecture theater, clockwise or anticlockwise, stopping now and again to peer disapprovingly at the students from a different angle. And they'd always hover a bit longer behind the back row, on the principle of "You can't see *me*, but I can see *you*!" Cheats in the back row were the easiest to catch, because you could come up behind them and you had an almost unimpeded view of what they were doing.

La Plouvier was particularly good at catching cheats, and when she did, your heart bled for them.

First of all, she would berate and humiliate them with well-chosen words, in a loud voice, and *in German*, so that every last student got the message.

She'd confiscate the student's exam paper, and send the miserable person packing. The exam would count as a "Fail," which was bad news if it was one of those tests where you were only allowed a limited number of attempts.

Finally, if you were really unlucky, the relevant examination board might be notified of your disgrace, which could lead to all sorts of nastiness.

No, if you wanted to cheat, you sat in the middle of the theater, where the proctors couldn't see you clearly and couldn't creep up behind you. Then you could cunningly arrange your cribs for maximum effectiveness, with notes tucked unobtrusively into your pencil-case or open on top of the bag at your feet. Some idiots even inked stuff on the back of their wrist (on the non-writing hand).

How could any of that be of help in a language exam, where you needed to demonstrate an advanced skill, and not just spout a few names or facts? There were really only two methods that could be recommended, and neither with a complete guarantee of success.

The first, for big-scale cheating, was the good old smartphone, with an internet connection to all kinds of useful websites about French irregular verbs or whatever it was you needed. Unfortunately, there was something about the way people *looked* when they were gawping at a cell phone (even one held under the desk) that proctors could spot a mile off.

The second, for cheating on one or two small items, was the short, unsupervised comfort break that everyone was allowed (two, even, though that was pushing your luck). Students were only permitted to leave the room singly, so that they couldn't confer outside, and the proctor was supposed to write down their names, with the times that they were gone. If you were out of the room for more than four or five minutes it was suspicious—bad luck if you had a tummy upset!

You needed to use those precious minutes, so you went online as quickly as you could.

Occasionally a boyfriend would be skulking outside, at a prearranged approximate time, with a bag of reference books.

Or you rang him at home with your beast of a question and hoped that he would be quick in finding the answer.

One or two brave souls had even been known to sprint across to the nearby library to check some essential fact, returning to the lecture theater sweaty-faced but smiling.

Best of all, back in the day, had been the stockpile of paperback dictionaries and other useful materials sequestered in the toilets. These would be placed out of sight on the window ledges in the cubicles at the beginning of each round of exams. No-one knew the identities of the noble-spirited people responsible for doing this, bless them, but it had been a good system. (The main snag was that the window ledges were quite high up, so that smaller students weren't able to reach them very easily, even when standing on the toilet seat.)

Those days were gone. A cache of science books in the Ladies' Toilet had been discovered, after someone forgot to put a physics handbook back where it had originally been. A systematic search was carried out by the *Grande Madame*, revealing a small library of essential texts obviously not left there to help the constipated. A search of the Gents' by a male colleague brought to light a similar collection of academic materials, plus, in one alcove, a pile of hardcore gay magazines.

Since then, there had been regular searches of the toilets at examination time.

Lisa and Steffi found themselves seats not too far apart and near the front of the room.

Lisa spread out what she needed on the desk: her pencil-case, somewhat grungy and ink-stained, but she'd had it for years; a bottle of carbonated water; two bananas (brain-food); some chocolate (for comfort); her little soft-toy mascot, a smiling tiger (for luck); a couple of paracetamol tablets (in case she got a headache); a packet of paper hankies; and her watch. She was ready. Let the Frenchies do their worst!

She knew that she wasn't going to pass. Fortunately this was one of those exams that (in her degree program) you could go on taking until you finally cracked it. The record was held by some guy who'd passed at the seventh attempt—and had then celebrated by giving up the university altogether. No-one knew what happened to him after that, but he was still a hero.

The room was full. Where was *La Plouvier*, with the exam papers?

Milo had told her once that, if they were in England, in situations like this the students would disrespectfully start singing "Why are we waiting? Wh-eey are we waiting?"

But they weren't in England, they were in Germany, and everyone waited patiently.

The door opened, and in came not *La Plouvier* but her young colleague (and gofer) Jean-Luc, carrying a huge pile of papers, accompanied by Richard Orwell (why him?), carrying a similar pile. Behind them sauntered: Harlan! Unimpeded by exam scripts.

What was going on?

Jean-Luc began babbling away in French, then sensibly switched to German. (Probably out of consideration for his Anglo colleagues, who were not likely to be any good at French.)

His dear colleague *Madame* Plouvier was indisposed. He had therefore been asked to take charge of the exam, and he would be assisted by two kind colleagues from the English Department.

A few cheers went up. Cheating was back on the menu! *Any* proctors would be easier to fool than the *Grande Madame* was.

What was wrong with Plouvier? She was *never* sick. You had to be human to catch human infections. Maybe she had Mad Cow Disease?

Lisa wasn't planning to cheat. She knew she was going to fail, but she wanted to see what the exam was like, and what she'd need to do to pass at some future date. Perhaps she could go to France for the summer; her dad would pay.

Now she had a rare opportunity to compare Harlan Kurz and Richard Orwell, before they all went off to Flossengamme together. Strangely enough, she'd never seen them standing side by side.

Orwell wasn't bad-looking, but he was sort of... *dull*. He stood quite still, and had a serious expression on his face that didn't change much. In fact, he looked rather depressed—even more gloomy than he usually did—and a bit what the British called "under the weather" (Lisa was proud that she'd remembered that idiom). His movements were slow. She noticed that he was wearing the stupid gray pullover that her mum had darned and patched so expertly. He had been friendly enough, in a distant way, when they'd talked during the pullover business. But he wasn't the kind of guy that you'd meet and think "Wow, I have to get into *his* pants!"

Standing beside him, Harlan couldn't keep still. He kept fidgeting about, this way and then that, grinning at students, smirking at Jean-Luc, and ignoring his British colleague.

God, if they disliked each other so much Flossengamme was going to be awful! But she had a lot of faith in Steffi. That girl had so much experience with men, she'd know what to do.

And Harlan Kurz was the right choice, she finally decided. OK, he wasn't the man she was going to marry. Her mother would have a fit if she brought him home for Sunday lunch (and Mrs. Meyer had an annoying habit of usually being right about most matters in the long run). But he was a live wire, and he'd be a laugh, she told herself. After all, she wasn't going to have his babies, was she?

There was no-one else on the horizon, at least not as far as reasonable-looking guys were concerned. With regard to men, she knew that she had some catching up to do, but her present options were very limited.

Micha had continued to ignore her, until she'd finally given up going to badminton.

Sebastian still leered at her. Ugh!

Milo obviously fancied her, but he was badly screwed up (though she wasn't sure exactly *how*). She wouldn't want to be alone with him. Anywhere. Ever.

Rico was rather sweet, but he was gay.

Why were there so few decent men around?

Steffi seemed to have fewer problems finding men, though she wasn't fantastic-looking.

One thing about her friend puzzled Lisa. Why was Steffi so interested in Richard Orwell? Did she see something in him that Lisa had completely missed?

I COULD HAVE SCREAMED

As we now know (but Lisa couldn't), Richard had a good reason for feeling depressed. Despite what sundry great minds of the past had to say on the subject, Richard was seldom a victim of post-coital sadness. In fact, he often felt quite pleased with himself. It was the usually laborious business of *getting-there*, not the deed itself, that occasionally made him unhappy.

He would have liked to have had more carnal activity in his life, perhaps on a routine basis. Monika had been so convenient. He had laughed out loud the first time he heard the rude German poem that began "*Nach dem Essen soll man rauchen / Oder eine Frau gebrauchen,*" loosely: "After mealtimes you should smoke / Or a friendly female poke," and he felt a lot of sympathy with the sentiment it expressed. (The poem continued, more clumsily: "No smoke or bird available? / Then drill a hole and fuck the wall.")

The trouble was that establishing such a routine would probably involve him having to install a long-term girlfriend, someone nice—and *that*, Sonia and Monika notwithstanding, was something that he regarded as a move into dangerous emotional *terra incognita*.

But on this occasion, still crushed by the enormous black cloud that had descended on him the night before (and which a very short night of fitful sleep had failed to disperse), Richard as he left the lecture theater might even have welcomed being swallowed up by that proverbial hole-in-the-ground. At least (be thankful for small mercies!) he wasn't carrying that most depressing object of all: a huge pile of unmarked student scripts.

The *Grande Madame* being out of action, the dismal duty of having to correct and grade the rubbish that he had just helped to proctor would probably fall to poor old Jean-Luc. Por sod! The French *Sprachkompetenz* exams were reputedly even more dreadful than the English ones. But Richard had plenty of exam scripts of his own to deal with. Stil, a partial rescue was at hand. His mood was considerably improved by what he found in his mailbox: another letter from "S."

She had, it would seem, been there at the last-but-one session of his British Studies course, a double-period in which he had encouraged some of the students to give short presentations. This was obviously not a normal procedure in a lecture, but he was always looking for ways to make his classes more interactive, beyond the usual, and seldom rewarding, closing few minutes ushered in by "Does anyone have any questions?" and generally followed by silence.

He had meant well, but "S." had not been pleased. She had written:

My darling Richard,

No!!! I could have screamed, but the cry of panic stuck in my throat. PRESENTATIONS? It took a moment for me to realise the extent of this catastrophe. I had forgotten it, I had completely repressed the thought, but now the bare facts lay before me like a death sentence. I had been looking forward to it for days: seeing you again and being able to hear your voice. I sat closer to the front in the lecture, but it didn't help. I had to listen to the croaky voice of some nervous fellow-student, instead of yours. I was grateful for every one of her mistakes, because you would then correct her! At these moments, seeing and hearing you, my heart beat faster. If only she had made MORE mistakes!

To make things worse, I was sitting on the wrong side of the lecture theatre. To listen to her stupid presentation, you had sat down on the steps on the other side. How I envied the girls sitting there, near to you! They had no idea how happy they should count themselves, or how much I would have given to be able to change places with them. And because I was sitting on the other side, I couldn't look at you without twisting my head back awkwardly—and I couldn't risk that, because you would have noticed that a student was gazing at YOU and not at the front. I could only watch you a little out of the corner of my eye. You laid [sic] back on the steps like a pasha, like a king in his kingdom: relaxed, challenging, dignified, majestic. If only I had been beside you! Like a woman of your harem, one of the many. Yes! You would only need to say my name once. Today you called out the names of several girls. Oh, how I regret not offering to do one of the presentations, when I had the chance. Then you would have called out MY name too.

But how could I have volunteered to do even the shortest, the easiest of the presentations? It would have been pointless. Knowing that you were looking at me, I wouldn't have been able to produce a single proper sentence, let alone one in English.

During the second presentation you sat right at the back of the room! You can't imagine how I cheered every single mistake that the student made, because you had to correct him, and then I could turn round and look at you directly without you noticing it, because at that moment everyone else was doing the same.

Then you dimmed the lights. Really, I don't need the lights on, I know your face so well that I see you before me every time I shut my eyes, and when I open them again you're still there. And yet: every time I actually see you I realise once again how SURREAL the image is that I have of you. Not even in moments of the most painful longing can I see you before me as you really are. There are limits set to my imagination. A face like yours—so beautiful, radiant, perfect, manly, full of energy—is more than my mind can grasp, let alone reproduce. I dream of your face over and over again, your smile, your laugh, yet I see that the reality is a thousand times better. You are simply UNDESCRIBABLY attractive.

For that reason I was in second heaven, even though it was dark. I watched you the whole time, listened to you, smiling, laughed at your jokes. And everything in me was tingling. The famous butterflies in your tummy. But that wasn't all. A bittersweet yearning flooded through my limbs. Oh, if only I could give myself to you! I would have done anything for you! Anything with you! ANYTHING! Anywhere and as often as you wanted! I wouldn't have denied you anything! Nothing! And that moment when you sat on the steps, so sexy-casual, I flipped. I imagined you, in that pose, on my bed, relaxed, a gentle smile on your lips. You were there on my bed, and I started stripping you...

I wake up.

The lights are back on.

The whole room is laughing.

My eyes turn to you, but you're not sitting at the back any more. You're standing there on the steps on the left-hand side once again. A discussion has started. That's great, I mentally encourage the student standing at the blackboard, yes, go on talking to the man of my dreams, so that he goes on talking too, so that I can enjoy his voice for a few more happy minutes!

But then it's over. The lecture theatre empties, and I have to go to, because staying here still sitting down would be too obvious. I go very slowly. I don't want to go! Every step takes me further away from you, but still I climb those steps at the back. At the top, I turn round one last time. You're talking to someone.

Now the time of waiting begins, the waiting for the next class with you. And as I leave the room, three questions are battering at my brain:

1) How will I survive until I see you again?

2) Did you look at me directly, or was I imagining it?

3) What was the lesson all about? All right, next time I'll pay more attention, I promise, word of honour!

S.

THE SNATCHERS

When Richard got back from his exam supervision, Eddie was waiting for him.

"We need to talk."

Holmes and Watson were getting nowhere. None of the main "suspects" were truly suspicious.

Richard had made it clear that he strongly believed (and hoped) that Kajo's "secret life" would turn out to be harmless.

Neither of them were convinced that the guy they were hunting was a student. The male students all seemed so *wet*.

Milo was the only student who couldn't be ruled out completely—for the moment.

On the other hand, no-one suspicious had been seen leaving the hostel, so didn't that mean that it was an "inside job," by either a student, or some-one brought in by a student and staying overnight?

"Maybe some guy came in during the day," Eddie suggested, "and hid in an empty room until it was late, and then slipped out. And afterwards he hid in the same room."

"Empty rooms in the hostels?" Richard queried. "Do you really think that's likely?"

"Well, it would be easy to find out."

Actually, it wouldn't. The organization that ran the hostels wasn't particularly cooperative with the university authorities, and Richard and Eddie were hardly "authorities" of any recognizable kind.

So: since they hadn't had much success by asking "who?," perhaps the question of "how" might lead somewhere.

Could the intruder have got in some other way, through a ground-floor window for example? All the incidents had happened in the autumn or early winter. Would the students have left their windows open during the night, even on tilt? The weather had been mild, but probably they wouldn't have. The wardens always told the students not to do that, because of break-ins. Lots of the girls were quite paranoid about this, and in one of the hostels the rooms on the ground floor were only assigned to boys.

"Is there any other way in? Do the hostels have cellars that you can access from the street?"

Südstädter Ring 27 had a cellar like that. You could access the cellar from inside the house using your apartment key, or you could climb down some steps at the back of the house and and come in through an outside door, using your house key.

No, Eddie said, the hostels weren't built like that. But...

"Yes?"

"It's just an idea. You know that the hostels and the university buildings are all kind of in a row, sort of sitting there on Gallows Hill?"

"Yes. And?"

"Well, they built them during the Cold War, and everyone says they built a big nuclear shelter under the university."

"What?"

"Yeah, you know you've got the basement floor with the language lab, the porters' room, and the storerooms, right? And under *that* is a cellar, right? No-one goes there much, apparently. They say that it's very big, because that's where the nuclear shelter is, but most of it is locked up. Now, what if the shelter was *really* big and extended all the way across to the hostels? Perhaps they keep it locked up, because there's a secret government control center down there, for use in a nuclear war. You know, with bedrooms and kitchens and water and electricity and everything."

Eddie realized that he was getting carried away slightly.

"You read too many trashy novels, mate! In a moment we'll be on to aliens, or secret US-government experiments. Or (since you're such an H.P. Lovecraft fan) you'll soon be telling me that there are monstrous-tentacled 'Great Old Ones' of Cthulhu lurking in a pit beneath Gallows Hill!"

Which Eddie then did (almost).

"Well, there are: the Snatchers!"

"I beg your pardon? The *what*?"

"The Snatchers. You know, *die Greifer*. Come on, how long have you lived in Reichsstadt? And you've never heard of them?" He sighed. "OK." He'd have to bring him up to speed.

Eddie fetched his laptop and showed Richard an online article (in German) about the "Myths and Legends of Reichsstadt." Most of these dated back to the seventeenth century, if not to the Middle Ages. They were bogeymen tales to frighten children with.

There was the witch-like Finger Lady, who lived in the local river, the Ebbe, and would catch children foolish enough to dip their toes in the water. Entangled in her slimy fingers, they would be dragged to their deaths.

There was the Grunter, that would spring out in front of you on certain lonely tracks through the forest. He would ask you a question, and if you couldn't answer it correctly he would chew off one of your limbs. Then he would ask a second question...

There were the little green Forest Folk, who stole newborn babies.

There was the Wind Goblin, who came on stormy nights and would prowl round the outside of the house, wailing dismally and noisily trying the windows and doors. Sometimes he would succeed in breaking into a byre or barn, and next morning you would find dead livestock there, horribly mutilated.

There was the Ogre of Gallows Hill, who could be seen during thunderstorms, squatting like a immense troll on top of the hill. Only children and virgins could see him, and he didn't cause any immediate harm, but any sighting of the Ogre was a reliable forewarning of some terrible disaster about to happen.

And there were the Snatchers. Few people who actually saw them ever lived to tell the tale, but many had heard their shrieking voices, or smelt them, or seen their shadows. They were vile, cruel, dirty creatures that lived in the caves alongside the river Ebbe at the base of Gallows Hill.

Belief in the myths and legends had been eroded after the Enlightenment and had not survived into the modern era of telegraph lines, steamships and railways. Except for the Snatchers. There were elderly people in Reichsstadt today (so the article) who claimed to have encountered them, and local children were still frightened of them (especially around the time of Hallow'een).

"Fascinating," Richard said. "But so what?"

"They lived in caves under Gallows Hill. Under the university! Under the hostels!"

Richard seemed to find this hilarious.

"Ah, so you're saying that these creepy monsters have been sneaking up out of the abyss to sniff at our girls' knickers? That's not very ambitious of them, is it? But it doesn't work: some of the girls caught a glimpse of the intruders, and they looked like ordinary human beings. Normal size. No tentacles. Also, the girls are still alive. Besides, how would these Snatcher-thingies get into the hostel?"

Eddie was disappointed.

"Yah, you're not following me, are you? I'm not saying the Snatchers are still there. I'm saying that *something* lived under the hill for ages, and there's probably a whole load of tunnels and caves down there and maybe they connect up with the cellars. So our guy could get in from the riverbank, and out again the same way, and no-one would see him."

Richard was completely unimpressed, but presumably to keep Eddie happy he said, "I'll go and talk to *Herr* Geisler about the cellars. Who knows, maybe he'll give me a grand tour? But I tell you: you're clutching at straws."

Herr Geisler was the Head Porter, and also the housekeeper of the university, with his own small apartment in the grounds.

Eddie shook his head. "He won't show you the cellars. They're all shit-scared of what's down there. You'll see."

"No way! Do *you* believe this stuff?"

Eddie pointed at the laptop.

"Here—this article's on the website of the Antiquarian Society of Reichsstadt. I used to go to their meetings sometimes. Look, they've got one coming up at the Town Hall. Tomorrow." He read: "The President of the Society, *Herr* Dipl.-Ing. Hans-Peter Dietrich, will be giving a lecture on 'Reichsstadt in the Seventeenth Century'. Wow, why not, let's go!"

"Oh, come on! A sodding history lecture? It's end of term: exam time, remember? The days are getting longer. The *working* days! I've already had one free evening hijacked by a bloody lecture: Professor Dr. Dr. Piesacker, and a right bundle of laughs *he* was. Where were *you* that evening, by the way? I don't think you ever told me."

Eddie ignored that last question.

"He's OK, is *Herr* Dietrich. And if you can at least *pretend* to be interested we can ask him to tell us more about the Snatchers. Over a beer, of course." He added, "I'm paying."

"Well, that'll be a first!"

How unfair that was!

THE ANTIQUARIAN SOCIETY
OF REICHSSTADT

And so it came about that the following evening Richard and Eddie, Sherlock Holmes with markedly less enthusiasm for their undertaking than Dr. Watson, took the bus into town.

They walked through the pedestrian area and across the Market Square to the Town Hall. This was a large Baroque building that had been flattened by British bombs in 1945 and rebuilt in the 1950s. The exterior was pompously imposing (which had indeed been the intention when the building was originally constructed); the interiors, however, were disappointingly shabby.

That surprised Richard somewhat, as their main purpose was clearly representational. There were Chambers of this and Halls of that, even a small municipal museum, but hardly any offices. Most of the municipal offices, including those that Richard, as a resident of Reichsstadt, had occasionally been obliged to visit, were located in an ugly concrete block two streets away.

The venue for the meeting was announced on a board in the main foyer, but Eddie knew the way.

"It's always on the first floor, in the Small Meeting Chamber."

Richard marveled at the numerous paintings lining the corridors.

Pride of place was given to a certain Hans von Barby (circa 1670), resplendent in full plate armor (though he had apparently been a judge, and a lay leader of the local church).

Next to him, though several generations earlier, was the merchant Traugott Wippel, looking very pleased with himself in a black, fur-lined ensemble.

Then there was the first postwar Lord Mayor, Ernst Egon Gutknecht, who had presided over the rebuilding of the shattered city (as was suggested by the discreet cityscape of Reichsstadt in the background of the picture), making himself a fortune in the process (he was a building contractor)

There was a whole batch of majestically-bearded nineteenth-century worthies, including at least one local writer, presumably Gottfried von der Linde, the renowned "Bard of the Ebbe," whose tedious "folk ballads" were the bane of elementary schoolchildren.

Less impressively, the Lord Mayors after Gutknecht stared out from large black-and-white photos.

There were several severe-looking Protestant clericals, but noticeably not a single Catholic Prince-Bishop or cathedral functionary.

You could be forgiven for assuming (as Richard did) that the picture-lined walls told the story of Reichsstadt. Far from it—the paintings were not arranged in any obviously systematic way or in chronological order, they were simply a mishmash of portraits of interesting characters, most but not all of whom had had some connection to the city.

Many of them were not even figures of *minor* historical significance. One self-important local dignitary, for example, had had himself painted at great personal expense, along with "great ones" of earlier generations, and then left the resulting artwork to Reichsstadt in his will.

Some of the pictures had been acquired when the city purchased the house and studio of a recently deceased portrait painter.

Not all well-known local figures were represented in the collection. Apart from the Prince-Bishops, the most notable absence was that of Konrad the Black, a crusader, donor of numerous reliquaries to local churches, mercenary thug, and serial rapist, to whom a well-known quotation was attributed: "The Lord's mercy is boundless; *this* lord's mercy is not" (which sounded better in German). To Konrad was attributed the only still remaining city gateway of Reichsstadt, the Tower of Tears, so named because of the countless local women and girls that he had abused there.

Also missing (for obvious reasons) was the huge oil painting of Friedel Grützmann, the Nazi *Gauleiter* of Reichsstadt, a man whose character was if anything even less appealing than Konrad's, which had once hung in a prominent position in the main foyer.

With malicious glee, Eddie told him that the painting, in a "heroic-classical" style, had been bought by a gay sauna club in Berlin, but Richard (while wishing it were true) didn't believe him.

When they reached the Small Meeting Chamber they found it packed, so that Richard wondered why they hadn't chosen the *Large* Meeting Chamber, if there was such a room. He noted with dismay that it was a mostly male, mostly elderly audience. The men were starchily dressed, and sat stiffly, showing no interest in their neighbors, as if completely intent on the "entertainment" to come. So this was how the wrinklies of Reichsstadt spent their evenings!

A few of them had brought their wives along (under duress?), and these ladies—not one of them much under sixty—sat equally stiffly, but with heads rotating as they surveyed the room in search of something or someone to disapprove of. All those eyes now focused on Richard and Eddie, who had arrived at just the right moment.

There were no young women to be seen, but half-a-dozen younger men were busying themselves with various activities, such as passing round information sheets and attendance lists, or setting up a microphone for the speaker (why did he need a mike in a room of this size, and with such a docile audience?).

Among the young men was Monika's new boyfriend Hans-Robert.

Richard and Eddie found themselves a couple of seats at the back. If they believed that no-one would notice them there, they were mistaken. There was a moment of considerable embarrassment when the lecturer, after making a few general announcements in his capacity as President of the Society, welcomed the "new faces" (everyone swiveled round to look at *them*) and expressed the hope that this "young blood" would soon be considering applying for membership.

Hans-Peter Dietrich, retired engineer, proved to be a hearty, no-nonsense speaker. The microphone was indeed wholly superfluous, and his jovial bellowing so loud that it occasionally seemed more like an address to a Nuremberg Rally than a lecture. The wrinklies didn't seem to mind (or had they switched off their hearing-aids?). The speaker used an over-freighted PowerPoint Presentation that contained most of his text as well.

He said a few words about the development of Reichsstadt in the Middle Ages. The name of the city was peculiar, in that it was strictly speaking a so-called "Free City" rather than an "Imperial City" proper. Despite the decibel level, Richard found himself nodding off as *Herr* Dietrich tried to unravel the complexities of Reichsstadt's civic status.

In the great religious civil war of the seventeenth century, the notorious

Thirty Years War, Reichsstadt's central location and unclear allegiance to either side had made it distinctly vulnerable. The old legal principle of *Cuius regio, eius religio* (that the religion of the ruler should be the religion of his people) had been hard to apply.

As an Imperial Free City, Reichsstadt still had certain feudal duties, admittedly of a very vague nature, owed to the conveniently distant (Catholic) Emperor, though (in the opinion of its burghers) none at all owed to the hated (Catholic) Prince-Bishop of Reichsstadt. (The Prince-Bishop saw that very differently.) The reason for this was that, while the surrounding villages and country districts remained predominantly Catholic, the City Fathers had since the Reformation become overwhelmingly Lutheran, if not actually Calvinist, and now chose to put themselves under the protection of the local (Protestant) Prince, adding their considerable financial clout to his substantial military resources.

When war broke out, Reichsstadt was therefore occupied and plundered by both sides, as marauding Protestant and Catholic armies rampaged backwards and forwards across the land. The very word "marauder" supposedly entered the language, from French, as a joking pun on the name of a particularly undisciplined commander, Merode.

Reichsstadt, however, was never "totaled" like the unfortunate city of Magdeburg, an event that gave rise to the verb "to magdeburgize" (ah, the lecturer declared, how the language was being enriched as the country was being despoiled!). And why was this? It was because the Catholic general would at the very least try to restrain his troops from pillaging in the area around the Catholic cathedral of Reichsstadt and the palace of the Prince-Bishop, while the Protestant general, when his turn came, would do his best to ensure that the streets near the Market Square and the Town Hall, including the guildhalls of the various crafts and trades and the offices of the merchants, were similarly protected.

In any case, after several rounds of looting there was nothing much left to steal.

The final "sack of Reichsstadt," by a mercenary army theoretically on the Catholic side, came to an abrupt and ludicrous end when the Imperial pikemen, unable to enter and search the little houses because of their long weapons, which were the tools of their trade and which they were unwilling to put aside and risk losing, turned resentfully on their brothers-in arms the Imperial musketeers (who could carry *their* weapons with them into the houses, and therefore generally secured the lion's share of the loot). An internal riot ensued, to end which the commanding general was obliged to withdraw his troops from the city altogether (though only after payment of an appropriate "sweetener" by the City Council).

After the lecture, Eddie introduced Richard to the speaker. Did *Herr*

Dietrich have a few moments to spare? Yes, he did, though he would eventually have to rejoin his fellow-members in the Ratskeller (the famous Bierkeller beneath the Town Hall). *Herr* Orwell (OR-vell) and *Herr* Hodgkins (HOJ-kints), potential new members as they were (!), were naturally very welcome to come too.

Richard got straight to the point: the Snatchers.

"Ah," and *Herr* Dietrich suddenly had a twinkle in his eye, "*that* old tale! You're asking me whether I'm a Believer or an Unbeliever? Personally, I prefer to see the matter in its historical context."

All the old myths and legends of Reichsstadt, he explained, were inventions of the Middle Ages, when most of the population lived at subsidence level, and were regularly exposed to threats that they couldn't understand or control: epidemics and fluctuating harvests, storms, floods and famines, wild beasts and human madness. With the limited intellectual resources at their disposal, people tended to come up with rather naïve explanations for these phenomena.

A drowned child had therefore been *taken* by malignant forces.

A vicious wild boar, protecting its young from a noisy intruder, became the Grunter.

Wolves or foxes became the Wind Goblin.

"And the Snatchers?"

"It's no coincidence that they were believed to live in the caves under Gallows Hill. As its name suggests, it was a place of execution, and it already had an evil reputation, because of the nature of the work that was done there. The executioners stored their gear in the caves. Sometimes prisoners would be held there, and maybe tortured to extort money from them, or for revenge, or raped if they had once been pretty. When the executions were not in season, it was a good place for criminals, vagrants or deserters to hide. Consequently there would often be sightings of evil-looking creatures along the riverbank. Innocent people would occasionally be attacked or even murdered there. But by the time that armed men went to search the caves, with torches and clanking weapons, they were empty of course."

Eddie: "But that was hundreds of years ago!"

To which Richard added that belief in the Snatchers had apparently survived into modern times.

"Yes," *Herr* Dietrich agreed, "and for that too there are possible explanations. You know: highwaymen in the eighteenth century? Fugitive convicts? And there was an interesting development at the end of the Second World War. When Reichsstadt was bombed, early in 1945, some people briefly took refuge in the caves. They may not have stayed there long, but they set an example. A few months later, as civil order in the city collapsed, hundreds of slave-laborers—mostly Poles and Belgians—escaped from their barracks and fled to the caves. They were joined by dozens of Nazis and their families, who were terrified of what the advancing Soviets would do to them. You remember what the Red Army did to the villagers in East Prussia?"

"Murdered them?"

"Umm, well, a bit more than that. There were naked women crucified to barn doors. Dozens of dead children. And the rapes in Nemmersdorf: women from eight to 84."

"Wasn't that just Nazi propaganda?"

"Not entirely, it seems. When the Red Army briefly withdrew, for tactical reasons, Dr. Goebbels sent in camera teams. They made the most out of it, of course! He wanted to make sure that the population in the Fatherland knew what was coming to them, if they didn't stand and fight. What matters is that in Reichsstadt they sincerely believed, at the time, that the Reds would get there before the Amis or the Brits—it was indeed close—and that the Russians would be merciless."

Richard wasn't too familiar with local history, and he found one detail puzzling.

"Wouldn't the slave-laborers have turned on the Nazis, and taken revenge on them?"

"In a logical world, yes. But these people had all been traumatized, by bombing, by hunger and fear. Perhaps they even hugged each other for comfort and warmth. Most of those who went into the caves came out again." He paused. "Maybe some of them *didn't*."

"What?"

Herr Dietrich shrugged.

"Now I must play *Advocatus diaboli*. You are familiar with that expression, *Herr* Orwell? It is the same in English: 'the advocate of the devil.' Because, you know, I am not one of the Believers! But they have a crazy theory, which goes like this: a few of those sad refugees, perhaps only some of the abandoned children, who were frightened almost to death, mentally disturbed even, stayed in the caves. They became wild. Feral. At night they hunted along the riverbank. They killed stray dogs, They stole livestock. They turned *cannibal*. Somehow they bred, and their children bred. And *their* children. They became accustomed to the darkness, and their eyesight adjusted itself. Perhaps they lost the power of speech."

"This is complete nonsense." Richard found the whole story ridiculous. "They've stolen it from a horror movie!" He paused, but there was no response from *Herr* Dietrich. "Come on, it has to be nonsense?"

"Probably. Yes. I am an engineer, *Herr* Orwell. I prefer the simple, practical explanations. Like you British, we engineers are all for the famous 'common sense'!"

"Thank you! Ockham's Razor, Eddie, remember?"

"But I have to say that the cave complex may be big enough... Ten years ago a team of speleologists was hired by the City Council to explore the caves. They came out after only three or four hours, and said that it was too dangerous. There were too many *human* adaptations to the natural caves, and it was like a crumbly honeycomb. The surfaces were treacherous, and unstable. Speleologists do *caves*, they said, not man-made death-traps."

"And so they just gave up?"

"Between you and me, *Herr* Orwell, I think they wanted to be given more *time*, and promised more *money*, and so they exaggerated the dangers, but the City Council said no. Yet the stories they told have discouraged explorers ever since. Some of our younger members are now forming a team to investigate the caves, but more as a kind of *observation project*, you know, like with your famous Loch Ness Monster?"

Richard grinned.

"Ah, yes, and the first person to get a clear photo wins a million dollars?"

Herr Dietrich smiled wanly.

"No, in this case there is no prize-money. Where do you get that idea from?"

Eddie, who had been untypically quiet for a while, butted in.

"But there could be! If you had photos, you could sell them for a lot of cash. There are magazines—"

"But photos of *what*, young man? Some tramps using the caves as a shelter? Because that is all that this amounts to, I'm sure. Nothing more than that."

"Sorry: but why now? Has something happened? Is there some new reason for observing the caves?"

The President of the Society sighed dramatically.

"Whenever things are quiet, young men go stirring up trouble. Yes, there have been rumors. Actually, there have *always* been rumors. There is something deeply unpleasant about those caves. Now people are claiming that there have been sightings again. In particular, since last summer—"

"Like in the hostels—"

Eddie got no further. Richard had trodden on his foot with as much weight as he dared to apply without telegraphing it too obviously to *Herr* Dietrich. *Herr* Dietrich noticed, nevertheless.

"The hostels? I don't understand. We are talking about the caves beside the river. The university hostels are all on the *other* side of Gallows Hill."

Eddie tried to repair the damage.

"Sorry, boss, I was getting my geography confused. Go ahead, just ignore me!" Then, as an afterthought: "Perhaps I could go along on one of these expeditions?"

Richard hadn't expected that. And *Herr* Dietrich gave no sign that he approved of the suggestion. Or of Eddie.

"The Society welcomes new members, *Herr* Hodgkins, but we are not an adventure club! And now I believe I really should be going down to the Ratskeller to join the others. *Herr* Orwell?"

"Oh, I don't know..."

"Come, come, a single beer will hardly kill you! And the pickled pork in cucumber aspic is excellent. Served with remoulade sauce, and roast potatoes! And they have apple strudel. Can I not tempt you?" He added, with slightly less enthusiasm: "You too, of course, *Herr* Hodgkins. And if your heart is really so set on this foolishness, either of you, *na ja*... But I have nothing to do with these hare-brained activities. You must speak to *Herr* Eberle about it. Hans-Robert Eberle. He is the main organizer. Unofficially, we call them the Young Antiquarians. Eberle is a *very* keen young man."

"Yes," Richard put in quickly. "I've already met him. Very keen, indeed. Eddie, why don't you go and get acquainted with Hans-Robert?"

Eddie gave him a quizzical look.

"You think I should? It does sound like fun."

"Oh, most definitely. This is so much more up your street than mine, Eddie. You know, Lovecraft and Atlantis? And only one of us needs to go."

Richard didn't tell him why he was so determined that the person interacting with Hans-Robert Eberle should be Eddie rather than him.

PART FOUR: THINGS THAT GO BUMP IN THE NIGHT

HERR GEISLER

If Eddie was going to start getting involved with the Reichsstadt Anti-quarians (if only to allow Richard to steer well clear of Monika's new beau, Hans-Robert), then the least that Richard could do would be to investigate the notorious caves from the other, less dramatic, side, by talking to someone who ought to be knowledgeable: *Herr* Geisler.

He went looking for the *Hausmeister* and, for the first time ever, found *Herr* Geisler almost immediately. That would normally have been quite an achievement—the Head Porter was a busy man, with heavy responsibilities. He was almost invariably "out on a job" when you needed him, and when you called him on his cell-phone all you'd get would be a few seconds of squeaking and crackling noises, and fragments of bad-tempered muttering, before *Herr* G. ended the call. But Richard had not simply been lucky in choosing just the right moment to catch him; on this occasion he had *known* where the *Hausmeister* would be—in the porters' room on the basement level, presiding over a porters' team meeting—because he had had a tip-off.

The tip-off had come from one of *Herr* Geisler's team of porters, Fred (pronounced by Germans as a short "Frayed"). Fred had helped him when Richard had moved into the office that he shared with Kajo Christenkorn. He had needed a new desk, and Fred had found one for him. Richard had pointed out that the window didn't close properly (this had apparently never bothered Kajo) and Fred had promised to get it repaired. Richard had thanked him, not expecting much, and he'd disappeared—only to return fifteen minutes later, with his toolbox, to carry out the repair.

Perhaps Richard's amazement was a reflection of experiences that he'd had with university porters in Britain, where even getting a light-bulb replaced could turn into an undertaking on the scale of the Normandy Landings, but he was so grateful that he'd cracked open a bottle of *Schnapps* that he'd bought at Real that same morning and offered Fred a shot. And they had gone on to have a couple more.

Drinking on duty was sternly forbidden, as was emphasized in regular email circulars from the President, but—sod him!—it was still general practice. Plenty of lecturers had a bottle of something in their desk for a quiet mid-afternoon tipple; *Frau* Professor Jordan in Protestant Theology was so frightened to face her students that she was incapable of lecturing without being half-sodden; and there were departmental meetings in certain institutes that almost always culminated in toasts being offered, in *Sekt*, to celebrate the arrival of a new colleague, the publication of a new book, or the successful completion of a doctorate.

After this excellent start, Richard and Fred had remained on friendly terms. They would greet each other in the corridor, and if Fred's soccer team Werder Bremen had lost that weekend (as happened more often than not) Richard would commiserate with him.

Richard had asked him when he might be able to catch *Herr* Geisler "in a good mood" for a five-minute chat, and Fred had told him. This was valuable information, since the Head Porter wasn't widely known for doing good moods. He was an unpleasant individual, and generally bad-tempered. It was said that he was only passing on the kickings that he got from his bitch of a wife.

Students hated it if they had to go and see him about something, because he'd bite their heads off. He was careful with Professors, but he'd snap bad-temperedly at any junior faculty who approached him, perhaps out of fear that they were trying to inveigle him into some kind of unscheduled work. Anyway, who were they to order him around? He had a technical diploma—that was how he'd got the Head Porter job in the first place—so they weren't any better than he was, were they?

"An unpleasant individual." Was it fair of Richard to pre-judge him like this? Yes, it probably was. He knew of nobody in the university who had a good word to say for the man

Yet when Richard spoke to *Herr* Geisler, he was friendly enough, by his own low standards—at least initially. The "good mood" was easily enough explained by the empty beer-bottles and full ashtrays on the table in the porters' room. So much for Presidential circulars!

They stood in the doorway to talk. Behind them, *Herr* Geisler's team had brought out the playing cards and, ignoring the bottles and other rubbish, were settling down to a quick game of *Skat*.

It was nothing important, Richard said, just a silly personal thing of his. He'd joined the Antiquarian Society of Reichsstadt ("Huh, *that* lot!"), and they'd been discussing the university, and Richard thought it might be an idea to talk to the person who was the greatest expert on the university buildings: the man who was in charge of them!

"You think so, do you? Well, all these buildings are modern, so why should the Antiquarian Society be so interested?"

"Yes, that's true, but, you know, Gallows Hill and all that? The university has levels that go right down into the hill, don't they?"

"What do you mean by 'right down'? There's the basement, where we are now, and there are the cellars."

The cellars: there was a lot of mystery about them, wasn't there?

Herr Geisler looked puzzled. Was there? Not in his book there wasn't. They were just cellars.

"I mean, for example, how *big* they are. Don't they extend all the way under the hostels as well?"

Perhaps they do, *Herr* Geisler conceded, and perhaps they don't. But the only part that they ever used was right next door—he pointed to a locked steel door next to the entrance to the porters' room—and it housed the older part of the university archive. Once every couple of months one of his lads would go down to fetch a file at the request of someone in the administration.

"That's the only door that we use, and we don't go far. Through there, down some stairs, and then just as far as the archive."

"But in theory, if you wanted to you could access the hostels through the cellars?"

Herr Geisler laughed.

"Have you been drinking, young lad? What a crazy question! Maybe you could. Maybe you couldn't. It might not *all* be locked up. But who would want to go down there?"

"Well, why not? Aren't you curious?"

"Why should I be? Do you really want to know what's down there? Rats, for a start. And no ventilation. The air's not good. No proper lighting any more. Builders' gear lying around for you to fall over. Stairwells and shafts to fall down. Fall down one of them, and no-one would ever find you—would your cell-phone work down there? No map of the layout that I know of. The damp. The smell. Isn't that enough for you, young man?"

"Stairwells and shafts? So there *would* be access to the level below the cellar? To the catacombs, even?"

Herr Geisler started. "You must be joking!"

"Have you checked?"

"I've never gone down that far."

"Why not?"

"Stupid question. I've just told you why not. You could have a serious accident. Are you tired of life?"

"Do you believe in the Snatchers too?"

"The Snatchers? No, of course not! But it is creepy down there. Dark and slimy."

"How do you know?"

"One of my boys said so. He went down a couple of times. A bit further. He said it scared him, and he was a big, crazy bloke."

"Bigger than me?"

"Probably. He had to stoop to go through the cellar door."

"Does he still work here?"

"No, there was a funny business, and they asked him to leave. That was years ago."

Herr Geisler looked at his watch. He was no longer giving Richard his full attention.

"A funny business?"

"Yeah, he drank too much and he was too friendly with students. *Girl* students, if you get my meaning? Usual nonsense. Someone complained. It was nothing much, he left before it got awkward. We don't talk about it. Anyway, why do you need to know? As I said, years ago." He added. "I keep my boys on the straight and narrow, but there's always a bad apple. A beer now and then, fair enough, I can let that pass. But funny business with students? We needed to nip that in the bud."

"What was his name?"

"Volker."

"Volker what?"

"Look, I think that's enough for today. You've wasted enough of my time, young man, and now, if you'll excuse me, we have some clearing up to do. It was pleasant meeting you. Next time you want a chat, tell me well in advance and I'll arrange to be out when you come knocking!"

And with that he pushed past Richard back into the porters's room and shut the door behind him, rudely, and in Richard's face.

Richard gave him a couple of seconds and then punched the air in delight. A suspect at last! Someone who had been in the catacombs, someone who might still have access to keys, someone who had had "funny business" with students (even if it had been years ago). Yes!

All he still needed was the man's full name, and he got that an hour later through a chance meeting with Fred at the *Mensa*.

The man's name was Volker Cordes.

"He left before I got here, but I did see him once. He came in for a drink with some of the lads when the boss was away. He was a big bloke. Bigger than you or me. Bigger than Geisler, too. Not too bright though."

Herr Geisler was very powerfully built, which made him even more of an object of terror to the students.

"Why did he leave?"

"I dunno. Maybe the boss didn't like him." He looked at Richard earnestly. "The boss said you were asking about the cellar. And the catacombs. None of us ever go down there. It smells horrible, and it's full of rats. That's what I've heard."

"He said he sometimes asks people to fetch files from the archive. Have you ever done that?"

"No! None of us wanted to go. *He*'s the only one who goes down there now and again."

Oh, that's interesting, Richard thought. And it didn't fit with what Geisler had told him. Perhaps it was even interesting enough to make *Herr* Geisler a suspect too?

"Just one other thing: is this Volker character left-handed?"

Fred laughed.

"What, you mean, like me? Or Rudi Götze? Or Geisler? I dunno. I don't think so. It would be funny, that would, like, you know, if half the porters were left-handed!"

There was no way he could see Fred as a suspect, but—Geisler was a big man. And he was left-handed (Richard had noticed that when he'd looked at his watch). And he knew his way round the cellars...

Geisler? Hell, why not?

Forget Kajo, this was more progress in a couple of hours than they'd made in months! He needed to tell Eddie.

There was still Volker Cordes. They ought to try and find him, if only to rule him out. The man had once been employed by the university, so there should be a file on him somewhere in the administration. But he could hardly ask the Personnel Department to show it to him. It would have to be done sneakily.

Hoping that the President would be away he went up to the *Präsidium* to ask *Frau* Henkel for her help, but his luck was out. Before he could do more than say hello to her, the Fat Man spotted him and beckoned him imperiously into the inner sanctum.

Surely Richard had not been avoiding him? Had he been neglecting the task he had been given? The President was not amused, and no-one should be fooled by his amiable exterior (what amiable exterior? Richard thought). He was directly descended from Manfred von Glöwing—the ruthless "Manfred of Eppingen," whose mass flayings and impalings of rebels during the Great Peasants' War made the Reichsstadt bad boy "Konrad the Black" look like Mother Teresa.

Richard would have to give him something, fast.

Yes, he had a suspect. No (he added coyly), he wasn't quite ready to reveal the man's identity yet. (How would the *Präsi* react to being told that the suspect was his own Head Porter?)

The Fat Man gave no sign of being satisfied with the morsel he had just been fed, but Richard was rescued by Kyra Henkel, who poked her head round the door (when had a woman ever looked so angelic?) to ask whether the President had forgotten his scheduled meeting with members of the local Chamber of Commerce—in the town center, in thirty minutes? The car was already waiting. Perhaps she could offer *Herr* Orwell a coffee, and so allow the President to get himself off to the meeting on time?

When he had gone, Richard thanked her profusely.

"No problem," she said. This matter of the hostel intruder had been preying on the Great Man's mind, especially in connection with the not insignificant subject of student applications. She couldn't help hearing, through the open door, that Richard now had a suspect? That was good news! It was no business of hers, of course...

No no, Richard was happy to share his thoughts with her. He knew that she enjoyed the full confidence of the President. He nevertheless balked at naming *Herr* Geisler—it was too early for that, he needed to talk to Eddie, perhaps they could set a trap for the *Hausmeister*?—though he did ask her, in passing, about Volker Cordes. Did she remember the guy?

"That's a long time ago, but I do actually. I met him once, with his wife, when I was shopping at the Reichsstädter Mall. It's funny how such big men are so easily intimidated by small women! She almost had him on a leash."

"Is he left-handed?"

"Now how should I know?" She gave Richard a funny look. "You don't think he's the, you know, the guy that His Magnificence is so worried about?"

"No, not really. He doesn't seem to be in Reichsstadt any more. I'm just tying up loose ends."

"I can't remember whether he was left-handed. I mean, we met, and we must have shaken hands, so I suppose I would have noticed if he was. I normally do." She thought for a moment. "Then, no, he wasn't."

"Would that information be in his file?"

She laughed.

"About his being right- or left-handed? You must be joking! We're not the *Stasi*," she said, referring to the much-feared East German secret police, "collecting information on how often you go to the loo!"

"I'd still like to take a quick peep at his file, if I may? If that could be arranged discreetly?"

His file would have been transferred to the old archive in the cellar. She said that she would ask the Chancellor's secretary to put it on the list next time she sent for stuff from the archive.

"But I do remember something else: that he left because he had a drinking problem. He was a bit of a lost cause, I fear. A silly man! And the other porters couldn't help you? A pity. But I'll do my best."

It would probably take a while before the file was brought up out of the cellar. Richard resigned himself to having to wait. Then, suddenly, only two days later, the help he needed came, and it was indeed because of Volker Cordes's former colleagues.

Richard received a letter, with (unusually for Germany) no sender's address on the back of the envelope or in the top left-hand corner on the front. It was postmarked "Berlin," and was from Volker Cordes.

Dear Mr. Orwell,

Some of my old mates said you asked about me? Why are you so interested? I've moved on, I've got a new life now. I don't like the university. They didn't treat me well. They showed no respect. I never did anything wrong and they still booted me out.

Why are you so interested in the catacombs? They're EVIL. I'm not going down there ever again and you shouldn't either. Only that arsehole Geisler ever goes down there (he has a key). And he has his reasons. I can tell you some VERY interesting stuff about that shitarse. Next time I'm in Reichsstadt I might just do that.

With friendly greetings from Berlin

V. Cordes

A bit of an anal fixation there, Richard thought to himself. And Mr. Cordes and Mr. Geisler were obviously not the best of friends. Under the circumstances, that was understandable.

When he told Eddie (with a certain degree of pride) that he thought he'd "cracked the case," Eddie was less than impressed.

"I don't think it's the *Hausmeister*. He's a miserable old bugger, is old Geisler. He *broods*. He hates everyone, especially his wife, but I don't see him actually *doing* anything."

In his opinion, they should keep up their observation of Kajo, the New Hostel and the Kronprinz Johann—basically, what Dermot was doing—though soon the hostels would be emptying, after the period of exams, with most students going home or on holiday. Things would be quieter then.

Richard was disappointed. Was Watson jealous of Holmes? Richard decided not to share with Eddie his idea of setting a trap for Geisler, at least for the time being.

He had to think about the best way to do it. One problem would be that they would have to organize a long-haired blonde bait with which to set the trap!

AN EXCHANGE OF LETTERS

Dear Richard,

You're a lazy sod, aren't you? Here I am doing all the work, pouring my heart out, and what do you do? Nothing. I don't think you're even TRY-ING to find out who I am! So now it is your turn. I want a letter from YOU, big boy. Write and tell me what you want from me, if and when I decide to reveal who I am. Don't hold back. Remember I'll do ANYTHING for you...

OK, I haven't got a mailbox like you have. So here's what we do. Write your letter, and sign it "M." (for "mystery man"). Because if someone finds it, I don't want to cause you trouble. (See what a nice girl I am.)

Put it in an envelope, close it, and stick it behind the picture of bloody Max Weber at the far end of the Sociology corridor, by the Disabled Toilet. That's a very quiet corner. The frame of the picture has got a thick rim on the back. You can tuck the envelope behind the rim so that it doesn't fall down.

Don't bother hanging about to see me collect it. I won't come till I know you're somewhere else, like in a class.

I give you 24 hours to write. OK?I want to hear from you! I want you to pour out your heart, the way I've been doing!

S.

P.S. When I read this again I thought it sounded a bit unfriendly. Sorry! So to make it up to you, I've got a little surprise. Have a sniff at the letter. I rubbed it against my MUSCHI. You like?

Richard wrote a reply, and deposited it behind the picture of Max Weber in the Sociology corridor, just as she had suggested, like a spy using a dead letter box.

Dear unknown person S.,
What lies hidden behind that single letter?
Your name, perhaps?
Or does "S." stand for SEXY which I'm sure you are?
Or for a STUDENT, which I guess you might be?
Or for a SURPRISE?
Or for my SLAVE, which is what you want to be!
What do I want from YOU? How can I answer that if I don't know who you are? What you are OFFERING me you have made very clear. Show yourself, tell me who you are, and I'll give you a full and satisfying answer. I long to meet you, and when I do, who knows what might happen?
Then YOU'LL be surprised!

M.

Her response came a day later.

M.,
ARE you "dear" or "my dearest"? I've opened myself up to you in my letters, I've let you into my most secret places, and what do I get in return? A load of "yes, um, maybe, it depends who you are" crap. Just like your fucking Prince Charles messing with Diana ("Whatever being in love means," haha).
Fuck you!

How can you be so cheap, hedgeing [sic] your bets like that? Did you never think that maybe I have my reasons to be careful, too? Reasons why I need to protect my identity, at least for the moment?

I'm only asking you to be honest with me. But it seems that you can't even be honest with yourself. You cheapskate!

Fuck you! But that's my problem, isn't it? I $_{do}$ want to fuck you, very very much. I stay awake at night, longing for you, rubbing myself and putting my fingers into where your prick ought to be.

Maybe I'm making a big mistake, but I can't help it.

S.

P.S. If you value what we have, at all, write to me, c/o Max Weber. Whatever you write, however pathetic it is, it will warm my heart and bring you closer to me.

HUPEY

Steffi and Lisa were holding a last-minute conference about Flossengamme: nothing should be allowed to go wrong.

Steffi had made a huge effort to tidy up her room, though she could sense that Lisa (who lived by other, more bourgeois, standards) was unable to appreciate it. For example, no dirty washing was anywhere to be seen—it had all been thrust at the last moment into a convenient holdall-cum-sports bag that Steffi's parents had bought her for Christmas and which she had never used for anything before.

(Might that not actually be a good place to keep dirty clothes in future? If Steffi could only remember that—she wasn't good at bringing order into her daily routine, an expression that was itself a contradiction in terms as far as her life was concerned.)

All the more cause for praise to be awarded, because it was Steffi who was now going through the checklist for the excursion.

Lisa, in contrast, was in a kind of moony daze, and barely able to concentrate. Fair enough, the prospect of a romantic encounter with Kurz would be a big deal for her. She'd beeen um-ing, er-ing and ah-ing for days now. Did she really want to? Was he the right one?

How pathetic was that?

For Steffi, the "right one" was a concept she'd always found difficult. Harlan Kurz was... well, Harlan Kurz, and his qualities (such as his bum) and his drawbacks (almost everything else) were plain to see. After all, she had been there herself, got the T-shirt (almost), and had no regrets about not taking the matter any further. Lisa was a grown-up girl, and she could make her own decisions, and her own mistakes. Could she *learn* from them was the question, though.

Lisa's sex-life obviously hadn't been terribly rich or varied, if she could get so ridiculously worked up over a leg-over with Harlan Kurz. But, then again, it might all turn out to be a fantastic revelation for Lisa. Harlan was quite possibly an energetic lover. In his classes he could barely keep still, bopping about as if totally deranged. He might even be capable of giving Lisa an orgasm!

Orgasm. That was an experience that Steffi was pretty sure her friend had not had in her life so far. It was an assessment that she based on what Lisa had told her (in confidence) about her past involvements with men.

There hadn't been many.

There had been a loathsome married man, a neighbor, who'd taken advantage of her for a quickie. Presumably he was her first. (Married men had their uses, as far as Steffi was concerned—and they were easy to dump.)

There had been a stupid boy from her class at school, with a colored stripe in his hair and a nose-ring instead of a personality. While Lisa was in the bathroom, washing herself after their mucky little interaction, he rang his mates to boast about shagging her. She had overheard every word.

And then there'd been that Sebastian creep. OK, Sebastian was quite good-looking, that had to be said. Steffi herself had chatted him up once, at a disco, but he hadn't shown much interest, and he'd told his friends that he didn't go for girls without tits. Haha, what a sophisticated fellow!

Lisa had even admitted to worrying in the past that she might perhaps be a lesbian?

"A lesbian? Wow! You do realize what that means? It means you fancy making out with Leathergirl Gundi, or going down hard on *Frau* Schlichting's pussy!"

Lisa was indignant.

"No it doesn't!"

"Look, if you were a lezzie, sweetheart, you'd know it, believe me." (Though Steffi didn't tell her *how* she'd know it. You just *did*, surely? Once or twice, at boring parties where there hadn't been enough boys to go around, Steffi had groped or been groped by other girls. It was a lot better than just sitting there playing with your drink, but the earth had definitely not moved. And a bit of groping didn't make you a lesbian.)

Might a full-on encounter with Harlan actually be what she needed? An important step in her personal development? No, that was most unlikely, but if you didn't make mistakes you'd never make anything, and Lisa did have some serious catching up to do. Anyhow, Steffi would watch out for her like a big sister.

It showed how naïve Lisa was that she freaked out when Steffi mentioned the little rubber things. Sheaths. Johnnies. Condoms. Whatever you chose to call them

Well, what was wrong with asking about that? No, Lisa, *of course* it's not about your getting pregnant or not. (Had *that* been her mum's main advice to her on contraception? God give us strength!) I know that you're on the pill. It's about catching infections.

Men do like to think they're taking the lead. But a sensible girl should have all the options and possibilities worked out in advance.

Let him ask whether you're on the pill, or show you his packet of condoms. If he doesn't ask, or show you the johnnies (and he hasn't been sterilized!), you'll know that he's selfish, or childish, or a psychopath, and that it would be better to give the whole thing a miss.

There would be no harm in that. No-one would lose face. As far as the world was concerned, the point of the excursion was to see Flossengamme, wasn't it (and not to get laid)?

There was a knock on the door. Fuck! Thong had been playing in the background, one of Steffi's favorite tracks from *Attitude* ("Stomp on it, baby, yeah, stomp on its tiny head"), with the volume turned down (a little) out of consideration for Lisa, who was more into the likes of Joni Mitchell. But while it wasn't loud enough for Steffi, it had obviously been much too loud for her difficult neighbor from next door.

Sod it!

Steffi asked Lisa to go and deal with Saint Agathe, please. Lisa would be polite, and would agree to turn the volume down, whereas Steffi couldn't trust herself not to do or say something drastic—and they really didn't need a stupid hoo-ha just before the big day.

The Agathe crisis was thereby averted.

Steffi's car, "Hupey," was fine. She had given it that name because she loved using the horn (*Hupe*) whether it was appropriate or not. In fact, bombing happily down the road on a sunny afternoon, she just couldn't resist honking away. She was expressing her joy in life! And why not? (Lisa knew very well why not, and had told her many times to be more careful.)

Hupey had been given the once-over most conscientiously by some engineering guy named Philipp, who was known to be desperately in love with Steffi.

"You're just using him," Lisa admonished her. "Taking advantage of him. What does *he* get out of it? Haven't you ever—"

"No! But I let him near me, don't I. Isn't that enough? He is an engineer, after all."

Poor Lisa sometimes had no idea how things worked.

"Well, I dunno," she muttered.

"Look, I'll send him a Christmas card. With love and kisses. He can show it to his friends in the *Mensa*. OK, happy now? Are you like this with puppies and kittens too?"

They'd discussed the matter of refreshments, and there was now a crate of beer in Hupey's boot, but the question of food was trickier. What could Kurz and Orwell possibly have in common, food-wise? Kurz probably lived on junk food, crappy U S of A-stuff. Orwell could well be a food snob, a "proper English gentleman," with crustless cucumber sandwiches on the lawn, or he might be into fish 'n' chips. How could they know?

They decided to take along some potato crisps and biscuits as snacks, also a small bottle of *Schnapps* each, to use as a secret weapon (Richard in particular might need "warming up"). They could also look for a place to pick up food on the way. Lisa vaguely remembered there being a snack bar in Flossengamme (in the village), which did curry sausage, *Bratwurst* and chips. (OK, *German* junk food.)

Though perhaps the gentlemen would feel inspired to invite the ladies to lunch at a suitable hostelry?

Steffi doubted that very much. In fact, she was worrying whether the two men would be talking to each other at all.

When she had invited Harlan, she had dropped a heavy hint that Lisa was besotted, and had eyes only for him (although she had expressed it more crudely than that). She had also, trying to do it as casually as she could, mentioned in passing that there would be one or two other people in the group, like Marlene Sanders (an invented name), Ulrike Sandmann, and his colleague Richard Orwell.

Harlan had not exactly chortled with delight when he heard that last name.

"Well, rightee ho, what fun! You ladies really know how to organize a party, don't you?" he had commented sarcastically and, putting on his familiar Richard Orwell funny voice, he had added, "One does feel so jolly *un*jolly with a stick up one's jolly bum half the time, what, eh? Anyone for tennis?"

Dear me, it was going to be such hard work.

AN UNHAPPY LIFE

Why am I talking to you? And what sad fuck gave you the right to judge me? You have no idea at all what my life is like. And you'll never know, will you? But if you could somehow crawl into my thoughts, what you found there would make you sick.

So don't try to judge me until you know me, and know how I live.

Who am I? Well, who cares? And who is asking? I could have been someone. I could have made something important out of my life, instead of being stuck forever in this shit-hole, surrounded by scum and losers. Oh yes, they think I'm like *them*, but I'm not. And I'm onto them. How surprised they will be when they find out!

They think I'm some hardworking, reliable, decent guy who didn't make it. They look at me, and they don't see anyone special. They even laugh at me behind my back. But I was destined for much greater things that this pathetic job that I do now. Believe me.

Know me by my deeds! Well, the world will soon find that out. And how shocked they will be! Still, I'm honest. I'm not some filthy hypocrite. I stand by what I've done, and who I am.

You haven't seen much of it yet, just a small but how enjoyable taste. I've touched on a few lives, here and there, a few people were frightened (how easy that is!), and they don't know where to find the bogeyman, even though he's right under their noses! I'm so close, I can smell your farts. I can taste your fear, and it tastes good!

You don't realize, no-one realizes yet, that there is a huge power in me, a power that I suck up out of the darkness that is deep down inside me, in my core, and when I release it the world is going to know.

The witch has been holding me back. She is clever and cunning. She thinks she has power over me. She gives me a little here, a little there, and thinks that she has me under control. But I need more than that. I could destroy her so easily, she is only a woman like you, but when my days of glory come I want her to be there to see it.

Why am I talking to you? Why do I bother? You don't know me. Actually, we have met. But you wouldn't recognize me. You won't know that I am the one who is causing your dread until it's too late.

Could it be that I am telling you this because I have chosen you as the first? You will be the first proper one. And you won't be the last. Oh, I'm not going to hurt you. I'm going to fucking consume you! I have only been playing with matches, but now I am going to light a whole furnace.

DISSATISFACTION

The evening before the great expedition to Flossengamme, Richard found another letter from "S.," this time in his mailbox.

Once again, it struck a different note. He found her mood swings puzzling. Was she really like this (in which case she'd be a whole heap of trouble if they ever became involved in a relationship)?

Or was she toying with him, trying to manipulate his feelings?

Either way, there could be trouble ahead. And there was no-one he could talk to about this; Eddie least of all.

If he was sensible, he'd start to ignore her letters—throw them away without reading them, even—but he couldn't deny that they turned him on. They spoke to a need that he had, to be admired and wanted.

He had never been sure of that with women, and maybe that was the reason why, with Sonia, or Monika, or any of his other girlfriends, he hadn't been able to open up and give himself (the way it was supposed to be in relationships, he'd always assumed). The damage caused by the debacle with Miriam Burkhardt would set him back even further, unless...

Was "S." the answer? She had written:

Dear Richard,

I was feeling pretty happy yesterday because at long last I had had the chance to see you again and to listen to your melodious voice. And while listening to your elucidations in your lecture, I had a daydream of living with you in a tiny cottage with a pretty little garden. You might find that silly, but these are the kind of daffy thoughts that women sometimes have.

Oh I can imagine what you are thinking: "This girl is really getting on my nerves. All these boring letters are a pain in the neck. When will she stop filling my mailbox and my waste paper basket with her weepy letters written in bad English?" Well, I do not expect you to waste your valuable time on reading any or even all of my letters. But allow me to point out one last thing.

I am very afraid that you could find out who I am. I am afraid you will then kick me out of your lectures. And how could I then keep on living without—at any rate—seeing you sometimes and enjoying listening to your voice? Is it really that wrong that I love you?

I am not addlebrained or boring or pudgy or unalluring. I fancy you could find me attractive or at least an interesting interlocutor (big word!). I think you would take on me [?].

If I only were able to talk to you! If I only could pull myself together and say something (anything!) in your presence. But I often think I'll never make it. And that is actually totally insane because by nature I am everything but shy—as long as YOU are not around. If so I always become as mute as a maggot!

Nothing else remains to be done for me but to look at you from afar... By the way (lest I forget to tell you that): I loved the new dark-blue polo shirt that you wore in your lecture. It's very becoming. It makes your light-coloured eyes even more beaming [sic] and you look quite sporty. The polo shirt really suits you excellently. Almost as good as the long-sleeved shirts you normally wear. What an adorable man you are, my love, and what I were readdy [sic] to do for you—or even better: with you...

I can't wait to see you soon! Has the time come for us to meet, if you still want me?No, better if we never do! Better that we say goodbye and forget this all. Better for both of us.

S.

The reference to his lecture showed that she hadn't sent this letter right away. She had written it a while ago, then sat on it, unsure of what she was doing and how to pursue her obsession. Just as Richard too was now unsure what to do. Wasn't the whole business pointless? He would write to her again, by way of Max Weber. Perhaps after the Flossengamme trip, when a day out would have helped him to clear his mind?

No, it was time to sort this out. She was playing with him, and he didn't know whether he *wanted* to play with her. Was it worth it? Or was it just a complete waste of his time. He was even beginning to feel threatened by her.

He wrote a quick reply to her letter.

> S.,
>
> I have a lot going on in my life at the moment, and I don't know if I can do this "relationship" (for want of a better word) any more. We need to talk, face-to-face. I don't know what you REALLY want from me but, until I've met you, and I know who you are, I won't know what I want from YOU either.
>
> We should stop playing games with each other. Isn't it rather strange, weird even, what we're doing? Perhaps it would be better for both of us to end this now. Whatever happens, know that I'll always treasure your beautiful, funny, passionate letters though.
>
> So—name a time and a place, please. If you don't want to meet me, please stop writing to me.
>
> The place can be anywhere you like, but it should be somewhere quiet and discreet. Am I right in thinking that we are both nervous about this meeting? Somewhere in the university would be OK, because in a few days most of the exams will be over and the buildings will be nearly empty. We shouldn't meet in my office, of course!
>
> The time? Any day after tomorrow, whenever you prefer, but not too early in the morning PLEASE.
>
> M.

He drew a little smiley face at the end of the last sentence, and then "posted" the letter care of Max Weber.

Walking back to the Südstädter Ring, he suddenly felt doubts about what he had written. Should he have put in that jocular final sentence? Or added the smiley face? The tone of his letter was otherwise stern and serious. He was trying to put pressure on her. But that last sentence gave the game away, didn't it? It showed how much he was still in two minds. That the fish was still caught on her hook.

Should he go back and retrieve the letter? He could write another one after Flossengamme.

No. What was done was done.

* * * *

At breakfast the next morning, the morning of the great day, Eddie was sulky and petulant. Richard was forced to remind him that the two of them had agreed that they would "do" Flossengamme in the summer, when the weather would be much better. Of course they both knew that all this wasn't about Flossengamme; it was about Richard going off on a day-trip with two girls, and Eddie having to stay at home.

"And would you really want to spend the whole day with Harlan Ray Kurz?" he added, knowing it was a rhetorical question.

Eddie sniffed, and stuck his head in a newspaper.

Newspapers seldom found their way into the Orwell residence, unless Richard happened to find them at bus-stops. TV and the internet were his main sources of news information.

Eddie was more of a newspaper man than he was, though he never actually *bought* the things. He had found this copy of the local paper yesterday, downstairs in the foyer, and had promptly "liberated" it, but had then gone to bed early, saving it up for breakfast reading. This was an occasional routine that he and Richard had. He would read out the "funny bits" (and the "naughty bits," if there were any) for Richard's and his own amusement.

This morning, though, he had punished Richard by *not* reading out anything amusing (so far). It couldn't have been that the newspaper didn't contain anything suitable. Because it was local, it was bound to be full of the most ridiculous stuff: pompous local dignitaries sounding off over trivialities; feuds between neighbors over the misplacing of a garden fence; overblown obituaries for local businessmen; letters from tiresome old biddies complaining about everything imaginable; tedious coverage of local sporting events.

Best of all were the statements boastfully reviewing the activities and achievements of the university (because Richard and Eddie often knew the reality behind the gushing prose). The doings of the Esthetic Practitioners were unfailingly good for a laugh,

Eddie suddenly sat up sharply and said, "Oh!"

Good! Richard thought, he was getting over his pique.

"You find something tasty?"

Eddie gave him an unusually serious look.

"Our guy. I think he's done it again."

A crime of violence. A brutal attack on a woman. An unsolved mystery. He read out the short article in the paper.

A local woman was in hospital, having been the target of a murderous and unprovoked assault. Her attacker had fled, leaving her for dead. She had been able to provide the police with useful information, and a spokesman for the police said that although the investigation was ongoing they were confident of being able to make progress in solving this horrific crime.

"That means: an arrest is imminent."

"But what makes you think this is our hostel guy? Did he do any funny stuff on the woman?"

"It doesn't say so here. But they wouldn't give that sort of detail."

"Well, then," Richard said, "Reichsstadt may not be the Bronx, but you do get these news stories occasionally about people being mugged or attacked. I wouldn't read too much into this one. Probably it was the boyfriend. You know, pissed off with her for two-timing him? That's why the police think they may be able to catch the guy."

"No, it says the man was a stranger. They must have witnesses, or forensics."

"I bet it's the boyfriend! Maybe she's covering for him? The silly bag wants him back!"

"It says the woman was attacked in a hotel bedroom. It doesn't say which hotel, but it says which street the hotel is in—"

He leaned across the table, holding the newspaper so that Richard could read the address for himself.

"But that's—surely not?"

"Yes. That's the street where the Kronprinz Johann Hotel is. Interesting, don't you think?"

Richard didn't want to concede anything. He thought Eddie was just looking for something to make a fuss about because *he* wasn't going away for the day.

"There are dozens of hotels in Reichsstadt. Probably several just in that street. So what?"

"Don't you think that it's a coincidence that this may well have happened in a hotel that we were already watching, because our main suspect was going there without a good reason?"

This was getting a bit much for Richard.

"For heaven's sake, Eddie! 'Our main suspect'? The chances that *Kajo* is this creep that the police are now chasing, or the psycho that we're looking for, are pretty remote. Kajo won't be arrested today! And it's probably a completely different hotel. Come on, our hostel guy is just a weirdo, he's not a murderous thug. I'm pretty confident that Geisler is the man we should be looking at. You can follow up your Kajo lead—you and Brother Dermot—if you want to, but don't imagine that anything will come of it."

"I'll do just that."

"Still, wouldn't it be just dandy for everybody concerned if the police caught this character," he tapped the newspaper that Eddie was holding, "and he confessed to dressing up as a Snatcher every couple of weeks and sneaking into student hostels to suck toes and steal underwear!"

"Ha ha. And it's fingers, not toes. You know, sarcasm is not your strongest point, Richard. You shouldn't make fun of this. The girls are really frightened of this man."

But Richard thought: Miriam Burkhardt isn't frightened of him. However, all he said was: "Oh, whatever."

At which moment the doorbell rang.

Eddie looked puzzled.

"If that's them, weren't you supposed to be meeting them over at the Real carpark?"

THE ROAD TO FLOSSENGAMME

They were now on their way.

Generally, it is easiest to tell a story from the point of view of one person. Who may get it wrong. Who may be "unreliable." But there'll be time to fix that, to modify the story from another viewpoint, to let other characters get a word in edgeways. Which is not the same as saying that there will always, inevitably, be contradictions, or that there are bound to be as many "truths" as there are perceptions. (The postmodernists have a lot to answer for.)

Sometimes, at the end of the day, if you could put all your protagonists together and let them compare notes you would find them agreeing that, broadly speaking, this or that is what happened. As simple as that. But that doesn't mean that those events wouldn't be the result of the interweaving of their motives and actions, or that they wouldn't have different feelings about them, and might carry the mark of the events, the burden or the hurt, in different ways.

Four people in a car were heading for Flossengamme, with differing hopes and expectations of what the day would bring.

* * * *

Richard, perched nervously in the front passenger seat, beside someone who was clearly not the world's most accomplished driver, was beginning to have doubts about the whole enterprise.

Lisa was not going to open up to them about her trauma in the hostel. And the idea that she might be deeply moved by Flossengamme and then, when (or if) she happened to find herself alone with Richard later in the day, tell him everything, was patent nonsense. Why should she be moved? She'd been to the place twice with her school, hadn't she?

Anyhow, unless she could identify Geisler as the intruder, anything vague that she told them would be of no great use. And Richard had more or less made up his mind that Geisler was the man they were looking for.

Now that he'd had a chance to take a look at Steffi Albertz, he felt sure that she wasn't "S." Or, to be honest, he was *hoping* she wasn't. "S." had existed safely in his imagination. Steffi, on the other hand, was there in the flesh, and while there was something sexually-charged about her, she was hardly his type. (He didn't actually know what his type was, just that it wasn't Steffi.) Besides, the encounter with Miriam Burkhardt was still preying on his mind. He shouldn't have done it, should he? Even if she'd had nothing to do with him academically, theoretically she was still one of his students. And Steffi Albertz quite undeniably was.

"S." was a different matter, but all of a sudden it came to him that, whether she replied to his last letter or not, he didn't want any more casual adventures.

Richard was also feeling a tiny bit queasy. He'd never owned a car and never wanted to either, and didn't even have a driver's license, so he was normally reticent about criticizing anyone's driving. But Steffi's driving was in a class of its own. She seemed to think she was Michael Schumacher, though she was at the wheel of a vehicle for which the word "jalopy" could have been invented. Hupey might be a write-off, but the jolting and choking and aggressive gear-changing were entirely Steffi's contribution.

There was a fourth person in the car—and it wasn't Harlan Kurz, who would have been the other factor in the equation. Instead of the revolting pseudo-American, it was Richard's obnoxious fellow Brit, Jonathan Snoad, who had already made himself comfortable in the back with Lisa.

A less well-matched pair Richard could scarcely imagine! She was slightly *bigger* than he was, for a start. And she had a clean-limbed, healthy look to her (even if she eventually turned out to be utterly boring as a person), a straightforwardness. What she needed, Richard thought, was some decent-looking, honest, plain-dealing jock with zero imagination and fantastic teeth, not a smug, superficial character like Snoad.

Snoad instead of Kurz. And they weren't even heading directly to Flossengamme. Both of these small surprises need to be explained.

Standing in the doorway to Richard's apartment, Steffi had apologized for the change in plan (which was not of her making). Harlan Kurz had called off at the last moment, pleading a tummy upset, but said that his good friend Jonathan was willing to make up the numbers. It would save her a long haul out to the Weststadt, and Jonathan would be able to meet up with them at the arranged rendezvous, the Real carpark.

What was in it for Snoad? That was Richard's immediate reaction. Jonathan never did anything without a good, selfish reason. And there was an obvious reason, he soon learned: Snoad needed to pick up his car from a specialist repair shop that was half-way to Flossengamme (sort of), so they were essentially giving him a free ride. But he'd continue on to Flossen-gamme with them afterwards (since *he* hadn't been there either).

Steffi and Lisa had decided to pick Richard up first (his address was no great secret) to spare him any surprise or embarrassment at the carpark.

What a miserable day it was going to be!

They might not need to go to the Weststadt, but they still had to make a considerable detour. Snoad's BMW (his "Bimmer," as he ludicrously called it) was waiting to be picked up at the Nielsen Garage. They'd go there first, and then (he suggested) they could leave Steffi's car there and travel on "in rather greater comfort," picking up the other car on the way back.

Steffi had said "no"—she preferred being in her own car, thank you, it let her feel she was in control of the situation, she said, and not imposing on someone. Then Lisa had suggested the obvious, that they use *both* cars. So after they had found the garage, and Richard had been forced to endure a long and tedious conversation between Snoad and the senior mechanic about the relative merits of different models of Bimmer, the party divided into two, Lisa going with Snoad "in comfort" and Steffi and Richard trun-dling along behind them, trying their best to keep up.

After a brief spin northwards on the *Autobahn*, they took a well-sign-posted exit and then, almost immediately, the first of a series of poorly-signposted turnings into muddy country roads that seemed to go nowhere. Steffi had originally muttered something about "map reading," but Richard wasn't called upon to do any; gliding on ahead, Snoad seemed to know the way well enough.

Whatever horrible old Nazi had built Flossengamme, he had chosen the site well, placing it not in the hills and charming little villages south of Reichsstadt but on the huge, flat plain to the north. Unless you were a yokel from some neighboring farming hamlet, you'd never find yourself "popping in" or "calling by" in Flossengamme, or "stumbling across it" on your way to somewhere else—nobody would ever find themselves there unless that had been their intention all along.

The poor sods sent to the camp undoubtedly hadn't wanted to go there, but who *else* in their right mind would want to?

The weather wasn't helping much. The sky was gray, and it was driz-zling slightly. Steffi's car skidded several times on the wet, muddy roads, on which there were also crushed lumps of sugar-beet that had fallen off the trucks during the winter harvest and not been cleared away. The whole day was, in a word, *leaden*.

If he had been in a literature class, Richard would have said that the weather was an "objective correlative" of his feelings, and that his mood was "homologous" with the rain and the gray sky.

Back in his BA days, Richard's favorite English prof had had a peculiar habit of attaching single-word labels to famous writers. Thus, Coleridge's poems were "tensed"; Swinburne's, in contrast, were "slack" (morally or metrically? Richard couldn't remember); D.H. Lawrence's work, which the Professor didn't like, was "restless" (if the Professor was feeling generous) or "uneven" (if he wasn't); and "leaden" was just the word to describe the atmosphere in Thomas Hardy's novels.

The Professor expected his students to come up with these silly tags in seminars and exams, and Heaven protect those who didn't! (Though Richard, a favorite of his, had once been excused his use of "coiled" in a class on Coleridge; "That's near enough, dear boy," the Professor had said. "You've grasped the point.")

Today, "leaden" would do very nicely.

* * * *

Sitting beside him, Steffi wasn't sure what to make of Richard. Without actually being unfriendly, he sat stiffly and was uncommunicative. What had ever made her think of targeting *him* of all people for a little adventure? On their way to the garage, neither Richard nor Lisa had offered her any moral support when Snoad had started teasing her about her car: "Chitty-Chitty-Bang-Bang" he had called it, a reference that she didn't understand but which was obviously not intended to be flattering.

Unlike his buddy Kurz, Snoad was an unknown quantity. Was this sneering perhaps an obscure way of flirting with her? Was he *hitting* on her? No chance there, mate! Or was it Lisa he was trying to impress with his arrogant version of macho?

Steffi had a bad conscience. The whole trip had been set up more for Lisa's sake than for her own, and now that Mister Jiggle-Bum had dropped out Lisa might well be wondering whether there was any point in the exercise? It wasn't about seeing Flossengamme—*she* was the one who'd been there twice before. And it wasn't *Steffi* who needed a fancy excuse before she would make her move on a bloke—a bloke who had decided not to come.

Steffi was furious with Harlan Kurz. What a bastard! She'd dropped more than enough hints about Lisa having a crush on him. She'd almost gone too far. OK, if he didn't fancy her, why didn't he just say so? Or had he dropped out when he heard that Ulrike Sandmann wouldn't be in the group?

And what was Snoad's motive in agreeing to stand in at the last moment? Was it just a convenient lift to the garage, with a few hours of cultural sightseeing tacked on? Or did he actually fancy Lisa?

That could hardly be. As far as Steffi knew, there had been very little contact between them. He didn't teach anything of much interest to either of them yet (there was still plenty of time for them to hook up with him as an examiner later on).

Perhaps Harlan had told him, look, there's this student, a real good-looker, and she's just *gagging* for it. She really wants to be put on her back by one of her lecturers. She's not my type, old man, so you could do me a favor here. And the other chick's a right *goer*, if you happen to prefer her...

Hmm. Steffi was pretty sure that the lecturers drooled over the students in just the same way as the students drooled over the lecturers. Eddie Hodgkins was a classic example.

Be that as it may, it would help a certain amount if Snoad could at least try to be charming, and flirt with Lisa a bit. Would he do as a replacement for Mister Jiggle-Bum? Lisa definitely needed a man. Could Snoad be The One? Her Mister Right? He was more conventionally good-looking than Harlan (or Richard, for that matter) and you could understand what he was saying, but he didn't seem like a particularly nice person.

Would Lisa care about that? Probably not. It had never mattered much to Steffi either. For example, Steffi would never have thought of Harlan Kurz as "nice," and she had still let him grope her after the party in Freshers' Week.

Steffi reminded herself that she had *other* reasons for not fancying him any more. He had blown it, and no-one ever got a second chance with Steffi Albertz.

She knew that Lisa, even if she did find Snoad appealing, was never going to make the first move, so Steffi was probably going to have to set it up for her. But how, and when? And how co-operative would Richard be?

It was going to be a long, long day, involving a lot of hard work for her—and not just the driving. Flossengamme in February was hardly her idea of a fun drive.

Richard, bugger him, didn't seem to value the sheer work she was putting in behind the wheel. In fact, so far he had hardly said a word. On the way to the garage, it was obvious that he and Snoad didn't get along. Snoad had made almost all the conversation, most of which was aimed at her, while Lisa sat beside him in a sulk. And whenever he had addressed a remark to Richard, it had contained some kind of sneer.

He'd never had a chance to talk to Richard, he said, about school and family and all that boring sort of stuff, but he had noticed, to his surprise, that Richard pronounced "garage" the same way that he did (GA-rage). Didn't most people in Richard's "back of the woods" say "GA-ridge," though?

"Denying your roots, eh?"

Steffi didn't understand what he was getting at, but from Richard's response ("No, not at all," followed by a broody silence) she deduced that it had been a put-down.

How strange the British were!

"Harlan Kurz says 'ga-RAGE', doesn't he?" she ventured, in a spirit of "keeping the conversation going," but with no success.

Well, now Lisa was sitting on her own with Snoad in his flashy Bimmer, and it was up to her. Perhaps he had a CD or a radio channel playing? His taste in music was bound to be closer to Lisa's than it would be to hers. His car was disgustingly comfortable, and it was full of what Steffi called "advanced electronic *schnick-schnack*." (Steffi's main requirement of a sound system—anywhere—was that it should be *loud*.) If the man would just make a tiny effort and concentrate on Lisa, she would so easily be charmed and impressed. The girl needed cheering up. Who knows? There might even be magic in the air. And Lisa would enjoy the day out too.

* * * *

Lisa was well aware that sulkiness was not a manner that many people found becoming in a young lady. She couldn't help it, though, as long as the four of them were in the car together and Mr. Snoad—she was still trying to get used to the idea of calling him "Jon," as he had immediately invited her to—directed all his remarks at Steffi or at Richard.

He didn't like Richard, there was no doubt about that!

Did he like Steffi, though? Perhaps he liked her a bit too much? Had Harlan told him that Steffi was an easy lay? Someone else might even have done. Admittedly, she was a bit of a slag.

Lisa was most emphatically *not* an easy lay. OK, Sebastian... But that was in the past. If she was an easy lay, she told herself, Milo would have been in her knickers long ago (he certainly tried hard enough). Nuff said about that.

She had got the message that Harlan Kurz wasn't interested in her, and that hurt, but she had already begun to have a few doubts about him. She was sure that he'd regret it one day! Eddie Hodgkins had once read a weird poem with them where some pervie guy regretted having "missed his chance with one of the lords of life" (weird, because it was about a snake). Those lines had stuck in her memory, and it was a good way of describing how Lisa felt about getting the brush-off from Harlan.

His loss, not hers.

But it was asking a lot to have to switch her focus now to being with this "blind date" (if that is what it was), a guy whom she'd never stopped to think about before.

Yes, he was quite good-looking, handsome almost, though she'd noticed a dead, pasty quality to his skin. And he was bright (he made Richard Orwell look like a complete dozy idiot, which she knew he wasn't). And he had an absolutely fantastic car.

She had suggested that they use both the cars. That was mostly because she was fed up with being ignored, but also because she wanted a ride in

Jon's gleaming BMW. What had it cost? She didn't dare to ask. How could he afford it on a lecturer's salary? Her dad made pots of money, and even his Mercedes wasn't as nice as this. It had a fantastic smell (from the leatherwork?) and you just *sank* into the seat. Oh wow! Was this how the rich lived? She imagined herself as Kim Kardashian or Oprah Winfrey.

Jon was growing on her fast. Her mother would like him. He was neatly dressed, his hair was short, and he probably had truly exquisite manners. ("May I pass you the salt, Mrs. Meyer?" and "I can see where Lisa gets her looks from, Mrs. Meyer!")

Her father might not be so keen. Her dad (she sighed inwardly) was so *work-oriented*. He admired guys who were dynamic and hardworking and got things done. She was ashamed to say that what would really turn her dad on would be if she brought home some over-achieving engineer with a PhD and his own company. He wouldn't know how to value someone as laid back as Jonathan Snoad was.

Hey, what was she doing, daydreaming about whether he would charm her mum or her dad? He was supposed to be charming *her*!

She gave Jonathan a starting push.

"It's so nice, Mr. Snoad—"

"Jon, please."

"OK, Jon. It's so nice that you could come along today."

Without taking his eyes off the road, he said, "You were expecting my friend Harlan, weren't you? I do hope you're not too disappointed?"

"Oh no, not at all!" she blurted out, and felt herself blushing—good that he wasn't looking at her! She was too flustered to follow up what he might have been insinuating (she hoped!), so she dropped back into small-talk. "Steffi and Mr. Orwell have never been to Flossengamme. Mr. Kurz hasn't been either..."

This time he looked at her.

"And nor have I. That makes me a good substitute for my friend Harlan, I reckon. I'm really looking forward to it!"

Was that a signal, or wasn't it? She decided that it was, and took a bold step.

"I'll let you into a secret, Jon. *Jon.* It still seems strange saying it! This trip is not really about Flossengamme; it's about something else."

"You don't say? Come on, I like mysteries!"

"Well, maybe I shouldn't be saying this... but Steffi has a, you know, sort of soft spot for Mr. Orwell. This is a chance for her to get to know him a bit better."

He laughed—a thinner laugh than she'd expected, but a laugh nevertheless.

"Wow! How strange! And there's no accounting for taste. So you're playing Cupid? And the chaperone too?"

"Oh, Steffi never needs a chaperone!"

This time they both laughed.

"I see. I was led to believe that you'd be giving us a long guided tour of all the barracks and gas chambers and whatnot, but maybe an extra-*short* tour is what is called for. So that they can then go off and amuse themselves."

"You wouldn't mind?"

"Oh, I expect you to show *me* around properly. I like being spoiled. You're the boss! Put me on a lead, but feed me treats and give me a pat or two. I'll be a good boy."

"I'll do my best."

He didn't need to say, "I'm sure you will." The smile said it for him.

* * * *

Jonathan Snoad had at first been slightly reluctant to oblige his friend Harlan.

He had had other plans for the day. He didn't like Orwell, and had no wish to have to put up with him for a whole day. He couldn't understand why Harlan had ever entertained the thought, even for a single second.

And who were these wretched students?

All had soon been made clear. Ulrike Sandmann—the *goddess* Ulrike Sandmann, the bum and tits (not just the face) that launched a thousand ships, the Venus of Reichsstadt—was to have been in the party. A day in Orwell's depressing company would not be too high a price for a day spent in *hers*. (They were both agreed on that.) When Ulrike dropped out, Harlan's interest in the excursion had quickly evaporated.

As for the two girls who would still be going, one of them was a student he'd already had a fling with, which hadn't worked out.

"I don't know about you, bro, but I never warm up the can a second time."

"No, right, I take your point."

Steffi was not only unappreciative of his qualities, he explained, she was also difficult and unpredictable, and he didn't want to risk getting involved with her again. But she was "hot," genuinely fuckable. *Jaan* might like her.

"She's got a crush on Orwell, though," he added.

"How unusual! And the idea of Mr. Dull bonking a student—I'd never have imagined!"

"Not your style, *Jaan*, I know, but if you want her, you can segue in on that one, no probs! I doubt that Orwell has got to first base yet. Bend your pinkie," and Harlan made a gesture of beckoning with his little finger, "and she'll soon come running."

And the other girl?

Lisa? She was just a bore. A big, blonde, not at all Harlan's type, even though she had the steaming hots for him, apparently. Still, seeing that she was Steffi's buddy, it stood to reason that it wouldn't be too hard for anyone to get *her* pants off.

Jaan could therefore pick up his car, spend a cool day out in the country, and have two sluts to play with, if he felt so included. He could rub Orwell's nose in it. What was not to like, man?

Jonathan acknowledged the sentiment, even while thinking that Harlan's way of expressing himself was sometimes a bit over the top.

He gave it some thought. Having to put up with Orwell's tedious company for hours would be a major turn-off. However, it would be a good opportunity to pick up the car. Nielsen's Garage was an immense distance from Reichsstadt, but it so happened that Nielsen's were the only people in the northern half of Germany that he would trust with his car. They loved Bimmers and handled them sensitively, as well they should, whereas the mechanics he'd encountered in repair stations in Reichsstadt were all yokels, hacks and cretins.

As for the two girls—despite what he'd said, Jonathan had no qualms whatsoever about screwing students. It was one of the perks of the job, wasn't it? Despite all the earnest tut-tutting by Deans and Presidents, every second Professor that you ever met was married to a former student of his. And when had *they* first got it on, if not between all those lectures and seminars? So much for the preachers of the moral high ground!

Even so, under normal circumstances Jonathan wasn't in the habit of screwing his students. True, it had happened once or twice—he took what was on plain offer quite ruthlessly—but doing it too often could lead to dangerous complications. And he preferred his women to be older, and classier—in fact, he preferred women to girls. He liked sex, because it boosted his self-esteem, but what he really liked most of all was having a trophy girlfriend on his arm for everyone to envy and admire. You don't get that from being seen out with some sweaty, crumpled student who didn't even know how to put her make-up on properly, and wore grubby jeans half the time.

When in doubt, don't bother, was his motto. Don't take the risk. And there were good reasons for this attitude that he lived by, because beneath the smooth surface of Jonathan Snoad there were no murky depths; there were only muddy shallows, and these were full of ugly lumps of self-doubt and insecurity.

Jonathan knew, and accepted, that he was condemned to a lifetime of comparative non-achievement.

Condemned by his wealthy, brutal estate agent father; by his greedy harridan of a mother; and by his appalling siblings. A typical Essex family: affluent and vulgar, working-class but right-wing Conservative. Gold-plated fittings in the —bathroom. Scarcely a book in sight. God how he hated them all! And he had been happy to escape them by finding a job in Germany.

Even his name irked him. Snoad. Why were there so many unpleasant words in English that began "sn-"? Sneak and snake, snot and sneer and snigger, snob, sniff and sneeze. At elementary school they'd been merciless. He'd been "Snotty Johnnie," and when he complained to the teacher they switched to "Johnnie Sneak" and held his head in the toilet.

He would have taken his mother's maiden name, but that was even worse: Higginbotham. Perhaps he'd change his name from Snoad to Snow. "Jonathan Snow" sounded fine.

He had been sent to an expensive grammar school, rather than to one of the élite public schools. This was not because his father couldn't afford it, but because he was an inverted snob. Jonathan knew that he had missed out—hence his loathing for public schoolboys like Eddie Hodgkins.

He had wheedled and maneuvered his way through school and college (Oxford, no less!) by taking care to ingratiate himself with the right people. He had always done just enough, no more, and never anything that stood out, or caused controversy. He had a reputation for being "sound," but he seldom had opinions on anything that didn't affect him personally—hence his dislike for Richard Orwell, who loved his subject, English literature, and took his teaching seriously.

Whenever the threat of work or of having to take responsibility loomed up on the horizon, you would see the famous Snoad shoulder-shrug in action. And over the years, Harlan Kurz had been a good ally. He, too, was a great shoulder-shrugger.

Two girls to choose from? Harlan was suggesting. Bedding neither of the grungy little madams would bring him any particular kudos. He'd have to keep quiet about it afterwards, and he certainly wouldn't go around bragging. But he hadn't had sex for a while.

Despite her undeniable loveliness, his current girlfriend, Veronika, was not putting out. It was mostly "look, but don't touch" with Veronika. Oh, there was plenty of good stuff to look at—they'd been in the sauna together, after squash, a game at which she excelled—but she wasn't letting him get too close, physically or emotionally.

Emotion was always one-way traffic for him, but it would be nice if she could get hung up on him, so that she could be persuaded to give him what he wanted. Annoyingly, whoever, she wished to "take it slowly." She had "issues with her sexuality," she told him, but she *knew* he could be trusted to understand!

Well, he *couldn't*, damn it! There had been some mild petting, and she'd gotten him all worked up, but then she'd refused even to give him a hand-job, let alone a blow-job, and he'd had to resort to masturbation, like some pimply kid at school. He'd have dumped her ages ago, of course, if she hadn't been such a fantastic looker. (The way those men in the sauna had stared at her...)

Jonathan was nothing if not an opportunist. If there was going to be any nookie on offer, he would seriously consider it. He took Harlan's word for it that both girls were attractive. It would only be a once-off, in any case. But it would have to be the blonde girl, Lisa, who sounded less complicated.

As for the other girl, yes, he could probably steal her away from the flat-footed Orwell. That guy didn't have a clue, and he had zero sex-appeal. But would it really be worth the effort?

Jonathan had spent his whole lifetime being lethargic, and choosing, wherever he could, the path of least resistance. It was a good recipe for survival, in a world full of more energetic people, out only for themselves, who'd shaft him if he got in their way.

"I like you, Lisa," he said. "We're going to have a great day, you and I."

When they reached Flossengamme, they had to wait for the others, who were a long way behind. Jonathan took a moment to check his smartphone. There was a text-message from Harlan: "You like?"

He replied: "I like."

AT THE CAMP

Richard was a bit pissed off about the way things had gone so far. He hadn't much enjoyed the drive, partly because of Snoad's sneering at him—which he couldn't respond to in front of the students, could he? That wouldn't be right—and partly because of Steffi's highly erratic driving.

Why couldn't they have left her car at Nielsen's Garage, and traveled on in the comfort of Snoad's fancy Bimmer? *Jaan* might have been more passive if he'd been driving, rather than lording it over them from the back seat. But Steffi plainly loved her old wreck of a car, and at least it had spared them Snoad's company for a short while. It had been a hairy drive, though, as Steffi, pushing Hupey to the limit, had had to struggle not to lose sight of the car in front. (If she had, his vaunted map-reading skills might have been needed after all. Steffi didn't have a navi.)

Steffi burbled away cheerfully. She was a lively little bundle, and by no means ugly, but he couldn't imagine himself in bed with her. She had been in classes of his (as she proudly reminded him), but she hadn't distinguished herself there (as she *didn't* remind him, but he vaguely remembered her un-obtrusive back-row presence).

No, this girl was not "S."

Lisa Meyer and Snoad were waiting for them in the gravelly Flossengamme carpark. He thought they looked rather relaxed and comfortable together. Poor girl! If she developed a thing for Snoad, that could only end in tears.

Admission to the site was free, but you had to register your name and read through the instructions on how to behave while visiting Flossengamme.

No shouting. No alcohol. No games or simulations. No dogs. No disrespectful behavior. No picnicking. And so on.

Before they went in, Lisa, who was now by common agreement "in charge," raised the question of food. It was already midday. Should they perhaps have something to eat first? And a beer or two? Outside, of course. They'd just passed a snack bar in the village of Flossengamme—which was more a cluster of houses than a village, Richard thought—so if anyone fancied a *Currywurst*?

A second option was the "office" at the entrance to the camp, which sold (expensive) light snacks, to be consumed outside.

A third option was that they had potato crisps, biscuits (Snoad: "Harlan would say cookies, I imagine"), a few apples, and plenty of beer.

It seemed like a harmless decision, but reaching agreement proved to be quite a hurdle.

Richard would indeed like to eat something, he said. He didn't say why, though (it was to settle his stomach after the bumpy ride).

Snoad (predictably) said "no"—unlike Richard, *he* didn't want to waste any time.

Steffi said that if they ate anything, and later they saw some photos in the camp museum of rotting bodies of dead Jews, or poor guys with all their ribs sticking out, then she'd thow up.

She added (unconvincingly), "I'm a sensitive soul, you know."

Lisa rather fancied a *Currywurst*. She was *so* hungry. Couldn't they...?

Not a bad idea, Richard said.

The two *Currywurst* enthusiasts had no car, of course.

Snoad said that he had never eaten a *Currywurst* (what a revolting idea!), and didn't plan to start now.

This highly weighty matter took a quarter of an hour to resolve. Eventually a compromise was reached, as follows.

Richard and Lisa would snack quickly on an apple each, those who wanted to could have a beer, and then they'd all go in and take a look at Flossengamme.

Lisa announced that she would keep her remarks brief ("I don't want to bore anyone").

Afterwards, they would have plenty of "free time" to wander about the site, Lisa said, "taking in the atmosphere" as they pleased.

(What did she mean by that? Eddie had given Richard a thorough briefing on concentration camps, with more information than he really wanted: for example, that at Auschwitz if you "wandered about" near where the crematoria had once been you could still find fragments of human bone. Now that *would* make Steffi throw up!)

An excellent plan, Snoad said. And if Lisa should then still be suffering from the pangs of hunger, he gallantly offered to run the young lady down to the *Currywurst* place in the village and buy her one of those objects, though he personally would observe rather than partake. (Richard noticed that he didn't say "Lisa *and Richard*," though he was sure he had made his own interest in a *Currywurst* abundantly clear.)

They would all meet up at the carpark when the site closed at 4.30, which was just before sunset.

Naturally they could also stop on the way back for a proper meal, if people so wished, and everyone would still be home punctually for the 8 o'clock news on television.

They went into the site and Lisa was as good as her word. To be honest, there wasn't a great deal to see anyway. Especially as Steffi stubbornly refused to go into the museum.

"Don't mind me," she said. "You can go in without me. I've seen photos like that on the internet and in books. It's too yucky for me, but you go ahead."

The others indeed went inside the museum without her, but came out pretty quickly, either out of consideration for Steffi, or because some of the photos they saw made them queasy.

Lisa pointed out several low mounds that marked mass graves. Small signs gave estimates of how many bodies were buried there, and which categories of prisoner they belonged to: so-many-thousand Jewish women and children here; so-many-thousand Russian prisoners-of-war there; four hundred gypsies in that one; there was a grave of "mixed" victims, including homosexuals, "politicals," Jehovah's Witnesses and others; and so on.

Richard found it all totally depressing rather than moving. It was so impersonal, and the day, the weather, the light, the statistics, the graves and sheds, the dull, flat plain... everything was "leaden." They should have stayed longer in the museum, he thought, and read more of the short texts about individual prisoners, who those people were and what their fates had been.

He said: "It's hard to imagine all that horror happening *here*."

Steffi disagreed with him.

"No, you get bastards and murderers everywhere, so why not here too? The Nazis weren't unique. But some of them got what they deserved, after the war."

Eddie had told him that the women were often the worst, and had shown him photos online of "Grete the Beast," or "Ilse with the Boots." They had both been hanged. Ilse, who had a face like a pig's backside and always carried a whip, had had it in for women prisoners, especially those more attractive ones who might still be noticed by the male guards even after being reduced to walking skeletons. She would torture them in pairs.

The two prisoners would have to toss a coin. The one who lost would get her face kicked to a pulp. The other woman would then have to lick the blood off Ilse's boots, before she herself got whipped, or burned with cigarettes (depending on how energetic Ilse was feeling).

Richard said: "In my opinion, not enough of them were hanged."

Steffi laughed, but Lisa seemed upset.

"I don't think it's fair, the way we Germans are always being made out to be monsters and villains. The Russians did terrible things in the war, too. But all we ever got at school was this stuff about German guilt and German crimes."

Snoad naturally had to weigh in in her support.

"Yeah, just lay off the girl, colleague. You don't have to make a fetish out of it. We can be more differentiated about war guilt, can't we? Just chill out. Times have changed. We've moved on."

While he was speaking to Richard, he held a protective arm over Lisa's shoulders. It looked silly—even wearing flat shoes, she was a good inch taller than he was.

Aha! He was going to make a play for her, was he? Well, sod him, Richard thought, let him do it. Why should *he* care?

They continued the tour, and Lisa made a few more points about the history of the camp, and listed a few of the famous people who had died, or been murdered, there. Snoad nodded after each name, as though he recognized them all. A couple of the names were actually familiar to Richard, thanks to the briefing Eddie had given him.

A French socialist politician, who had been allowed to starve to death.

Some guy who'd been on the fringes of the 1944 plot to kill Hitler, but not prominent enough to be sent to die on the meathooks at Plötzensee Prison.

An "inconvenient" German journalist, whoe had probably died from typhus.

A minor, but promising, young Czech novelist.

A nun who had rescued dozens of Jewish children before she was trapped by the Gestapo.

Lisa did her best, but after the little spat over German war guilt it had become obvious that their tour was now a tiresome exercise that everyone was hoping would end very soon.

As it soon did.

The light was slowly fading. They walked to the carpark together, and discussed what to do next. Lisa wanted her *Currywurst*, and Snoad would be happy to oblige her. Lisa asked considerately whether Richard and Steffi wanted to come with them?

No. The sights of Flossengamme had made Steffi feel queasy, and a walk and fresh air were what she needed, she said. A walk out of sight of the graves and the barracks. Away from the reminders of death, disease and torture.

They would meet up again at 4.30.

When Lisa and Snoad had disappeared in the Bimmer, Richard began to make an apology for causing an upset.

"No, you didn't," Steffi interrupted him. "And why are saying this to me anyway? It's Lisa who's the sensitive one. I don't care. I didn't do any of that stuff—"

"You're a bit too young, aren't you?"

They both laughed.

"But nor did my grandparents. They were just Bavarian farmers."

"Well, I hope I didn't hurt her feelings."

Steffi said she was cold and suggested that they sit in Hupey for a moment to warm up. Richard could have another beer, if he liked.

But what about the walk?

"Oh, sod the walk! We can have a chat, can't we? If you don't mind, of course. I know I'm not your cleverest student."

"Come, come!"

"No seriously, have you ever really noticed Lisa or me during your lessons?"

"Well..."

"Always hidden in the back row? Never saying anything? We're not the brightest stars in the academic firmament! Me in particular. Lisa works quite hard, though." She laughed. "But only in short bursts!"

They climbed into the car, and Richard stretched his legs out as best he could. She told him to push the seat back: there was a tiny lever underneath it.

"Ah, that's better!" He stretched his legs sensually, closing his eyes for a moment. "But what's *that*?"

She was holding a bottle under his nose. It was alcohol. She had already unscrewed the cap.

"*Schnapps*, of course! Come on, it's cold, and you're an uptight old Brit! A couple of sips of this will help you relax."

"I can't sit here boozing with you, you're my student! It wouldn't be right."

"No, what wouldn't be right—if you're a gentleman, that is—would be to let me sit here boozing on my own. I can't drink too much of this anyway, because I've got to drive—so I won't get so sloshed that you'll be able to take brutal advantage of me!"

"Steffi, really!"

"Oh, come on, don't be such a wimp. A few sips won't hurt you. Or are you trying to reinforce my stereotype of what Brits are like? Come on, just a sip. Are you a man or a mouse? *I* certainly need one, because you're now going to explain to me what a lousy student I am."

What the heck! So much pressure was too much for Richard, and he took several generous swigs from the bottle.

"Oh!"

It was good stuff.

"What do you mean: oh? This North German junk is completely harmless. In Bavaria we wouldn't even classify it as alcohol."

"Very well, let's be serious for a minute or two. You suggested it! Now 'lousy' is not a word I would use, but maybe you do need a slight change of direction. If you adopted a more—how can I put it?—*businesslike* approach to your degree, you would still have plenty of time. And I'd be only too willing to be your examiner—if you wanted me to be, that is. There's no waiting list for Orwell. I'm not terribly popular as an examiner, you know that."

"Yes, I know that. Not like Jonathan!"

Although it was true, Richard still felt slightly piqued.

"Well, I think some of the students regard him as being easier..."

"Oh, he's easy all right! And in more ways than one. I expect he's already put *Lisa* down on his list. They were getting on like a house on fire!"

Richard was genuinely shocked.

"You're not saying—"

She glowered at him with unexpected ferocity.

"I'm not saying *anything*! But I wouldn't go to that guy if he was the last examiner there was!"

"There are other examiners, you know."

"Well, it doesn't matter anyway, because I won't get that far. I'm going to chuck it in soon. Go back to Passau. Or go round the world. What's the difference, one way or the other? For me, all roads lead to nowhere. I have lots of fun, but studying's not for me. I haven't got what it takes, and I don't think this university wants me either."

Richard gave her a serious look—the stern "adult look" that he sometimes used in his office hour to bring a student to her senses, or when he was telling a girl to pull her socks up (those often being the girls "whose pants you'd most like to pull down," as Philip Larkin once observed).

"Steffi—"

"Richard?"

And he laughed. Sternness was not going to work here.

"OK, do what you want, it's your life. I'd be sad if you left. It would be a waste. And I know someone who'd be really unhappy. Who thinks a lot of you."

"Who's that?"

"Mr. Hodgkins."

"What? *Eddie*? After what I did to his English Conversation class?"

"You beat up Jeannine Garbe, I've been told."

"Shit! I think the whole bloody university must have heard about that. So there's no future for me here now, is there?"

"Eddie would be truly sad if you left. He really likes you."

"Between you and me, Richard, I think he likes *all* the girls. The trouble is, none of them like *him*. Not *that* way, at least."

To his amazement, Richard found himself launching into a eulogy of his irritating temporary tenant.

"Eddie is not everyone's cup of tea, I know that, but he's kind, he's funny, and he always means well. You just have to ignore the silly way he talks sometimes."

"Some of the girls call him Eddie the Shagmaster. Which is an example of irony, I think."

"He's a good person, he knows a lot, and he values the right people. Incidentally, people like *you*, Steffi. And no-one that I respect dislikes him."

"OK, I get the message. Actually, only too well. Because I've noticed a couple of people who don't like him, like Snoad and Harlan Kurz, and that tells me a few things about you, Richard, doesn't it?"

"Stop!"

This was going off the rails. He'd already had too much to drink (he wasn't used to *Schnapps*) and he could hardly talk to a student about which colleagues he disliked, even if was obvious.

It was now dark outside, but it was cosy in the car. And the inevitable happened.

"Eddie likes me. OK." She paused, and then in a husky voice asked, "Do *you* like me, Richard?"

And she placed her hand gently but demonstratively on his thigh.

He lifted her hand away.

"No! We can't do this, Steffi. *I* can't do this. I'm your teacher."

"Then *teach* me, Mr. Orwell. I'm here and I'm willing. No-one needs to know, if that's what's worrying you. We can keep it to ourselves."

"Stop it! Look, they'll be back in a moment."

"No they won't. I'll let you guess what they're doing now. Lisa is one poor, sad, frustrated girl, and your dear colleague Jonathan is nothing more than a predator. He's shagging her right now, wanna bet? Or he's warming her up and he'll shag her tonight back at his place." Then she changed her tone. "OK, I'm being silly, Richard. You're not that kind of guy. You'd never take advantage of a student, I know that. And Hupey here is not ideal for close encounters of the physical kind—I can tell you that from past experience! I've always fancied you, Richard. If it happens it happens, and I don't think I'm going to be your student much longer anyway, if that's what's holding you back. And if nothing happens, that wouldn't be the end of the world either."

She took his hand and made to place it between her legs, but he pulled his hand away.

He almost *didn't*. He imagined the softness of her thighs. And what lay between them. Was it the alcohol?

He found himself saying—foolishly—"It would be nice. But still wrong."

"It would be nice, wouldn't it? Don't worry, if they come back, we'll see the lights of his car. And if they're driving back to Reichsstadt without us, she'll text me first. So—relax, Mr. Orwell. We could cuddle a bit? Do you get many cuddles?"

"Not recently."

What had happened with Miriam Burkhardt wasn't a cuddle.

"I thought not. You do realize that all this was *planned*, like a campaign? Two young ladies, and two gentlemen. She's got a bottle of *Schnapps* with her too!"

"You girls are wicked."

"One thing, though. She was love-sick, but not for Jonathan Snoad. It was Harlan she was crazy about."

Richard started with shock.

"Is she completely mad?"

"No, she's not mad. You know that she was attacked by this monster in the hostel? She's still terrified. She needs to be with a man. Why she picked Harlan Kurz, though..."

Richard felt a chill go through his veins. For a few hours he had forgotten the hostel predator: an actual predator, vicious and dangerous, not a stupid pest like Snoad. For a short while it had been cosy in the car, but now the real world had broken back in with a vengeance.

"Steffi, perhaps you should text her? We need to be sure that she gets back safely tonight. Do it please—now."

"Oh, you're such a party poop, Richard Orwell. A real mood-killer," she protested, but she texted Lisa nevertheless. She also tried to ring her, with no success. "Hmm. Maybe she's switched her phone off?"

He suggested that they hit the biscuits and potato crisps while they were waiting. The temptation of other pleasures had come, and gone. Now both of them were feeling distinctly hungry.

IF IT HAPPENS, IT HAPPENS

They found the *Currywurst* place very quickly. The village was so small you could hardly miss it.

"Look," Lisa said, "if you're a vegetarian or something, why don't you stay in the car? It won't take me long, I promise."

"Oh no, I wouldn't miss this for anything in the world. You like this kind of food so much, you can explain it to me! And I'll have a Coke."

The snack bar stank of fat that had been used far too often. There were a few small, ready-made salads under the glass of the display case beneath the counter; otherwise, it was all meat: mostly sausages of various kinds, waiting to be grilled; and lumpy meatballs. On the counter were plastic dispensers for tomato ketchup and mayonnaise, and plastic cutlery, including tiny, brightly colored plastic tridents for spearing french fries, also two-pronged wooden works for eating pieces of sausage.

"Would you like some fries, at least? You know, 'chips'?"

"No, just a Coke. So, which of these delightful objects is your famous *Currywurst*?"

None of them were, yet, she explained. You had to grill the sausage, chop it into chunks, and then add the spicy red sauce, and some curry powder. It was the sauce that made it a *Currywurst*. Here in Reichsstadt they normally used a plain grilled *Bratwurst*, but in the Communist East they had preferred a skinless sausage, so in Berlin you often had to specify which sort you wanted.

If you were more sophisticated you could ask for a different kind of sausage, but served in *Currywurst*-style, something tastier, like a *Schinkenknacker*, that had swollen under its skin while it was being grilled and would explode its juices into your mouth when you bit into it; or a delicious *Krakauer* from Poland; or a thin sausage that was a meter long.

The normal accompaniment to a *Currywurst* was fries, served either "red" (with tomato ketchup) or "white" (with mayonnaise). Or even "red-white" (with both).

"When my dad was a medical student, they also called that a 'Fortuna', after some soccer club that played in a red-and-white strip."

"And this delicacy is now the national dish of Germany? Like fish and chips in Britain? Or spaghetti in Italy? Oh wow. Hard to believe. Well, you go ahead and order, and I'll enjoy watching you eat the stuff!"

But he paid for her food, like a proper gentleman.

He drove the car onto a secluded but well-lit patch of ground, a sort of improvized parking lot, behind the snack bar and, as he had said he would, watched her closely while she was eating.

This was amazing! Did he fancy her? If he was going to kiss her, this is where it would happen. It wasn't as dark as she would have liked, but there was no-one about.

"If you want to wash that down, you can have a swig of my Coke. Or we can share this."

And he suddenly produced—a small bottle of *Schnapps*! It was uncannily like the one that was still nestling unopened in her bag. And he had two *Schnapps*-glasses too.

"Oh yes, rather! You first, though."

"I can't drink too much if I'm going to drive."

"We can stop for a coffee somewhere on the way back, can't we?"

"You think of everything!"

She ate very slowly, giving herself time to think. And she drank, to give herself courage. There was obviously going to be a kiss.

She congratulated herself on the way the day had worked out. Steffi seemed to be getting on quite well with Richard, and Jonathan Snoad was (to be honest) a vast improvement on Harlan Kurz. What had she ever seen in that guy?

OK, he had a nicer bum than Jonathan (in fact, Jonathan hardly seemed to have any bum at all), but he was so *weird*, and you couldn't understand him half the time; her student friends wouldn't accept him (especially the ones who went to his classes); she didn't know what kind of person he was; her parents would hate him (which in itself was almost a pleasing thought, but which would prove to be a nuisance in the long term); and he didn't have a car.

Jonathan, in comparison, was such a cool character. He was always relaxed, and he had something witty to say about almost everything, usually as a funny put-down. There was a lot to be said for a man who could make you laugh so often and so easily. He was good at imitations, too, just like Harlan. That was his style, she decided: *cool*. How her friends would envy her! And his car, his Bimmer, was out of this world.

She didn't like his reedy voice, or his reedy laugh, but then you couldn't have everything.

She finished eating. She was ready for him now. She saw what the time was on the dashboard clock. There would be a kiss, and he'd grab her tits (didn't all men do that?). There wasn't time for much more than that, and she couldn't imagine doing it in a car. She was a fairly big girl—there just wouldn't be room to do it properly, even in the Bimmer. And it would be so uncool, wouldn't it? They weren't teenagers.

After that, they'd have to go back to meet the others. But he'd make a date to see her—tomorrow, perhaps? For a romantic supper? Could he cook? No, too much work, he was too laid-back for that. He'd send out for something smart, Thai food, or some *sushi*. They'd drink some chilled white wine. And then they'd go his bedroom...

She was curious what his apartment would be like. Very stylish, for sure.

He scrolled down the window on his side. He reached over, took the cardboard serving plate and the plastic cutlery from her, and to her surprise threw them out into the night.

My, what a lordly gesture!

Then he said, "Shall we make ourselves more comfortable, milady?"

He stepped out of the car, went round to her side, opened the door like a chauffeur, and asked her to climb out. What did he mean? She soon found out. He opened the rear door, and indicated that she should get in. Then he joined her on the back seat.

She had now committed herself. He leant over and kissed her.

As he nuzzled her lips, she was painfully aware that her breath must smell of curry ketchup, or of *Schnapps*. His breath didn't smell of anything in particular, she noticed. That was a surprise. Lisa was sensitive on that score, and she could remember the smell of each of her handful of lovers to date. But Jonathan smelt of nothing.

He pushed her lips apart, licked at her teeth and then thrust his tongue into her mouth. Well, yes, *lordly*—that was the word!

He hadn't said anything so far. Fair enough, his mouth was busy. But she liked to hear words expressing delight, or passion.

She was excited, and curious, but she didn't actually feel aroused yet. What would be needed for *that* to happen?

As if on cue, he threw himself onto her. They thrashed about, sucking and biting at each other, his hand roaming all over her body in a frenzy, palpating her breasts through her pullover and rubbing at her crotch through the jeans.

Finally, he said something.

"This is fantastic! But couldn't you, sort of, undo a few buttons perhaps?"

She was dressed for February. In July or August it would have been so much easier!

OK, she needed to give him something to play with. She slipped out of her pullover and undid the front of her blouse, also the fastening of her jeans at the top. While she was doing this, he removed his jacket, folding it carefully and placing it on the floor behind him, and unbuttoned his shirt to the waist.

Then they grabbed each other again.

He soon had her bra off, and was massaging and kissing her tits. She was very aware of his erection. She stroked his hairless chest and bit gently at one of his nipples.

"Ow! Be careful there!"

"Why? You're never gonna breastfeed, are you?"

But he didn't laugh, as he should have done.

"So you like it rough, do you?"

He yanked open the front of her jeans and pulled them down to her knees. Thrusting his hand under her knickers, he pushed his fingers inside her.

Talk about the direct approach! He was kneading her labia and poking his fingers into her. She didn't find it pleasant.

"Look, shouldn't we be getting back? We can always—"

He grunted, and wriggled on her as he pulled his own pants down. She felt the touch of his erection against her skin. She had never felt so helpless in her life. This was worse than with that man in the hostel. Was he trying to fuck her? How could he? With her jeans bunched around her knees there would be no room for him to enter her, even if he ripped her knickers off with force.

He must have had the very same thought. Just as the position she was in was becoming almost unbearably uncomfortable, he raised himself on his hands, giving her room to move.

"Shit, this isn't going to work. Turn round. We'll try something different. I bet your bum is as nice as your tits!"

"No!"

She wasn't going to do it.

"Oh, come on. This little fella needs a home to go to."

He pointed at his erection, then drove it suddenly against her crotch. At that moment, feeling a cramp in one of her legs, Lisa moved to change her position. As she raised her hips slightly, and twisted them, she caught the end of his weapon full-on. She felt it buckle, and twitch, and then suddenly his come was gushing out onto her bare stomach.

"Oh, fuck that! Look what you've made me do!"

Jonathan was furious. She tried to apologize.

"I'm sorry, but—"

It didn't help. He seemed to take it personally. In fact, it got even worse when he saw that his come was smeared all over the upholstery of the seat, too, and some had even landed on his jacket.

"I don't believe it! Man, this can't be happening. Are you a fucking virgin or something? Come on, get out. I need to clean this."

He reached over and opened the door on her side. He didn't actually *push* her out of the car, and slam the door behind her, but it came close.

Then he hunched himself over the upholstery, muttering, and tending to its needs as best he could with a paper handkerchief. He was trying to soak up as much of his semen as he could without rubbing it into the seat and leaving even worse stains.

"Look, Jonathan—" she started, peering in guiltily to see how bad the damage was.

"This is a catastrophe! I'll never get it out like this. I'll have to take it in to be cleaned tomorrow. Well, thank you for *nothing*! All I wanted was a simple blow-job. Was that too much to ask for? What a fucking waste of time you are! I knew it was a mistake."

She tried to remonstrate with him, but he wasn't paying any attention. All that interested him now was the state of his car's upholstery.

"No, really—"

"Just shut up, you stupid cow! I need to concentrate."

And now he did shut the door on her.

Lisa was shaking. She pulled up her jeans, and buttoned up her blouse, but her pullover was still in the car. It wasn't dark, but it was cold. Was anyone watching them? She hoped not.

She opened the door again.

"Jonathan, we need to talk about this. *Please?* And I need my pullover."

He threw the pullover in her face.

"Just sod off, will you?" he shouted at her, and she burst into tears. She collapsed into a little heap of despair. How could he treat her like this?

Jonathan got out of the car, and what happened next took her completely by surprise. Instead of walking over to her, comforting her, and picking her up, he walked round to the other side of the car and climbed into the driver's seat. But before shutting the door he shouted, "Find your own bloody way back—you don't need me. I'm going!"

And then he drove off.

She cried, and cried, and stayed sitting in the dirt for quite a while. Of course he was going to come back. He was pissed off because he'd had a premature thingie. He'd been hoping for much more than *that*, naturally.

His come was now drying on her stomach.

Why did men have to be such pigs?

He'd been "wounded in his manhood" or something (she'd read all about that in a novel). He was British. He was a gentleman. He would come back for her, after he felt he'd made his point.

Except that he didn't.

After what seemed like hours of sitting abandoned on the ground in an impromptu carpark, sinking deeper and deeper into misery, she decided that he wouldn't be coming back after all. Then her mood changed spectacularly.

What a Total Fucking Bastard! He had forced her. Basically, he had *raped* her. And then he'd driven off, leaving her squatting in the dirt. She would go to the police! Her dad knew all the senior policemen from Rotary meetings. Jonathan Fuckface Snoad was going to get himself *disembow-eled*!

However, first she must find her way back to the entrance to the camp, and the other car. Best if Steffi came and collected her, in fact. She'd ring her.

But shocks seldom come on their own. Fumbling for her smartphone, she realized that it was in her bag, along with her wallet. *And her bag was in the car.*

Lisa started to panic. Which way *was* the camp? Instead of being sensible and asking in the snack bar, she rushed off in what proved to be the wrong direction, tripped in the murky light over a low metal railing, and went sprawling on the concrete pavement.

Her whole body ached. Her fashionable jeans were now ripped open at the knee, and she was bruised and bleeding. She had also grazed her elbow.

Now she had no choice but to go back to the snack bar and ask the nice Turkish gentleman for directions. She must have looked a right state! But he didn't say anything about that. He told her how to get to the camp, and he would have driven her there himself, he said, but he was on his own that night and his uncles would murder him if he left the shop.

If she liked she could come behind the counter, though, and keep him company, and later on he'd drive her wherever she wanted.

He leered. He had a lot of gold teeth. She left the snack bar immediately. She'd had enough of getting into cars with strange men for one day!

She walked, but it took her ages. She felt terrible, inside and out, and she wanted to cry again. Anger alternated with panic.

It was still early, but the streets were empty. Flossengamme was a dead place. What if the man with the gold teeth followed her and jumped her? She brought that spasm of paranoia under control, and was faced with an even more horrific one. What if *that* man—the one from the hostel—had followed them to Flossengamme, and was stalking her now? She had to keep telling herself to calm down, that it was utterly unlikely.

Nevertheless, she glanced about her constantly as she walked, even though she saw only shapes and shadows.

Because she wasn't concentrating, she took several wrong turnings. Such a small village, and so many ways to get lost!

By the time that she reached the carpark at the camp, she was exhausted. Steffi and Richard were still there, waiting. Steffi jumped out of the car and rushed over to her, shouting something, tapping at her watch and looking angry—but then looking puzzled.

"Whatever happened to you? Hey, you're crying! And where is bloody Prince Charming."

Now Richard was standing there, too.

Lisa spoke the thought that had never left her mind the whole time that she was stumbling through Flossengamme, looking for them.

"He raped me and left me lying in the dirt."

Then she collapsed.

NIGHT AND LEMURS

Richard and Steffi had bundled her onto the back seat of the car, where she rambled incoherently about what had happened to her, before falling asleep.

They had decided to drive straight back to Reichsstadt. It was dark, but Richard's skill with the maps wouldn't be put to the test. Directions how to get to Reichsstadt, the capital of the Bundesland, were there on every road that they took; on the outward journey, directions on how to reach Flossengamme, a dump with a snack bar, some cows and a former concentration camp, hadn't been much in evidence.

Without taking her eyes off the road, Steffi said, "Ring the bastard, we need to sort this out."

But that was easier said that done. He didn't have Snoad's mobile number saved on his smartphone, he said. Why should he? Nor did he have the number of anyone who would.

"Snoad's friends—"

"Like Harlan Kurz!"

"—are not *my* friends. Dr. Christenkorn might have his landline number, but not his mobile number. He's not into cell-phones."

Steffi pulled over to the side of the road and took out her own phone.

"I'll ring *her* number. If her phone is in her bag and in his car, maybe he'll answer it."

But he didn't answer.

"Either he can't hear it ringing or vibrating," Richard said, "or he doesn't want to talk."

"That bastard has a lot to answer for!"

Lisa slept almost the whole way back, but woke as they drove in through the grubby industrial estate in the eastern suburbs of Reichsstadt.

"Good morning, princess, something stirring back there?"

"I wasn't asleep," she said, unconvincingly.

"No problem. We're almost there. I'll tuck you up, make you a hot drink, and we can talk if you want to."

"Almost *where*?"

"The hostel, of course. Gutie! Where you *live*, sweetheart."

"No, I don't want to go there," she whispered hoarsely, sinking back on to the seat. "Somewhere else. Anywhere else."

"Your parents', then?"

"No."

Richard looked puzzled, but Steffi knew what was going on. Her friend didn't feel safe in the hostel, because of the attack, but nor did Lisa want her parents to see her like that. They'd ask too many questions.

"Then we'll have to find a hotel."

"No," said Richard, "there's another alternative: she can come back to the Südstädter Ring. We've got hot drinks there too, you know. We can talk, if she likes, or just sit and watch TV. And if she wants to sleep there, she can have the sofa."

"I thought you shared with Mr. Hodgkins?"

Snoad had sneered about that. During her little guided tour, when Lisa had mentioned the hundreds of homosexuals who had died in Flossengamme, he had asked Richard rather pointedly whether he was "still living with Hodgkins."

"Yes, Eddie's got my spare room." He turned to look at Lisa, whose eyes were wide open and gleaming. "Would you like that, Lisa?"

"Yes, I would, thank you."

"Then I'd better ring Eddie, and tell him that we're coming. I hope his phone is switched on, just for once."

It was. After he'd finished, Steffi asked him what Eddie had said.

"I mean, does he mind?"

"No, I told you—Eddie is a kind person, and a gentleman. Unlike some people we both know!"

Lisa was staring out of the window at the dark streets of Reichsstadt flitting past. She was shivering.

"Lemurs," she said.

"I beg your pardon?"

"Night and lemurs."

Was she suffering from concussion? Had she bumped her head when she tripped and fell in Flossengamme?

But Richard said, "I think that rings a bell with me. It's from a poem, isn't it? Aren't lemurs those little furry creatures, like koala bears but with big, staring eyes?"

"No, they're monsters," she said.

"Oh, I think not—" he started, but Lisa wasn't listening.

"We read a poem in school. I can't remember much. I didn't like German lessons. The teacher was awful. It was about some tropical island. There was stuff about shadows falling, and animals making noises, and then just: 'night and lemurs'. I've never forgotten that line. I don't care what *real* lemurs are. For me, lemurs are out there in the darkness. Monsters, that come for you in the night, when you're alone and frightened. You know you'll never be safe from them. They're always going to come back, on some dark night when you're not expecting them. *You* can call them something else if you like—but for me they're lemurs."

Her "lemur" was the man who'd come to her room in the hostel; the man she was sure was going to come for her again.

"Then perhaps you *should* crash at Richard's tonight, with two big strong men to protect you!"

Lisa was still shaking when they arrived at the Südstädter Ring. Richard had apparently never "entertained" students there before, and obviously felt uneasy about it, but Eddie was welcoming and attentive. Anyone would think they were a married couple, and he was "mum"!

He bustled about, fussing over Lisa, making a kind of nest of blankets for her on the sofa, and organizing the hot drinks.

He praised Steffi for deciding that Lisa should come to the Südstädter— she needed to be with people—rather than go back to the hostel. (It had been Richard's idea, but she didn't say it.)

He gave Steffi a telling-off for drinking and driving. He had smelt the *Schnapps* on her breath. Had Richard encouraged her? That wasn't very responsible behavior, was it now?

He clucked over Lisa like a mother hen. She didn't need to talk, but perhaps she should try to tell them in simple words what had happened, while the events were still fresh in her memory? After all, she had used the word "rape." That could have serious consequences.

At first, Lisa said nothing, except "You're so kind," and "Thank you" (for the hot lemon tea). When Steffi pressed her to speak, she looked past her with dead eyes and said only "night and lemurs."

Richard had made himself scarce. Was it all too emotionally stressful for him? Steffi thought. The uptight Brit? It had been a heavy day for him too. Uppity students trying to get him drunk, and making passes at him!

But then he beckoned to her to come to the other room with him. His *bedroom*. Wow, surely not?

No, he had something to show her, and it was in a book. A book of poetry translations.

"I knew I'd read about 'night and lemurs' somewhere. Look! It's a translation of a poem called *Palau*, by Gottfried Benn. I can find the German original online, if you like?"

She read:

> *"Evening is red on the island of Palau*
> *The shadows are sinking*
> *Sing! From a woman's cups, too*
> *You can be drinking*
> *Death-birds are screaming*
> *The death-watch hammers*
> *Soon night will be coming*
> *Night—and the lemures [...]*

OK. So what about it? Bit weird, I'd say."

"Palau is an island in the Pacific. But you only find lemurs on Madagascar, in the Indian Ocean. So it's not the cuddly lemurs, it's 'lemures', with an 'e'."

"What are they?"

"The spirits of the dead."

POST COITUM

Lisa was dreading having to talk about it, but she knew she was going to have to. She had said "rape." Not "mistake," or "quarrel," or "fight": words that you could leave hanging in the air without the need for an explanation. But "rape" was a very heavy word indeed, and it wouldn't be going anywhere until it had been dealt with.

Besides, there was something else that oppressed her far more, and had done for months. Maybe it would help to get the one thing, the lesser hurt, out of the way? And they were being so nice to her—she owed it to them.

Her anger had dimmed a little, but was still flickering. She didn't want her father to know, even if that meant keeping the police out of it. Perhaps the university authorities would be the right people to speak to? He had forced her. He had hurt her. She had had an hour of nightmare because of him, and she wanted to hurt him back.

Get it done with! All she wanted now was to sleep.

She told them everything, in a rush. No-one interrupted her, except to ask whether she wanted another drink. Eddie, she saw, was taking notes.

When she had finished, there was silence for a few seconds, and then Steffi shouted, "Fuck the bastard! Crucify him!"

Richard said, "Someone should talk to him."

Steffi: "Yeah, someone with a baseball bat!"

"You should go to the police, " Richard continued. "I'll come with you if you like."

And then Eddie said, "But it wasn't rape, was it, though?" (Steffi: "*What?*") "No, bear with me, can we just go through what happened, step by step?"

And she had to tell her story all over again, with frequent interruptions from Steffi, who seemed to have appointed herself her counselor.

It was Steffi who reminded them how cold-bloodedly Snoad had set it up, cutting their tour of Flossengamme short so that he could be alone with her.

Lisa shook her head. No, to be fair, *she* had done that.

Why?

Because she wanted Steffi and Richard to have some time together, because she thought they might, you know, hit it off?

Steffi laughed (why did she do that?). Richard looked embarrassed, but didn't say anything. He raised the next point, though: Snoad had plied her with alcohol, hadn't he?

(Steffi: "Just as I did with you!")

Again, Lisa had to admit that she'd had a bottle of *Schnapps* with her, too. But he had been quicker with his bottle than she had with hers.

Eddie looked glum.

"So far, not so good. Did he force you to go on the back seat with him, or did you go willingly?"

"He didn't force me."

"Did he force you to kiss him?"

"No."

"Did you kiss him back?"

"Yes."

"He touched your body. Did you touch his?"

"Yes."

Steffi interrupted: "Look, mate, whose side are you on? Is this some kind of male solidarity thing?"

Eddie was indignant.

"What, solidarity with Jonathan Snoad? *Me?* He hates my guts. And I'd push him off a cliff any day. But if Lisa goes to the police with this, they'll ask the same questions."

Lisa shook her head at the word "police." "No. No police."

Steffi suggested that she could go to the Gender Equality woman, Kerstin Dröge-Daschmeyer.

"She's as hard as nails, and she hates men. If we want him crucified, she'll do it for you!"

But Richard had seen her in action, he said. She was a Rottweiler, but she would never go for her target unless the case was rock-solid.

"And you know why? She's got so many enemies, if she slips up even once they'll boot her out. All those old MCP Professors in the Senate. She hates them, and they hate her. They're just waiting for a chance to bring her down."

"Look," Eddie said, "I'm sorry to get personal, but did *he* loosen your clothes, or did you do it?"

"I did it."

"So you were giving him access to your body? At this stage, you still wanted contact with him?"

"Yeah, I suppose so."

"Sorry, no 'suppose' about it—it has to be either 'yes' or 'no'."

"Yes. I still wanted him. But I was drunk!"

"And when he touched you... *there*, did you say 'no'?" Lisa didn't answer. "This is important—we need to be clear about when you said 'no' the first time."

"I said 'no' when he asked me to turn round."

"Why did he do that?"

"He wanted to do it from behind."

Steffi was outraged.

"The pig! What a disgusting—"

"No," Lisa cut her short, "not like *that*. He just needed more room."

"But you said 'no'?"

"Definitely."

"And what did you mean by 'no'? That you didn't want to have sex with him? Or that you didn't want to have sex with him *in that position*?"

"Both, maybe. I dunno. I just didn't want to. 'No' means 'no', doesn't it?"

"Yes, it does. You don't have to justify yourself. If you say 'no', he has to stop. *Did* he stop?"

"He squirted his stuff all over me. And all over his bloody car! I still feel sticky."

(Steffi: "I'll run a bath for you."

Richard: "Sorry. I haven't got a bath. Just a shower."

Steffi: "OK. Then we'll take a shower!")

"So: there was no penetration?"

"No."

"Did anything else happen after he'd had his premature ejaculation?"

"He shouted at me."

"But he didn't hit you?"

"No." But she added: "He threw my pullover in my face!"

"Did he pin you down?"

She hesitated.

"Well, no, not really."

Eddie looked at each of them in turn.

"So that's all there is? M'lud, I rest my case. This was not rape."

"You stupid sod!" Steffi shouted at him. "If it wasn't rape, what the fuck *was* it then?"

And it was Richard who answered.

"It was bad sex. We've all had that in our lives, haven't we? I know that I have. Crossed wires. A misunderstanding. The wrong person. The wrong place. The wrong time. A stupid mess."

"I know what you mean," Eddie said. "Sometimes you try too hard..."

Lisa sniffled. She wanted to cry, but she was too tired.

"I don't think I've had any *other* kind of sex. Ever."

Eddie: "I know the feeling."

"It's up to you whether you report him," Richard said. "He was a pig. He's a nasty specimen. But he didn't rape you. That doesn't mean that I think he should get away with it, but I'm not sure what you can do about it, Lisa."

She sighed.

"Pick someone nicer next time? Let's just forget about it."

Steffi was still fuming.

"Forget about it? He forces himself on you, throws you out of his car, insults you, drives off leaving you alone after dark in a strange place with no money and no smartphone... 'Just a bit of bad sex?' That's the way *men* talk, Lisa. I'm surprised at you! That guy needs his balls cut off with rusty garden shears!"

"Oh, just let it be, Steffi. All I want to do now is sleep."

"But not at the hostel?"

"No, not tonight."

Eddie, like a perfect gentleman, offered her his bed in the spare room. He had changed the sheets that very morning. He would sleep on the sofa. And he disappeared immediately, to check the arrangements for her.

"You can sleep for as long as you like," Richard said, "and you'll get a fantastic breakfast. That's the least we can do! You showed us Flossengamme, and we all learned something today."

"Look, he still has your phone," Steffi said, "and your wallet, doesn't he? I'll get them back for you, and while I'm about it I'll tell Fuckface what I think of him. Oh, and while I might not get round to cutting his balls off, it's not true that there's nothing we can do about him. He worries about his image, doesn't he? So, a few graffiti, perhaps? And we can put the word out on the grapevine about him. Gundi would be a good person to start with."

"What was that about my old friend Gundi?" Eddie asked, as he came back in. And to Lisa: "I've opened the window to air the room for a few minutes!"

Steffi got up.

"I need to get back to the hostel. Love you and leave you. OK? Can't say that *everything* was fun today. Next time: better organization, eh?"

Eddie offered to see her safely home ("There are some nasty people about"). Steffi laughed.

"My, you *are* in cavalier mode today! You should do it more often, it suits you! Actually, I'm driving. But if you want to escort me across the perils of the Gutie carpark, you're very welcome."

When they had gone, Lisa said "thank you" to Richard. It was so kind of him to let her stay. She wouldn't tell anyone about it. She didn't want to embarrass him. And maybe one day she'd like to have him as an examiner?

Richard showed her the bathroom and explained how the shower worked (basically, not very well). The graze on her knee wasn't as bad as she'd thought, and wouldn't require any special treatment, but he gave her some antiseptic and a couple of sticking-plasters just in case. He also handed her a brand-new toothbrush and some fluffy towels, and fished out a huge T-shirt for her to use as a nightie. (She preferred sleeping nude, but she didn't say that.)

She shouldn't be alarmed, he said, if there were any strange sounds. That would just be Eddie, letting himself back in and using the bathroom. He tended to be noisy. And he sincerely hoped that Eddie wouldn't forget that she was there, and try to climb into his bed in the spare room. ("Just my joke, of course!")

At first, she found it hard to get to sleep. She was in a strange apartment, in a strange bed, and it had been a pretty hairy day. She didn't sleep well, and something woke her during the night. For a moment she thought she was back in the hostel, and that *he* had broken into the apartment and was looking for her.

She got up and went to reconnoitre (wisely remembering to slip on the improvized "nightie" first). There was no-one on the sofa. Eddie had not returned yet from the hostel. She peered at her watch and was able to make out that it was 4 a.m. Now *that* was interesting! Steffi, you naughty girl.

She found the bathroom, and had a wee. She peeked into the bedroom (the door had been left ajar). Richard was sleeping soundly, like a baby. Could it be that he was wheezing slightly? It wasn't exactly snoring. The bed was large, and looked temptingly comfortable. Much better than the old mattress in the spare room.

It had been a day of silly things. Why not add a final silliness? Very carefully she climbed into the bed. Could she risk a gentle cuddle without waking him? Why not?

As she drifted sweetly into sleep, the thought came to her that in twenty-four hours she had "bedded," so to speak, not one but *two* of her lecturers, and neither of them the one she had originally intended to seduce.

A TRAP IS SPRUNG

Eddie rang him late the next morning. He and Steffi hadn't got up yet, and they weren't really planning to for a few more hours at least. They were quite happy enough where they were! But Eddie had a strong need to tell someone, and who else could that be but Richard? Smartphones had their uses, and Eddie had recently gotten more into the habit of remembering to switch his on, ever since the surveillance project with Dermot had started.

There was so much to tell, but Steffi saved Eddie the trouble of finding a tactful, roundabout way of telling Richard that he was in bed *with a girl* by shouting, "Is that Richard? Give him my love!"

He hoped Richard was suitably impressed. He had presumably reached the same conclusion anyway, from the fact that Eddie hadn't returned that night.

All the same, he said, "That was Steffi, of course. Look, you and I need to talk. Did you get a chance to talk to Lisa? No, not about yesterday. About the hostel business."

To his surprise, Richard told him that, no, he hadn't a chance yet, but that Lisa was still there and maybe they'd get an opportunity later, over lunch?

Now *that* was interesting. What had they been up to? The "need to talk" now took on a whole new dimension. But Steffi was having none of it. She snatched the phone out of Eddie's hand.

"Sorry, Richard, the bullshitting will have to wait. Eddie and I have a lot of stuff to talk about. So unless it's super-urgent university business, or your Sherlock investigations, later please, OK? Give my love to Lisa. Bye-ee."

Eddie couldn't be annoyed with her, though. They did have a lot of "stuff" to talk about it.

She was a good talker (he thought) but an even better listener. They had so many interests in common, he was amazed to discover.

She liked (and disliked) the same people that he did.

They enjoyed the same books. (Not that she had read as many as he had, of course.)

Her taste in music was comparatively undeveloped. There was nothing wrong with Razorblade or Thong as such, but they were so derivative. He would introduce her to Velvet Underground, John Cale, Patti Smith, and some of the more interesting Punk bands. They would blow her mind.

Obviously, she would love his sound system.

She had a great sense of humor, and it wasn't so different from his.

And she *liked* him.

He hadn't had a proper friend for such a long time. Though Richard meant well, he didn't really count. He wasn't a good listener, and even when he was pretending to show an interest you could sense that his mind was somewhere else. Steffi was the real thing, though. And not only had he found a "mate"—he'd won the sweepstake and found one who was a *girl*!

When was the last time he'd woken up to find himself in bed with a girl who *didn't* say, "Why did we drink so much last night?" and ask him to leave before anyone saw him? It didn't bear thinking about.

So the next few days were going to be spent in her company (he hoped). She'd already declared that she wanted to join him on his next trip with the Young Antiquarians.

"I always thought Gallows Hill sounded spooky!"

Heck, he was telling her everything! He hadn't even told Richard that he'd not only joined Hans-Robert's little team, he had already been inside the caves with them on a first, brief exploration (before they realized that they needed better lighting gear).

Naturally, he'd also told her about their search for the hostel intruder. She hadn't been surprised.

"Someone's got to find that guy. You saw how frightened Lisa is. Even if it's only some harmless pervert, some Peeping Tom, he's gotta be stopped."

But she couldn't contribute anything useful: Lisa hadn't really confided in her about what had happened.

And she was amused to find out that Jeannine Garbe had been one of his victims. That explained why the girl was so totally screwed up, she opined. Maybe she should have gone easier on her?

"Maybe you should."

"You know me! Well, you *do* know me now, don't you?" she said, pinching his cheek amorously. "But there's plenty more to find out. And when my brakes are off, *Herr Doktor*—they're *well and truly* off."

There followed a couple of minutes of pretended fleeing and chasing, accompanied by shrieks and giggles, and, when the hunter finally trapped his prey, which was not a difficult task, given the modest size of the hostel room, a longer period of intensive and strenuous "finding out."

Saint Agathe the Virtuous had fortunately already gone home to her parents.

The next few days were similarly enjoyable. Steffi admitted that she'd probably be spending the holidays in Reichsstadt (Passau and back was a long slog for poor old Hupey, and she couldn't afford the train), so it would be up to Eddie, wouldn't it, to see that she wasn't too bored—assuming that he felt up to it?

Eddie had never felt more up to anything in his life.

He returned to Richard's apartment every day, but only to pick up clean clothes. He and Richard, who now had his head down getting exam papers marked, didn't talk much, at least after the first meeting, when Eddie had naturally quizzed him about Lisa.

"So, how was it? If you had to describe it...?"

Eddie had evolved his own "taxonomy of leg-overs," as he called them: the *duty* one (it was the girl's birthday); the *routine* one (it was Saturday night); the *drunken* one (self-explanatory); the *tactical* one (you wanted a favor from her); the *earth-moving* one (as in Hemingway!); the *trophy* one (where you notched the bedpost afterwards); the *comfort* one (someone had just failed their exam again); the not-so-nice *revenge* one...

At first, Richard had been reluctant to answer.

Eventually he said, "You're making a lot of assumptions, aren't you? I didn't say that we did anything. did I? And even if we had, I wouldn't be telling people about it. *Der Kavalier geniesst und schweigt* ["A true gentleman takes his pleasure, but keeps his mouth shut about it"]. She's my student, and she wants me as her examiner. But, yes, she was in my bed when I woke up. That much I'll admit to. And we had a cuddle. Which was nice. Well, better than a poke in the eye with a blunt stick."

"But the earth didn't move?"

"Oh for Chrissake! Does the earth always have to move? Sometimes it's good just for it to be there, you know? Solid ground, not moving? So that you feel safe. That you can trust someone. That they like you. But what about you and Steffi? Come on, fair's fair."

Eddie had put on a show of indignation.

"Fair's fair? Sherlock, you haven't told me zilch, so why should I tell *you* anything? But I will, because you're my mate, and because it doesn't matter any more."

It didn't matter any more, he said, because he was going. Eddie had decided to leave Reichsstadt. The Snake wanted him out (everyone knew that). So why should anyone care?

Richard had looked quite hurt.

"*I* care, Eddie. I'll care a lot. and I won't be the only one."

"Steffi is probably leaving, too. She says she'll give it one more semester. But she said that before she goes she intends to take down Snoad. His days here are numbered."

"Good for her!"

"Actually, the earth did move a bit."

"Hmm."

That didn't sound to Eddie like the reaction of a man who was enjoying a week of fun and games with a new girlfriend, but maybe the exam-paper marking was getting to him? Eddie saw so little of Richard that week that he couldn't judge.

He was just beginning to write Richard off and make his own plans for the coming weekend, plans that involved going away somewhere quiet with Steffi, when an unexpected late-afternoon phone-call plunged them both back into cold reality.

Dermot rang, to say that "person number one"—his code-name for Kajo Christenkorn—was in room 26 at the Kronprinz Johann, *and he wasn't alone.*

How did Dermot know that? Because he'd slipped past the reception desk, followed Kajo up the stairs, and observed him entering the room. When he had put his ear to the door, he had heard muffled voices, one obviously Kajo's, the other voice higher-pitched.

Eddie should come at once. Dermot would stay near the room, which was on the first floor, and wait for him.

Eddie immediately rang Richard, who grumpily thanked him for so kindly disturbing him while he was marking, but he snapped out of it at once when Eddie told him the news.

"Good that this has happened now. If we hurry, and we catch Kajo playing around with a bird, we can rule him out, as I said we should all along! And since you're leaving anyway, you can do the confrontational stuff, OK? Meet you in the Gutie carpark in eight or ten minutes."

Those eight or ten minutes were needed for Richard to run down the hill from Südstädter Ring 27; Eddie, on the other hand, would scarcely need two minutes to saunter out to the carpark.

In those two minutes he mulled over two major problems that they faced.

Firstly, how to get from Gutie to the Kronprinz Johann? Richard was probably assuming that Steffi would drive them, but Steffi was crashed out on her bed sleeping off the three-quarters of a bottle of Soave that she'd had with her lunch (Eddie had stuck with beer). Neither Richard nor Eddie had a driver's license, and even if it had been a matter of life and death, Eddie (who could barely remember his driving lessons) wouldn't trust himself to drive Hupey.

The second problem was how to handle the situation at the hotel. He had read often enough about private eyes crashing into a hotel room to get documentary evidence of an adulterous assignation. That might have been perfectly all right for Philip Marlowe and his colleagues, but all it would do today was get them arrested for disturbing the peace, breaking and entering, trespass, threatening behavior, assault and God knows what else.

He tried to explain this to Richard.

"What, no Hupey? Hell's bells! Then we'll take a taxi. And you are paying. This is *your* show, remember?"

But what number did you call for a taxi? 7070? 7700? 7007? Then they realized that both of them had left their smartphones behind.

They ended up taking a bus.

During the short but infuriatingly slow bus-ride, Richard emphasized (for the umpteenth time) that Eddie was now in charge, and that he must "sort it," one way or the other. Kajo was *his* suspect, and Dermot was *his* buddy, not Richard's.

And weren't they wasting their time? The police were already investigating a crime in that street, maybe even in that hotel. Wouldn't the criminal be crazy to go back there again?

Richard obviously didn't understand the criminal mind, he was told. Serial killers loved to return to the scene of the crime, and they had favorite hunting grounds.

"What, so Kajo Christenkorn, who can't even operate an overhead projector, is now a serial killer?"

They literally ran all the way from the bus-stop, and arrived at the hotel panting and gasping. There was no-one at the reception desk (wasn't it always like that at cheap hotels?). Confusingly, the rooms with a "1" as the first number were on the ground floor; those with a "2" were on the first floor.

Dermot was waiting for them there as promised, a hulking, shambling figure in a greasy gray overcoat. He greeted Eddie with enthusiasm.

"Great, I've done my bit and now it's all yours. (Go easy on Rita, man, you know you said you would?) See you at Murphy's? Oh, and you couldn't oblige me with some change, like? As expenses?"

Eddie and Richard looked at each other.

Eddie had bought the bus-tickets. Richard blinked first. With bad grace, he fumbled in his wallet and extracted the lowest denomination banknote he could find—20 Euros.

"We'll take it from here."

But how?

Dermot left, and they waited. Yes, there were faint voices coming from inside the room, and was that laughter?

A plump lady of uncertain age approached them. She had immense breasts. Could breasts be that large, Eddie wondered, without surgical intervention? She offered the two young men her services. 100 Euros included the charge for the room. Depending on what they wanted, if they were quick she could accommodate both of them.

Er, no thank you, they were meeting a friend.

"Aren't we all, *Schätzchen*? Love is a cruel mistress. Good luck then."

Richard was seething.

"This is nonsense, and you know it," he hissed. "To think that I left my marking, just as I was getting into the groove, for *this*! I don't even believe that Kajo is in there."

"Just hang on a bit. Have patience."

And so they did. If whoever was in there was hiring the room by the hour, he must be getting near to the end of his second hour by now.

"Come on, this really is ridiculous! We've been sent on a wild goose chase—by an *Irishman*, of course!" (what was he rambling about?) "And did you smell the booze on his breath? He's down at Murphy's now, spending my hard-earned money! Have you been drinking too?"

"Shh!"

The door was opening. The voices were suddenly louder, and one of them was definitely Kajo's. Eddie and Richard remained where they were standing. There was no point in running—they would be seen anyway.

Two men came out of the room and stood, staring at them in surprise. One of them was Kajo Christenkorn. The other was Rico.

REVELATIONS, AND AN INVITATION

All four of them gawped in astonishment. But if Richard was quick to grasp the situation, Rico was even quicker.

"Hey, you guys, what a nice surprise! I knew you were living together, but I didn't realize..."

Eddie shouted, "This is not what you think!"

Kajo reached out and touched Rico's forearm in a restraining gseture.

"It doesn't matter what we think, Rico, they can do what they like."

"I'm sorry if we surprised you, Dr. Christenkorn—"

"Karl-Johannes, please."

"Eddie and I are not a gay couple. We're just here by accident."

Kajo smiled. Richard had never seen him smile so sweetly.

"Rico and I are *not* here by accident. We *are* a gay couple."

Eddie slowly offered Rico his hand in congratulation; then, even more hesitantly, he did the same with Kajo.

"I'm sorry I shouted."

"Thank you Mr. Hodgkins. Or may I say Eddie? You youngsters are so informal! It takes some getting used to."

"Eddie, of course."

"Look, Eddie, Richard, it doesn't matter whether you're a couple or not. If you are, your secret is safe with us. But it wouldn't matter if people knew. Rico is still my student, so for us it's different. Next semester he'll be switching to Esthetic Praxes, where," and he smiled again, "the Love That Dare Not Speak Its Name is one of those praxes that they seem to cultivate. Until, then, we'd be grateful if you could keep this to yourselves? Until the Student Matriculation Office has confirmed the move, in April or May? I appreciate that, in the meantime, the temptation to gossip about this will be overwhelming."

"Not a word, Karl-Johannes. Scout's honor."

Eddie reached out his hand once again.

"On my honor as an officer and a gentleman!"

Rico couldn't resist: "Ooh, now we're on shaky ground!"

"I'm sorry, Karl-Johannes, but I have to ask: does Tilde know about this?"

"Yes, she does, Richard. I moved out a week ago. I've left her everything that I own except my clothes and my laptop. I'm staying with an old school friend. He understands about Tilde, but I haven't told him more than that. So I can't bring Rico under his roof. We're looking for a small apartment for the summer semester. Tilde will be happier without me. Over the years I've disappointed her, and she's made my life miserable. I have ten years left in this job, and I want those to be happy ones."

He looked affectionately at Rico, who smiled back.

"Why shouldn't they be, Kajo?"

Wow, he was calling him "Kajo," and Kajo didn't mind!

"Yes, why shouldn't they be?" He paused. "So, gentlemen, *mum's the word*? I think that's what they say in Britain, don't they? We'll be on our way."

Rico offered them a lift to the university. Kajo wanted to check his mail. Richard accepted the offer, but Eddie said that he would find his own way back. There was someone waiting for him, and they had a sort of date. More of an *activity*, actually, but he didn't want to miss it.

He used the German word "jemand," which is not gender-specific. Rico still winked at him, and said, "You don't want to keep her waiting, do you?"

Rico's car could well have been Hupey's elderly aunt, but Rico got the three of them to the university in one piece. The two lecturers retrieved their mail, while Kajo's friend-cum-lover-cum-chauffeur hovered in the background.

"Thank you again, Richard. You're a decent man. I don't know how long it will last, but he makes me really happy."

"Yes, I can see that."

"I owe you. I won't forget this."

There was no letter or card from "S." waiting in Richard's mailbox. She wasn't prepared to meet his challenge. Had this just been a childish game for her, tweaking him with erotic fantasies and images, but not prepared to risk meeting him? If she really was so crazy about him, was she frightened that he might just look at her and say "You're not my type"? Or, even worse, put her on her back, take what he wanted from her, and move on?

There was a faint chance that she'd written "care of Max Weber," but he couldn't imagine that she'd dare to put details of a time and place for them to meet in a letter left in a public corridor, even if it was hidden behind a picture-frame.

He'd go and look, though he didn't expect to find anything.

It dawned on him that, to be honest, he didn't care one way or the other. He'd had his fling with Miriam Burkhardt, and look how that had turned out! And he felt comfortable with Lisa. He wasn't sure which direction that might take, but he had a feeling that it could be positive.

"Feeling"—that was the key word. In a subtle way, Lisa had woken emotions in him that he hadn't felt since... when? He couldn't even remember.

What there was in his mailbox, amongst other stuff, was what looked like a second letter from Volker Cordes. He couldn't open it while Kajo was standing almost next to him. He would go and check out Max Weber!

"Good night, Karl-Johannes. I'm off now!"

"Good night, Richard. And you can call me 'Kajo' if you like. It probably fits the new me better than 'Karl-Johannes' does."

There was no-one to be seen in the Sociology corridor. And of course there was nothing from "S." Fair enough.

He wandered about, looking for someone to sit down and read his mail in comfort. No chance in Sociology! Did those guys *never* feel the urge to just sit down, make themselves comfy, and take a time-out? What the University of Reichsstadt needed was a British-style Junior Common Room, with armchairs, newspapers and a proper coffee-machine.

The *Mensa* was shut, and the cafeteria was shut too. It was a Friday, long after six, in the holidays. Why should they still be open?

Thinking about coffee-machines, he remembered that there was one (a terrible one!) outside the library, with a few chairs and benches. The chairs were nearly always taken, but since the library would also be shut he might just be in luck.

The university seemed to be empty. They'd already switched off all the lights in the library. When did they lock up? He thought it was at 10. The duty porter would go round checking everything after 9.

Even if you got yourself locked in, there was a small side-door near the main entrance that could be opened from the inside, to let people out (but not in). That arrangement had been put in place many, many years ago, before the era of mobile phones. A girl had had a French oral exam late on a Friday night, had failed, and had fled to the Ladies' to cry her heart out, copiously and at great length. When she finally emerged, the poor girl found that her examiners, who had a master key, had already left, effectively locking her in for the night. Talk about adding insult to injury!

The side-door had been installed, and the porters instructed to make their final round slightly later in the evening. So there was no danger of Richard finding himself locked in, even though he'd left his smartphone behind.

He opened the letter.

Dear Mr. Orwell,

I promised to get in touch again. I'll be in Reichsstadt on Friday to visit my sister. If you want to know more about Mr. G., we can talk for half-an-hour. I need to catch the last train back to Berlin. Meet me outside the language lab at 8 o'clock. You've got a key for that I expect. It'll be nice and quiet. The porter won't come round before 9.

If you can't make it, no problem. But I won't be in Reichsstadt again for months, and there is some stuff you don't put in a letter, if you understand what I mean?

Be there at 8. I won't hang about. I don't want to miss my train.

All best

V. Cordes

Oh hell. That was today! The bloody letter must have been sitting there waiting for him for a couple of days, while he was gallivanting about in Flossengamme. He hadn't checked his mail for how long? You just *didn't* in the holidays.

He looked at his watch. It was twenty to eight. And his watch might be a few minutes slow. But he still had time. He could make it easily, even allowing for a short trip to the nearest Gents' restroom.

He had known that Eddie's "Kajo lead" would prove to be worthless. Which made it all the more important to find out what Volker Cordes knew about Geisler. The Head Porter was now their main suspect. If Volker Cordes had some incriminating information on him...

Maybe he'd tell him that that hypocrite Geisler had been trying to hit on girl students too, the offence for which poor Volker had been given the push.

Or that Geisler had been involved in some minor hanky-panky like stealing technical equipment, or fiddling his accounts.

Or that he'd been downloading kiddie porn.

Probably it would prove to be nothing. Cordes was bitter about his former boss and was out to hurt him.

What if he knew, though, that Geisler had a secret hobby? That he'd been accessing the hostels through the cellars? Maybe he'd seen him there? He was supposedly the only other person brave enough to venture down there.

It was time to find out.

Richard found the wide stairwell that led down to the basement. He switched on the lights and descended the stairs. At the bottom he turned right, walking past the door to the porters' room. He tried it very cautiously, but it was locked. At the most there would be only one porter still on duty, who in about an hour would start his final round; in the meantime, he'd be having a quiet snooze at reception by the main entrance.

More likely, since it was the holidays, the final circuit would be made by *Herr* Geisler, who would come over from his apartment on the campus to do the honors. Richard's meeting with Volker Cordes would need to be brief, not just because of the train business—it wouldn't do for Geisler to catch them talking. Richard was perfectly willing to believe that Geisler was capable of serious violence.

Beyond the door to the porters' room was the locked steel door that led down to the cellars. This too was locked. Richard shuddered at the thought of going down there, at night, alone, with the campus in darkness and the buildings virtually deserted.

A few yards further along the corridor was the entrance to the language lab. The corridor ran further down to a series of storerooms and workshops assigned to different departments, but in actual fact seldom used. As far as Richard knew, they were mostly full of out-of-date junk.

He stood in front of the lab and realized that he didn't have a key. That was because he had found the letter so late. His language lab key (most of the members of the English Department had one, whether they needed to use the lab or not) was in his desk, in his office.

Did he have time to fetch it? He looked at his watch: it was six minutes to eight. No, he wouldn't be able to manage it. And he didn't want to miss Volker Cordes, who might be impatient to get to the station to catch his train. He would stay where he was—and suggest that they find a quiet corner by the storerooms to talk.

He walked down in that direction. The corridor was lined with dusty glass display cases containing geological specimens and stuffed animals: a fox, an owl, a ferret. Or was the ferret a stout or a weasel? He had no idea, and the light was too murky for him to be able to read the grimy labels. There were huge canisters of rolled-up wall-maps, for history or geography teaching, and a couple of maps (perhaps more often or recently used) were suspended from a hook in the wall. The one on top was "Asia: Physical Features."

Suddenly he felt a presence behind him, and a flickering of the light. He turned round. Looming up in front of him was the large figure of a young man. He must have been at least the same size as Geisler.

"*Herr* Orwell?" He pronounced it "OR-vell," but Richard was used to that. His voice was unexpectedly high-pitched.

"Yes?"

"I am Volker Cordes. I wrote to you."

"I'm very pleased to meet you!"

Richard held out his hand, and Cordes took it in a large paw, but then released it without actually shaking it. For such a big, muscular-looking man, he had a surprisingly smooth, babyish face. Richard would have taken him for educationally backward—perhaps he'd been to a school for pupils with special needs—except that his eyes, small, deep-set, piggy eyes, told a different story.

He was was rocking backwards and forwards slightly on the balls of his feet. Poised. This was a man, Richard reminded himself, who was bent on revenge.

"Have you got the key then?" he asked.

Richard explained how he'd not been able to bring the language lab key with him. But they could find somewhere else to talk for a few minutes, couldn't they? Perhaps one of the storerooms would be unlocked? There were at least five of six of them. He set off in that direction.

He heard Cordes behind him saying, "I haven't got much time" and then: "I want to do this properly."

Richard was puzzled.

"Why? What do you mean?"

"I want this to be *just right*."

The way he said it made Richard turn in surprise, but not quickly enough to see what hit him, knocking him smack into a black pit of shock and pain before he lost consciousness.

BELOW STAIRS

When Richard came to, his head was hurting like it had never ever hurt before, and he was in complete darkness. He was tied up, with his hands behind his back, and sitting on, but not bound to, a standard wooden class-room chair. He knew that it was a classroom chair from the curved form of the seat and the back-rest.

He could hardly breathe. There was a lot of cloth around his head: a gag, cutting into his cheeks, and a blindfold. That was why it was so dark!

He could nevertheless smell the damp. He was below ground. Had Cordes taken him down into the cellars or, deeper still, into the catacombs? Richard had been hunting a predator, and without knowing it he had found him—or, rather, it was the predator who had found *Richard*. And now the man was going to kill him.

Or had he just left him to die?

He wasn't sure which prospect was *less* terrifying.

No-one would find him here. No-one would even be looking for him. No-one ever came down here, except for *this man*, Volker Cordes, and Geisler. And now Richard himself, of course, though not of his own free will.

The cellars were always locked, and the porters were frightened to enter them because of the Snatchers. Except maybe Geisler, and Geisler wouldn't come down here unless he had a reason. He must have already done his evening round, and now he would be sitting watching television, drinking a beer. How many weeks or months would it be before he opened the locked steel door to go down and retrieve a file from the archives? And would he venture beyond those few yards, deeper into the cellars?

There would be no search parties for days. Eddie might eventually report him missing. It was Kajo who had seen him last, at the mailboxes. They would start looking for him, in the places they knew he went to, but why should they search *here*? By the time someone had the bright idea of checking the cellars as well it would be too late for him.

Richard wasn't tied to the chair, so he could probably get up and walk. How far could he stagger before falling down a stairwell, or knocking himself out against a wall, or cutting himself on something sharp? He had no idea how far the catacombs extended, or which direction it would be best to go in.

He realized that he could wiggle his toes. Cordes had taken his shoes off! As a trophy? Or to make it harder for him to escape? God, was he planning to cut his toes off (after chopping off his fingers)?

Richard felt like crying. Why hadn't he just left well alone, ignored the President, gone to the police, let the tough guys deal with it? He wasn't a tough guy.

Anything but.

Perhaps Cordes was watching him. Enjoying it.

"Is there anyone there?"

Except that it came out as "Uurh-thurh-ugh-ugh-ugh-thugh?" because of the gag.

He waited. He didn't sense any presence; he couldn't hear anything apart from his own breathing; and he couldn't smell anything, except for the damp and his own fear.

Cutting himself on something sharp—that gave him an idea. If he were to walk into something sharp or jagged, he might hurt himself, but perhaps he could cut through the cord or cloth tying his hands together? Yes, it was worth a try.

He tried to get up, but immediately flopped back onto the chair. He hadn't noticed that his legs had also been tied together, loosely, and that they had gone to sleep.

OK, he'd move his legs from side to side and try to get some life back into them. Then he'd make another attempt. But he couldn't wait too long. Cordes might already be on his way back.

There was a sound: the lightest of footsteps. Through the blindfold he was faintly aware of light. It was too late! He tensed himself for the blow, or the sharp pain of a cut. Now someone was in front of him. He heard their breathing, and smelt... what? It wasn't a man. It was a woman.

Hands were touching his face, gently.

"Be still, while I take these off."

It was a woman's voice, speaking English with only the slightest German accent. A familiar voice, but he couldn't place it.

She untied and removed the gag. Gratefully, he sucked in the damp air of the catacombs.

"Oh *God*, thank goodness. Thank goodness."

Now she was fumbling with the blindfold. Finally it came off, and she stepped back.

He blinked for only a moment. There was no bright light to dazzle him, just a feeble bicycle lamp or similar, which she had placed on the ground near him. She was standing in front of him, but the lamp illuminated mostly her feet.

Whoever she was, she was small, and conservatively dressed. He couldn't make out her features in the darkness, and he only realized who it was when she spoke again.

"Poor Mr. Orwell. You don't recognize me, do you?"

It was Kyra Henkel.

"Oh, *Frau* Henkel, thank goodness you've come. Please get me untied. Please hurry! He may be coming back."

"Who?"

"Volker Cordes. The porter. *He*'s the predator! He's the murderer, too! And I let him trap me and bring me here."

She knelt down at his feet and moved the lamp a little further away from the chair.

"Please hold still, Mr. Orwell, while I do this. No, don't try and get up. You'll only hurt yourself. I've nearly finished."

She fumbled with her fingers around his ankles, untying the cord that bound his legs together. She was wearing rubber gloves.

"How did you get into the catacombs?"

She laughed.

"In the *Präsidium* we have master keys for everywhere. Not that I like coming down here. No, keep still, Mr. Orwell."

Strangely, he had no feeling that she had untield him. He made to get up, and almost tipped forward. His legs were still bound together, and now they were also tied to the chair!

Richard was distraught.

"Hey, what have you done? Please hurry up, get me untied—he's coming back! He'll kill both of us!"

"No, I don't think so. Look, stop that! Please sit still, Mr. Orwell. We need to talk. Though first I need to do something."

He felt her running her hands over his legs; touching his clothing. "What are you doing?"

"Ah, here are your university keys. And a used paper handkerchief, shame on you! And this"—she held up a second small bunch of keys that she had fished out of his trouser pocket—"this is presumably the way you lock and unlock your apartment. One key for the house-door. One key for the apartment. And here's a teeny-weeny little key for your mailbox. Am I right?"

"Yes. But what do you want them for?"

A terrifying suspicion had elbowed itself into his thoughts.

"These will save me from having to break into your apartment. You ought to be pleased."

"I don't understand?"

"Then sit and listen, Mr. Orwell." She got up, picked up the lamp, and shone it in his face. "Oops, sorry! I'm not the Gestapo. But you were right about Volker: he is coming back, and it's time to let him finish what he started."

Richard was horrified.

"No! You can't mean—"

"Please don't interrupt me! Volker is a very violent man, and I don't wish to be here when he arrives. We don't have much time. Less than an hour, I would say? So we should make the most of it. Afterwards, you won't have very long."

"You—and Volker Cordes? That doesn't make sense."

"Why not?"

"Do you know him? Surely you're not—"

She laughed.

"An item? Oh, come on now, what a quaint idea! Let's say we are... *colleagues*. That girl Lea, and the detail about the fingers. The President blabbed to me about that, long before he told you. I think he was trying to impress me! And then I made the connection to Volker Cordes. You see, back then when he was sacked, I was the one who did the paperwork, because the Chancellor's secretary was sick that week. In the file there were all those written complaints from girls he'd molested. They made interesting reading! Someone wrote that he'd tried to lick her fingers. Another one, that he'd offered her money for her slip. I put two and two together, and made four. So I tracked Volker down and told him that I'd go to the police—unless we could come to an *arrangement*."

Richard's mouth was very dry. The way she was holding the lamp, he couldn't see her face to read her emotions. Was she joking with him? Was it all a game? Was she crazy? He licked his lips.

"An arrangement? You mean: money?"

"No, not money! He would help me with my little project, that was all. My *English* project. In return, I would make those letters disappear, and change what was in his file. 'Sacked for drinking on duty'! When I told him about my project, he was very happy to help. There'd be girls for him to play with. Fingers to kiss. Underwear to steal. Girls sleeping naked, unaware, in their hostel beds. But no violence, I told him. He still had copies of all the keys. He could access the hostels from the catacombs and through the cellars. If he was interrupted, he could make a quick escape—no-one would follow him, especially in the night!"

There was a twisted logic in there somewhere, but Richard hadn't grasped it yet.

"Why English? It was always *our* students. Why us?"

"*Why?* Do you really need to ask? It's because of who *you* are, and what *I* am. Imagine that you're an alcoholic, you work in a bar, and you're not allowed to drink!"

"I don't understand."

"Then let me spell it out. You can hear how good my English is. I wanted to study, I wanted to be an English teacher—that was always my dream. I could have been a lecturer. But I had a whole family of deadbeats and losers to support. There was no way I could go to college. I had to work. And if you're a woman, and you haven't got a degree, you hit the glass ceiling very quickly."

"But that's not *our* fault."

"Listen," she said. "Mine is the last friendly human voice you'r ever going to hear, and I'm doing you an honor. I've never told anyone this, not even Volker, and I'm never going to say it again." She paused. "But if you don't want to listen, I'll leave now, and you can spend these last minutes in the darkness."

"No, go on," he said, swallowing hard. "I'm listening."

While she was still there, and talking, there was just the faintest hope that he could convince her. That she might still change her mind. She had some crazy hangup about English students, and she needed to explain it to someone. Might that perhaps be enough for her, once she'd said her piece?

"Imagine my predicament, Mr. Orwell. I had to work for men that I *despised*. *Herr Professor*! *Herr Doktor*! Not one of those guys going in and out of the *Präsidium* was worth my little finger, for all their titles and their self-importance. Where else can lazy, arrogant social cripples find a job for life except in a university? But those bastards would look at me, and I knew what they were thinking. 'She's *smart*, that *Frau* Henkel, she holds the shop together. She's not young, but she keeps herself in good shape. I bet she's a great fuck! She could go a round with me any day. Why doesn't she flirt like the other secretaries? She must be a dyke. Pity, that.'"

Richard was glad that he couldn't see her face.

"Is that why you hate men?"

"Men? Oh, you mean men like that dollop of vanity that I work for, or you conceited little creeps in the English Department? No, you've got me wrong, I don't hate men as such. Women can be just as bad. But it was good fun making fools of you. I felt quite the feminist! And I'll tell you this, Richard: Volker is a man—the only real man that I've met in this university. He has strong desires, *unusual* ones, and he isn't afraid to live them out."

"But he's a psycho!"

"Of course he's a psycho. Aren't *all* truly great men a bit crazy?"

"You were helping him to attack our students!"

"Come on, let's not exaggerate. Your precious students: all those stupid girls pretending to 'study', throwing away chances that I never had, wasting their time and their parents' money, partying, fucking around, heading nowhere, except some lousy teaching job. There were plenty of dumb blondes there for Volker to play with—because that's the sort he likes—your department is simply full of them, and I suppose he also wanted revenge on students. So I would point him in certain directions. I know his taste. But I kept him on a leash. And while he was playing with the students, I could play with one or two of the lecturers." She put on the voice of a young girl groaning with lust. *"Oh, Richard, how you turn me on! Suck me! Fuck me! I want you inside me! I want your come all over my tits!"*

Richard was amazed.

"*You* are 'S.'?"

"Congratulations, Sherlock! It took you long enough!"

"Why me? What did I ever do to you?"

"It had to be someone from the English Department—after all, I have a personal point to make. You were the obvious choice—look at the alternatives. Christenkorn? No, his wife tortures him quite enough for one lifetime. Little Enno? My love-letters would have frightened him. And how do you seduce a guy like that? *'Dear Professor, I think your project is so wonderful! I so admire your research model! I'd love to be one of your assistants...'*

Snoad? Too many bimbo admirers, too much in love with himself. Too lazy. Too self-satisfied. Kurz? Too stupid. Hodgkins? A clown, though he won't be around for much longer. I even considered the women, you know. A passionate lesbian love-letter or two? But your boss is such a nasty specimen—she isn't made for love. As for the Schlichting woman: she has zero ability, she's the living proof that in our system mediocrity can flourish. That left you. And when the Fat Man invited you to be his personal detective, I thought: fantastic, two birds, one stone! Giving you 'S.' to chase after would distract you from your assignment, and leading you around in circles would keep me amused."

"You led me into a trap in order to kill me—*for fun?*"

"Show some respect, Richard! It was hard work. I had to research you. I even sacrificed some of my coffee-breaks for you, slipping into your lectures, in the back row, when the lecture theater was crowded. There was never any intention to kill you. I didn't want him to kill *anyone*—no more Lea Hartwigs! It was all just a game."

"This is a *game*?"

"Not any more. You see, I've been holding him back for months, and it hasn't easy. That girl Lisa doesn't know how lucky she was—he almost lost it there. He was getting obsessed with her. So perhaps it's time to throw him a bone, to let him get it out of his system. He prefers girls, but it'll have to be you, I'm afraid, and for that you have only yourself to blame. You were *so* close to finding him out. I couldn't allow that to happen! And you were no longer interested in playing games with 'S.', you made that perfectly clear. So when he gets back, I'll leave you lads to it."

"You're a monster!"

"No, I'm not a monster. But my friend Volker *is*. He's gone to his sister's, to fetch his tool-kit. Wire-cutters, I imagine. Maybe some new item that he wants to try out. And some heavy duty gear to portion up what's left of you afterwards. Plastic wrapping. Some cleaning materials. We don't want you to be found. We need to be careful."

She held up her hands.

"Rubber gloves."

"Just a precaution."

"They'll catch you, you know that?"

"Volker, sure. Eventually. Because he's mad, they'll catch him, sooner or later. But there's nothing to tie *me* to any of this, and he won't betray me. Even if he does talk, he rambles stupid nonsense about everyone." She put on a strange, demented-sounding voice. "'The President is the Antichrist!' (That's quite perceptive.) 'Walter Wichsler is possessed by demons! Professor Michael is a woman in disguise! *Frau* Henkel gave me my instructions! The End is nigh! The Day is at hand!' And so on. Who'll believe *any* of that garbage? He'll go straight to the loony-bin. I'll take my chances."

"But they'll find all your letters!"

"Letters from a hysterical girl named 'S.' to her teacher? So what? And there are no fingerprints on them, except yours. Perhaps you wrote them to yourself? But while you boys are having your fun, I'll pop over to your apartment and see what I can remove."

"Look, you can still stop this! No-one's been hurt. I'll cover for you. You're right, nobody will believe you're involved. It'll all be on *him*."

"Give me a moment to think about it." She rested her chin on her hand as though deep in thought. "Thinks. Thinks. Thinks. No! Let's do it as we originally planned—it's more fun that way! Sorry, Richard. My, how the minutes fly when you're in good company! So, hey ho, it's time to go." She picked up the lamp and stepped round him. The light grew dimmer. She must have walked several yards before she turned back and said, "Enjoy the silence. The next sound that you hear will be Volker."

But it wasn't.

Somewhere in front of him there was a faint light, and a voice called out, "Hallo? Anywhere there? You with the lamp?"

Then there was an explosion of movement, and light. He heard other voices. Through the dazzle, he saw figures coming towards him, and he recognized Hans-Robert Eberle. And Eddie. And wasn't that Steffi? The Young Antiquarians had been exploring the caves!

Eddie said, "Richard, is that you?"

He heard Steffi say, "I *told* you we should go in further," and someone shout, "Go after that woman!"

Was he delirious? It was too much to take. Richard blacked out.

DAMAGE LIMITATION

Kajo Christenkorn was enjoying a shamelessly late Saturday morning lie-in when his host's wife brought him the telephone.

"It's for you," she said, obviously embarrassed to see him in pyjamas, and whispered, "The President!"

"Come in to the university *now*," the *Präsi* barked. "That's an order! Hurry! Take a taxi if you have to. Did you get that?"

"Yes, of course."

"The main entrance is open. I'll be waiting for you in the *Präsidium*. Just come straight in."

Kajo did exactly as he had been told.

Sitting in the taxi, he asked himself what the Great Man was doing in the university on a Saturday in the holidays? Had he found out about Rico? Was he about to be sacked? No, even the *Präsi* couldn't do that.

The *Präsidium* was empty: there were no Vice-Presidents to be seen, no Chancellor, no *Frau* Henkel, no *Frau* Binsenweis. If the President had come in to do some urgent administrative work, or because of some sudden crisis, wouldn't he have arranged secretarial backup?

"Come in, shut the door, sit down, and *listen*. Oh, and I can't offer you any coffee."

"No need, *Herr Präsident*, I've just had breakfast," he lied.

Kajo sat back and listened, and was told the following. The President of a distinguished university in a major city inevitably had friends in high places, *good friends* who would, on occasion, and off the record, keep the President informed of matters of interest pertaining to his university—and do it long before those matters became public knowledge.

"And thank goodness for that! It is only by such means that we can meet, and master, the challenges with which we are confronted on an almost daily basis."

"Of course."

In this instance, the President continued, it was the information that the police had made no fewer than three arrests, at two different locations. The first location had actually been on the university premises, late on Friday evening—

"*What?*"

The *Präsi* ignored his interruption.

"—while the second arrest was made several days ago, in connection with the brutal attack on a young woman in a sordid downtown hotel. The identity of the suspected attacker has not yet been made public, but I can tell you—in strictest confidence—that he is a part-time lecturer at this university. A part-time lecturer whose contract will naturally be terminated with immediate effect! I have called you in for this urgent consultation because of the embarrassing involvement of" he paused to take a breath "the *English* Department."

Kajo was deeply perplexed.

"*Herr* Hodgkins would never do such a thing! Or are you referring to our Visiting Scholar, Dr. Dong?"

"No, no, Christenkorn, you're not following me. I didn't say that the man *taught* English. The name of the suspect is Lothar Baumgart, who is—"

"—the husband—"

"—of your present Head of Department. Good heavens, you're slow today! So the nature of the game is now: *immediate damage limitation. Frau* Professor Dr. Reiss-Baumgart has already been to see me, of her own volition. She has asked me for a sabbatical semester, to start at once, and on the grounds of compassionate leave. An unusual request, but since she assured me that she will also use the time for a new research project I saw no reason not to grant it. This will have to be confirmed by her Faculty Council, of course. Which means—"

"That an Acting Head of Department will be needed."

"Don't look so miserable, man! I'm offering you an opportunity here."

Yes, like last time, Kajo thought. Or maybe *not* like last time.

"Which I would be honored to accept, *Herr Präsident*. Damage limitation indeed. The English Department has been going through turbulent times. I shall need to reassert discipline within the team. Crack the whip. Bring a few hotheads to heel."

"Absolutely! You weren't always able to convince me in the past, Christenkorn, but I like what I am hearing now. Confident, dynamic leadership. Excellent!"

"And I know that I can rely on your full support, *Herr Präsident*?"

"Of course. One hundred percent, *Herr* Christenkorn. You have my word."

Kajo took a deep breath. Why not? But he had a favor to return.

"*Frau* Professor Reiss-Baumgart has added considerably to that turbulence by making unnecessary threats, for example to get rid of several of the junior staff. I'm thinking of *Herr* Hodgkins, and young Orwell. With your approval, I would like to be able to reassure them that their contracts will be renewed."

The President positively beamed at him.

"Whatever you need, Christenkorn! Curiously, those two young men were involved in the other, more recent affair."

"The one that took place on campus?"

"Yes, yes, we are trying to keep that small detail under wraps. Away from the media. We have to think about the next round of applications. So, not a word about this to anyone, Christenkorn! Orwell was attacked, in seems, but was rescued through the brave efforts of Hodgkins and his young girlfriend. A man has now been arrested. He is possibly a mental patient on the run. Unfortunately, the police claim that there is a link between this lunatic and" (his voice dropped to a whisper) "—this now in the *very, very strictest confidence!*—our own dear *Frau* Henkel, who has also been arrested."

"*No!?*"

"I'm afraid, yes. Naturally, she denies any involvement. I can't imagine that there is any truth in this, but we shall have to let the police do their work, Christenkorn. My informant tells me that they believe that one of the two men they arrested might also be the murderer of poor Lea Hartwig, may she rest in peace. Forensics can perhaps throw further light on that."

"These things always take their time, *Herr Präsident*."

"By the way, did I tell you that *Herr* Orwell is a special protégé of mine? Such a promising young scholar: a rising star of Conan Doyle Studies! I had asked him to look into a small matter for me, of no great significance, but that seems to have resolved itself now. We really should encourage him to get his PhD finished. We wouldn't want to waste his talents, would we now?"

AUTHOR'S NOTE

This is a work of fiction, and none of its characters represent real persons, alive or dead.

Not all of the plot is invented, however. The predator plot-line and the excursion to Flossengamme are fictional, but many of the other situations happened more or less as recounted.

If some of the descriptions of university life seem far-fetched, I can only say in my defence that they are based on many years of experience, as a student or a lecturer, and that, when it comes to modern universities, I am reminded of Juvenal's comment that there were some subjects about which it was "harder *not* to write satire."

The messages sent by "S." are mostly translations or adaptations of anonymous letters. These were sent to me at different stages in my teaching career by at least three correspondents, none of whom ever revealed who they were. They too are fictional texts, but they are from someone else's imagination.

As a German colleague once remarked to me, "You know, doing this job, we really ought to get danger money."